THE FALSE MOON

The Immutable Moon, Book Two

Jacqueline Rohrbach

A NineStar Press Publication

Published by NineStar Press
P.O. Box 91792,
Albuquerque, New Mexico, 87199 USA.
www.ninestarpress.com

The False Moon

Printed in the USA
First Edition
May, 2018

Print ISBN: 978-1-948608-70-1

Also available in eBook, ISBN: 978-1-948608-65-7

Warning: This book contains sexually explicit content, which may only be suitable for mature readers.

Outsiders call them False Moons, but Garvey's kind call themselves Moondogs. Moondogs hunt. Moondogs live free. Moondogs stick together. Moondogs are half-breeds, not completely accepted by those who consider themselves "true wolves."

Garvey is a Moondog to his bones. He and the unexpected get along just fine. That's why when Molly, the vampire who should be a mindless eating machine, turns out to be an oddity, Garvey decides to hide her away instead of killing her.

But that leaves him needing another vampire to carry out the schemes of the two powerful werewolf rivals he's caught between. What's an improvising Moondog to do other than find some poor sap and create a new one?

Garvey might be a Moondog to his bones, but to defeat his enemies, he must navigate their world and be the stupid, subservient beast they expect. At least on the surface. Behind the scenes, Garvey intends to turn their plans against them and bring the two greater packs to the brink of war.

To Mom and Dad:
Rock by rock, we can make amazing things. Thank you for raising me to
be the person I am today.

Part One

The Children of the Formless

The Varcolac

Chapter 1: Jouska But Not Really

KIJO

Kijo stood in front of the gateway Mazgan stole from the Boo Hags. Lacking descriptive language, she could only call it doorish but smaller. As it was, when she became wolf, it was what she felt and not what she saw. Surging electricity pried apart large spaces inside of her to make room for itself amongst her being. This sensation wasn't intoxicating. It was terrifying. Without knowing how she knew it, Kijo understood the presence with her wanted to rip her apart.

You do not open it. It opens you.

It was one of the few things Kijo remembered Lavario saying with any force back when he was still her father. Normally flippant about bright-line rules, he was stern, even afraid, when he cautioned her against tampering with the sentient powers immured within the gateways.

Back then, pride kept her from asking him more. As a new wolf, she wanted her pack to think she was in control, secure in her ability to fight any enemy the world had to offer. *Varcolac.* What a fool she'd been. Now it was too late to ask for guidance, too late to admit her fear, too late to do anything other than move forward. Under her nose, Mazgan had already brought a gateway there and left it where anyone could access it. Worse, he'd selected Garvey—a brazenly careless wolf—to travel through it and bring back a vampire of all things.

"Here is proof of Mazgan's foolishness," she said to herself in the darkness. "Here is proof he's tampering where he should not."

In her head, she considered her pack's response. *It's nothing,* they'd say.

She stressed the significance to them. "It is a gateway. *Here.*"

Their retort played out in her head. *It was past time for Varcolac to have dominion over one. We are due. You are looking at your birthright. Your rank is not just some silly title. It is a destiny,* Guardian.

Furious, Kijo paced the length of the hall. Her imaginary conversation with her subordinates became reality if she approached them now. Pack pride surmounted their caution. An honor they'd been denied all these years, a right reserved by the much hated Isangelous, was in their possession. Having did not mean tampering. Even if it did, the wolves of the Varcolac—mostly younger, brasher—might not understand the danger.

Mazgan hadn't exactly hidden it either; the damn thing was literally a door to a storage room. Inexcusable hubris.

"You will need so much more to persuade them of the danger," she concluded to herself.

This time, her pack did not answer her. She was alone.

No, not alone. An unknown entity stirred nearby. More curious than concerned, Kijo scanned the hallway, narrowing her eyes while she sniffed the air in measured, stable inhalations. Her nostrils barely twitched. Although she didn't see, didn't hear, didn't smell anything, instinct demanded she listen.

Kijo straightened herself, haughtily raising her chin. She walked up to the gateway the same way she'd approach any other enemy. *Touch.* The energy sent her staggering backward. It was an impulse as strong as anything she'd ever felt, more demanding than even her body's need for blood.

"No." Defiant, Kijo said it out loud. Cold liquid ran down her spine. Sweat, she realized.

The energy shifted, tipping her direction as though to acknowledge her refusal. Softer this time, the request was seductive. *Touch.*

Kijo's hand twitched at her side. With effort, she forced herself to walk away. Lavario's words repeated, *You don't open it. It opens you.*

EACH TIME KIJO turned her head, a quick flash of movement, a flutter of a shadow, caught her attention. Imagination couldn't run away with her when she didn't have one. Sour with the whole experience, Kijo pursed her lips, annoyed with whatever followed her home. Once she determined the unseen was most likely unseeable, she went back to her studies.

Tip-tapping—nothing more audible than the sound of mice running inside the walls—didn't turn her head. Some of the art she selected for her ever-shrinking personal space toppled to the ground with a muted clap. She heard something, perhaps glass cracking. Annoyed, she sniffed indelicately. Not even Geri or Freki would come clean it up if it were to shatter.

"Yes, yes," Kijo said to the unknown entity, "I understand you're here."

When the knock at her door came, she assumed it was still her guest trying its best to toy with her. It came again, loud enough for the reverberations to shake pencils on the desk. A voice accompanied it.

"Kijo, it is Mazgan. Open this door."

She preferred the specter. But there was no ignoring rank.

As soon as she cracked her door open, he pushed his way inside, using his superior bulk to force her against the wall. His facial features were muddied and sloped like the face of a mountain.

"Alpha Guardian," she greeted him with an icy formality.

"Guardian Kijo." Mazgan's tone was strict and self-consciously commanding.

The giant apartment Lavario created for himself within the Varcolac stronghold was no more. In its place was a modest single-wolf dwelling with blasé showroom-white walls cut into cold ninety-degree angles. Per his suggestions, she'd divided the space amongst her pack.

Various relics from the bonfire were scattered around it: bits and pieces from Lavario's collection of things that once were. Items too valuable to burn, too much Lavario's to display. Nostalgia tugged at Kijo, increasing her ire.

Mazgan assessed it all, stopping to glower with disapproval at the unused paint cans and unhung art. Decorations were frivolous, unwelcome in the Vercolac compound.

The long hairs on his arms and neck stood at attention. Claws and teeth wanted to come out. His body was trying to tell itself there was danger in the room. Fool that he was, he probably assumed it was tension between them. Indeed, he smirked to himself in a way that made her want to slap sense into him. What was the point of having the wolf inside of him if he ignored it?

"How can I help you, Alpha Guardian?"

"I'm here to offer you another chance to stand by my side. I held off challenges for your benefit. This will end soon. I cannot hold the gate forever," he chided her.

A glass fell off the counter, sparing her from having to answer promptly. Mazgan pushed past her to follow the noise. Perhaps he expected a lover to dominate, maybe a traitor to cow when he patrolled the kitchen. What he got was an empty room, barren of anything except for the tenebrific presence that made the small space gravelike.

Hoping he'd listen to his senses, Kijo waited for him to notice something amiss.

Seeing nothing obvious, Mazgan went back to assuming the tension in the room was somehow between the two of them. The glass was a mere curiosity. By the time he walked back her way, she had mastered her tone, readied her response.

Calmly, she said what was needed. "I accept whatever challenges await, Alpha Guardian."

His eyes grew wide in his shocked anger. "They have my leave to kill you."

"Then I give myself leave to kill them, as is my right, Alpha Guardian."

"Kijo…" For a moment, he looked uncertain. He reached out one hand to take hers. "Kijo, my darling, through me, you will have the power you want. No need to make our relationship contentious as it was with your father. Do not make his mistakes."

What he offered was a glimpse at the sun through blinds. Filtered under the best of circumstances, blocked in the worst. Kijo pulled away. "I will not make my father's mistakes, Alpha Guardian. Send the challengers."

Minutes later, after they'd already said their terse, formal goodbyes, Kijo went back to her work. Something that smelled of wet dog eating rotten meat leered over her shoulder. Tired of the unknown's games, she snarled over her shoulder and demanded it leave. Whatever it was didn't obey. Whatever it was vanished the moment she turned her head to confront it.

A word to describe what was happening wormed its way to the front of her mind, pushing aside her conflict with Mazgan. *Lifestealer*. The supposed soul of a vampire. Every fiber of her being screamed that this thing was more a threat than the careless Alpha Guardian would ever be. She knew it. Politically cut off, she was trapped.

"I have to deal with Mazgan before I can properly address whatever this is," she said to herself. "Him and his idiotic schemes."

Her current world was a convoluted mess. Kijo needed to simplify.

Chapter 2: Between Two Camps

GARVEY

Outsiders called them False Moons, but Garvey's kind called themselves Moondogs. As half-breeds, they'd always be weaker than the werewolves of the Vercolac and the Isangelous, the true wolves as they called themselves so they had to be smarter. Garvey was Moondog to the bone. Since he couldn't physically dominate his enemies, he'd manipulate instead.

With Molly, the last remaining vampire, in tow, Garvey made his way to the chamber of Mazgan, the Alpha Guardian of the Vercolac. Doing his best to sound subservient, he tentatively rapped on the door and waited as Mazgan pointedly exerting his control over the situation in the most petty way possible and made Garvey stand around. Eventually, Mazgan flung open the door and gestured for Garvey to come inside.

He took one look at Molly and said, "Where is the other vampire?"

Timothy, the vampire Mazgan spoke of, was now in the great beyond, whatever that was, no doubt yammering on about food, humans, and hunger. Poor re-dead Timothy with his limited vocabulary. Garvey didn't linger long on such things, though. Tim's death wasn't part of the plan, but life was like that.

"One second, you have a scheme that involves two bloodthirsty vampires clamoring for human blood. The next, you have a plot that only ever realistically needed one," he explained to Mazgan.

"Meaning?"

"Meaning the other vampire died, Alpha Guardian. Now Molly over here is the only one left."

"Left," Molly repeated.

Pissed as predicted, Mazgan fumed. His eyes alternated colors as he struggled for control over his emotions. Mazgan wanted them to stay brown so badly that Garvey almost felt sad for him when they inevitably slid to gold. Alpha Guardian Not Lavario could never achieve any level of mastery over his transformation. Hell, he struggled to manage his human side, let alone the wolf.

Such anger might have worried Garvey if the Alpha Guardian didn't need someone to do his dirty work. The wolf lord was known for little else besides being pugnacious, violent. Fortunately, Mazgan had no other lackey. The wolf lord would bluster, yell, and get the fuck over it. Meanwhile, Garvey poked.

Garvey lifted his thumb and jabbed it in Molly's direction. "You still have one vampire, Alpha Guardian."

Mazgan looked at Molly with disgust. He was none too pleased to have a corpse in his chambers, which, Garvey noted with some amusement, was now decorated with expensive furnishings. Varcolac wolves were meant to have no use for comfort and frivolities. Hard lives made stronger warriors who earned rank through battle rather than by birthright, the way Isangelous wolves did. This way of thinking was what supposedly separated the two packs.

From all appearances, Mazgan had embraced the Isangelous way of life when it came to luxury and decadence. The beyond-king-size bed was draped in furs from all sorts of creatures. There were pictures of Mazgan all over the place. Perhaps the best thing was the random giant-octopus coffee table in the middle of the room; its tentacles held up a giant slab of marble. Awesome. Garvey loved everything about it.

Mazgan shook his head. "What happened? I told you to bring both. This was not the plan."

"Plans change, Alpha Guardian. Especially when part of it dies."

Molly nodded. "Dies."

"How did it die?" Mazgan bit it out with effort.

This required some truth bending. Mazgan would not be pleased to hear Tovin had been the indirect cause of a botched endeavor. Little human boys did not thwart werewolf kings, either directly or by going through open doors. Garvey had already thrown poor Tovin under one toothy bus too many.

"Molly killed it."

"Killed," Molly confessed without apology.

"Why on earth did it do that?" Mazgan was exasperated, the way Garvey liked him to be.

"Grudge, Alpha Guardian," Garvey explained.

"Grudge," Molly agreed.

"Vampires do not hold grudges." Mazgan sounded so sure.

Garvey wasn't quite there with him. Part of Garvey thought he might actually be telling the truth and his vampire companion really did axe old Tim to settle a score. Molly was different. He wasn't quite sure how or why, but he knew his girl was an exception. At least she certainly had her likes and her dislikes. She parroted Garvey eagerly while snubbing Mazgan.

"This one does, Alpha Guardian," Garvey reassured him.

"Does," Molly confirmed.

"By the goddess! You do nothing right!" Mazgan was to the yelling part. Good times.

"It's my curse, Alpha Guardian. I suppose I should go find the original screwup who bit me and cut off his head. I hear he took up residence in Oliver's quarters."

Without regrets, Garvey winced as Mazgan's face rolled like a wave into its true form. While it was expected—Mazgan always resorted to violence when pushed—the blow and subsequent kick to his ribs stung.

Garvey was on the floor coughing up blood by the time Molly said, "Quarters." Thanks, Mol.

"And shut this stupid thing up." Mazgan hit Molly too. Beyond pain, the undead woman understood the gesture well enough. She hissed at the wolf lord before jumping up to bite at his torso and arm. Her clawed hands tried to gain leverage around his back—digging in, hopefully with enough force to get under the rough coat of fur that protected vital areas. Mazgan threw her off.

That didn't stop Molly from continuing her attack. She was beyond many things besides pain—fear and reasoning included.

"Mol. Mol." Garvey ran between them before she could lunge again. "Come on now, settle down."

"Down." She hissed back at him.

"Oh, I know. I know, Mol. But chill." Garvey stood between her and Mazgan, hopefully blocking her view for long enough that she'd forget she was ever angry. It wasn't really working. The old girl apparently had a long and evil memory.

"Chill." She looked beyond Garvey and over toward Mazgan when she said it, as if instructing him. At least she was staying put. For the time being.

Mazgan lifted his lips to show his teeth. "Take this thing and sit on it. I'm going to work out how to fix this." With that, he kicked Garvey and the seething Molly out of his chamber and slammed the door behind them.

It was bad enough to have to travel with vampires. Now he was the thing's babysitter? Garvey wasn't sure what needed to be fixed. Mazgan's plan was as complex as releasing the vampire in a highly populated area to spread the infection. Humanity's civilization would collapse. Werewolves, specifically the Varcolac, could then take possession of the new world and the bloodservant trade. Felt like they could do that already.

"What else does that idiot need?"

"Need," Molly said back.

Garvey sighed at her. "That's going to get very annoying very fast."

He was waiting for it. Waiting. Waiting. But Molly sat there looking right back at him, saying nothing. As much as Garvey loved the unexpected, the vampire woman was truly starting to creep him out.

"Alright then, Mol. Remember me fondly."

Those eyes of hers, glazed by milky white cataracts, sharpened as she focused on his face. An unwilling shiver tingled all the way through his body, ending at the tips of his fingers. As if responding to his fear, Molly reached out to place a reassuring hand on his chest.

"Fond," she said after a bit.

HIS INJURIES WERE not as severe as he had hoped, at least not be-less-discreet bad. Blood from the beating Mazgan had given him smeared nicely on his face. For good measure, he clawed a slit down the middle of his shirt and rubbed some into the tattered edges of the mangled garments.

"Fabricated. Get it, Mol?"

She did not laugh.

"Some pal you are."

Kijo wasn't much more impressed. When she opened the door to their meeting place, a shack on the edge of the woods, the look on her face said she'd clawed out of her mother's womb bored and displeased. Her gaze did linger on the side of his face where Mazgan's claws had made their mark. Moondogs, or False Moons as the greater packs liked to call them, healed much more slowly. For all Kijo knew about his kind, they didn't heal at all.

Sniffing the air was a habit, an action as automatic as breathing. The results of Garvey's brief, unintentional scan surprised him. There were two others there. One of them was a wolf wearing rather expensive floral perfume. But Garvey couldn't make out the other scent. Kijo caught him trying to sort it out. Rather than express displeasure as Garvey expected, she viewed him with a type of grudging appreciation.

"Who's the other wolf?" he asked her.

"Her name is Vanu. She is here to witness the existence of the vampire."

"Ah. And the other thing?"

His sister's lips twisted in anger. She didn't answer, which Garvey took to mean she wasn't in a sharing mood. She gestured to Garvey's torn clothes and injuries. "I take it Mazgan was upset," she asked with zero concern, perhaps even a tinge of pleasure. It was hard to tell.

"As expected. Things didn't go according to plan."

She sniffed the air, winced. "And this thing is a vampire?"

"Affirmative."

"I thought there were two?"

"Not anymore."

She didn't even blink. "Bring it in."

Young for a werewolf, this was Kijo's first time seeing one of the undead. To her, they probably seemed a creature of legend, existing only because older wolves passed on the stories. If Kijo's expression was anything to go by, the experience was a bit of a disappointment. Molly hopped from one foot to the next with barely constrained agitation as Kijo inspected her. Yellow teeth snip-snapped whenever fingers came too close to her mouth. Like a spooked horse, she reared her head, eyes rolling backward.

"What's wrong with it?" Kijo asked, lifting her lip. "Is it sick?"

"Hungry," Molly's response was wrapped in a drawn-out moan.

Kijo gave Garvey a hard, unforgiving look. "You did not feed it before you brought it here?"

"Totes did, sis. No less than a few hours ago. She can't be anything other than hungry."

"Hungry," Molly echoed, a childish whine to her voice. Garvey felt a stab of pity.

Vampires could survive months without feeding, surviving on whatever magic kept them reanimated, but they were consumers by nature. Created by Atrophia to destroy humanity, Molly's kind were little more than mindless killing machines forever trapped in an endless loop of torment: yearning, yearning, yearning only to be ever so briefly satisfied right after feeding.

Garvey didn't want to explain all of that to Kijo. She could pick up a damn book. "She'll be fine," Garvey reassured her as Molly continued to snap at the end of her tether.

"Tie the thing up outside. It stinks."

Molly crinkled her nose.

Kijo gestured to a chair across from hers as he reentered the room. It was as close to playing the good hostess as she came.

Five seconds later, with Garvey's ass just hitting the chair, she tapped her clawed hand impatiently on the cheap wood. "Does Eresna know? I expected to hear something by now."

It was on the tip of his tongue to ask his sister if she was really counting on the Boo Hags, the common pejorative for Isangelous wolves, to solve her problems, but he already knew the answer. Kijo, darling of the Varcolac, didn't trust her pack to make the right decision even if they did know what Mazgan had done. She *was* counting on the Boo Hags to end the threat for her. Otherwise, she'd simply show the Varcolac Molly. An actual living vampire was as concrete as evidence came. Pointing this out to his sister would only be painful.

Garvey assured her of Eresna's knowledge. "I had Molly attack her bloodservant. Eresna should know soon enough."

"That is good. Is her bloodservant dead?"

"No, Molly killed it before it did any serious damage to the human. I guess she didn't care much for old Tim." When Kijo's eyes went golden in anger, Garvey rushed forward. "But the boy was very shaken. He will tell Eresna about it."

"I told you to be less discreet. I need others to have knowledge of this. This thing"—she gestured to the vampire—"needs to be a threat. Eresna must know of it."

"I did as you asked. It attacked Eresna's bloodservant. Plus, I traveled through the portal in the middle of the Boo Hag library." If that wasn't less discreet, Garvey didn't know what was.

Gold eyes turned to black, a transformation Garvey wasn't sure made him feel much better, as Kijo settled into her chair. "Playing me as well as Mazgan?"

Garvey took a cautious look at his sister, who looked back with hard, unwavering certainty. Her face was relaxed, even serene: no teeth poked out, no claws dug grooves into the wood of the chair, no light—golden or otherwise—touched the eyes. Time to tell the truth. Or die.

"Yes."

"That is surprisingly smart of you." She leapfrogged over his response and went to the task at hand. "I need you alive as much as you want to stay alive. Play Mazgan. Manipulate him. Treat me with the same disrespect, I will have blood. Release the vampire in Eresna's compound, make sure to keep casualties to a minimum. Double kill any collateral. Go." She waved him away.

As Garvey untied the impatient vampire, he wondered how he was going to get out of this mess. Mazgan wanted his perfect moment. Kijo wanted it done now. Not surprisingly, the vampire was no help at all. She wrenched her leash while crying out her hunger. Earlier, Garvey said Molly knew nothing but. He started to think it was true of them all.

Chapter 3: Torn Apart

KIJO

By the time Kijo locked her jaws around Bram's throat, she was sure he'd already changed his mind about the challenge. Just the same, she twisted her head left then right to embed her canines, pushing beyond the protective scruff of fur to his throat. Limbs sputtered—flopping, twisting against the floor in a series of dull thuds and grasping-clawed scrapes as he tried to use his body to pry her away.

Rookie mistake from a new wolf. That only made her hold on him much more intimate. Gasps and mutterings came from the crowd of onlookers, atypical for such a low-level challenge. Curious about what might happen, many of the pack stayed to witness. Would she, like Lavario, refuse to accept the pack's censure, or could she gracefully take the hint and come back to the fold? Their curiosity was about to be satisfied. Bram twitched his last twitch.

The faces of her packmates told her she'd made the wrong choice. Their ears lay flat. Their teeth were bared to her. Low growls rumbled deeply in puffed-up chests. Even Lavario, as hated as he was, never killed. He'd been content to magic disrespectful wolves about the room for his own amusement or to slap them around with one large paw until they stayed on the floor. Beaten, disgraced, but otherwise unharmed. Kijo gave them consequences.

She stood up, blood dripping from her jaws, to remind them she was not Lavario. Like them, she was Varcolac, and she showed power through force. They wanted to follow the strongest? Well, she was strongest.

One solitary howl reminded herself she was his daughter.

SCALP STUCK BEHIND Kijo's ears. Other bits and pieces of Bram shackled her to what she'd done, to what she might continue doing. Hand over hand, she scraped dry flakes of him off herself, splashing water up to her elbows and then her face. Although her mouth was clenched shut, diluted blood zigzagged along the contours, latching onto the sides of her lips, persistent in the way only water was. Although victory tasted terrible, Kijo opened her mouth to it while thinking, *What a waste.*

"Well, that was something." Vanu's tone lashed Kijo's thin skin.

She curled lips over teeth, the wolf inside of her leaping to its feet—as always, ready and eager to do battle. *Frenzy*, she chided herself.

Vanu was no sycophant. Old for a Varcolac, she was unlike the young wolves who showed their bellies either metaphorically or literally to Kijo whenever her temper surged.

Vanu raised her lip ever so slightly at the emotional display but continued their conversation as though nothing happened. "You know Bram only tried to express his disapproval for your actions. Your response was quite severe."

Another admonishment. Kijo's lips twitched again. This time, she kept her wolf in check, swallowing it up inside herself. Continuous outrage was a luxury emotion she could ill afford.

Challenges came as promised after she refused Mazgan's orders. One by one: that's how the rules told them to do it. That's how they did it. Before, Kijo would have lauded the strict adherence to tradition, believing what was pack was what was right. Testing one's strength, matching it against another's, was the only way to settle scores, determine rank, or express grievances and disapproval. Now that she was on the other side of it, she wanted to yell at them to put it in a complaint box and get the fuck off her doorstep. There was so much more at stake than their egos.

She tried to communicate this to Vanu while she paced from one corner of the room to the next. "I have other concerns. As I said, Mazgan is tampering with the gateways."

Dismissive, Vanu fluttered her fingers. "Younger wolves won't care."

"You are not a younger wolf. You know the danger."

"You sent the danger, the vampire, away with Garvey. Your proof." The older she-wolf grimaced at the stupidity. "Why do such a reckless thing?"

Kijo had invited Vanu to witness the presence of the vampire to secure an ally in the fight against Mazgan. Old as she was, the Vanu understood the potential threat. More importantly, even though she was Varcolac to the bone, Vanu understood the need for the bloodservant system. Having a true ally necessitated honesty on Kijo's part.

She had no other option but to admit, "To circumvent any argument Mazgan might make for keeping it. To ensure its destruction at Eresna's hands."

"Grievous, Kijo. Some could call it treason."

"Would you call it such?"

"No," Vanu admitted after a long pause. "I understand your need for certainty. But I cannot go to the pack with no evidence. You need a real threat to get them back on your side. Simply showing strength will not be enough."

Kijo forced herself into an unnaturally calm state, breathing deeply in a way she was sure Vanu noticed. Once she'd settled, the charged atmosphere around them became more obvious. It was a sensation she had taken for granted, nothing more than a part of her daily life, much like her own smell. To Vanu, it should be new.

"Feel the air around you," she instructed. "The real threat is here."

Tiredly, Vanu did as she was told. After a few seconds, her brow furrowed and a scowl made the corners of her mouth slouch. Before too long, her gaze darted around the room, trying to find the unseen enemy her senses told her was there.

"Feel it?"

"Yes," Vanu confirmed. Now on full alert, Vanu's body tensed. Her claws dug into the wooden arms. "What is it? It feels...hot."

"I believe it's what my father called a lifestealer, an entity he described as cunning, powerful, very angry. Almost unstoppable once it finds a host. It's been with me since I investigated the portal."

"Hasty leap, Kijo. It's leftover energy from Garvey's travels to the Door and back. Nothing else."

Shoulders tense, eyes darting, Vanu's demeanor suggested more concern than her words allowed. She twisted in her seat, the sound of wood scooting across the floor reverberated in the empty room.

Kijo leaned forward. "Lavario told me I'd know the energy if I ever felt it."

"How?"

"I'd feel it reach for my life. Can you feel it reach for yours?"

Vanu turned away. "No. It's harmless."

Cognizant of the ruse, Kijo gave her companion a knowing look. Normally, she'd have little patience for denial under these circumstances, but that was when she had more than half the pack on her side. After her disgraceful fight with Lavario and her fallout with Mazgan, no other wolf heeded her call.

She pressed her companion. "And if it isn't harmless?"

For the first time, Vanu sounded genuinely apologetic. "Guardian Kijo, I cannot go to the pack and say with confidence that whatever's here is a threat or that Mazgan caused it through his involvement with the portals."

"You have my word."

"Based on something Garvey told you," Vanu gave her a pointed look. "Based on a vampire you sent away with him. Based on vague feelings of a presence in your room. Chasing ghosts."

Kijo needed more, much more. It was her fault. She should have been more specific in her directives to Garvey. Shock, along with time constraints, rushed her decision. It was coming back on her now, and she was feeling it.

Desperation put a sharp edge in her voice when she turned back to her companion. "I need you with me on this, Vanu. Your pack needs you."

"I am with you fully the moment it's certain. Up to then, I am with you behind closed doors."

Circumstances being what they were, it wasn't the worst response. Kijo nodded somewhat curtly before finally sitting across from her guest.

Always eager to be on the move, she fidgeted in her seat as she spoke. "Have you seen my—" Kijo stopped herself before she called him father. "—Lavario recently?"

"Yes."

Kijo hated herself for asking, "How was he?"

"Hard to say. He's certainly decorated. Not quite to the extent you have."

Kijo let the sarcasm slide without comment. She'd bought a lot of weird things since Lavario's disgrace, since her pack's abandonment: a couch, a lounge chair, a comfortable mattress. A few scattered paint cans, unopened, had gotten tossed to the side of the room along with some unhung wall art that slid, then flumped whenever she slammed her door.

Mostly, though, she had bought booze. Lots and lots of booze. And a cabinet for her booze, which leaned against the wall on its gimpy, uneven leg. Her space was a disastrous, ridiculous blend between her two factions. Aware of the divide, Kijo was not willing to fully acknowledge it, let alone defend it to another of her pack.

Silence settled between her and Vanu as they retreated to their own respective thoughts, neither of them really caring where the other vanished. One of the things that made their partnership work, aside from Vanu's ability to weather the storms of Kijo's temper, was the Vanu's level of comfort with prolonged periods of quiet. Instead of trying to chatter nervously the way most of Kijo's subordinates did, Vanu sipped her tea, which she had gone to the kitchen to brew herself, while Kijo gathered her thoughts.

Vaguely, Kijo remembered Vanu saying, "What will you do with other challengers?"

And her responding, "I will kill them."

Brow raised in an admonishment that Kijo chose to ignore, Vanu said, "And what does Garvey want from all this?"

Kijo couldn't be certain of anything, but her time spent with Lavario as his daughter taught her the finer points of strategy. He had warned her to always be ahead, to predict the movements of her opponents.

"Garvey wants the Varcolac and Isangelous to kill each other. He wants war."

"Kill him," Vanu said and left afterward.

Unable to get drunk, Kijo settled for the burning sensation of the alcohol as she poured it down her throat.

Chapter 4: Children of the Formless

KIJO

Wolves knew their origin. No mystery. No mythology. No dispute.

Born as a continuation of their species' story, a tale of science and magic gone awry, Kijo's kind kept to the script. Atrophia created vampire to destroy humanity. A sect of druids known as the formless took the infected and fused them with wolves, a creature naturally immune to the undead's plague. Idealists, the druids left their creation with the bloodthirst of the vampire but the intelligence to protect its food source. A perfect watchdog. Or conquerors as it turned out. That's pretty much all there was to it.

That's why it puzzled Kijo to learn she was a child of the formless rather than the unintended consequences of its mistake.

The wolf inside her entwined itself in her spinal column, letting her know the animal was closer to the surface than she might like, current conditions being what they were. One blink to make sure she was seeing correctly. Yes, Mazgan had created a chapel. He was in the middle of a sermon.

"This is our world. Our time." He'd said variations of that for the last half hour or so. From the looks of it, they'd have to hear it for another hour before it was over. "We are the children of a powerful goddess, destined to rule this world."

Newer wolves lapped it up. Chosen had a better ring to it than miscalculation. Glamorous as Mazgan's version was, it was also wrong. And dangerous. Under his rule, young wolves might never grow up to accept their role in the pack or the world. Kijo took heart to see older wolves like herself frown at their leader's carelessness, at the younger wolves' mounting excitement.

Was it enough to sway them back to her side? She doubted it.

Whatever followed her from the portal was there too. But it was farther away from her, almost indistinguishable from the hum of magical energy her own kind gave off. Anymore, she made a point to search for it amongst the white noise of everyday living. Never again would she let it slide itself into the familiar category.

She risked a glance in Lavario's direction. Bored, he rested his chin against his fist, one eyebrow raised in an expression of pure disdain. Amber, his bloodservant wasn't with him as she normally was. Almost as stubborn as Lavario, the girl was probably at Wraith Loch, trying to commune with the dead.

Occasionally, Lavario's facial features constricted and he twisted in his seat as though uncomfortable. Against all odds, Kijo hoped he found the foreign signature of the lifestealer amidst the cacophony of magic in the room. It was in her mind like a prayer. Saying over and over, *Feel it. Sense it.*

His eyes met hers. For an instant, they were like they always were, sharing an understanding and a love despite their stark differences. Concern for her brought his brows together. Small moments like this allowed him to be her father again. Never out in the open, not after he'd lost all rank, but in a mutual understanding that didn't require a verbal exchange. Once more, Kijo found herself angry at his unwillingness to overthrow Mazgan. Had he done so, their position might be radically different. There'd be no vampire, no lifestealer, no discord. Side by side, they could have kept such threats from harming the pack.

She wanted his counsel as badly as he wanted to give it. She rived her gaze from his, feeling the split down to the core of her being. Pack edict was clear. He was dead to them.

The mood in the room changed.

Mazgan said her name a few times. At first, she thought he might be calling her to his side to show his control over her. But the message broke through.

"It is with the blessing of the Formless that I issue this edict to all her people. Anyone who defeats Kijo in a challenge, killing her, shall stand by my side as this pack's second, regardless of his current rank."

Her packmates assessed her reaction. Far be it from her to disappoint the audience Mazgan gathered. Kijo smiled.

UNTIL MAZGAN'S PROMISE, challengers were few and far between. Flood, to trickle, back to flood, now back to trickle.

Gene was one of the few remaining after the spectacle she'd made of the first wolves who'd dared come her way to seek her rank. Teeth bared, ears flat on his head, he did a presentable job of posturing. To show her contempt for his display, Kijo didn't bother transforming.

Like Lavario, Gene relied heavily on magic—an atypical strategy for a Varcolac wolf, who exalted physical strength over mental. The scar she'd kept from her fight with father burned, as though to remind her what it was to take sorcery for granted. Lesson learned. Kijo prepared herself to counter every battle spell she knew.

He rushed at her, a blur of fur and teeth.

Surprised for the second time that day, Kijo found herself sidestepping Gene's rushed frontal assault. If he expected her to be thrown off by his tactics, he was sorely disappointed. Effortlessly, Kijo recovered into an offensive position, watching as Gene's momentum sent him tripping toward the ground. In a matter of seconds, she was full-blown wolf, charging at speed into the small of his back. Bones cracked on impact, the force propelled Gene headfirst to the floor.

Quick to recover, Gene transformed back to human. Magic was in the air, the energy of it buzzed around Gene. Although the animal inside of her raged, wanting to close in for the kill, Kijo forced herself to take heed of the power she felt, no longer sure that spells were the recourse of weaker wolves.

Patiently, she waited to see what her subordinate planned.

Nowhere near as powerful as Lavario, Gene was inexperienced, as green as her hands were red. Rattled, fear radiating from him like warmth from a nearby fire, Gene struggled to control his magic. A weak blowback, which barely had enough force to send Kijo staggering backward, was all he could manage.

Once she'd countered, Kijo bolted forward to take advantage of the time he'd have to spend gathering up energy for another spell. On impact, she hooked her claws into his flesh, simultaneously opening up deep wounds along his belly while dragging him to the floor. Even if he could manage another spell, he'd bleed out within minutes.

He did nothing. He'd given up.

Kijo opened her maw wide enough to clamp down on his throat.

"Please, listen to me," he whispered. "I am on your side."

Kijo snapped her teeth together, willing to hear last words but impatient for him to get on with it.

Gulping, Gene tried again. Eyes closed, he shot out information as quickly as he could in short, staggered bursts. "This was the only way to talk in private. Let me submit to you. Don't kill me. Talk with me in the cabin where you met Garvey. Tomorrow. Please."

On guard, Kijo stood slowly, releasing her hold on him in increments. Ready to strike, Kijo listened to her instincts—any inkling he was still a threat would be met with force. But he did nothing.

"I submit," he said loud enough for the entire pack to hear.

"I accept," Kijo responded. A quick glance was all she spared him before stepping over him to exit the arena.

Chapter 5: Temporarily Useful

KIJO

Patience wasn't a virtue to the Varcolac. Powerless wolves waited. Powerful wolves made them wait. The heat of Kijo's anger steadily rose until it leveled and ticked like a bomb. Only her own nagging desperate situation kept her from leaving.

When Gene finally appeared, he had a dimpled, apologetic smile where there should have had a tense, wary frown.

"Greetings, Guardian—"

"Get to your point." Kijo interrupted any other introductory material he had planned. "Keep in mind I can change my mind about your submission for another two days. Choose your words as if my jaws are at your throat."

Licking his lips, he swept the room with his gaze as though he were a paltry human bound by the limits of vision. Any small noise induced a fit of nervous twitches. He was as poor of an ally as Kijo could imagine.

"I recognize you don't think much of me," he said as if guessing her thoughts. To highlight his ineptitude, he fumbled with a nearby lamp after backing into it.

"Accurate," Kijo confirmed.

Confidence tried to find its way to his voice when he assured her, "I'm smart. Like your father. Very useful if you'll allow me to be."

Gene and Lavario were pack eccentrics. Both preferred magic and each used charm and wit more than tooth and claw. But Gene lacked the easy confidence of Lavario, the assurance he carried with him wherever he went. In short, he lacked a spine.

Eager to be on her way—indeed, even questioning why she'd shown up in the first place—Kijo walked to the door. "You are nothing like Lavario. Challenge me again and you will die, pup."

"Wait!" Gene snapped the open door shut in Kijo's face. It was a slight she forgave after hearing what came next. "I'm lovers with Vanu. That's how I knew about Garvey, the shack, the vampire. She has her own agenda, Guardian."

At last, he had Kijo's full attention. "She and Mazgan collaborate?"

"No... she wants his rank. She asked me to offer you my services and, uh, spy on you."

Kijo felt her fangs protrude. "And here we are."

He went back to licking his lips and looking for exits. Kijo couldn't blame him. Even she felt the room alter around her fury and hers could be a rage devoid of boundaries.

Backed up against the wall, Gene rushed out, "I'm not, though. I'm...not spying on *you*. I mean, I'll have to act like I am. But I'm *not*."

Stammering irritated Kijo. Each stop and start reminded her why it was wiser to kill him. A bumbling ally might prove more damaging than none at all. She stopped herself. There was an intricacy in the dance they'd done in battle, all the ducking and weaving that brought him to the floor with her. Perhaps a wolf like that could find his gumption in times of stress.

"Show me your teeth," she commanded.

He balked. "What?"

She transformed. *Do or die*, was the general message.

The struggle for control over his fear played out before he finally made a decision. The thin line of his teeth turned jagged. Hair turned to fur, nose to snout, hands to paws; he transformed with slow, deliberate ease. Done. He growled, forcing his snout into her face.

She didn't ease up on him. She forced him to face her without flinching.

Gene did a presentable job of it. Close enough.

No one understood how he managed to pass his test let alone survive seventy-five years. Kijo suspected it was because he didn't have anything worth taking—no rank, no belongings, not even his life. Ambition was something he did have. Lots of it too. Enough to exploit.

Kijo felt as close to happy as she could. The feeling persisted until it came to an abrupt stop.

The energy from the portal was gone.

VANU CALLED HER assumption hasty; jumping straight to lifestealer was rushed, unnecessary. Kijo didn't agree. Back in her younger years, when she was still his daughter, she'd asked Lavario how she'd know the strange creature he described if she ever encountered it. *The lifestealer hunts us*, he told her.

We are wolf, she'd replied. *We can destroy it.*

No, we can only contain it. We are its prey, us and every other living creature.

Lavario's warning rang in her ears. At the time, what he said hadn't made much sense—she couldn't fathom being anything's prey. After feeling the eyes of the lifestealer upon her, she understood.

Kijo ransacked every room in pursuit. Too worried for protocol, she barged inside the dwellings of her subordinates. Wolves suspecting Kijo might follow in the footsteps of Lavario prepared for battle.

"Stop." Kijo pushed them aside. "I am not here for your belongings."

"What is the meaning of this?" one of the bolder ones asked.

"Survival."

Each search came up empty. There was no trace of it in the corridors of the lower compound either. Hallway after hallway was clear of the magical energy, such power lingered. The lifestealer wasn't with any of the lesser wolves of the Varcolac pack.

She went back to the portal. *Touch,* the chameleon in its door-like skin commanded. Kijo gritted her teeth through the impulse. Against her better judgment, she got closer, halting a mere inch away from it. She sniffed indelicately. No new lead to follow. Nothing but the repeated command, *Touch.*

The only places left to search were the homes of the guardians. Lavario said the lifestealers, souls of vampires, sought out energy, much like their undead shells sought blood. They were attracted to power-hungry individuals who were easy to seduce and possess or to humans who had a very specific genetic defect.

Kijo started with the most obvious place for the lifestealer to go.

"Guardian Kijo." If Mazgan was surprised to see her, he hid it well. "I am delighted to see you come to me at last. Now I am afraid you need to beg to—"

She shoved past him without an invitation and began her search of the room. The decadence of the surroundings, the over-the-top tackiness of it, riled her. She shook it off. Hypocrisy shouldn't shock her. He was every other type of wrong, every other stripe of useless.

The lifestealer wasn't there.

"I look forward to killing you. You are a miserable excuse for a wolf," she let him know as she left.

There was one place left to go.

Minutes later, Kijo stood at the entrance to Wraith Loch. Amber stayed on its shore, fixated on her task to contact her dead family. Begging echoed throughout the cave, each iteration was more broken than the last. Kijo thought back with some regret on the night she ordered the slaughter of Amber's family. Although Kijo had done it to secure her place in the pack and maintain power, she couldn't help but feel entirely responsible for Amber's situation. One day, she hoped to call her sister. Until then, their relationship needed to be chilly at best, hostile if needed.

Amber continued to plead. "Please talk to me. I'm sorry. I'm so sorry."

Did Amber's message reach her family? Kijo didn't know. She assumed it was possible. What she felt told her Amber had caught the ear of the lifestealer. It searched for her, ready to tangle itself in the gut of her wants. Eventually, it would find her.

Kijo thought about intervening but stopped herself. She'd let Lavario deal with the creature.

The Isangelous

Chapter 6: Annoying, Useless Pets

YURI AND NADINE

The old ways never quite left Yuri.

Lemon tea brewed on the stove. Its aroma gave the air around her home a crisp summery scent. Carefully, she toyed with the brew until the honey balance was as Nadine liked it, slightly sweet undertones cutting through the biting acidity.

Nadine made no secret of her dislike for fancy décor. Tiptoeing, she'd say, *I feel like I'm playing frogger with your stuff, only I'm the car.* Breakables got stashed in the bedroom. Porcelain plates got set aside for cheap clay ones. Before too long, Yuri transformed her entire home into a klutz's paradise, complete with plastic cups she'd bought from a restaurant going out of business.

Last, but not least, she locked Mr. Fluffbutt, her cat, away. He meowed indignantly. "Sorry, buddy. Nadine says you're a soulless killing machine and it gives her the creeps. Harsh criticism from her." The cat clawed at the door for ten minutes afterward. "Mommy will get you after dinner," Yuri said to the door.

Her efforts were worthwhile in the end.

"Yum!" Nadine boomed, her voice enormous in the small room. Two courses before, she'd made her typical fuss; a long stream of you-shouldn't-haves followed by satisfied belches. "That meal was outrageously good. And...nice flowers." She nodded to the various flower arrangements, a compliment she threw in to please Yuri.

"Thank you. You said you needed to talk to me about a matter of importance?"

She was stuffing puff pastries into her mouth when she responded. "Right. Yes. It's about Tovin."

Yuri's hands shook uncontrollably under the table. Unbeknownst to Nadine and the rest of the pack, Yuri had snuck Tovin into the bloodservant pool. She'd found him as a child, cold and alone, and had followed him throughout his life, which only ever became marginally better as he aged. Because of her interference, she lived in a constant state of fear, worried that they'd find out and kill them both. It took a great deal of effort to make herself calm when she invited her friend to continue.

Tongue on tooth, Nadine called out Yuri's ruse. Her eyes shone with good humor. "Don't play indifferent. Each time he gets in trouble, you throw your hands up in the air, rushing toward him practically screaming, as Garvey said, 'My poor stupid cub!'"

Yuri lifted her chin. Quoting Garvey of all wolves stung her pride.

"Don't be like that, Yur. I'm only here to tell you that I've got it covered. My eyes are on the kid."

"How…" for once it was Yuri stumbling over her words. "How is he doing?"

"Well, you know. He's…well…he's really weird." Nadine's expression indicated there wasn't much else to say about it. She picked a bit at a few of the crumbs on her shirt, flicking them off onto the floor. "But at least he's not trying to run anymore. Dunno, maybe I miss that a bit. Got me three seconds of exercise in a day, five if I wanted to boost his confidence a bit. Most of the time he reads."

"Is Eresna pleased with him?"

That earned her a chuckle. "She thinks he's the Voltron of failure, a giant robot made of suck and whose individual parts are also suck. Curses you almost nightly for bringing him into her life. Wants to tie a big bow on his dick, then regift him to Lavario." She paused in her playful ribbing and continued in a more serious tone. "Mazgan put her over a barrel by forcing her to introduce Tovin to the other companions. She'd hoped to pawn him off on an underling. Stuck now."

While the news didn't surprise her, Yuri wanted desperately to hear something different. Ever since the extraction, she'd been left out of the loop—too far fallen from the queen's graces to warrant explanations. Selfishly, she hoped her leader could forgive all transgressions while embracing Tovin. Neither seemed all that likely given Nadine's description.

"What can you do for him? To integrate him? To make him appear more regal?"

Nadine groaned. Afterward, she gave several suggestions consisting of getting the boy ready to mingle with the other companions, mostly centered on his social skills and clothing choices. And then more about his clothes.

"His wardrobe is a distress flare that can be seen from space," Nadine concluded.

"I get it. His fashion needs work."

Nadine drummed her fingers on the armrest. Nails clicked on the wood's varnish. Both noises made Yuri's teeth protrude from her gumline. Guest or not, she was about ready to say something until, finally, her friend's shoulders heaved, indicating resignation.

"I suppose he's not a total lost cause. Eresna likes the kid. We all *like* the kid. He's doesn't serve his function. That's all." She stood to leave. "I'll see what I can do."

Mr. Fluffbutt, still trapped in the bedroom, yowled indignantly. At this point, he was no longer asking to be let out. He was demanding. The door vibrated with the force of his paw swipes. No doubt the carpet would be in squiggly threads around the edge of the door.

Nadine made a face at the ruckus. "What is it with you and annoying, useless pets?"

"Tovin isn't a pet."

"As long as you'll acknowledge the other two are on the nose."

Smiling a bit at the joke, Yuri thanked her friend for coming.

Once the door shut, she let Mr. Fluffbutt out of his prison. The irate cat, black fur vertical along his spine, jumped up on the table, swiping at anything in his path. Forks clattered on the floor. Hissing followed. Done reprimanding her for the dinner he wasn't invited to, the fickle creature jumped to the floor and groomed himself as though nothing had happened at all.

"Poor baby," Yuri clucked at him.

"Yow!" he agreed.

After a treat or five, he was purring while rubbing his head against hers. The soft clicks of his contentment made Yuri wish her relationships with everyone else could be as simple. What she wouldn't give to have a queen who could be so easily placated by a few fish treats or a friend who forgave her after a few belly rubs. But when it came to pack matters, nothing was that simple.

The previous night made things a great deal more complex. Tovin had been out of his room. "He's a mess," she told Mr. Fluffbutt. "But he's our mess. Isn't he?"

Chapter 7: Not so Special

TOVIN

The door, the door, the door.

Hyperventilating, Tovin managed to blunder his way back to his bedroom. He looked around with panicked eyes, so certain Eresna—the werewolf queen who kept him captive—was there with him and she knew he'd broken free and left the confines of his room. Against his chest, he hugged the box of records he brought back with him up. Panicked, not really thinking, he shoved the box under the bed and hoped no one would find it until he thought of a way to get it back to the closet. Sleep wasn't something he ever thought he'd do again. Cramped up in a corner, his knees drawn up against his chest, he stuck to the thought until he woke up the following morning.

The ghost was once again with him. "You're evil," Tovin told her as forcefully as he could while being quiet. "Why show me something that'll get me killed?"

That was not the Door.

"Certainly looked like one!"

Typical ghost, she went through a wall. "That's perfect!" he shouted at her, but it wasn't enough. He went right up to the place where she'd vanished and pounded loud enough to collect rent money.

That's how Kurt found him. "What on earth are you doing?" He'd never looked so puzzled or put out. He assessed the situation with a manager's eye: cold, detached, critical, but looking for an opportunity for growth. "We let you out at the same time every day. You should know the schedule by now."

Kurt was the only other human Tovin had been allowed to see so far, and he couldn't say he cared much for the other man's company. Anxiety made Tovin snappier than he wanted to be when he said, "I *do*. Thanks for reminding me, though."

Kurt opted to ignore the tone and go directly to another topic. "I'm going to introduce you to Jerald and Alpha. Start your integration. Up to the task?"

No, he was not ready. His heart pumped like that of a small animal—faster and faster to compensate for its insignificance. Sweat staggered down his spine, stopping and starting like a drunk failing at his sobriety test. Eventually, it pooled in Tovin's ass crack. And it itched. Oh god, it itched. *Yup*, his entire body said. *You are definitely freaking out.*

He managed to respond, "Uh. Oh. Maybe."

Kurt's brow knitted together into a vee, as in very vexed. "I need confidence from you today. This is happening, Tovin."

"Fine. I'm *super* ready. Couldn't be more eager or excited. Confidence galore."

Kurt gave him one last level look before running off to fetch Alpha and Jerald. Head buried in his hands, Tovin leaned against the wall and slumped. Why had he tried introducing himself to adventure? He'd gone from being a somewhat happy salesman to a captive of blood-drinking monsters after one bad date with Garvey, his would-be rebound fuck who turned out to be a werewolf. The problems just kept coming: the ghost who didn't communicate what she wanted, the strange doorway that called out to him, the box of death records containing files that said people who touched the strange doorway, which he'd just done, died. And now he had to socialize. Fuck life. Fuck adventure. Fuck everything.

At least his heart rate was back to normal. Tovin was grateful for that. Clarity returned in pieces, bits of logic where he recognized Kurt's presence and his demands were good signs. No one knew he'd been out of his room. Otherwise, the conversation would be much different.

Tovin clung to the hope Eresna might change her mind and give up on the idea of making him socialize. According to her, the other bloodservants learned of his existence, and their jealousy forced her hand. Tovin didn't care about the reason. Mingling with the other humans felt as wise as adding water to acid. So far, he'd only seen Jerald and Alpha from a distance. Where he was concerned, that was enough. Both of them seemed like real assholes.

Turned out they were what they seemed.

Alpha's name suggested as much, but Tovin held out hope for Jerald, who was kind of sexy for a slope-headed Neanderthal. Real old-school humanity. He looked like he could hit rocks against larger rocks to make a firepit of some sort.

Jerald assessed Tovin in one brief glance. "Don't look so special ta me."

Alpha, a very skinny skinhead in skinny jeans—he had a theme and was sticking to it—agreed. "Not at all. Normal as herpes."

Tovin agreed too. "I'm not special."

The ghost caught up with the times. *Herpes is normal now?*

Kurt bottled his snark. No doubt, Tovin would have to drink it later. For now, though, Kurt calmed himself by going to his happy place. It was probably a wondrous land where people completed assigned tasks in the proper order, then left in a single-file line without complaint.

Eventually, Kurt's private-paradise expression faded. He scowled when he suggested, "How about a movie?"

Tovin assumed Kurt chose the activity because movies demanded silence from polite people. It didn't stop Tovin from feeling like a babysat child. For extra awkwardness, it was a horror about ghosts.

Jerald and Alpha talked, talked, and talked. Whenever they thought something was especially funny, they'd bounce off each other's shoulders. Eventually, they were shoving, both taking the force right up to the line of a blow.

This was fine until Jerald jabbed his thumb the general direction of the screen asked, "What do you think of this dumb chick?"

"Oh," Tovin said once he realized the question was for him. He studied the pretty young lady. Eyes wide in the dark, she walked down the stairs, using the wall to guide her way. "She's not dumb."

Wrong answer. The two men rolled their eyes. Jerald vocalized their shared contempt. "She's going right toward the danger!"

Defensive, Tovin countered, "When your fuse blows, do you think there is a vengeful ghost in the basement trying to lure you? Is that the first thing that comes to your mind? Because, personally, I'm going downstairs to throw the switch."

They gave him a hard glare.

"Look, it's not like *she* hears the cellos playing in the background. That's all I'm saying."

Both men snorted. Again, Jerald spoke for them both, snide mockery laced through his voice. "Good point, Tovie."

At least the real ghost was on his side. *Damn skippy. I am not accompanied by spooky music.*

"Thanks." Tovin kept his response as enigmatic as possible. Aimed at the ghost, the comment hopefully satisfied Jerald as well.

Luckily, the subject dropped when the woman in question had her soul sucked away by the lurking demon chilling in her basement. As it was in most cheesy horror movies, her eyes bubbled out of her head. Jerald and Alpha guffawed at the misfortune. Soon after, they started up their jabbing again.

Tovin made a sour face at their stupidity.

Jerald tried to be funny when he said, "What you lookin' at, Tovie? Checkin' me out?"

"No, he's checkin' me out." Alpha followed his lead, laughing without really laughing.

"You're both pretty," Tovin assured them with a bit of sawdust in his voice.

The offhand remark upset both men. Jerald's fists crunched together. He looked at Kurt to gauge how he'd respond if things became physical. *Very poorly*, Kurt's expression said. Jerald sneered in response.

A bit more reckless and a great deal more impulsive, Alpha pushed himself up from his seat. Spittle boiled out of his mouth. Red-faced, Alpha puffed up his scrawny body as though to warn away a bear.

"What you said, Tovie... Take it back."

Tovin obliged. "Okay. Neither of you is attractive."

The situation did not improve afterward.

Kurt interjected himself between shouted threats. "Cut it out," he warned Alpha, who kept trying to push his way to Tovin. When Alpha didn't listen, Kurt took him by the shirt and used the man's own momentum to fling him to the couch. "Enough."

This time he listened. Soon afterward, Alpha and Jerald were gone.

Overflowing with ire, Kurt came back into the room with a mouthful of questions he'd archived throughout the whole ordeal. Of course, the first and the most pressing was "Are you just stupid?"

"No."

Kurt ran his hands through hair he didn't have. After a succession of nods—during which the man kept saying *right, okay, right*—he was ready to try again. "That did not go well. Are you at least aware of that?"

Tovin indicated he was.

"Good. That's something at least. I can build from that." For once, Kurt looked worried. Genuinely worried. Back in his private world, people were jumping the line. Maybe they weren't standing in line at all. "Tovin," he said when he came back out to reality, "I have to report this."

Kurt left after Tovin promised he'd try harder, do better. He told himself the same lie, and he halfway believed it before remembered the box he'd stolen and shoved under the bed. Once everyone had left and he was reasonably sure they weren't coming back, he pulled it out to stare for a while, trying his best to think of some type of plan that would bail him out of his predicament.

There wasn't really anything to say about it except "Shit."

Right, the ghost said. *You did that one on your own.*

Chapter 8: Team Tovin

TOVIN

The ghost had the bones of destiny, a constrictive rib cage only teasing at the possibility of escape. So Destiny is what Tovin named her. She never left him. Whenever he went to sleep, she was there at the foot of the bed. As he woke, she greeted him to start a new day. A nuisance. She was also the realest thing to him in his new world.

Being watched, Destiny warned him. *Redheaded werewolf.*

The sound of stomping combat boots followed. Nadine burst into the room. "Hiya, kiddo."

Nadine rubbed Tovin's head as though he were a dog, cuffing him playfully afterward as though he were a *bad* one. Despite her many flaws, Tovin found he'd warmed to Nadine. With her, he could be himself—no corrections, no reprimands, no stress. The only other one who made him feel that way was Yuri, but her visits were rare. Tovin didn't understand why. One day, she'd come to warn him away from the door and urge him to play the part of a brainwashed idiot who believed he'd been brought there to become a werewolf. She'd said she was a protector, someone who'd watched him his whole life. Afterward, she all but vanished, only to be seen on the sidelines, watching but never interacting. Like everything else in this new world, she confused him.

Nadine let gravity take her to the chair. One somewhat bushy eyebrow rose, and her blue eyes sparkled with good humor. She shook her head at him and said, "Hey there, track star. You feeling okay? Your face is a bit red."

Anxiety made him look continually flush. Tovin tried to pin it on a fever, hoping Nadine might leave him alone if she thought he was sick. "It's getting worse."

Nadine licked her tooth. "Uh-huh. Heard you had a good time with Jerald and Al."

"They're both dickpickles."

Nadine tossed her head back to laugh. Tears were in her eyes before she was done. One finger swiped them off her cheek windshield-wiper style. Tovin knew it wasn't that funny; Nadine always looked for an opportunity to laugh.

"Holy shit." She stopped herself before the episode morphed into giggles. "So what's their beef with you? Yours with them?"

Quickly, Tovin gave her the rundown: their snideness, their vulgarity, their undeserved sense of self-satisfaction, and—worst of all—the violence lurking under each and every gesture.

"Their beef with me is they think I'll make them gay somehow." Tovin rolled his eyes.

"So what...they think you were bitten by a radioactive gay spider and now you're supergay?"

"I'd like a better origin story please."

"I want to know how it works. Do you have to bite them or...suck their—"

"I get it."

"—cocks," Nadine finished. She put the tip of her tongue on one sharp tooth to show her amusement.

"Groan." Eyes rolling, Tovin summed up his reaction.

Undeterred, she launched into this complex story where Tovin's superpowers backfire. Before long, he had a sidekick named Dickpickle and they were saving Manhattan from a giant ape. She acted out each part until Tovin couldn't help but laugh with her.

"At the end, the ape drops the girl because you gayed him. She's falling down, arms flapping in the wind. White dress billowing around her like a falling cloud. Then splat. And you're just like, 'Eeep!' My bad.'"

"And we live happily ever after?"

"If that's your kink."

Nadine let the joke run its course, smiling in a sad, patient way. The mannerisms signaled she came there on a mission. Humor sugarcoated the medicine she'd come to push down his throat.

Tovin muttered, "What's up, Nadine?"

"You're making yourself an adversary."

"I am not—"

"You are, kiddo. You are."

Tovin bristled, falling silent. The idea he needed to go out on play dates with other captives nettled him with its absurdity. He didn't know who could be so delusional to believe they'd been brought there to become werewolves. As far as lies went, it was one of the most nonsensical he'd heard.

Nadine waited for his response. When she didn't get one, she continued. "Look, Eresna only wants you to suck less at your job. She doesn't believe you're stupid enough to needle Alpha and Jerald without knowing exactly what you're doing. You're right to hate them—they're terrible—but..." She rolled her hand. "You can't keep isolating yourself."

"So...what am I supposed to do? Agree with their nonsense?"

Nadine chuckled and leaned back in the chair. She placed one large boot up on the fragile glass table. "Boss them around. Make them fall in line behind you. You'd have Eresna's support. She's team Tovin once Tovin becomes team status quo."

Sour as Eresna was, Tovin sort of doubted she was anything other than team bureaucracy. "Look, I know you think I'm some weak do-nothing no one, but—"

"I actually think you're quite nice," Nadine corrected him.

"So a *nice* weak do-nothing no one, but—"

"Don't be a dickpickle, Tovin. Being kind takes a tremendous amount of courage in this world. All I'm saying—and what's been said to you many times before—is that you need to be more pragmatic. Eresna isn't an infinity pool of patience. Don't hit the edge. When you do, it'll be time to get the fuck out of the pool. Want to stay swimming, kiddo?"

Admitting defeat, Tovin bobbled his head.

"Good! So are you ready to be social?"

"Hurray." Tovin swirled his finger in mock celebration.

Once she left, Tovin pulled the box out from under the bed. Photos of hundreds of dead people spilled out from each folder. Tovin arranged their faces, searching for some pattern other than what was written. Different sexes, races, ages. The people were separated by vast swaths of time, some by as many as 200 years.

Seeing no connection other than the obvious, Tovin wondered, "What's the fuss over a door?"

It's not the Door. It's a portal. Destiny came out of lurking to correct him. *You have the mutation. You've touched it. You're open.*

"What?"

You're a conduit.

Tovin waited for more of an explanation he gradually realized wasn't coming. "Oh. Okay. Thanks. Cleared things right up. Understand fully now."

Destiny drifted right through his sarcasm.

After minutes of making faces at her didn't yield results, Tovin began the task of putting the folders back in the box, meticulously organizing each one back to how he originally found it. Somehow, he'd have to get the box back to the storage room.

"Any suggestions on how to get rid of this?"

None.

Perhaps being dead made one sour and unhelpful. Not to mention annoying. Resolved to continue with his life the best he could under the circumstances, Tovin laid out clothes for his social event. Nadine had told him the first would be a Christmas party.

"Does this look festive?" He held up a green sweater he'd matched with black pleated slacks. The face she made suggested it didn't look too great, so he added a loose-fitting collared shirt paired with a green and yellow plaid tie.

"Better?"

She stuck her finger down her imaginary throat to signify vomiting.

"Harsh."

Don't go, Tovin.

"Not optional anymore."

It'll be bad if you go.

"Yeah, well. It'll be worse if I stay. Nadine said I'd drown, which I'm almost sure is literal."

Wrathful, her colorless eyes fixed on his with a thousand lifetimes worth of unresolved grievances. Hers was a slow burn, a steady one—the emotional equivalent of leaving water on the stove to boil away until fire took your whole house.

Tovin tried to reason with her. "Not like anything else has changed. I'll come right back. You're being very *possessive.*" He chuckled at his own terrible joke.

Tovin. Destiny said his name like a warning. *Don't go.*

He ignored her and went back to fretting over the next day's party. No matter what, he'd do something wrong then. He knew it. Anxiety looped: he worried about worrying, and that made him worry more, which caused him to be unable to sleep. And being unable to sleep worried him.

Oddly, he didn't consider the ghost. She was off to the side, the way she always was, waiting for another day.

Chapter 9: Social Obligations

TOVIN

There was a bit of fuzz on Tovin's robe. It clung to him through a million miles worth of primping and grooming. Maybe the werewolves wanted him to be the picture of perfection, but the fuzzball wanted him to be real. Tovin hid it in a pocket as Kurt approached.

"Today is a big day." Kurt came to underline what was already in italics, bolded, and in a different typeface.

"It sure is," Tovin responded, minus the enthusiasm.

This day, he got to meet his fellow captives. Not too long ago, Kurt had said there were others like them—people who knew the lies behind the grins—and those people were either dead, useful, or compliant. Tovin wondered if he'd recognize his peers by sight. If they would be internally rolling their eyes along with him. Unfortunately, he had to meet all the captives, even the ones as dumb as Alpha and Jerald, and his directive was to aid in the con or die. He was ready. Ready. Ready. Ready-rino. Or so he told himself over and over again. Whatever expression he'd fixed on his face began to slide; he could feel it drift away but didn't know how to hook it back.

Kurt gave him a harsh finger wag. "Smile. Stick to the script. Do you remember what we talked about?"

"Yes."

"Good."

Tovin yo-yoed his weight from one foot to the other while Kurt checked him for abnormalities, any visible sign that he was botched goods. Seeing nothing report-worthy, Kurt patchworked a smile on his face and thumped Tovin on the shoulder.

Tovin gave Kurt another forced smile. "Pass inspection?"

"You'll be fine. Wait here. I'll tell Eresna you're ready."

Tovin took the fuzzball from his pocket and put it back in its place. He didn't have to wait long. Eresna came around the corner, Kurt trailing behind, moments later.

"Hello," Tovin greeted her as she walked toward him.

She skipped greetings. "You are nervous. Why are you nervous?"

Tovin's eye twitched. She expected him to love her already. The authority, the power, and the prestige of being her servant should have theoretically puffed him up and quelled any objections he ever had to the entire ordeal.

As far as he could tell, the connection they theoretically shared, what the werewolves called bonded, allowed her to glean some of his thoughts or at least his general emotions. It bothered him that she might be able to detect his moods at any particular moment. Tovin could never pin down for certain how extensive the ability was. Like him, she said very little about what she knew.

"Only a little nervous, Guardian," he said. "I'm sure it'll pass."

"Good. Here." She handed him what looked like a scepter, a gaudy bejeweled thing that he might later use to prop open his door, hold down paper, or crack nuts. Tovin rolled his eyes at it.

Her lips tightened. "Someone other than me will be watching today. Remember what's expected of you."

Tovin took the item with a disingenuous thank-you, holding it up over his head—mockingly triumphant.

A dark look was all the response she had time for. The doors opened. Before he could retreat, she took him by his hand and pulled him through.

Thousands of little blue and white lights blinded his eyes. They decorated the small trees along the pathway, which lead to a massive evergreen in the center. Draped with tinsel and blue lights in the shape of icicles, it was quintessential Christmas. Beneath, there were hundreds of brightly wrapped gifts.

"Tovin would like to welcome you all to his first Christmas with us." Eresna introduced him, then stepped aside.

"Welcome." Tovin began and concluded his speech.

Beside him, Eresna cleared her throat.

"And Merry Christmas," Tovin added, waving the scepter in front of him in an arc.

Showing no sign of irritation, Eresna clapped, and most of the others followed suit. A few in the crowd looked at each other with raised eyebrows, smirks, the occasional scowl. Jerald gave him a resentful curl of the lip.

"Now Tovin will hand out the gifts," she prompted him as he remained silent, standing as much off to the side as he could possibly get.

"Oh. Right. Presents."

One by one, Tovin called out the names of his peers and handed each a decorated box. The other servants accepted the gifts with various levels of ceremony. Some bowed, some shook his hand, some did a weird type of dance, some gave him a flower in return, some simply offered him a big smile. Jerald and Alpha each gave him a terse nod.

Tovin thought he'd reached the end of it until one last woman made her way up to the small stage area. Unlike the others, her dress was modest, almost bare-bones in its simplicity. No jewels on her fingers. No crown on her head. No diamonds looped around her neck.

Finally, Tovin thought. *Someone like me as Kurt promised. A person I can relate to.* A genuine smile sprung to his lips, the first spontaneous one he'd had since being brought here. Tovin reached back to retrieve her gift. He turned his head left, right, up, and down. Tovin even looked under the tree skirt. There were no other presents there.

"Sorry," he told the woman as she waited. "I'll find it here in a sec."

Eresna grabbed his arm with a pinch. "Tovin was delighted to meet all of you."

He pointed to the young lady. "But the—"

To him, Eresna whispered, "Stop pointing at nothing." To everyone else, she said, "My dear sweet one, I was too eager and already opened the gift you got for me." She laughed, inviting everyone else to do the same. Most did. "My apologies."

"Oh, that's okay. That's good. That's fine. I hope you liked it." Tovin sputtered out a string of banalities. His attention locked onto the giftless woman in the crowd, who stood there without comment until she finally morphed into a face Tovin recognized. It was Destiny.

"I loved it. Thank you." Eresna glared over at him. Her expression went from reproachful to worried the longer she studied his face. Her grip on his arm slackened, and the compressed line of her lips relaxed.

Once again, she addressed the crowd for him. Her light, musical voice carried the room away from what might have been a disaster. Everyone but Tovin traveled with her. He stayed behind, him and the woman in blue.

Chapter 10: More Social Obligations

TOVIN

Gone. No, not gone. Gone. No, not gone. Gone?

Destiny came and went—one moment hovering beside him in calm stasis, the next vanished. Sometimes, she reappeared off in the distance as one of the crowd, the hem of her blue dress visible between parted legs. Other times, he'd turn his head and she'd be right there with him, listening as one of the other companions chatted about his great future. Or, as was the case now, in line with him for the shrimp buffet.

"Stop where's-Waldoing me," Tovin said with as much hush as he could, cognizant of those around him, especially Kurt, who was rarely out of earshot. "Just tell me what you want."

Company, she replied.

"Tovie! Tovie! Tovie!" A redhead pushed past everyone else in line, clanking as she walked. When she stopped moving, the jewelry she wore went *tic-tic-tic* like the balls of a Newton's Cradle.

Lonnie. Tovin remembered her from the gift-giving ceremony. How could he forget her? Jewels on top of beads, beads on top of lace, lace on top of silk, silk on top of what sort of looked like a ball gown: she wore an aggregate of textures and styles that left her looking like some fashionable abstract painting everyone complimented in the presence of the artist, then speculated how it became popular once they got into the car.

He didn't have time to correct her about his name.

Wearing a wide, generous smile that bordered on insane, she squeezed Tovin up against her breasts. "Tovie! Tovie! Tovie!" she said again as though he hadn't heard her the first time. "We're happy to see you're feeling better. We were all so devastated when we were told that your illness might be fatal."

Not as devastated as he was to hear it. "Thank you. I'm pleased to finally meet you as well. I hope what I had is no longer catching."

Beside him, Kurt coughed. The man was never too far away.

"Oh no!" Tovin exclaimed. "Kurt's come down with it!"

At least the ghost laughed.

Kurt's look was dark.

Lonnie blinked dumbly and continued to talk. And talk. And talk. Big gulps of air punctuated subject changes; they went from what Lonnie liked to what Lonnie wanted to be to what Lonnie thought of this or that. Like a child trying to get attention, she grabbed at the sleeve of the robe he wore and pulled on it whenever she got really excited.

"We're so going to be besties! I can feel it!"

Oh no. No. No. No. Before the ceremony, Tovin practiced a wide array of facial expressions that were all some variation of happy for this exact reason. He hoped the one he chose from the stock responses conveyed delight rather than the deep, bottomless dread he felt.

Eresna saved him. "I'm sure you two will be great friends. Now we need to make the rounds and introduce Tovin to the other companions."

"Sure! Sure! Yes! I was so happy to meet you, Tovie." Lonnie stepped aside but not totally out of the way. She continued to bee hover over their shoulders, darting in and out but always there each time he turned around—sort of like the ghost, only alive and more terrifying.

At once ethereal yet somehow mundane, the actual ghost drifted behind them, looking at her surroundings like a tourist on vacation.

Eresna looped her arm around Tovin's to steer him back to the crowd. Other introductions followed until Tovin had heard every rehearsed variation imaginable of "we're so happy to meet you" and "we'll have to do [insert thing here] some day."

Tovin thanked them all.

They continued to look at him. Why? They invited him to something, and he said thanks. What else was there?

"Tell us about yourself, Tovin." Nadine rolled her hand.

"Oh. I'm a salesman. I mean, I *was*. I sold stuff as a salesman. Household stuff." Yep. That pretty much covered it. Tovin shrugged. The scepter, which he'd tied with the sash of his robe, bobbed at his side.

Lonnie was there for him. "Neato!"

Eresna gave Nadine a side-glance.

Tovin got the idea. "But now I'm here for my great destiny. On my way to becoming a werewolf like Eresna and—" Tovin gestured to the other werewolves in the circle, whose names he realized he didn't know. "—everyone else."

They looked at him.

"I'm really excited about it," he assured the perplexed faces.

Rolv, Lonnie's master, took up the mantle. "We're all thrilled, Tovin. I can't wait for the day I call you brother."

Lonnie clapped her hands together for him—it was her job as his bestie after all—while Tovin made a mental note to take her with him wherever he went in case he needed his own start-up claque.

"Wonderful," she said, "simply wonderful."

Wasn't it, though?

AT SOME POINT, the werewolves left the humans to socialize amongst themselves.

Eresna graced him with a tender pat on the cheek, behind which she slid in a warning. "Be good, love."

As soon as the door shut, Jerald advanced. He used his shoulder to push Tovin against a wall—hard enough for him to know it was no accident, soft enough to look like one to onlookers. Very few turned the direction of the commotion. They were busy congratulating themselves for various feats of nothing.

When he was on his own, stashed away in a hidden room, Tovin had plenty of time to ask himself, *Who would be dumb enough to believe they're here to become werewolves?* Now he had an answer. These guys. All of his fellow human companions seemed sure they were the smartest, wittiest, prettiest people to ever exist and that it took a group of immortal beings to finally realize that about them.

Jerald was one of the worst of the delusioners.

One lip too thick, the other too thin; skin too smooth on his head, too potholed everywhere else; fingers too short, nails too long; head too large, neck too small: Jerald's features were a nest of contradictions and overcompensations. Taken all together, he wasn't an unattractive man. It's when you looked too long things came unraveled. Tovin made it a point never to look too long.

"You ain't nobody," he whispered. His words were wet and stank like a million years worth of garlic plaque. "Nobody."

Tovin kept it cordial. "Agreed."

Destiny kept it unhelpful, *Call him an asshole.*

Looking at her was a mistake.

Jerald followed the direction of his stare. "Who's there, Tovie? Your invisible friend from the party?"

Alpha wasn't too far behind. "Yeah, invisible are the only types of friends he got."

"True enough," Tovin told them both.

Even Lonnie started to look like good company. Between the gap the two men left with their bodies, she waved at him with zealous hope. She wanted to be the best friend of the enigmatic companion of the powerful guardian of Eresna more than she wanted to breathe.

He could make that work. Tovin tried to make his way back toward the harmless-but-deranged woman. Jerald and Alpha blocked him.

"Stay a bit, Tovie. Let's talk."

"Sorry, I don't know much about protein shakes or steroids," Tovin quipped.

Unnatural laughter pealed from Jerald's mouth, curling upward at the edges. It was an unhappy, violent noise more like cawing. One large hand grabbed the loose slack of Tovin's robe, pulling him upward on his toes.

Tovin looked the big man in the eye. "Put me down."

Jerald obeyed. "Okay. You got it, Tovie."

Well, that wasn't so bad, was the last thing Tovin thought before Jerald's hand thwacked the side of his face. Ears, as it turned out, really could ring. Whose number they dialed was anyone's guess. Blood welled up in his mouth, poured down the front of his shirt. Droplets of it pooled on the slick surfaces of his buttons.

"You hit me." Stupefied, Tovin looked down at his own hands. The room refused to come into focus.

Destiny was ready to brawl. *He did! Hit him!*

"You're not helping," Tovin snapped at her.

Sharks were attracted by the smell of blood, so were drama enthusiasts. The other companions gathered to rubberneck the altercation.

"He's nuts," Alpha told the growing audience, asking them to take sides. "Talking to nothing. It's what happened at gift givin'. You all saw him there, jawing at the air like he was high."

Instead of backing down, Tovin doubled down. The dead woman wasn't much, but she was what he had. "She's a ghost. Her name is Destiny. And, uh, she can smite you."

I can't smite them, Tovin, Destiny said.

"Oh. Well. You can sure as hell open doors and get me into trouble!"

Destiny glared down at him without apology. Tovin strongly felt she owed him one.

Luckily, Jerald appeared to be superstitious. He retreated to the group, crossing his fingers over his chest as he muttered some type of prayer. Whenever Alpha tried to advance, Jerald held him away.

"He's touched by the devil," he told Alpha.

That's the way Nadine found them when she opened the door to end the "party": Tovin on one side of the room, beaten and bloody. Everyone else on another, shocked and scared. She licked her tooth.

"Well," she said, "another successful outing."

Chapter 11: Spook Yarn

YURI AND NADINE

Yuri saw little through the crack in the door. Pressing her face closer to the keyhole brought her friend and her queen somewhat in focus.

Eresna fumed. "There's a ghost now? What is it with humans and their ghost stories?"

Nadine confirmed. "He's calling it Destiny." Nadine's barking laughter echoed. Toward the end, she started snorting.

That's when Eresna cut her off. "The situation amuses you?"

Although her leader's tone was stern, a slight smile was visible—the lurking humor, the kindness behind the administrative outrage. Nadine must have seen it too.

Her response was cheerful. "Hell yes, I do. He told the others Destiny would smite them. Freudian little dork."

"He actually said that?"

"Affirmative."

Eresna put her hand to her temple. "What am I going to do with that kid? And Jerald." She shook her head. "Something must be done about him too."

Nadine wasn't a troubleshooting type of wolf. "I dunno. Tell Tovin to knock it off. Jerald—" She rolled her hand. "—gobble that turkey."

"My dearest Nadine. You can't eat all your problems."

"You can when they're edible."

Eresna grunted. Afterward, she went quiet. Real solutions were what she needed—the type Yuri usually provided. But Eresna couldn't forgive Yuri. The Alpha Guardian should have received a handsome, dignified man worthy of her rank. Instead, because of Yuri's carelessness and her outright deception, she got saddled with Tovin. Although Garvey, the False Moon who hunted with them, had caused Tovin's injuries, Yuri had been the one who snuck Tovin inside the bloodservant pool. Worse, at least in Eresna's eyes, she'd allowed Garvey to have free rein during his date with Tovin, trusting him to follow the script the way they had so many times before.

Yuri winced as Nadine tried to gesture her direction. Reckless as she was, Nadine knew better than to ask how long her queen would cling to her grudge. Instead, Nadine tilted her head to the side and nudged her chin toward the door, indicating Yuri was outside eavesdropping.

Eresna knew as much. Finally, with a sigh, she said, "Join us."

Yuri kept formal—her back straight, her tone starched like a stiff collar. "Guardian Eresna."

Eresna did not greet her in return. "You've heard the problems. What do you suggest?"

Yuri did her best to act as though she hadn't given the situation much thought. She kept her response matter-of-fact, indifferent. "Encourage Tovin with the ghost. He's hardly the first to see one, but it gives him something to talk about. As for Jerald...no one likes him except Alpha. Vilify him. Isolate him. Give Tovin credit for his eventual removal. Work with the situation as it is rather than try to change it."

Eresna's response was enigmatic. "Interesting. And when everyone starts to see ghosts?"

Yuri shrugged. "Annoying but not unmanageable. By then Tovin will be integrated."

Nadine, as always, was on board. "I say we rename the ghost. Something cool. And only Tovin can keep its bloodlust in check."

Even though Nadine was on her side, Yuri struggled not to roll her eyes at her heavy-handed overdramatization of events. "Keep the name as it is," she suggested. "Make it literal. The ghost is real. Its name is Destiny, and it chose Tovin."

There was bite to Eresna's voice when she said, "There's something between you and this boy. More than you've said."

Yuri kept her voice level as she lied, "No, Guardian. I bonded with him during the extraction. Garvey kept him awake. He was such a sweet—"

"Yes, I know the story." Eresna cut her off.

Appearing uncomfortable, Nadine fidgeted in her seat. Yuri understood why. She and Eresna were the two Nadine loved more than anything else in the world, and the tension between them drove her mad. Unable to bear it any longer, she let out a short laugh that sounded like a thunderclap on a clear day.

Yuri winced at the noise. She lied to them all, but her lies to Nadine clawed at her more than the beast inside herself. An urge to confess rose inside her, but she beat it down by a pragmatism greater than her guilty conscience. Dead wolves were nothing more than pelts.

"My relationship is as I said it was. Nothing more," she told her queen.

Eresna closed her eyes and opened them again. "Very well, Yuri. We will try it as you say. There is a ghost, and it chose Tovin. Go work your magic."

NADINE CAME OUT of Eresna's chamber a long time after Yuri left. Her expression troubled, she staggered toward Yuri. Her normal steady-forward stride was filled with stops and starts as though she'd forgotten something important and was on the verge of remembering any second now.

"Everything okay?" Yuri asked her.

"Yeah. Uh. Yeah." She rolled her hand a bit. "Eresna wants to vet replacements for Jerald and Alpha. And, uh—" She rolled her hand in the air. "I'm in charge of the extraction."

Heat rushed to Yuri's face. Her tone was brittle when she replied, "A promotion. Congratulations. Who is on your team?"

"Well...Garvey for starters."

"And?"

"And you."

Fighting back a reflexive wave of anger, Yuri swallowed two or three replies before she was finally able to say, "Oh, that's good. Very good. Very big step."

Conversation was sparse. The two of them untangled the knotted hallways leading to Tovin's room with minimal interaction. They briefly talked about the weather the way humans might; meanwhile, the animal inside paced, snapping impatiently at the social constraints keeping them at bay. Maybe it was Yuri's imagination, but each passerby looked at her as if they already knew. Wolves probably smelled rank the way salmon knew to swim upstream.

Yuri sniffed.

"Here we are," Nadine said with relief. She knocked a few times on the door. Immediately afterward, her voice exploded, "Hey, Tovin. We're coming in. Make yourself pretty. Five, four, three, two, one..."

They both heard scurrying, the sound of frantic, up-to-no-good dragging of something from here to there, during the countdown. Nadine smiled. Yuri did not.

"Hiya, kiddo," Nadine greeted Tovin the moment the door swung open. Because she'd been carelessly forceful, as always, the knob hit the wall. No doubt it left a circular imprint. Yep. It sure did. Yuri guided her fingers along the edge of the crater, frowning with fierce disapproval.

Tovin gave them a nervous half wave. "Hello." His voice shook, like jello. His face was bruised, his lip bloodied from his altercation with Jerald.

Different people had a strange habit of seeing an altered version of the same situation.

Nadine probably saw a pup with glittering green fearful eyes. She tilted her head to the side, approaching the way one might a skittish, beaten dog. Yuri knew better. Whatever his other faults, Tovin wasn't deterred by rough handling. She cataloged the totality of his appearance—the sheen on his forehead, the uneasy smile, the trembling hand—and recognized someone hiding something.

Yuri took the lead in the conversation, cutting Nadine off. "You did better than expected at the party."

"Jesus. How bad did Eresna think I was going to do?"

Everyone smiled. Tovin had seen a ghost and spent the rest of the night trying to get others to fill the silence, which had to be the social obligations version of duping someone else into doing your work. In the end, he'd done his best, but his feelings remained obvious. He didn't like them.

As if picking up on the thread of Yuri's thoughts, Tovin said, "Where do you even find those people?"

Nadine filled him in. "Dating websites, online quizzes, social media."

Tovin gave her a disbelieving look, which she responded to with a chuckle and further explanation. "Technological advances have really streamlined the process. They want to know the colors of their soul or what fictional character they most resemble. We want to know who's vulnerable—the insecure, the egotistical, the unattached, the needy."

"Sounds predatory."

Yuri was in no mood to coddle. "We are predators."

Nadine cut back in with her cheerful voice. "Yes, anyway. We're here to talk about the ghost."

Tovin looked suspicious. "The ghost?"

"Yeah, the dead person you gave a smart-ass name."

"Oh. She's not here now."

Fake enthusiasm made Nadine's voice sound salty when she said, "Awesome. Why don't you tell everyone more about her? Really chat it up. Tell them how great she is. Not in the she's-going-to-smite-you way. More like how nifty you are because you can see her."

"Why?"

"Because if you don't, Eresna's gonna kill ya, eat ya, poop you right back out. Yuri and me will bring a variety of sauces to your BBQ."

"Plain enough," Tovin responded.

Nadine ruffled his hair. "Knew you'd see sense. And put some ice on the side of your face. You look like something Yuri's cat yucked up."

Nadine left right after those encouraging words.

Yuri lingered. What she'd said to Eresna was true. Lots of humans saw ghosts after being abducted by werewolves. Whether they were lying for attention or plain crazy wasn't something Yuri troubled herself to find out. She incorporated their stories and repackaged them to be sold.

Tovin's ghost felt different. Tovin remained perfectly still and quiet while his eyes followed something around the room. He didn't make a show. If anything, he self-consciously downplayed his connection to the other world.

"Come on, Yur!" Nadine shouted from the hall.

Yuri touched Tovin's shoulder. "When did you start to see this ghost?"

"Well—" As though he'd been interrupted, his mouth hung open in an aborted response. He stammered like he wanted to take another run at an explanation, but stopped himself again and pointed. "Er, I think Nadine wants you."

"Sure do." Nadine grabbed her elbow. "Come on, Yur. We have to go."

With a low growl, she allowed herself to be led out of the room by her friend. Not that she had much of a choice. Nadine gripped her tightly and walked her out, her gait uncompromising. Going willingly kept her from being dragged out like a drunk at a bar. Once they were outside, Nadine relaxed her hold.

Her voice sounded atypically serious when she said, "Whatever's going on with him needs to stay with him. Don't involve yourself, Yur."

"You did notice something amiss?"

"Subtlety isn't exactly his strength. He's into something and he's in it deep. Right now, my plan is to give him space to work shit out on his own. In the meantime, our motto has to be 'plausible deniability.' You remember what that means? You should. You taught me."

Impressed by her friend's cautious approach but annoyed with the lecture, Yuri grunted. "When did you become so political?"

"When you stopped. Herding you out of this minefield, Yur. Like it or not."

"You care about him too."

"Yep. Hence the giving him space rather than snapping his neck."

"This ghost—"

"Is a secondhand spook yarn. Don't stress over it."

Yuri dropped the subject. She wanted to believe Tovin's ghost was the product of an overzealous imagination sparked to flame by his fellow bloodservants' tales of apparitions. It didn't fit. Tovin didn't behave irrationally. He was merely a daydreamer.

Telling Nadine would agitate her more. Yuri forced conviction into her voice and said, "You're right. He's adjusting to his new life in an odd way. It'll pass."

"Good. Yes. Exactly."

As they walked, Yuri thought about what new lies she'd have to tell and where they might lead her.

Chapter 12: Dead Asshole Scientists

YURI AND NADINE

Before going too overboard, either with accusations or cover-ups, Yuri reviewed security footage from the last few months. So far, the tape showed Tovin asleep in his bed from midnight until eight o'clock—well behaved, normal. Each time a new day started, she was fearful of what she would find all over again.

Yuri leaned back in her chair, stretching her arms outward. She'd yawned so much her jaw hurt and her eyes watered. Another swig of strong, black coffee gave her a bit more pep to keep going, but it didn't warm her. Its burn wasn't unwelcome in her dry throat.

Mr. Fluffbutt sniffed and gave a liquid a dissatisfied *yow.*

"I know, baby. It's not for you, is it?"

"Yow!"

Yuri took a break to scratch under the offended cat's chin, promising him cream and tuna after she was done. Purring, he bopped his head against hers. "You forgive me? Thank you, Mr. Fluff." When she turned back around, the screen was blank, but the timestamp ticked forward.

"Huh." Far too tired for the delicate touch, she hit the machine a few times.

"Yow." Fluffbutt didn't like the noise.

"Sorry," she soothed him with a few long strokes down the arch of his back.

Yuri squinted. Beneath the matte screen, she swore she saw two figures moving. One had the outline of Tovin, his characteristic anxious gait that jittered here to there. The other distorted every second or two. It was a translucent blob one moment, an elongated cylinder the next.

They moved together toward where the door should have been. Three hours later, they reemerged. The feed cleared. Tovin rested in his bed as he'd done every other night before.

She didn't realize she'd been crying until a fat drop of water landed on her thumb. Irritated at her sentimentality, Yuri shook it off. "None of this means anything," she counseled herself. "There was a malfunction in the feed. It happens. Technology isn't perfect."

"Yow." Fluffbutt rubber-stamped her conclusion.

Dread wouldn't be cast out so easily. It clamped itself down around her stomach, squeezing the bile up to her throat. Nothing she'd seen was definitive proof, but her instincts screamed.

"It's real," she told herself in a shocked stupor, "the fucking ghost is real."

THE TICKING SOUND her heels made on the marble floor announced her purpose. Yuri took off her shoes. Too bad she couldn't as easily slip away from the treason she was about to commit.

She entered Tovin's room without knocking. Guilty as charged, he sat on the floor with files strewn all around the room. Yuri didn't have to study them too long to know they were death records from the sealed closet in the library. Like all the others before him who'd seen the ghost, Tovin had somehow accessed the files despite the many locks and failsafe measures put in place to prevent such a disaster. Hopefully, Yuri could prevent him from suffering the same fate of his predecessors—death.

"Where did you get these?"

He stood up suddenly. From a different angle, the injury on the side of his face spread all the way from his chin to the tip of his ear. Sickly white, his skin appeared bleached everywhere the bruise wasn't. His right lip was swollen, red. He stumbled the moment he got to his feet. Good thing he didn't flee. Yuri thought if she had to chase him down, she'd kill him.

"The...the Eresna gave them to me. To study."

"Bullshit. You got them from the closet in the library. How did you get in there?"

"By accident."

Angry beyond reason, Yuri let her claws help Tovin get the point faster. A thin red line welled up on his shoulder, and she hated herself for it, but she didn't have much time to figure out how to help him.

"The truth," she demanded.

He put his hand over the wound, applying pressure. Blood welled up between the gaps in his fingers. "The ghost let me inside."

"Did you touch the portal?"

He hesitated. "I...uh..."

"Did you?"

He tilted his head upward, looking defiant. "Yes."

"Ask the ghost why."

"She's not here."

The deep roar from the pit of her stomach shocked even herself. "Listen. And actually listen this time. Shove the box under your bed. Do not go near it again. Talk to no one else about it. Go forward with your ghost stories as we discussed earlier. Do not alter them at all. Understood?"

Eyes wide, face pale, Tovin moved his jaw up and down, but no sound came out.

"Understood?"

"Yes." It was barely above a whisper.

"Good. We'll talk later."

Yuri denied herself the urge to comfort him. Ignoring his stricken face, she stormed out of his room and walked to hers as quickly as she could without rousing suspicions. Anyone watching the cameras would see her leave the apartment in a huff, not unwarranted given his nonsense with the other bloodservants.

When she was once again in her own space, she collapsed. "What do I do? What do I do?" she repeated until she came up with an answer.

Yuri got out her phone, a flip one straight out of the 90s. Practical minded, she didn't need disembodied heads, things Nadine and Garvey called emojis, to represent her current mood. Texting was childish, and she sure as hell didn't need to play silly games. It was a phone. She used it to make calls. That's what she'd do.

"Garvey." She greeted the False Moon when he answered.

"Yu-Yuri."

"Yes, I need your help."

"Holy shit. I'm going to go make sure the sky isn't red and there are no comets streaking across the horizon. Hold up a tick."

Much to her anguish, he sat down the phone and left her with only the sound of a blowing fan on the other end. No doubt he enjoyed drawing out the encounter, allowing time for her predicament to stew inside of her. Yuri swallowed a frustrated scream. She needed to believe Garvey, who'd been Tovin's date the night of his extraction, suffered some guilt for the trouble he had caused. Minor, no doubt, but present.

She was about to hang up and go to plan b when he picked up again and cheerily said, "Back. Okay, go."

"Tovin is seeing a ghost."

"Are they serious?"

Yuri wasn't really even paying attention to his replies. He could have been a wall for all she cared. "The ghost is real."

"Come again?"

Yuri ignored the question. She didn't have time or the desire to convince him. "If you are a ghost, what do you want?"

"Dunno. Not to be a ghost. Seems like the type of thing that would suck."

"Yes, it does seem like that type of thing." Yuri kept her gaze distant, fixed straight ahead. "We said there was no connection. All of the bloodservants who went to the portal did different things. But what if the lack of pattern is a pattern? What if the ghost doesn't know what to do? What if she's theory testing? Throwing herself, and whatever human can see her, at possibilities?"

"Dead asshole scientist. Got it."

"What can we do to keep her from killing Tovin as she's done the rest?"

"I have no earthly idea, Yuri. Why do you think I'd know?"

"Perhaps I thought an asshole, living or not, was someone you'd relate to."

Garvey chuckled but sobered quickly. He started a reply but aborted it. When he spoke again, his voice sounded atypically serious. "Are you sure it's a ghost?"

"What else would it be?"

Silence. This time it didn't feel like he wanted to milk her discomfort, but the long stretch of quiet still made Yuri's skin crawl.

"Garvey...what else would it be?"

"You're right. There's no other explanation. Why did you call me?"

Gritting her teeth, she bit out, "I need you to tell Eresna you want a visit with Tovin. Ask her if you can bring sex toys."

"Keen on this plan already. What sort of toys?"

"The important thing is you bring a white banker's box, fifteen by twelve by ten."

"Very specific fetish."

To save herself on sanity, she kept ignoring his replies. "Once you're there, I need you to swap out the contents. Tovin has the death records from the library, the humans who died at the Door."

"Wow, he's determined to put a checkmark in every dumb-thing-to-do box, isn't he?"

"Take the records. Put them back or destroy them."

Hesitant, Garvey asked her, "Do you understand what you're asking me to do?"

"Yes."

"Yuri...I know we haven't always been the best of buds, but—"

"Do this for me, Garvey. Do it for Tovin."

"Eventually, this will bite you. Once again, you're sure?"

"Yes."

"Okay. Done deal."

Pressing the end-call button on her phone seemed final. More than that, it felt reckless. False Moon or not, Garvey was older than her by a significant amount of centuries. Him saying the ghost could be something else entirely gave her pause. But what else could it be? Yuri didn't know.

Chapter 13: A Gratuitous Amount of Social Obligations

TOVIN

Ghosts were naggers by nature. Always fixated on something, whether it was premature, tragic demise, unrequited love, trauma of another flavor. Destiny probably came back because she forgot to turn off the oven. She was that level of tenacious. A real natural haunter.

You're in deep shit, she told him the moment he woke up, as if he didn't already know. *Put that box away like she told you.*

Unceremoniously, Tovin kicked it under his bed. "Done. Happy?"

The dead are never happy.

"Bummer."

My troubles are yours.

"Oh, shush, you," Tovin scolded her at the exact same time Kurt materialized and greeted him.

"Pardon?" The man's voice rose in indignation.

"Oh no. Not you. The ghost!"

How awkward.

"Everything okay?" Kurt asked.

There was a frown ready to appear in case Tovin gave him an answer other than yes, so that's what he said. For extra reassurance, he added, "Lost in a daydream. That's all."

"Clear your head. You have an event to attend."

"Another one? I went to that party with Lonnie."

"A week ago."

Tovin nodded. "Right."

"You have to socialize more than that."

"Dammit."

A chuckle broke free from Kurt's personality slammer. The noise was snuffed out and replaced with an irritated grunt. "Stop dragging your feet. Today is especially important. We're doing damage control for the whole ghost nonsense."

Destiny bristled. *Nonsense? Don't go, Tovin. I don't want you to. You're an open conduit.*

The last part sounded like a threat. Tovin wanted to shout at her that he didn't know what she meant. So far, being a conduit only seemed relevant when he was about to do something she didn't want him to do.

Torn between two conversations, Tovin's reply to Kurt was annoyingly—at least judging by the man's expression—fragmented. "Oh. Er. How?"

"Leave the talking to Eresna. Stand there looking regal. That's your job."

Regal? More like bedraggled. At least that's what Tovin thought after an hour of grooming. The suit Kurt jammed him into probably weighed more than he did. At least it wasn't ornamental. Always sensible, Kurt made selections based on whether the mirage got others to stumble toward Tovin's waters.

"Think they'll drink?"

Tovin hadn't shared his analogy, but Kurt was intelligent to get most things through context. His reply was accompanied by a slight smirk. "No one's getting drunk, but they'll sip. Remember to keep your mouth shut. You're a chronic truth teller."

"Easy enough."

The two of them walked toward the community center.

Hallways were ten miles longer while wearing a heavy suit. Overhead, the heat from the lights wiggled its way under the suffocating threads. Sweat ran down Tovin's back. Dry wool itched. Wet wool tortured. He backed himself against a wall and rubbed against it. Scratching felt so gratifying he never wanted to stop.

"Very inconspicuous," Kurt commented on his technique.

"Gah! It never ends," Tovin bellyached.

"You need to get your nerves under control."

"What I need are jeans and a shirt."

Kurt's glower was half knock-it-off, half I'll-see-you-later. Wholly committed to Eresna's subterfuge, he slung an arm around Tovin's shoulder and used the leverage to pull him along. Kurt greeted interested onlookers with a cheerful hello. Only seeing two best buds out for a stroll, they waved back.

By the time they reached Eresna, Tovin's hair was damp and curling. The Alpha Guardian studied his disheveled state with pursed-lip concern.

Kurt reassured her. "Nerves. He'll be fine."

"Tovin?"

Dry mouthed, he went along with Kurt's analysis. "Yeah, I'm good."

Playing the part of a mighty leader chosen by forces beyond understanding was easy enough when it was a silent role. Tovin stood behind Eresna while she explained how his call to be a werewolf overtook him.

"I too was visited by a ghost. This is a sign of Tovin's great future," she explained to the other bloodservants. "His destiny is to be as I am. One day, he will make a strong guardian."

Showmanship wasn't Tovin's forte, that was putting it mildly, but he couldn't recall being nervous to the point of fever. Kurt radiated confidence like the Grenoble of coolness. Meanwhile, Tovin melted down like actual Grenoble.

You okay? Kurt mouthed.

Very hot, Tovin mouthed back and shrugged.

His eyebrows pinched together in a worried frown.

Thankfully, Tovin didn't have much longer to wait. Eresna concluded, "And everyone's great destiny is at his choosing. None of you"—her gaze lingered on Jerald and Alpha—"make it without him. May he forgive you all for how you've treated him."

Several of the bloodservants shuffled their feet, no doubt upset their great futures were compromised. Tovin had to hand it to Eresna. She was slick. And she knew it. The tilting smile on the edge of her lips said as much.

"The hard part is over," she whispered in his ear. "Mingle, offer them your hand in friendship. Be generous, benevolent."

"Got it," Tovin responded.

Lonnie was the first to approach. Characteristic of her, she pushed her way to the front, going so far to shove a smaller man off to the side. "I'm so happy for you, Tovie! Unlike these fakie snakies"—she tossed those behind her an over-the-shoulder scowl—"I never stopped believing in you."

Good hell, Destiny said. *She makes me want to die all over again.*

Tovin couldn't be as forthright. "Thank you, Lonnie. Your continued support means a great deal."

Eresna gently guided the fervid woman off to the side. Eyes wide, Lonnie gave the Alpha Guardian a nasty, "Harumph!" and stood on the stage near the podium, as front and center as she could be while still obeying Eresna's unspoken command to move.

Men and women who were nameless to Tovin approached in droves, each extending their hand, hoping he'd take it into his. Real or not, the power lured Tovin to its snare, stringing him along with compliments and supplication. How easy it was to get sucked into this world that offered so much for so little.

The odd fever climbed. He continued to sweat. His mouth got dryer.

"Doing great," Kurt whispered in his ear.

Surprising even himself, he actually was. Almost everyone was in his thrall.

Jerald and Alpha were the only two bloodservants away from the pack. Arms crossed over their chests, they simmered in hostility. Tovin winked at them, knowing full well the gesture, sarcastic or not, would enrage the two self-proclaimed alpha males. Sure enough, Jerald rushed forward, eager to prove he wasn't cowed by a few words.

Flirting with disaster, as always.

Tovin ignored Destiny.

"Jerald." Tovin greeted the stampeding bullheaded man. "Do you have an apology for me?"

Niceties were off the table. Jerald went straight to threats. "You'd look better with the other side of your face bashed in. Nice and even. Ya know, like matching socks. Want me to arrange that for you?"

"No thanks."

Jerald snorted. Words weren't really his thing, so he made use of his height and muscle, hovering over Tovin in a way that chanted *violence, violence, violence.* The other bloodservants heard it too. Uncomfortable, they focused on Eresna for answers. She wasn't providing any. Relaxed, hands folded in front of her, the Alpha Guardian watched the exchange from a distance.

Tovin didn't mind. He didn't think he'd need her. "Do you want Destiny to take your soul? To drag it down to the abyss where it will be fed upon for all eternity by demons?"

The superstitious man backed away. "Eresna said the ghost ain't like that. She's here to speak to the chosen."

"Right. And I'm chosen. She's whatever I want her to be. Right now, I sort of want her to be a bit soul snatchy." He lifted up his hands in front of Jerald's face and made grabbing motions.

Nearly always stoic, Kurt turned away from the scene. Tovin saw his shoulders shake, suggesting he was either laughing or crying. Eresna patted his back, trying with all her power to make it seem as though he were in the midst of a coughing fit.

Bloodservants had more malice than humor. They ignored the werewolves and fixated on how things would play out between two of their own. Eresna had brought Jerald there to play the role she thought someone as meek and intellectual as Tovin couldn't handle. Only Jerald proved himself to be hard to control and even more difficult to like, a combination that made everyone eager to accept lies about him.

Tovin pressed this advantage. "You were brought here to serve me. Apologize, apologize to everyone for how you behaved."

Jerald turned to Eresna, perhaps hoping she'd contradict Tovin's claim. She said nothing, did nothing. The man's nostrils flared at the snub—in and out, in and out. The way he ground his teeth reminded Tovin of a saw cutting through a rock.

He wasn't exactly contrite when he spit out, "Sure, why not? Sorry."

Be generous. Be benevolent.

Tovin took Eresna's advice. Instead of jabbering off from his list of mean things he wanted to say, he inclined his head and acknowledged Jerald with a gracious, "Thank you."

The event ended soon after.

"Good work," Eresna congratulated him.

"Finally!" Kurt echoed the sentiment in his own way.

Tovin gave them both an ear-to-ear grin and then collapsed. When he woke, he was back in his bed, a cool rag on his brow, saline pumping in his veins.

"What happened?" he said to anyone within earshot.

Destiny answered. *I told you...you're an open conduit, and I can drain you.*

"What do you mean?"

I mean exactly what I just said.

"What do you want from me?" Tovin asked.

The ghost smiled at him. Almost as though they were having a nice brunch and she were corporeal, she did a lovely impression of someone sitting across from him, hands folded in an old-fashioned, ladylike way over her lap.

His voice croaked when he said, "There has to be someone better than me to haunt."

No one else listened, she responded. *Sometimes, that's how destiny works.*

Part Two

The World Provides

The Moondogs

Chapter 14: Be the Raptor

GARVEY

White mucus dangled from Molly's upper teeth, drifting like unfettered spiderwebs in the wind. Jaw dangling open, she snorted in the night's smells through her nose and mouth. Although the air was cold and bitingly dry, the noises sounded pulling-your-foot-out-of-mud wet. Whatever eventually tickled her sniffer must have been delightful. The cracked corners of her mouth twisted upward, mischievously disgusting.

"Mol, pay attention." Garvey elbowed his undead companion. "I'm the raptor, systemically testing fences. You're more the stripe of the incompetent computer geek who thinks he can plow his way through the park last minute during a storm. Rich in madness, poor in method is what I'm trying to say. Sit here and wait."

"Wait," she grumbled back.

Lights blinked off until the streets were dark. Only one streetlamp guarded the entire neighborhood. It loomed over the gas station, a lonely sentinel well away from all the cookie-cutter, barred-up homes and their tiny cluttered yards. Garvey knew the area well, right down to when the lights turned off and when Jim, the night manager, pulled from his driveway. He'd stalked a couple for months, knowing he needed a neighborhood where no one cared about anyone else. Someplace easy to hunt with a hungry vampire: high turnover, high apathy, and plenty of dark places to hide.

Not too far off, a homeless man coughed. Garvey didn't worry too much about his presence. High as a kite, the man whistled and jabbered to himself.

Garvey pulled Molly forward, concealing her leash the best he could in the folds of his long coat. Unaccustomed to baggy clothing, he tripped on his own ruse. The slight stumble gave Molly enough slack to rush forward, an opportunity she took advantage of almost instantly. He criticized her tastes.

"Poor people are food for amateurs."

Molly struggled to repeat his last word. She gave up pretty quickly. "Food," she said instead.

"Yes, we'll get some. I know just the couple. Picked them out especially for you. Come on." Garvey dragged her to the alleyway behind the homes. Once they were there, Garvey pointed to the scene in front of them.

Any pervert can see us! was something the wife said angrily and often to encourage her husband to get on board with the whole window treatment idea. She had a point. Nighttime light made the couple's cramped life a thrill-less, plotless movie.

"Cheap spouses are a godsend," he whispered to Molly while they watched the show.

"Send." Molly licked her lips.

Creatures of habit, the two humans started their nightly routines on time. He went to the bathroom to stealth masturbate. She sat at her arts-and-crafts table to sew yet another quilt. These patchwork works of art were always some faceless girl with peppy sayings stitched onto floral skirts. Shit like, *She springs happiness!* Then, of course, it would be a spring scene—daisy-picking bullshit. Ad nauseam.

Garvey tried to picture himself in a similar domestic scene where Tovin attended to his hobbies, probably bird watching, while Garvey stealth-ate someone in their bathroom. "Can you see that, Mol?"

She snorted her snot back inside her nose.

"Right, he'd have to be outside to bird watch. It would be something like that, though. Something real boring."

"Boring."

Garvey turned to Molly, whose lacteous eyes were manic with eagerness. "Steady," he told her, "stick to the plan."

"Plan," Molly loudly reiterated. Her leash snapped when she reached its end. The woman inside looked up from her project briefly before deciding that whatever she'd heard was the wind, the television, or the moans of her self-satisfied husband.

Garvey shushed Molly. She responded with a small, annoyed moan. Apparently eating Tim, her deceased companion, didn't do anything for her. Garvey started to think it was just a gesture on her part, a sort of vampire dick move.

"Soon. Very soon, Molly."

"Soon," she said back.

As if responding to their conversation, the woman got up from her project to go back to the bedroom. This was the next step to the ritual. Time for her to fix the sheets, pull up the blankets, remove the dolls, and then call her husband to bed. Garvey moved quickly, practically sprinting, as her shadow along the hallway wall vanished. Once there, he grabbed the house key stashed inside an obviously a fake rock. No need to break in. Garvey pushed the door open, then walked inside, pulling Molly along with him.

"Eat?" she asked once they crossed the threshold.

"Shhh." Garvey attached her lead to one of the wall sconces. In a tizzy, she'd be able to pull the thing out easily enough, but it at least bought him some time to get things settled.

"Shhhh," she said back to him.

There were neighbors to consider. No one especially liked the couple, who were prone to violent squabbles lasting well into the night, sometimes into morning. From the time he had spent casing the place, he'd only ever seen the couple interact with the mailman. Still, Garvey wanted to keep the noise to typical domestic dispute levels—something familiar, nothing alarming. So he and Molly would wait some more. Eventually, as she always did, the woman came back to the room to turn off the television.

Garvey hit her in the throat, dropping her to the floor almost soundlessly. Being remarkably patient for a vampire, Molly stayed put through the whole thing. She'd walk to the end of the leash, let it tug, then stop. A befuddled expression twisted her face around.

"Okay, Mol. Time to eat." Garvey cut her loose. Self-control instantly went out the window; Molly was on top of the woman in a matter of frenzied seconds, ripping at the throat to drink the blood. There were a few scattered thuds and bangs against the wall as feet, legs, arms, and elbows jerked around in the struggle, but—overall—a successful feeding. Garvey congratulated himself before moving on to his meal.

The man was almost finished. As a matter of courtesy, Garvey waited until he heard the muffled sighs and groans that signaled the end of the process.

"Honey," the man called out, "we need more toilet paper from the store tomorrow."

"I'll pick some up." Offbeat with most of his kind, Garvey loved to talk to his food in wolf form. It was all part of the oh-shit-this-can't-possibly-be-real service package he provided. This guy was no exception to how it generally played out. He screamed, fell backward, crab-crawled until he ran out of floor and bumped into the place where he'd be found. Quickly, Garvey descended, then clamped his jaws over the throat to stop the screaming, squeezing and drinking until he felt the body beneath his slacken then fold.

Molly found them soon after. Apparently, she was already done with the woman. Garvey growled at her to let her know the man was his kill. She gave him a low hiss in return, blowing out bits of flesh and blood in the process, but she went on her way without violence.

Forced to hurry through his own feeding, Garvey swallowed as much blood as he could. Notoriously impatient, savage creatures, vampires got quickly bored. Who knew what she'd do once she finished her scan of the house for more food?

"Molly," Garvey called out to her.

"Garvey!" she shouted back. It sounded like she was in the bedroom somewhere.

Garvey sighed. He supposed he was close enough to done.

He found her going through the dresser drawers, dead-elbow deep in the woman's quilting projects. Molly held up one of the finished projects.

"That's lovely." Really, Garvey thought it was stupid. The idiot woman had a billion of those things. Quilts with stitched-on trite sayings were one of the primary reasons Garvey decided to kill and eat her.

"Keep." Molly pulled it to her chest.

"Go nuts." What did it matter? If compliance could be bought so easily, she could haul around the entire drawer for all he cared. "But we need to get moving."

"Moving."

"That's right. Come on." Without incident, she followed back out to the living room where Garvey looped the leash around her neck again and swaddled her in her cloak. It was a weird sight—an image humans would most likely remember if they got caught. Garvey had no desire to end up on the nightly news.

"Stay quiet and stay low," he told Molly.

Quickly, quietly, Garvey shut the door behind them.

Chapter 15: The World Provides

GARVEY

The world provided. Where others saw setbacks, drawbacks, cutbacks, Garvey saw opportunity.

Not fans of organization, structure, or sense in general, his pack pretty much had him pull a job out of a hat. He got truck driver. Awkward since he knew nothing about big rigs. But he made it work. Then he'd made it function: free time, a ready explanation for a life on the go. In the end, it was really everything a hunter like him could need.

He'd bought himself a hat that said #1 truck driver, some mud flaps with silhouettes of naked ladies, and a lot of flannel. He ate fast food, like the gyro he crammed in his mouth.

He transformed Molly the same way. Well, at least he dressed her in a baggy T-shirt and a wide-brimmed hat. The undead gal looked better than most on the road. And she was at least twice as sane. The illusion was frail, though. Whenever her head tilted up to reveal her face, any onlooker would see a corpse—white eyed and rotting.

"Whenever you get in a pinch," Garvey advised her as she clawed at the door, "say, 'I like guns!'"

"Guns."

"There, you got it."

She went back to fiddling with the door latch. Groaning, she called out in her hunger in a way that made Garvey uncomfortably compassionate.

He brought the truck to a jittery stop to consider his current situation.

Normally, new plans came to Garvey the way fleas came to strays. Figuring a new course was an itch he couldn't quite scratch. He needed to unleash Molly on some poor, random humans in Eresna's camp but couldn't quite part with his undead companion, unique as she was. Garvey loved the unusual.

"Well, Mol. Any suggestions?"

"'Estions Guns."

"Good team effort."

She grinned. Her mouth was still covered in bloody goop from their meal. The mess made Garvey look at his gyro a second time. "Eh," he shrugged and took a bite.

Molly looked at him with disgust.

"Really? What? I already paid for it. May as well eat it."

"Eat," she said.

"Yeah, you're damn right I will."

Molly's head bobbled as though she agreed. At least that's how Garvey decided to interpret the gesture. This was one of his favorite things about the vamp; she left everything wide open to his whims.

His butt tickled. Because it was pleasant, he let the phone ring up to the point it almost went to voice mail. "Hello hi," he said to the other whatever on the line. He never bothered to check caller ID. Life was more exciting that way.

"Garvey," Eresna's aristocratic voice answered. "I thought about your offer to entertain Tovin, and I think he needs your services. It will help to see a familiar face. You may have heard already... Jerald struck him. Thought I'd tell you in case the bruises were not healed."

"Consider me booked."

She hung up immediately afterward. This was fine by Garvey, who fought back his protective instincts. Jerald struck his sweet treat? Garvey shook his head and resolved to forget Tovin's troubles and be 100 percent more cheerful.

"Goddamn. Thanks, Universe. Do-him ex machina. That solves pretty much all our problems, Mol. We're getting in—more ways than one, if you know what I mean."

Molly grunted. She sniffled, and it sounded like she was huffing a century's worth of snot through a very small straw.

"Yeah, my joke was lame, but no need to be so gross."

She curled her lip a bit when she repeated, "Gross."

"That's right. What are we going to do about you?"

Garvey drummed his fingers on the steering wheel. Chewing his straw normally annoyed any companion, assuming he had one. Molly watched the thing waggle in his mouth like a tail. She seemed more intrigued by it than anything else. She reached toward his mouth with grabby crud-covered wiggling digits. Garvey swatted her away.

"Hungry!"

"Damn, girl. Settle. Thinking about your future over here."

She slumped back in her seat with a dissatisfied groan.

Garvey waited for another streak of good luck, some other world-wrapped present to drop into his lap. No phone call. No text. Email? No.

"Welp," he said after a bit, "guess we'll have to make our own luck on this, huh, Mol?"

He got out of the truck in a quick hop. Glass crunching under his shoes told him what type of place he'd stopped at. The eating establishment next to the fill-up station was once called Restaurant. Now the sign only said *Rant*. It could be the name of an upscale hipster place downtown, though they'd probably find the condoms thrown into dead bushes a little too ironic.

A man approached the moment Garvey got close to the convenience store. He stepped out from behind what had to be the world's last pay phone. "Hey, hey, man. Hey. Got a couple bucks? I ran out of gas."

Agitation was stamped into this guy's DNA—the way he twitched, bent his head, and sniffed constantly. Any moment, he could turn violent or loud, drawing unwanted attention. Difficult as it was to part with the money, Garvey gave him a few dollars.On the road, he wanted to be invisible. Nothing more than one of the nameless, faceless transients constantly in and out of the gas stations and local diners. No one paid much attention to anyone else.

When Garvey opened the door to the convenience store, a tiny bell rang, alerting the attendant. The man took a moment to assess Garvey's features, as though committing them to memory in case he later needed to identify Garvey in a lineup. Smiling, Garvey half waved, half saluted as he strolled to the magazine rack, whistling as he went. Everyone else in the store minded their own business. That's why the person watching him stood out. The man had a predatory gleam in his eye Garvey's brain was hardwired to understand.

"Sec, friend?" he said casually enough as he approached with hands raised to his sides, preemptively presenting himself as a nonthreat.

"More than a sec for a friend." Garvey put down his magazine.

The human had the same appearance as most of the others inside the gas station: paunch belly, stringy hair, meth-torn teeth, and eyes that were deep pits of questionable sanity.

"I wondered if you came from up north?" The human looked over his shoulder in a quick jerking motion.

Garvey gave him an affirmative.

The man continued to ask about the weather, the road conditions, whether or not some diners were still in business. Small-talk stuff. All the while, he looked around with nervous agitation. Then, suddenly, he wished Garvey a good day and went about his business.

"Huh."

If Garvey were a human, he might be worried for his safety at this point. Since he wasn't, he shrugged, then went right back to reading his magazine until the store owner presented him with the typical pay-or-leave option.

Four dollars was way too much to pay to find out who wore it better. Scowling, he flipped to the relevant section, gave the competing pictures a head nod, then put it back amongst the other gossip rags and paid for his gas.

As he neared the rig, he caught the scent of at least three human males, the one who chatted him up and two others.

With a raised eyebrow, Garvey pulled out his phone and texted the local werewolf sheriff: *prob going to have company. Lol.*

The response: *have fun. ;)*

"Alright, Mol, going to have to stash you away in the cargo bed. We're going to have some truckers over for dinner."

Ten minutes later, Garvey's truck broke down on the highway. He got out and waited. Ranting in the back of the rig about her hunger, Molly slammed against the metal, which buckled.

Unconcerned, Garvey bashed the dent back down with his fist. "Easy, Mol. The world provides."

Chapter 16: Highway Robbery

GARVEY

Here were men with a lot to say about the "goberment." Here were men fully committed to questionable choices in facial hair. Here were men whose smells pegged them as indentured, to each other and to the region. Here were men who started with answers, never questions; good ol' boys to whom reality bent its knee and agreed that because it was cold outside, global warming could not be a thing.

Things since the breakdown progressed pretty much as Garvey expected. Three men stopped, offered assistance, and then jacked him along with his truck. Now sandwiched between two passengers and the driver, Garvey went along for the ride all the while waiting for his own moment of opportunity. It couldn't come soon enough.

The passenger next to the window farted, sniffed right after as though confirming it did come from him.

The driver rolled down the window. "Hell's shit, Bear. Keep that in your cabbage shack."

Satisfied with all the attention, Bear rolled his cheek and did it again.

The only one dedicated to the idea that he and his colleagues were bandits of the serious and skilled variety, repositioned his shotgun, pointing it at an angle where he'd be far more likely to wham-blam-gone-man his own face or the driver's. Although the human declined to comment, his nostrils flared and his chin lifted.

"Here. Pull over." The man with the shotgun pointed to a work road. When the driver ignored him, failing to slow for the turn, the man became red in the face, agitated. He was in charge. "Pull over now. Now!"

The driver, who turned down the road with an eye roll and a sigh, was not impressed. "Calm your tits, Carl."

"Shut up. This is a serious situation."

Spit from Carl's *s*-words splattered from the side of his mouth, hitting Garvey on the cheek.

Too narrow, no place to turn around, the road Carl forced them to turn on was not rig-friendly. Halfway tempted to kill them all to avoid what was guaranteed to be paperwork, Garvey reeled in his impulses and waited for things to play out.

They stopped when the road forced them to. "Now what?" the driver asked Carl.

They walked. A lot. Bored, Garvey did his best to appear terrified, sagging his body so that the two men lagging behind Carl had to drag him from time to time. He wailed and shrieked *no, no, no please* like someone about to die. Rather than appreciate his efforts, his two guards shot each other uncomfortable looks. Garvey stopped his fake protests. Neither of them had any idea what they were doing there.

Carl finally stopped. Sneering, he turned to Garvey, "I know what you are."

"I doubt that, Carl. I really do."

"You're a werewolf."

Huh. Garvey, who rarely felt surprised by anything, cocked his head to the side. Was his jaw hanging open? It felt like it might be. How did Carl— a guy who probably thought his ancestors rode around on dinosaurs— figure out Garvey's secret?

"A what?" the driver asked. He backed up several paces, getting ready to run.

"A werewolf. He gets off on the moon and kills people. We're going to take him out before he eats 'nother."

Bear and the driver exchanged glances. Bear swiped at the shotgun. "Gimmie that, Carl, you've gone mad on bad drugs. Ain't no such thing as a werewolf. Ain't nobody who gets off on the moon and kills people."

Garvey sighed. "Can we revisit the whole 'gets off on the moon' phrasing? Not that I'm offended by the sexual undertones. It's just that the moon has nothing to do with it. It's kind of a sore point."

The driver whirled on Garvey, snapping his fingers in front of his face. "Have some sense and shut your mouth before this gets out of control."

"Okay, then," Garvey said. He raised his hands above his head as the two men fought it out.

Bear stood off to the side, scratching the span of belly that stuck out under his NASCAR hoodie. He shouted over the fighting, "If he were a werewolf, wouldn't he have killed us by now? I mean, he ain't done nothin' but stand there with his hands raised."

Garvey said, "Well, this is kind of amusing from my perspective."

"You're as mad as he is runnin' your mouth!" the driver sputtered at Garvey. Then, to Carl, he added, "I only came for the truck. Money. Cash. I don't wanna kill no one. You're on your own."

Carl turned to his other friend. "Bear, you with me?"

"He can't be a werewolf," Bear concluded simply. Garvey got the feeling that's the only way the big man knew how to conclude things.

Carl, exasperated, shouted, "We're going to have to kill him 'nyway. He'll talk."

Garvey thought this was where he could speed things along. "That's true. I'm a big talker. Johnny Blab, that's my nickname."

Bear and the driver each looked to the other for answers. Bear, seeing no help from his friend, gave another go at convincing Carl to back down. "We don't want to kill nobody. Let's leave him be and take the truck like we planned. He's plenty scared already."

Garvey shrugged. "Meh."

Both the driver and Bear glowered at him. He wasn't helping.

Carl said, "You don't want to kill nobody? He ain't a nobody. He's a monster. Get goin' then. I'll handle it."

Heartwarming as their refusal was, the two of them left fast enough.

Garvey waved at them. "They seem nice," he said to Carl.

"Shut up."

"You're the boss," Garvey assured the man. "But your friends don't appreciate that. They're going to leave you. They're going to take your share. They think, and I quote, that you're crazier than everyone's uncle Jim. Whatever that means."

Off in the distance, rattles sounded as the other two tried to break the lock on the back of the truck while they talked about exactly that.

"How do you know this?"

"Werewolf, remember?"

Carl gave him a little laugh. "Moon ain't full, chief."

"Right. Right. So...how did you know I was a werewolf?"

Instead of answering, Carl shot him.

Garvey remained standing. Golden eyes, twin red suns in the settling smoke. Canines out, gleaming white in the darkness, he said, "Come on, you can tell me, Carl. How did you know?"

Carl ran. Tough guy was gone, a shrieking baby still holding onto the gun was in his place. He shot it one more time over his shoulder before tripping into a face-plant. No matter how tough people talked in the theater, this was them nine times out of ten—crying and all.

When Garvey caught up to him, he wet himself and screamed a long series of tangled words that added up to, *Don't kill me!*

"Seriously?" Garvey wiped the man's urine off his pants. "Not cool, Carl."

Off in the distance, the lock on the truck scraped against the metal sides of the bed. Dammit. Garvey grabbed hold of Carl and dragged him back and clung to the fragile hope that the other two wouldn't be Molly food by the time he returned.

Chapter 17: Home Problems

GARVEY

Gravel plunked the underside of Garvey's truck as he and Molly drove down the driveway leading up to his home. Well, one of his homes. He rolled down the window, letting the breeze drag away some of the vampire smell. Not that what was underneath smelled much better. It was an old truck with years of smoke covered by sweet perfume.

Molly, who he'd thrown into country attire complete with cowgirl hat, sat on the grooved upholstery with barely contained hostility. Only a few minutes ago, she'd been wrapped up in the back, concealed so she didn't lunge at every human they passed through town.

"Hungry," she informed him.

"Hold on a tick, Molly. Soon."

A low growl let him know she didn't appreciate waiting.

Garvey focused on acting normal. His pack lived in a gated community tucked away in the forests of Idaho near the Snake River. Rustic stuff: log cabins, wooden bears holding up welcome signs, flannel, fire pits, and steel cut in the shape of moose. The works. Werewolves did what they needed to fit in with the locals.

For Garvey, it meant trading in his fine city clothes for jeans and jean jackets, his sports car for the truck, his actual sexual proclivities for more acceptable leanings.

Mercy, his packmate, doubled as his country wife; the type who always baked pies, teased her hair up into spun cotton candy that smelled like alcohol, and wore several fake precious stone rings on well-manicured fingers. An overzealous method actor, Mercy couldn't quite decide if she was a Southern belle, a western cowgirl, or some type of Frankenstein's monster of both cultures.

She looked at Garvey's casual clothes, really nothing more than a dress shirt with a plaid pattern, and seemed to question his commitment to their subterfuge. He looked at hers and questioned her sanity. He never, however, questioned her loyalty—to him or the pack.

"Darlin'." She pecked him on the cheek when he got out of the car.

They were always in character out in the open. While the community was gated, it wasn't exclusively wolf. Their human neighbors, mostly retired couples with mountain-cabin dreams, were always in someone else's business. Garvey couldn't see them, but he could hear them, smell them, sense their presence with a predator's inkling. He behaved accordingly.

"Babe." Garvey drawled it with a smirk. "This is Molly."

Although it had to be clear from the smell that Molly was neither human or wolf, Mercy did not miss a beat. "Howdy, Mol."

"How D," Molly said back.

Mercy smiled. "Atta girl, sugar pie."

Molly was done with pleasantries. "Hungry."

"You betcha. I'll get you some baked beans with grits n' biscuits."

Garvey vomited a bit in his mouth. Molly didn't look much more enthused.

Mercy waved them both inside, the eager hostess. "Come on then, getter done."

"Get our guest settled, babe," Garvey told Mercy. "I'm going to pull the truck around back."

Mercy ushered the undead woman into their home, and he smiled with benevolence the way he saw other country husbands look at their silly wives.

Only because he knew Mercy could he pick up on her annoyance, the flint sparking fire in her eye told him he was pressing his luck. Her expression conveyed nothing of the sort; she could simper and dote with the best of them. When the door shut, he hopped back in the truck, pulled it around back, and unloaded what looked like sacks of grain into their cellar.

It wasn't grain. Carl grunted in pain when he hit the floor. The rest did too. Garvey ignored them, shutting the wooden doors behind him as though it were the most normal thing in the world. To him, it was.

PIE WAS CODE for "I really want to know your shit" and was the traditional method nosy neighbors used to get into Garvey's happy home. Normally, he didn't mind. He liked pie. Considering presence circumstances, it was a massive nuisance. And the pie was rhubarb. Fucking rhubarb.

The baker brought her soapbox to his kitchen. "Young women these days. The liberal media tells them to dress like harlots and they wonder why no man respects them."

Their neighbor was a sixties-something sunbird with a sharp beak and a tendency to cluck. Her name was unknown to Garvey, but her stench was unmistakable. She gossiped with Mercy while he sat off to the side, neck planted firmly in a curled-up fist. His role there was simply to confirm whatever the old woman said, which he did with an occasional yep, uh-huh, or certainly. Molly-like, he occasionally repeated key words.

He did exactly that when he said, "Right. Harlots."

Mercy elaborated. "Why, I saw a young'un in our very town with a halter top! Can you imagine?"

The sunbird could not imagine. "Tell me, Mr. Garvey. Are the women you encounter on the road as shameful?"

"Not at all," Garvey assured her, "I find them very tasteful."

Mercy kicked him under the table. A light tap it was not. Garvey struggled to keep his expression happy despite the pain in his knee.

Mercy simpered at their guest with a sweet grin on her face. "He travels through small towns like ours where Christ and morality prevail. He stays away from big cities."

The sunbird nodded her approval.

Things went on like that for what seemed like enough time to kill the dinosaurs five times over. Garvey cringed at every little noise Molly made below them. Mercy was equally agitated. Human ears were much less sensitive than a wolf's, but he was sure the old woman could hear the wailings of hunger, frustration; not to mention the sporadic attacks on the walls. Being nearby so many available humans must have been torturous.

When the door shut and the sunbird's footsteps and smell faded, Mercy smacked him on the chest, a preemptive punishment for his many transgressions. "Right then, darlin', let's see what you brought home."

Garvey wheezed out an affirmative.

Molly rushed out at them the moment they opened the door. Hunger frenzied, she almost plowed right through them on her way upstairs where memories of human presence lingered the strongest. Soon enough, she'd catch a whiff of the guys right beside her door.

Panting, heaving with the effort, Mercy was finally able to get Molly back inside the small room.

The vampire wailed her frustration.

Garvey breathed heavy too. "Mol. Mol. Hold up a tick. We're going to get you food."

"Hungry!" Molly shouted back at them, an edge of betrayed trust in her voice.

"What the hell is that thing?" Mercy demanded. "Tell me that is the worst of it, darlin'."

"It's a vampire. Is she the worst of it? I'm going to say probably. Look behind door number two."

"Oh fuck me, you fucking fuckwit." Mercy's disguise finally dropped when she saw the three human men, now mostly out of their sacks, twisting around on the floor of the cellar. "Fuck," she said when one of them tried to snake crawl toward her, a muffled "help me" breaking through the gag.

Left without a defense for his actions, Garvey simple said, "Yeeeaaah," and hoped for the best.

"A vampire, Garvey. Really? And I assume these others are its food?"

"Yeeeah," he said it as an apology this time. "Also, I want to create another vampire to spare Molly here."

Disbelieving yet finally amused, Mercy shook her head. "Shoot. If this don't beat all. I'll get a tarp in the truck. You, mister—" She poked him in the chest with a short, pudgy finger. "—you owe me cameos at bake sales and competitions. Don't think I won't collect."

"I will be there with bells on, love."

While Mercy gathered up killing supplies, Garvey briefly wished she were the man he had met out on a Wisconsin lake on a day when the snow made the world white and flat. But the snow had melted, and the land had the curves of a woman.

Like him, she rolled with things. Vampires were said not to exist anymore, yet she accepted one was there without a trace of disbelief.

There was even a slight hint of excitement to her voice when she finally said, "Stop gawkin'. Let's getter done, cowboy."

Chapter 18: To All the People We've Killed Before

GARVEY

Garvey's phone beeped. "Check this, would you?" He handed the cell over to Mercy.

Mercy made a face, some cross between amused and befuddled. "It's those larping kids again, darlin'. They're inviting you to something called LARP-RI-CON. Huh." Mercy squinted at the text, her nose and mouth puckered in concentration as she re-read the words. "Oh, I understand. Like leprechaun. But real. And in Rhode Island. Oh-la-la, there will be a seafood buffet. Yum. Yum."

From stalker to stalked. Painters painted on without him. Dancers let him literally sashay right out of their lives. Quilters found someone else to hold their scraps of fabric. Bird watchers wrote him off as another loon. But these kids...they hounded him with numerous invitations. Blogs, social media, parties, and now some type of conference. Relentless.

One of them even had a kid, as impossible as that seemed, and had the audacity to send Garvey some type of gift registry. *Congrats on successfully reproducing. Here, have a toaster.* That was the card he had sent, hoping they'd get the point. He'd received a nice thank-you note two weeks later, a picture of the improbable spawn included.

"It smelled like Fritos," Garvey concluded his tale of woe to Mercy.

"The tit sucker?" Mercy did not like children.

"Sucker," Molly echoed.

They were to the point they simply ignored the vampire between them.

"No, the card. But probably the kid as well. Gah! I'm going to have to eat every last one of those nerdy fuckers."

Mercy gave him a playful slap. "You're so cold. I can understand that from a Boo Hag or a Varcolac. But you... You live with people; you see them every day."

"You're one to talk. You once ate guys named Mike because there were too many of them in your life and you kept getting them confused."

Mercy sniffed. "I needed to simplify."

"And then there was that time you brought a cake to the funeral of some guy you killed. Best cake in the place you said. You made me stand there next to it to count how many people took yours versus Betty's."

"I won that. Betty can suck on it. What about you? Oh." She snapped her fingers. "Those teenagers you ate because they trick-or-treated as werewolves."

"I was not there for their cultural appropriation."

Molly struggled with the last word that time. Garvey and Mercy waited for her to spit it out before they started up again.

"Or what about that cable guy who wanted to charge you thirty extra for premium channels?"

It was the principle of the matter. Garvey hit the wheel, remembering how pissed he was at the time. "They were included in the service when I signed up for it!"

Tirades about the evils of cable companies—the whole bit about packages, price hikes, service fees—were something to which Mercy had become accustomed. She knew when to *yup*, when to *uh-huh*, and when to give him a vigorous "amen, eat the power." She did that for him. Garvey only stopped when she tapped something on his phone.

"What was that? What did you just do?"

"I hit accept."

Garvey stared at her, so aghast he almost ran a stoplight. His country wife lifted up her shoulders to her cheeks, scrunching her face to a cutsie pose. "Picturing their excited lil faces now. Their good ol' friend Garv coming back after all this time to play faerie princess dress-up rescue with them. Still got your sasquatch ears?"

He growled at her. "They were wolf ears. You know they were."

She started to reply, laughter making her eyes twinkle, but stopped herself short. "Darlin'! This is it. This is our stop." She tapped on the dash, her fake nails clicked and scraped on the vinyl.

"To be continued..." Garvey warned her.

"Bated breath, lover. Bated breath."

They were at a place affectionately known—to wolves at least—as Teeth Cutter, a sprawling bit of desert paradise where sagebrush grew in random spurts alongside jutting volcanic rocks covered in moss. Hums from the electric wires overhead and the occasional musings of coyotes yip-yowling off in the distance were the only sounds for miles. Off the beaten path and in a place where law enforcement were of their own, it was the go-to place for new wolves to, well, practice their trade.

Both Mercy and Garvey breathed in the familiar territory. Times long past came to them on air currents—the dirty odor, ever so sweet in context, of coming home after a long trip. Wind gusts made the cloth covering their nakedness whirl and flap as a reminder to the bodies beneath that it was more savage, every bit as wild.

Garvey took off his shirt, letting it go where the wind took it. Prone to sprouts of romantic notion, he thought of his scent spreading across the desert, making himself a part of its story. Curiously, he thought about Tovin coming there and the two of them becoming part of the landscape's memory together.

Mercy asked him, "What are you thinking about over there?"

Garvey rarely lied to Mercy. "Tovin."

"Ah, the sweet treat."

"He's the one."

"Not like you to linger, darlin'."

"I know." Usually, he forgot about past lays the way others forgot about leftovers in the fridge. Nothing ever tasted the same after warming it up. Somehow, the second bite of Tovin appealed to him almost more than the first. "Unfinished business," he said, unconvincingly judging by the steep incline of Mercy's brow.

She let it drop without comment. One of the reasons he rarely lied to Mercy was that she hardly ever pressed him for more information than he wanted to give.

She allowed Garvey to stand there a while longer, lost in his thoughts before she pinched his elbow and said, "Enough of that. Let's get 'er done."

Molly watched them with growing impatience. Until this point, she'd been as good as a vampire was ever going to be under these conditions. Opaque slobber trails where Molly licked the glass clouded up the windows. Garvey thought he saw a bunny in one of them.

"Yuck," Garvey told the vampire.

"Yuck," she agreed.

"Stop gawkin' and start haulin'," Mercy huffed at him.

Bedazzled high heels made off-beat scraping sounds as she tried to navigate the uneven environment while pulling humans out of the van.

Anyone watching might think she wasn't strong enough to lift; her knees were bent into a squatting waddle, and she wrenched one of Molly's unfortunate meals back and forth from the seat. Her contortions helped her avoid getting what she called "human smell"—or any other types of unwanted mess—on her clothing.

Garvey took jabs at her. "Nice choices there. Practical shoes."

She took jabs back. "Says the guy who tossed some murder evidence literally to the wind. Good thing you brought a bag full of incrimination... I mean a change of clothes."

Eventually, the three humans they'd brought with them were sprawled out on the ground in front of them. Reminiscing in front of their kills, aside from being dickish and kind of fun, served some function: things went a bit faster at the end. There was less begging when they knew, as Mercy often told them, that this wasn't their first rodeo. Though terrified, the three looked somewhat resigned to death.

"Which one we going to vampirize, darlin'?"

"My vote is for Carl. His going-to-kill-me-a-werewolf shenanigans cost a lot of paperwork. And you know how I feel about paperwork." Garvey tsked the bound and gagged men.

"He really hates it," Mercy let them know.

"What about you? Any preference?"

"Well, I do like the idea of one of the immortal undead being some mutton chops fat guy wearing a NASCAR hoodie..." Mercy tilted her hand back and forth through the air to signal her wavering. "Still, Carl's the werewolf hunter. It's a bit of fancy for him to the vampire. Done deal."

Garvey wavered. He couldn't help but wonder if this would be the dumbest thing he'd ever do. He'd always confided in Mercy. Although her hair looked like it was one solid entity, especially now with the wind making it bobble up and down, she was one of the wisest wolves he'd ever known.

He voiced his doubts to her now. "Not sure we should do this."

"What's to know about it?"

He told her a story of another time where thousands of cloudy undead eyes fixed their gaze on a nearby settlement. The bodies they stood over crumpled up, only recognizable as human because a few had faces.

"I laughed when Lavario said they'd turn into a million soon enough. But day came. The town was no more. The one next to it was gone too. We had to walk a hundred miles before we came across a living human. Behind us, the undead said, 'Hungry, hungry, hungry.'"

"Damn," Mercy considered.

"Yes."

Her eyes fixed on the sky above them. She turned her head his direction when she was ready to speak again. "Ten years until the culling, darlin'. Our pack will die. Except you." She smiled at him without malice. It was well known Lavario protected him, even after their falling out. "You have to decide what's worth risking. Wouldn't blame you if you decided this is too much."

She wouldn't. Moondogs were a very forgiving lot, and they'd be happy—never resentful—he got to live.

"I couldn't live with myself if I did nothing," he finally told her.

"There's your answer, darlin'."

Yes, there it was. Garvey couldn't shake the image of undead eyes. He couldn't forget how it started. The single vampire that became a hundred. A hundred that became a million. Who knew how many after that. There wasn't a census for that type of thing. But a lot.

Chapter 19: Carl the Werewolf Hunter

GARVEY

Rules didn't govern the lives of Moondogs the way they did the lives of the two great packs. Flying by the seat of your pants was acceptable, even a virtue, in most contexts. Their current situation made him think they should have gone into this with some type of plan.

Nothing happened.

Bear—so proudly flatulent—was dead. Mercy lived up to her name by casting a sleeping spell before Molly fed on him. She'd done the same to the driver, who was still alive but didn't have to watch his friend get eaten or worry over his fate.

Carl was the only human awake. Earlier, Mercy tied Molly to a tree so that she could barely reach the man's arm, which Garvey forced into biting range. Puckered, torn, bubbling: the bite was not a pretty sight. Angry red lines drifted from the center and went all the way down to the human's elbow. Dirt was caked all around the wound—dark black where it was wet with blood, lighter brown where it wasn't. Without really knowing why, Garvey kept trying to clean it.

"Oh, hey. Better make sure that doesn't get infected." Mercy rolled her eyes at his efforts. "Are you even sure this is how it works?" She squinted at Molly's handiwork with doubt. She poked the very center of the wound with one ungentle finger. Carl moaned through his gag and buckled.

"Yep. It's a virus of some type. Takes a bit, though." As the wolf with the most experience with this sort of thing, Garvey felt it was his duty to guess how long. "An hour maybe?"

"You said that seven hours ago."

She wasn't calling him by any endearment or bothering to make her voice sound country; that's how tired she was. Even her hair was flat against her head, limp and unresponsive to her fingers' pleadings. Garvey was in the same boat. What felt like a homecoming eight or so hours ago started to feel more like an indefinite prison term. The wind annoyed him and flung dirt in his eyes, or in his mouth if he opened it to speak. Worse, it made it impossible to read the smut magazine he'd stolen from a local grocery store.

"Yeah, I have no idea," he finally confessed.

"I assumed as much."

During the exchange, Carl went from terrorized victim to someone who'd like to speak with their manager. With renewed vigor, he squirmed around on the ground while trying to communicate in muffled groans.

"Think he has something to say. Want to hear?"

Bored, Garvey shrugged his shoulders. "Meh."

Mercy ungagged the man. Newly free, Carl sputtered for a bit before launch. "Your marriage to him ain't real. He's a werewolf. Let me go. Let me go, and we can have a real marriage. I'll buy you nice things, take you nice places—"

"This the result of...." Mercy tapped her arm in the place where the bite was on Carl.

Garvey shook his head. "Our interactions were limited. But don't think so."

Mercy prodded the man with the tip of her shoe. "I'm a werewolf too, ya turtle. How did you know about Garvey here?"

Blinking, Carl declared, "I hunt werewolves. I have a web business and all. Other werewolf hunters are comin', so you better let me go."

Mercy burst out laughing. "No, really. How did you know?"

Carl spat in their direction. "The sheriff told me."

Now they were both laughing. Between gales, Mercy shouted, "The sheriff is a werewolf too, ya turtle!"

Garvey went so far as to slap his knee. "Oh, he pranked you good, Carl."

Mercy ran back to the car and came back holding her phone. Coated with dust, her bedazzled heels crunched on the parched earth. Up and down, up and down, up and down: her hair bobbled on top of her head. She was too excited to notice or mind.

"He's got a website! He's got a website!" she shouted.

The two of them bent over the small screen of the smartphone. Sure enough, Carl had himself a webpage for his thriving werewolf-hunting business. Pictures of him and another man graced the homepage. In one of Garvey's favorite poses, the two of them stood next to what appeared to be a bear rug altered to be a werewolf carcass.

Garvey and Mercy couldn't stop laughing. Meanwhile, Carl begged for his life. From heartfelt pleas to insult-filled tirades, the desperate man covered every angle on the before-death negotiations plus some.

After a bit, he caught on to their indifference. "Are you listening?"

They were not.

"Look at his," Mercy shrieked. "He has a pricing page!"

Carl drew his legs up toward his chest. Then, with as much force as he could muster, he released his body's coiled tension and shot dirt onto their feet. "I'll come back and kill you both! Cunt!" he said to Mercy. "Fag!" he said to Garvey.

It was at that point Carl fell over dead.

"Huh," Mercy said.

"Welp." Garvey was totally perplexed.

For a while, the body lay there as if giving the two of them the middle finger. *All that waiting for nothing*, it said. Right when Garvey was about to mea culpa the disaster, a leg twitched. The spasm moved upward until it seemed like Carl was on an invisible-magic-fingers bed. Blood geysered out of his mouth, coming out bright red at first and then a sort of russet color toward the end. Once its original path down chin and cheek was too congested, it spilled over to the rest of his face—the eyes, the hair—until his features were not even recognizable.

Purged of his old blood, Carl opened his eyes, which glossed over with milky white cataracts that obscured the brown iris beneath. He sniffed the air. Blood bubbles popped in his nostrils. Surprisingly fast, he crawled over to the driver, still asleep on the ground. Eating noises seemed to mingle— the slurping, crunching, licking, biting overlapping to one single action.

Mercy summed up the experience. "This is pretty messed up."

"Yeah," Garvey confirmed.

Mercy lept her wide eyes focused on Carl and said, "What now?"

"I get back to work," Garvey told her.

Carl turned the direction of their conversation and said, "Hungry."

The Isangelous

Chapter 20: Back to Work

YURI AND NADINE

Weeks went by without any incident. Yuri's guard slipped and she allowed herself to believe she could playact her way to normal. The ghost wasn't real. Tovin was fine. She, Garvey, and Nadine were back out on the hunt, searching for two new bloodservants to replace Jerald and Alpha. No problems.

Well, one problem.

Nadine and Garvey were crazy if they thought she was going to look over the selection list to make sure everything was above board, on schedule. If they failed, it was on them. No, it was on Nadine, who was her boss. *Her boss.* Yuri bit on her twisted lip, fingers itching. She checked the paperwork. Then she checked it again. With dismay, she realized everything seemed correct.

Nadine hit the roof of the car, startling her. Yuri dropped the damned clipboard, which clattered conspicuously. Her friend smirked, her tongue on tooth. Bright blue eyes twinkled.

"Everything in order?"

"Yes," Yuri confirmed tersely.

"Success!" She lifted her hand up in triumph. "Now come hunt with us."

"Where are you hunting? Daycare?"

As always, Nadine wore an outfit that playfully blended styles and colors. Eighties tube socks rolled up around bright orange leggings; her T-shirt said Eat Free Range, which she and Garvey thought hilarious. All of it was held together by her leather jacket with a wolf's head stamped on back. Now, more than normal, the childish attire annoyed Yuri. Unprofessional. That's what it was.

"Stop sulking. Come hunt."

Yuri sulked. "Go on without me."

With a massive sigh and a roll of her eyes, Nadine flopped herself into the passenger seat. The small vehicle sprung after adjusting to her weight.

A bright, genuine smile on her face, she grabbed Yuri by the shoulder and pulled her as close as the console would allow.

"What's up, boss wolf?"

Yuri sniffed indignantly, but she did not pull away from her friend's embrace even though it was crumpling the fine silk of her blouse.

"This thing with Eresna will pass. She'll—" Nadine rolled her hand through the air the way she always did whenever she struggled for the right words. "—get over it." She paused again. "One day." And again. "Maybe."

The smile Nadine gave her afterward felt like looking into the sun. Yuri squinted her eyes, trying to make out some sign of worry through the brightness. Seeing none, Yuri settled back into her seat and closed her eyes.

"Where is he?" she asked, referring to their target.

Excited, Nadine slapped her hands together. She was glad to have her friend back on the team. "He's trying to pick up some brunette. Really doing a shit job of it. Garvey is keeping an eye on him."

Yuri's lip curled at the mention of the False Moon.

"He's by the book tonight. I've seen to it. No playing," Nadine assured her, though she had her tongue on her tooth. "And if he tries to order you around... I will slap his teeth out of his head."

"Would you really?"

"Whack! Right out of his head!" She demonstrated how she'd do it by backhanding her open palm. It made a satisfying whip crack noise.

That made Yuri smile.

NORMAL DIDN'T STICK. Garvey scraped it off her bones, digging his claws right down to the marrow.

Nadine was nearly done telling him Tovin's ghost story. Garvey requested the juicy details while giving Yuri a toothy grin. His reflection in the rearview mirror continued to needle her. Whenever she looked up, his eyes met hers and the smugness behind the cheery good humor shone through.

"I didn't think he was the type to make up ghost stories." Nadine shrugged her shoulders.

The False Moon showed all of his sharp teeth. "Maybe he didn't make it up. Maybe there is a ghost."

"Pffffttt."

Garvey flopped back in his seat. "Right. That's impossible. I bet that's something our friend here—" He pointed to the unconscious human sitting next to him. "—said about us: 'werewolves! pffttt!'"

Nadine chuckled and licked her tooth.

Yuri gave Garvey's reflection a snarl.

"Get some humor, boss wolf," Nadine chided her.

"One of us has to be serious."

Plucky, Nadine stuck out her tongue until Yuri did the same. Tension cut, the two of them settled back into their easy friendship, filling their respective roles: Nadine the cut-loose free spirit and Yuri her anchor to the real world. It was a steady, reassuring groove until Garvey took it off its tracks.

"Come on, Yuri," Garvey pressed. "What do you think of Tovin's ghost?"

"Utter nonsense."

"Really? There's no part of you that—"

"No."

Garvey clucked his tongue.

"Break it up, you two." Nadine wagged her finger. "No more fighting until there's enough booze that the bickering sounds like angels singing."

"You're the only werewolf who can get drunk, apparently." Yuri's tone was still harsh from the fight.

"Whatever. You two make me long for the days of being shit-faced. Garv, don't be a suck bucket. Yur, cut Garvey some slack from time to time. After we drop this guy off, you two are coming with me to a ladies bar. Drinks are on me. And one"—she held up a single finger—"and I mean *one* appetizer."

One last shot from Garvey, masquerading as a concession. "You're the boss, Nads."

Yuri's nails dug into the leather fabric of the passenger-side seat at the offhand mention of the demotion. Blithely unaware of the tension, Nadine turned up the radio and "sang" along. Inaccurate lyrics. Off-key. Horrible.

"Quiet up front." Garvey planted his foot against Nadine's chair and pumped.

"Under attack here, Yur."

"Your voice is god-awful. A tin can on a cheese grater sounds pleasant in comparison."

"I see how it is. Glad I could unite you two against a common enemy."

Nadine didn't stop crooning even after they pulled up to the distribution center. She placed the newly abducted man on a medical gurney and filled out the attached paperwork, humming to herself through all the familiar actions.

"Done!" she notified them both, slapping her big hands together. Smiling, she sang her next command in a fractured whistle register. "We did it, you guys. First successful hunt back to together as a team. Back into the van!"

Garvey covered his ears. "I'll go, but no more singing."

Yuri awkwardly agreed with Garvey. "That's the only way you'll get me to go."

"Fine, *fine*. Deal."

The tires hummed on pavement.

"Okay," Nadine said the moment they stopped. "Team building exercise time. Your job is to pretend I'm interesting and that I just broke up with a hot lady whose name I wanna say is Jessica. Afterward, finish your appetizer and leave me 'alone,' like the backstabbing snakes you are, and let me cry my eyes out, friendless and without comfort."

Garvey wanted to know "Does this actually work on women?"

"Only the dumb ones, which is what I'm in the mood for. Any questions?"

Garvey raised his hand.

"Yes, you in the back."

"Can I get her information when you're done? Stupid people streamline the meal process."

"No, you can't murder my hookups."

"Had to ask."

"Good effort."

They went inside the bar together.

"Yuri." Garvey pulled her off to the side the moment they stepped over the threshold and the noise from the crowded place hit them full force.

"What is it? I'm in no mood for more of your shenanigans."

"Shenanigans?" The False Moon actually balked at the word. "You know what, whatever. Do you want me to bail Tovin out of his box problem or not?"

Facial ticks wiggled across her skin. Frantic, she checked and double-checked for Nadine, worried her friend was going to walk in on the conversation and learn how far she'd fallen.

"Can you say it a bit louder?"

"Give me ten more seconds without an answer and I can. And will."

"Yes," she hissed back at him. "I want you to take care of it."

"Then I need you"—he put his finger on her chest—"to get me in the back entrance."

"Why?"

"Because front-door debauchery is risky."

Yuri growled at the situation.

"I know. Treason is *so hard*."

Her growl tapered off to a grumble. Garvey was right. "We'll tell Eresna it's for the sake of Tovin's modesty. He's shy. She'll buy that. Tell Nadine the same."

Nodding, Garvey indicated the plan had merit. "Coy little sweet treat, isn't he?"

"Save it for later."

"Oh, I will."

Fury made the wolf inside of her nip at her heels. He wasn't any more serious about this than he was about anything else. "Tovin…"

"What about him?"

"Don't hurt him."

For a moment, it looked like he was going to hide behind another blithe comment, a sarcastic jeer. He didn't. His face cleared to the point he resembled something more or less human.

"I'll protect him the best I can. Yuri, I can't and won't protect you, just so you know," he added without malice.

"I understand."

Nadine danced with a busty woman who giggled and pulled away, a clear invitation for Nadine to reel her back into her arms. Grinning big, no doubt knowing where the dance might lead, her friend played her part with gusto.

Tears in her eyes, Yuri wondered if she could find comfort in those big arms after she was a known traitor. More likely, her friend's hands would wrap themselves around her throat. Maybe Nadine would cry while she choked her, but Yuri wouldn't bet on it.

Chapter 21: No Grudge Here

GARVEY

Being invited made breaking into the Boo Hag compound a hundred times easier. Being a Moondog meant going through the back entrance his lot in life. He didn't need to worry there'd be someone watching out for him. Too inferior to monitor. Too baseborn to matter. Yuri had done her job well.

Garvey emerged in the housing units for the scrogglings, the bloodservants of the lower-ranking wolves. Tucked away in the basement of the compound and gated off, the area was a perfect place to release the vampire, which was exactly what Garvey planned to do. Later.

First, he had a score to settle.

Garvey pulled on Carl's leash, urging him to shamble forward onto the elevator platform.

"Hungry." Carl's way of saying it felt a lot more like nagging than Molly's.

"Hold it." Garvey tugged on the leash hard enough to make Carl nose-dive. He didn't like undead Carl any more than he liked living Carl.

The feeling appeared mutual. "Hungry," Carl groused at him again.

"Yeah. Yeah. Soon enough." At least he hoped.

Ding! The noise told them they were on the right floor. It was also the sound that came right before someone said, "Order up!" in greasy diners.

Winging it was his signature move. Despite it, Garvey acknowledged the stupidity of changing his plans. Revenge should have nothing to do with any of this mess. At least, that's what Garvey told himself. A lot. The lurking romantic in him didn't listen. He imagined the imprint of a hand on Tovin's face, and he knocked.

Jerald, the bloodservant of Alpha Guardian Eresna answered. He didn't seem surprised, only put out by Garvey's presence. The door clicked shut in his face. Seconds later, it opened a crack only large enough to get an arm through.

Jerald thrust out a sack full of DVDs. "Here, False Moon. Take these. Get me some new ones. Something with naked chicks." He sniffed the air. "And what is that thing? It stinks."

"Hungry." Carl, the thing, pulled forward.

Garvey kept his voice level. "Let me in."

Jerald didn't blink. Demand-filled eyes that wanted this or that continued to glare as though the barefaced menace on display would dominate Garvey into delivering smutty movies. After a long-suffering sigh, he flung the door open, allowing entry.

Any Boo Hag could tell you the windows in Jerald's apartment were forty feet tall and that the cashmere and silk rug was six-hundred square feet. The room was designed to make anyone who entered feel small and the person who inhabited the space feel larger than life.

Garvey felt annoyed. He resented the wealth on display more than normal. *It's not because this brute struck Tovin,* he told himself. No. Nope.

Jerald wasn't helping matters. "What do you want?" he snarled.

Normally, rank forced Garvey to demure to the bloodservant of any guardian. Convincing them of their great destinies fell on everyone's shoulders, but especially a lowly Moondog like himself. Not today. Garvey grabbed the Jerald by his shirt and slung him against the nearest wall.

He checked his nose to see if it was broken. It was. "What the fuck, man?"

Was it worth it to respond? Yes. "Here to kill you, bro."

He backhanded Jerald, knocking him hard against the floor. To ensure a kill rather than a conversion, Garvey grabbed Jerald's leg and kicked down on the kneecap. He couldn't run anymore. Not far, anyway. Jerald's shrieks blared like a car alarm on an otherwise quiet street.

No one came out to check, which fit the analogy. Well, no one but Carl.

Surprise made Jerald's defense sloppy. The first bite took a finger. The vampire swirled the digit in his mouth, at last spitting it out before going back for more. Unpracticed, he picked for scraps, pulling away tidbits of flesh the way dogs gnawing on bones did.

Garvey criticized his technique. "Yucktastic job here so far, Carl."

Carl wasn't available for feedback.

"Get it off me. Get it off," Jerald bellowed.

Blood turned his blue shirt black. It pooled on the hardwood floor. He twisted his arms up and down in it, smearing the outline of an angel. Trembling made the brass buttons of his blazer *tick-tick-tick* as his whole world went kablooey.

Garvey determined he'd been enough of an ass for one day. Well, almost enough of one, he amended as he allowed himself a last jab. "Before you die, you should know there is no great destiny."

Jerald was too weak to do anything other than dribble blood and gaze up at him with dumb, uncomprehending hope.

"Oh, and this was for Tovin," Garvey whispered and stomped the man's head.

Carl fed until Garvey pulled him away. By that time, there was little left of Jerald other than scraps of his clothing and the overbearing stench of cologne. And piss. Always piss.

Carl surveyed the damage. Unsteady, he slipped around a bit in the mess he made. "Hungry," he contemplated.

"Yeah, you're right," he said to the vampire. "Eresna is going to throw a fit about the rug."

Garvey sniffed the air. His own scent damned him. The best he could hope for was a quick escape.

SCROGGLINGS WERE PAMPERED, not loved. Eresna felt their loss the way a banker felt the pinch of numbers not balancing. They were, however, Garvey's hope for the widespread carnage Kijo demanded.

He pushed Carl into one of the recreation rooms. Around eight or ten o'clock, it would fill with people, all of them eager to catch up on news from the outside world. The vampire would be there waiting for the bloodservants to enter the room. They'd scream. Maybe they'd get away. Garvey doubted it. The bloodservants of the Isangelous were pretty useless.

"Big day tomorrow. Bite lots of people, okay? Eat a few for old Garv."

"Hungry."

"That's the spirit."

Flesh fell out of Carl's mouth as he lumbered over to a dark corner of the room. Head tilted to the side, he stared at nothing with rapt attention. The milky white eyes of the vampire usually jittered, always on an endless quest for more to eat. Carl's eyes remained fixed, steady, intent.

An odd sensation held Garvey in its grip. Wind blowing through an open house carried the same feeling; the world could be wild even in a contained environment. A tingle like an electrical charge hobbled down his spine. Beneath his clothes, his skin jerked and twitched as the wolf inside him demanded to be let out.

Garvey searched Carl's face for the same glimmer of recognition, a small but present spark of life he had found in Molly's eyes. "Carl, do you still hear me? Do you know who I am?"

"Hungry."

"Still want to hunt werewolves, buddy?"

Carl drew his cracked lips back in a ghoulish smile. Very slowly, he stumbled forward, extending his hands in front of him as though to feel his way in the darkness. The tips of his fingers touched Garvey's face.

"Hunt," he said. Maybe it was only Garvey's imagination, but the voice sounded human. Only it wasn't Carl's.

Garvey backed away from the vampire's touch. "What's happening?"

Chapter 22: The Moon Is Full

GARVEY

Garvey smelled Tovin before he saw him, the simple whiff of hominess, like chocolate chip cookies fresh out of the oven. It was the type of scent that invited you to have another cup of coffee and make yourself comfortable. The unfettered wanderer in him resisted. And lost.

He knocked on the door. "Hello, hi, sweet treat," he said when Tovin opened it.

Tovin didn't seem at all conflicted when he snarled, "Garvey? What are you doing here?"

Garvey showed him the contents of the box, the sex toys Yuri asked him to bring. "Booty call. Eresna sent me, said you needed it."

Sputtering, Tovin denied it. "She...she said wrong!"

Garvey didn't want to hear the rest of Tovin's objections, so he swallowed them up in an impromptu kiss. The mumbled protests vibrated against his lips. Tovin's hand swatted him on the top of the head.

Groaning, Garvey broke the kiss and rested his forehead against Tovin's. "Still a lot of work, I see."

"Mm-hmm."

Heightened wolf senses weren't necessary to detect the hostility. Sweet Treat's entire face boiled with indignant rage. His cheeks heaved like bellows. Garvey hissed air through his teeth. He supposed he couldn't totally blame him. Last they met, Garvey had turned into a werewolf and chased him through the forest for a bit of sport. Other than that, it had been a night of magic.

Mockingly apologetic, he asked, "Holding a grudge because of the date? The vampire thing?"

Tovin's eyes narrowed at the reminders.

"Sorry about that." Garvey gave him a shrug. "Right. Made nice. Comin' on in, then."

Rather than wait for the rejection that was sure to come, Garvey pushed past Tovin and entered the apartment. Resigned but annoyed, Tovin stepped aside and shut the door with a heavy-handed *whack*.

Impressed with the luxury of Tovin's new home, Garvey whistled. The silk Isfahan rug alone was worth more than Tovin would have made in his lifetime as a salesman. Rather than resent the lavish lifestyle, Garvey found himself grateful that things had kind of worked out.

There was something else here too. Its smell shied away each time Garvey tried to pin it down. Familiar, like a name that kept darting to the back of his mind, the scent had an otherworld quality.

He couldn't help but wonder. "So there's a ghost?"

Startled, Tovin rattled off a long series of nos that amounted to a yes.

Garvey skipped past the step where they quibbled over the thing's existence. "Is it here now?"

Perhaps he was about to hold back again, but after one long look at Garvey's face, Tovin surrendered. He looked left, right, back to the left.

Befuddled, he said, "No, she isn't," in a way that suggested she usually was.

Garvey placed the box of sex toys on the nearest table. Tovin glared at it with mute rage.

"Well, you let me know when she arrives." Garvey clapped to signal a change in topic. "So...how you been?"

"Swell."

"Good. Good. Carnal pleasures being off the table, is there anything Garvey can do for his sweet treat?"

"Stop calling me that."

"Never."

Tovin pointed at the door. "Then leave. Go out and howl at the moon—I think it's full tonight. Chase some hikers or fuck with people down in the moors. Scram, basically."

Messing with people in the moors sounded pretty fun, exactly the type of thing he could do on a Friday night. Full moon references, however, struck the wrong chord in Garvey. "Just like a human. Your perception of an object changes and you think that's meaningful. The moon is always full, sweet treat. It can't be anything else."

Unimpressed with the tirade, Tovin shrugged. "Okay."

Arguing was useless. Garvey knew it. Tovin must have, too, since he leaned back in a chair, elevating his feet on an ottoman. He closed his eyes. Prepared to nap it out from the looks of it. A winning strategy.

Instantly restless, Garvey got up to meander around the room. He picked up one of the scattered books and flipped to the middle. Boredom kicked in soon after. He was about ready to say his goodbyes, defying Yuri's expectations, when Tovin sat upright. Eyebrows snapped together like magnets. He scrutinized Garvey as though he were doing a balancing act.

Decision made, he got up and rooted around for something under his bed.

Garvey realized he'd been waiting for Tovin to ask for his help. When Tovin came back with a box that looked like the one Yuri described, Garvey was elated.

He didn't let it show in his voice when he asked, "What is this?"

"It's a box."

"Very precise, sweet treat. What's inside it?"

Instead of answering, Tovin pushed the thing against Garvey's chest.

Garvey took the box with ill grace. Once the contents became clear—death records for humans who'd found their way to the Door—Garvey whistled low. "When I see your harmless face, I think you should be a natural at laying low. And yet here you stand with your going-to-get-myself-killed box of dumb things you shouldn't have. You misfortune-prone whackadoodle, you."

"Help me." Tovin made it sound like begging.

Garvey contemplated the desperation. He found himself doing something he rarely did with outsiders—telling the truth. "I can't help you. Not really. Look," he continued when Tovin's face fell. "Truth over certainty is Eresna's personal creed. She's a digger. A transgression of this magnitude gets her full attention. I guarantee it."

"What do I do, then?"

He almost said, *Fuck if I know*. Madness overtook him before those sensible words got out and replaced them with, "Come with me. I'll have to flee, go into hiding. We can do it together."

To say Tovin's expression was suspicious would have been an understatement. No doubt he ran through a list of the bad things Garvey had done to him up to this point, which was extensive. He averted his gaze, decision made.

Whatever madness possessed Garvey the first time forced him to explain himself. "Look, you got caught up in something big. I tried to get you out of the bloodservant pool. I really did. When I couldn't do that, I had to go forward. Tovin, look at me."

Very slowly, Tovin turned to face him. There was hardness in his eyes Garvey hadn't seen before.

"They are going to kill my family. Everyone I know and love. I chose them over you."

"And now?"

"I still choose them over you. I have to see this plan through to save them. Tomorrow, I have to take care of something. Assuming I'm not dead, I'll come get you afterward."

Tovin swallowed down the admission Garvey would always put his family first. He raised his eyebrows a bit, as if deciding whether or not the terms were agreeable. "Why do you want me to come with you?"

What was he going to say? Certainly not that he felt some strange animal connection he couldn't quite shake off. This time, he kept his madness, the more vulnerable part of his reasons, in check.

"I owe you. Deep down, I think you're a Moondog like me. You weren't built for the type of subterfuge the Boo Hags require. You want freedom more than this manufactured perfect-existence bullshit."

Tovin's level stare lightened up. Suddenly, he was shy and unsure again. "How do I know you'll keep your promise and try to get me out of here? How do I know you're coming back for me? How do I know you're even thinking about me at all once you leave this room?"

Garvey wrapped his arms around Tovin. "How do you know I'm thinking about you? How will you know I'm coming? Look to the sky. The moon will be full."

Chapter 23: Promise Kept

GARVEY

Sweet Treat's lips against his didn't make sense. Hadn't they been sparing a few moments ago? Garvey decided to let the unexplained remain a mystery and deepened the kiss whenever he thought Tovin would allow a tighter hold. Alternating between seeking intimacy and veering from it, Tovin pulled away only to press against the length of Garvey's body again moments later.

Suddenly shy, Tovin stopped. His pupils were large, black pools. "You said we'd finish what we started one day. In the library," he added, in case Garvey didn't make the connection.

"Right. And you're not dead yet, though you did try your best. Do you want me to make good on my promise?"

"Yes."

Garvey pulled their bodies back together. Apparently, he moved too fast. Tovin flinched from Garvey's touch, ducking his head to avoid eye contact.

Muttering tender reassurances, Garvey pressed his lips against Tovin's and said, "I won't hurt you."

"Unless you have to because of your family."

Honesty demanded he admit, "True. Otherwise not, though. And never in bed."

"Good enough, I guess."

Unrealistically high standards were not something Tovin struggled with. His skin recoiled wherever Garvey touched, shirking away as if expecting a blow. He averted his gaze whenever Garvey's eyes tried to find his. As he did in the woods, Garvey forced himself to slow down, to coax Tovin out of his shell, to give more pleasure than he got.

Top, middle, lobe: Garvey kissed each segment of Tovin's ear on his way down to the neck. He delighted in the frantic pulse beating against his lips and nibbled the tender skin there. Groaning in surrender, Tovin leaned in and combed his fingertips through Garvey's hair.

Garvey laughed into Tovin's mouth. "Is it still the best type of nonlethal keratin?"

"Very soft," Tovin muttered back. He curled one finger around a strand of it and tugged. The tiny bite of pain snapped Garvey to attention. With a low growl, he lifted Tovin and pressed him up against the nearest wall, forcing their erections together.

Gingerly, weary of a negative reaction, he punctured Tovin's shoulder using the tip of a tooth—enough to get a few licks of blood, nothing more.

"Do you like that?"

"Yes." Tovin pushed forward, grinding his pelvis against Garvey's.

Garvey laughed and kissed the small puncture wound. "Good, me too."

Removing Tovin's white T-shirt granted access to the very well-formed upper half of his body. Unlike the other bloodservants of the Isangelous, Tovin hadn't let himself get soft. If anything, his muscle tone had improved. The lines were sleek, elegant, tight.

"Very nice." Garvey congratulated him on his physique.

Tovin flushed at the praise.

Garvey took his time exploring Tovin, all the while taking sips of blood here and there. Each time he did, Tovin bucked against him.

Tovin's nipples stiffened under the strokes of Garvey's thumb; he shuddered when Garvey's hand glided along the bumpy ridges of his stomach muscles. Instinctively, he lifted himself on the pads of his feet, drawing Garvey's attentions nearer his crotch. Eager to accommodate, Garvey dipped his hand below the waistband of the loose jogging pants and massaged the tender ridge between Tovin's cock and leg.

His efforts paid off. Tovin once again pressed his erection against Garvey's. The pleased noises he made were reminiscent of their time in the library. He tried his best to stifle them. As if not fully in control, he licked, kissed, and nibbled at Garvey's neck in frantic succession.

"Like that, do you?"

"Yes."

"Good. Get on the bed."

Tovin fell backward haphazardly, and Garvey yanked off his pants and underwear, removing his own clothes right after in a quick, unceremonious fashion.

Tovin studied Garvey's erect cock. Something changed in his eyes. They narrowed and lost their glassy, aroused sheen. Garvey had seen the same transition in the forest and in the library. Tovin worried about penetration. Garvey didn't need to be an empath to see the signs.

"Has a man been inside you before?"

"Yes."

"Did you enjoy it?"

He shook his head. "It hurt." He stopped and considered and tagged on, "A lot."

"I won't hurt you," he repeated. "Promise."

He sounded doubtful but said, "Okay."

The way Tovin laid down face-first on the bed constricted Garvey's heart. Making murder personal in obvious ways was never wise. He'd already broken the rule today with Jerald.

Feeling decidedly unwise, he asked, "What was the name of the guy who hurt you?"

He twisted his head to the side to answer. "Miller. Why?"

Garvey put a pin in it, thinking to himself Miller sounded exactly like someone who needed a mouth hug. "No reason," he told Tovin. "Curious."

Gently, Garvey nudged Tovin over to his back. Once again, he ran hands up and down the length of his body, encouraging Tovin to a delirious state of lust. He trailed kisses where his hands had been, stopping at the juncture of Tovin's thighs. He licked the head a few times to test the waters. Tovin moaned. This time, he couldn't control the noise, it swelled up and filled the room. Enjoying the soundtrack, Garvey took the entire shaft into his mouth and sucked hard.

Tovin balled the sheets into his fists. Twisting, moving upward as if trying to get away, he slid his penis from Garvey's mouth. Garvey grabbed hold of his hips and tugged him back each time, simulating penetration.

"Oh, oh, oh." Each admission of Tovin's pleasure brought a smile to Garvey's face.

When Garvey stopped, Tovin whimpered in disappointment. His face was flushed, his hair curled around his temples where he'd been sweating.

Garvey licked Tovin's swollen lower lip. "Do you want to come inside me?"

His eyes opened wide. "What?"

"Don't look so horrified. It's not a trick question."

Garvey hadn't been penetrated much since his time with Lavario. Fumbling humans didn't do anything for him. He'd always missed the sure, confident strokes of Lavario's lovemaking. For some reason, though, he wanted Tovin in the same way.

He instructed Tovin. "Use your finger to work in the lubricant. Yeah, like that."

Uncertain, Tovin entered him and moved his hips in short, careful thrusts as if Garvey were precious and tender, rather than a monster. Garvey didn't expect the immediate spike of pleasure that followed. Surprise almost tipped him over the edge right away.

Tovin pushed deeper, his thrusts made use of the full length of his cock.

Clinically, in a way that left Garvey thinking they'd need to work on Tovin's sexy bedroom voice, Tovin asked, "Does that feel good?"

Breathless, very near climax, Garvey answered him in short bursts. "Yes. Feels good. *You* feel good."

Tovin reached forward to grab hold of Garvey's shaft. Garvey couldn't give him top marks on rhythm—the stroke of his hand was out of sync with the stroke of his shaft—but he gave Sweet Treat full credit for the overall sensation. Every last resource his body owned went toward keeping that one spot in his body alive.

Difficult as it was, Garvey—gritting his teeth—managed to fight off climax until Tovin released himself.

Garvey wrapped himself around Tovin, who nestled his head against Garvey's chest. His lashes shaped crescent moons along his cheek. Hearts didn't squeeze, so what was Garvey's doing?

Garvey tilted Tovin's face to the side, inspecting the lingering bruise around his eye where Jerald had struck him. He kissed it enough times to undo the harms of a lifetime. When Tovin snuggled up closer, he gave his head a quick sniff, committing the scent to memory.

"Sweet treat," Garvey whispered until Tovin stirred.

He blinked his eyes and looked at him with sleepy, dazed confusion. "What?"

"Stay here tomorrow. I'll be back after dark and we'll leave together."

He muttered what sounded like a yes before his eyes closed again.

As Garvey drifted off, he saw a flash of movement, a rustling fabric he swore was the hem of a blue dress. A smell he recognized followed. But it was clouded, hidden. He let it slip from his mind, telling himself he had a lot more to worry about. Later, he'd probably be killed. He'd hold Tovin while he could.

Chapter 24: Over the Top Dead

YURI AND NADINE

Yuri woke to the sound of blaring alarms. Mr. Fluffbutt, always vigilant in the fight against change, perched on the edge of her bed and yowled. Hair stood upright along his spine. His tail flicked left to right.

"No need to have a shouting match with the security system, Fluff." Yuri yawned at the cat's showbiz flair for the dramatic. He let her scratch his chin for ten seconds before he gave her hand a warning bite. "Ouch! You little devil!"

He licked her scent off his coat. "Yow."

With some assistance from the spray bottle, Yuri put an end to Fluffbutt's early morning reign of terror, but it was too late to salvage her sleep. Drowsy, she fumbled around for the coffeepot. She ignored the alarm almost completely. Much like humans, werewolves tested and retested security systems. The frequency of the drills resulted in an indifference to the noise.

Ten minutes passed.

The alarm pulsed in time with the throbbing vein in her forehead. "Enough," Yuri groused, covering her ears. From under the bed, Fluffbutt gave her a vindicated yowl. "Yeah, yeah. You told me so, Fluff. I'll go find out what's going on."

Confusion reigned in the hallways. The moment Yuri stepped outside, she got pushed against the wall by a frantic young wolf who swiveled her head left and right without paying any attention to the path straight ahead.

"Pay attention," she barked, but the pup wasn't listening.

Yuri smoothed the creases of her blouse and took a moment to consider the scene. Wolves of all ranks rushed room to room.

"Is this a drill?" she asked the first few she came across. None of them could say, just that they needed to sweep the area.

"What are we looking for?" she asked any who stopped for a few seconds.

Pity-filled derisive glares substituted a response. A new submissive, barely ten years a wolf, gave her a short answer before pulling away. "No one knows. We weren't told."

How unhelpfully vague. Her falling out with Eresna kept her isolated so she couldn't know for sure, but this felt like a real emergency. At least it had all hallmarks of chaos, and the guardians needed her to help sort the mess. Yuri pushed back her shoulders and resolved to go straight to the source.

Eresna's chamber was open as always. Inside, loud voices bickered. Yuri recognized a few, Nadine's was among them. It was a booming thing always stuck on shout.

"Yuri." Eresna's greeting lacked enthusiasm. The other wolves there didn't acknowledge her, not even Nadine.

"Alpha Guardian."

"What do you want?"

"To know what's going on. And, if you're being honest with yourself, you want that as well."

Eresna's nostrils flared. At first, Yuri thought she might have overestimated her own worth. The other wolves in attendance—who shuffled their feet awkwardly at her brash display—felt it was the case.

When Eresna spoke again, her voice was tight. "Come with us."

The procession marched down the hall. Mindful of her current situation, Yuri stayed behind the group. Nadine, who should have been toward the front, slowed her pace to walk beside her. Grateful for support amongst so much hostility, Yuri reached out and gave Nadine's hand a quick squeeze.

Nadine mouthed, *Close call, boss wolf.*

I know, she mouthed back.

Thumbs-up. *Glad you did it.*

When she figured out where they were going—the living quarters of the guardians' bloodservants—Yuri wasn't so sure she was glad she'd lobbied to come along.

The previous night, Garvey supposedly snuck away with the box of files Tovin took from storage. The False Moon promised to throw her under the bus if something went wrong. Suddenly, she worried that had been his plan all along. She was a bug he'd stuck a pin through. Squirming was all she could do. And that's what she did.

"You look close to meltdown," Nadine whispered in her ear. "Cheer up. Eresna knows she needs you."

Yuri's lungs had air for one response. "Okay."

They stopped at Jerald's door. Relief eased the tightness from Yuri's chest. Two wolves guarded the entrance, each gave her a curious glance.

The one on the right went so far to ask, "What are you doing here?"

"I brought her." Eresna's tone added "obviously" to the remark.

Heads bowed low, they stepped aside.

Yuri gasped at the carnage in the room.

"Yes," Eresna responded. "It is beyond comprehension."

Being a werewolf had placed her at more than one murder scene, but her kind were generally quick, merciful killers. Neither of those words felt apt to describe Jerald's death. Claw marks on the floor and the man's broken fingers told the story of a protracted, cruel demise.

Grief wasn't a problem for anyone, not even for those who had bonded with the violent man. Few troubled themselves to offer Eresna their condolences. The queen acknowledged those who did with a short nod of her head while her attention remained fixed on the dead bloodservant.

Nadine didn't bother with polite pretense. Reverence for human life wasn't her thing. "This guy is over-the-top dead," she observed and kicked a detached leg back toward the torso. Knowing her, she probably thought this made cleanup easier.

Eresna tensed at the disregard. "Enough, Nadine."

"Sure thing."

The Alpha shook her head at the cheerful tone but moved on. "Tovin couldn't have done this." It was a statement that sounded an awful lot like musing.

Yuri wanted to know, "Was that ever a consideration?"

"Yes." She locked eyes with Yuri. "Garvey was here last night as well. He came to have sex with Tovin. His smell is here."

"He wouldn't dare attack your bloodservant," Yuri stated, thinking it to be true. "Did you check the tapes?"

"Odd malfunction. No tapes."

"Hm. Strange. We should lock everything down, only allow wolves in the hallways, no humans. I saw several wandering around."

Such cloddishness made Eresna's lip curl. Her voice rose almost to the point of shouting. "Why do we have drills when no one pays attention to procedure?"

Rather than answer, they tucked their tails. Metaphorically, of course. Isangelous wolves preferred to remain human.

Eresna waved them away. "Yuri and Nadine, stay here. The rest of you get us on lockdown. Since none of you seem to understand what this means, I will spell it out for you. Make sure all entrances and exits are sealed, each human is in their home, and no one enters or leaves without us knowing. Understood?"

"Yes, Alpha Guardian Eresna."

Riding high on the incompetence of her peers, Yuri lifted her chin, happy to have found her way back to Eresna's good graces. She went down on her haunches to inspect the remains thoroughly. With some disgust, she noted the striation marks on the bones. Dull teeth made for sloppy bites.

"This is no wolf bite. A human did this."

"That's the way it appears," Eresna agreed. Her voice was precise, her eyes steadfast.

An inkling hopped into Yuri's mind. Her Alpha had an answer. Suddenly, Yuri had it too. All the wolves chasing after shadows made sense. They searched for something Eresna wasn't sure existed.

Yuri stood up. "A human wouldn't do this, at least without previous history."

Eresna nodded, indicating they were on the same page. "Tovin says he sees a ghost. Perhaps it's time we consider the possibility."

"You think a ghost did this?" Nadine's lips puckered. So far, she'd been content to watch the exchange, happy—despite the circumstances—that things were returning to their natural order.

"No," Yuri corrected her friend. "She thinks it was a vampire. But what does the ghost have to do with it?"

Eresna ignored the question.

Nadine didn't let the silence last too long. "A vampire? Like Dracula?"

"No, an actual vampire." Yuri shook her head, questioning her own words before they came out of her mouth. Dumfounded, she added, "And I agree."

"Find it if it's here," Eresna commanded, placing a great deal of trust in them both.

Chapter 25: Less Discreet 2.0

YURI AND NADINE

Vampire. Room by room, Yuri searched for a creature thought to be dead for centuries. Only stories—vague notions of how the creature hunted, behaved—guided her steps. She wasn't looking for caskets. Daylight and native dirt were the same as moonlight and regular dirt.

It went directly to the blood. Infection spread in its wake.

Ripped apart bodies and blood-smeared walls marked a trail of where it had been. A scroggling, the servant of a low-ranking wolf, crawled toward Yuri on her belly. Torn skin wadded on the woman's arms and back. It looked like cottage cheese.

"Help."

"Which way did it go?"

"Help me. Please." Blood spilled from her mouth.

Yuri stomped on her neck, killing her. She didn't want to be cruel, but more would die the longer the vampire remained on the loose.

Another bloodservant used a wall to prop himself up. What remained of his leg dangled from his hip. He'd been sliding Yuri's way, toward what he assumed was safety, until he saw her kill the other servant.

He tried to get away, but Yuri knocked him back on the ground. His nose was gone, part of the upper lip as well. Yuri focused on her task. "Where did it go?"

The man moaned. "I don't know. I don't know." When Yuri raised her foot, his screams became high-pitched bleats—a very annoying noise for about seven seconds. Gunk clung to the hem of her white silk pants. With some ire, Yuri kicked her expensive heels off to the side.

"Hold up," Nadine shouted, sprinting.

"I'm not human. Use your hunting voice."

Her friend gave her an apologetic shrug.

Yuri decided to let it drop. "Where were you and your boots? My Louis Vuittons are ruined."

Nadine looked over to the discarded shoes. Chunks of hair stuck out of the heel and a brain-blood combo saturated the rest. "Yuck. Yeah, that isn't going to come out." She shook her head, did a series of hand gestures to get herself back on topic. "Did you find the vampire?"

"No." Yuri punched a nearby wall. Tiny cracks exploded around her fist. "We need to find this fucking thing fast."

"Umhm," Nadine agreed. Her eyes turned golden. Not in anger. She was getting in touch with the animal inside her. "This way."

Nadine's pace forced Yuri to run to keep up, an indignity she forgave considering the circumstances. Unlike her, Nadine didn't bother to check behind each door. Nose in the air, she ran in seemingly random directions, sniffing. Sometimes, she took the air in through her mouth, sampling it like a fine wine.

Questioning humans wasn't something Nadine bothered with. She killed any servant they came across. Stories spread like infection; both disrupted the system.

"Stop killing our leads, Nadine. We don't even know what vampires smell like."

"Exactly, I'm following the only scent I don't know."

Yuri berated herself. She should have thought of that.

"This way," Nadine pulled at her arm. "We're close."

Lights in the hallway flickered as if on cue. Down the way, they could hear voices, which at first they took as a promising sign. That was until they realized it was only one word—hungry—and the rest of the noises were pained screams.

"This isn't good, Nadine."

"Isn't good? Fucking hell, Yur, this is a soundtrack for a goddamn haunted mansion. Vampires don't eat werewolves, do they?"

She didn't know. "No."

Nadine must have heard uncertainty. Instead of moving forward, she staggered back.

"Stop being such a pup."

"Don't see you scampering ahead, boss wolf."

Yuri straightened her shoulders and strode ahead with a confidence she didn't feel. Few wolves were old enough to know what to expect when it came to vampires. None of them knew what it was like to be prey.

Nadine, seeing her resolve, followed along. Soon, her longer gait overpowered Yuri's and she was in the lead. Yuri smiled to herself. She knew there was no way her boisterous friend would let her go first. Protective—certainly. But also because being one of the few werewolves to see a vampire came with bragging rights.

Ajar, the door to the recreation room dared them to enter. Nadine tapped it open with the tips of her fingers. Caution was a strange look on her friend. It made her focus dart, seeking out enemies. She placed a hand on Yuri's chest, gently pushing her back.

"Let me get a look first, Yur." Nadine poked her head through the doorway.

Yuri nodded but followed close behind. Her gaze skimmed over the redundant gore inside the room, searching for movement. One head popped up. Another. White eyes, flickering in the dim light, glanced at her and Nadine, but they skipped over, disinterested.

Air rushed from Yuri's lungs.

"Oh my god, the smell. Why didn't you warn me about the smell, Yur?"

"No one warned me." Yuri crinkled her nose and forced her way into the room. Testing the waters, she made threatening gestures toward the vampires. They ignored her and continued to shovel chunks of flesh into their mouths.

"Hey, dummy." Nadine shouted at one and kicked at it with the toe of her boot. Shrugging at the unresponsiveness, she transformed and took it up in her maw, snapping its neck. The other vampires didn't even acknowledge the death.

Gagging, Nadine spit and used her paw to rub the gunk out of her mouth. "Yuck, yuck, yuck. Next one is yours."

Yuri scrunched her nose. "All you."

"I insist."

"Remember when I drove you all the way to Vegas to see Celine Dion in concert? You'd lost your license and—"

"Oh no. Don't you dare…"

Yuri continued, "Yeah. That day you said, 'Anytime you need a favor, I owe you one, whatever it is.' Well, here we are."

"Jesus, you have a good memory. I expected you to ask me for something like… I dunno… to pick up groceries. Something equivalent."

"Celine Dion was worse than vampires. Get to the nom nom."

"Fuck. Fine."

For the first time in perhaps her entire life, Nadine didn't rush through the task. She was careful, even precise, when disgusted.

Yuri mocked her. "Pardon, madam. Would you like a lobster bib?"

"Oh, you wait. I'm going to get you so bad after this. You can't even imagine."

Yuri snorted she was laughing so hard.

Nadine finished. "Okay, well, I'm done eating forever. Do we need to do anything else here?"

"We should quarantine off this area for sure. Help me stomp on the heads of all the bodies."

The two of them slogged their way out of the mess. Nadine shut the door behind them with a bang. "So long room of horrors," she fussed.

"You poor—" Yuri stopped her playful ribbing to smell the air. "I think I smell another one."

"Or me. Or you. Because..." She pointed to their slimy clothing.

"No. Fresh. Get the scent and follow it. You're a faster tracker than I am."

"Got it." By the time Nadine had slowed down, they were in the upper level where the guardian's bloodservants resided.

"Shit," Yuri spat.

"We're on lockdown. They should all be safe."

To be certain, they checked over the doors, pushing and pulling to confirm the safety mechanisms had done their jobs. All was looking good until they got to the back entrance of Tovin's apartment, the one that went to the garden area. Someone had left it wide open.

Heavy with the unfamiliar scent, the air around them told a tale of disaster. "Suck bucket! That kid's luck is insanely bad."

Chapter 26: Cloud Nine

TOVIN

"Jerald is dead."

Dancing was bad manners, so Tovin said, "Oh no. Sorry to hear that, Kurt." Imaginary-him lit a sparkler and then took off his pants and whipped them around his head. Real-him ate a cupcake generously decorated with sprinkles and acknowledged imaginary-him would probably be on fire.

"Did you kill him?"

"You said he was eaten, Kurt. I don't eat people."

"Does Garvey?"

"He ate me."

"Tovin, I'm serious."

"Me too."

Frustration looked as difficult to swallow as a femur. Kurt's Adam's apple bobbed up and down several times before he could talk again. "Eresna will ask you questions. Prepare for it."

Touched by the actual concern he heard in Kurt's voice, Tovin thanked him for the warning. And of course he was right. If Tovin were leading an investigation, the crazy weirdo who talked to ghosts and just had sex with an admitted human eater would be his first suspect too.

He didn't linger on the gruesome details. It was a nice night. The smell of fresh lilac meandered around the garden on a gentle breeze. Little fish swam in the ornate pool. Tovin put the tips of his fingers into the water and let them nibble, enjoying how their little sucker mouths tickled his fingers.

He went back inside of his head, to the arms of some imaginary hunky man. He went to the city, to the woods, to the quiet place in the park where he could feed the ducks while watching the people go by. Places his mind knew by the desperate pull of his heart.

Destiny, meanwhile, reminded him, of where he was and what might happen. *They'll be here soon, Tovin.*

Tovin ignored her for as long as he could, enjoying what peace he could find in his own daydreams, before her interruptions became too persistent. "Yes. Yes. But they're not here now."

Kurt jumped at the sound of Tovin's voice. He said nothing, but he pressed his lips together like he wanted to say a whole lot.

Destiny talked enough for all three of them. *They'll be here soon, Tovin.*

"You said that forty-five minutes ago! Let me know when it's within the hour. Here, haunt this in the meantime." Tovin lobbed a shoe in her general direction.

Kurt's head followed the shoe's path, his expression befuddled.

The ghost drifted off to the edge of the room. Tovin wanted to say she did it gravely, but he supposed that was redundant. Looking beaten, she pressed herself against the wall like a scolded child and floated there. Cold shoulder. Worked for him.

Something is here. Tovin. It's not alive.

"Yes..." Tovin was about to say something snide about her being dead, but he heard it too. Light little scrapes on a wall somewhere accompanied by wet slaps, the sound his feet used to make when he ran along the edge of a pool. Nothing good had ever come from mystery noises so far. He was zero for two on that particular grab bag.

"Kurt..." The man ignored him. "Kurt. We need to run."

"Because the ghost told you to? Go back to playing around in the pool. Nothing can get in here." The man gave him a very pointed look. "Or out. We're on lockdown."

Go! It's a vampire! He'll chase you. It's his job.

Tovin ran.

For once, Kurt didn't do his job and stayed behind. Tovin didn't even notice until he heard a long-distance yelp. The calls for help started up soon afterward. Ornery as Kurt was, leaving him to die was out of the question. Tovin dug around in the sporting equipment until he found a ball bat.

Tovin, you're not good at this sort of thing. Destiny gave him an exasperated look. He got the sense that she'd place her hand on his chest to stop him if she could.

Destiny had a fair point. By the time someone more suitable for the task showed up, Kurt might already be dead. Tovin was Kurt's only available savior.

"I have to try," he told the ghost and practiced swinging the bat.

Don't let it bite you, she warned. *That's how its infection spreads, so keep it away from you.*

"Will do."

Tovin ran back out to the courtyard.

Kurt had a tall man with wild facial hair pinned against the wall with the lawn chair. The smell hit him like a fist. Pungent, it was a mixture of all things dead, all manner of things rotting. The milky white eyes fixated on Kurt. Its hands swiped forward in long arches.

Approximations to words gurgled out of the vampire's mouth. "Foo, foo, foo," it said. Tovin added the *d*; he was sure Kurt had done the same, judging from the desperate look in his eyes.

"It's strong!" Teeth bared with the strain, Kurt pushed backward, trying to keep the creature at a distance, but it was stronger than a mere human.

"Don't let it bite you, Kurt!"

"Why would I *let* the fucking thing bite me? Hit it."

Tovin swung the bat, which bounced back to him because he'd struck the chair. The vampire snarled at his efforts. Or maybe that was Kurt.

"For fuck's sake, Tovin. Hit it."

The next few wallops landed—one on the creature's head, the other on its arm. Seemingly more affronted than injured, the vampire snarled at him but kept lunging. Spittle flung from its mouth. At least it wasn't trying to say words anymore.

"I'm not doing anything to it, Kurt. It doesn't care."

With a grunt, Kurt lost his battle with the creature. The chair tipped to the side, and the thing beelined for Tovin. Since he didn't have the chair to navigate, his swings were cleaner. His next blow sent the thing flying backward against the wall. The one after that took it to the floor.

The bat was raised to strike again, but the creature caught on fire. Neither of them knew what the hell happened. Kurt looked to Tovin, Tovin to Kurt. Shrugging, Tovin landed one last wet-sounding smack on the thing's head, splitting it open. Perhaps it was overkill, but this seemed like a better-safe-than-sorry type of situation.

"Were either of you bitten?"

The two of them whirled at the same time. Eresna stood behind them, her hand extended outward. Her eyes were piercing. They took turns telling her no.

Eresna didn't listen to either of them. "Yuri, check Kurt. Nadine, check Tovin."

Once they'd been examined—poked and prodded, completely shaved, washed—Kurt went right in for the question. "What was that, Guardian?"

She spared Kurt a quick answer. "It's a walking contagion." She turned her gaze back to Tovin. "You. Tell me everything about your ghost."

Chapter 27: About the Ghost

TOVIN

Palpable fury made Eresna's direct transformation unnecessary. Wolf was in the air; an electrical current charged and transmitting via synapse right to the animal part of Tovin's brain that suggested, *Um, hey, uh, this could get really bad.*

"Hi." He gave her a friendly wave. "Sorry to hear about Jerald."

"Thank you."

"Welcome."

Tovin tapped his fingers on his knees and waited for Eresna to say more, which she didn't.

Everything in the Alpha Guardian's personal office gravitated toward practicality. Academic books that looked boring even to Tovin's studious eyes lined the walls. Nothing personal, nothing fun—row after row of cold, hard facts covered in tattered casings.

Paintings, the few she had scattered about, were informative maps and diagrams. Comfortable-looking cushions did grace a few nooks and crannies, but the shape of them dipped and buckled. Well worn. Luxury was apparently something she buoyed up in the common areas. Here, in her space, that shit drowned.

Scuffmarks eroded the floor beneath the queen's wooden chair, a monstrosity that yelped and screeched under each little movement. The sound it made when she pulled forward reminded Tovin of a gavel hitting a bench.

Eresna leaned forward in the chair. "The ghost's name is Destiny?"

Under her fixated glower, the smooth edges of Tovin's self-ascribed new cool melted away. He twisted in his chair. "Oh. I...err. Well, that's what I call her, Guardian."

Nadine licked her tooth. Standing beside her, Yuri cleared her throat and gave the redheaded werewolf a serious squint. Nadine spared Tovin a wink, a half-dimple grin, and a down-with-the-man fist pump to let him know she, at least, enjoyed the dig he took at their system.

Eresna was not at all amused. She paused briefly before her next question. "What does she want?"

"Beats me," Tovin responded.

The wolf queen pushed her lip out and ground her teeth. The bottom canines jutted forward, making her look a bit like an angry warthog. A very *lovely* angry warthog, Tovin amended in case she felt or heard his thoughts, sensed them or whatever.

"Ask her," Eresna finally bit out.

Tovin turned toward Destiny, who stood over Eresna's shoulder. Right when Tovin started to suspect she was going to Michigan-J.-Frog him and force him to make shit up, the ghost gave a response.

"She said she wants to be fully dead."

"And why did she appear to you?"

"She says I'm willing to see her."

The answer dissatisfied the queen, who probably wanted some type of scientific explanation for the haunting.

"But why are you able to see her?"

"Willing, not able, the ghost says."

Eresna shoved herself upright. The chair smacked against the wall with enough force to make a small indentation. "Why can't I see her, then? In my own home?"

"Oh. Uh. Because. Uh. Because. *She* said you're not very openminded."

Nothing about Eresna's expression was open for interpretation at that point. From the claws that dug into the wood of her desk to the teeth coated in bubbling saliva, all signs pointed to murderous rage.

"Is that so?"

Yes, Destiny said emphatically.

"No. No. Not at all," Tovin told the queen.

Liar, Destiny accused him.

"You're already dead," Tovin sneered at her. Out loud. He realized his mistake when Yuri cleared her throat again, and Nadine sucked in air. It sounded like water hitting a hot pan.

Calmly, Eresna leaned back in the chair. It hiccupped. The worn leather made little farting noises that might have been amusing in some other context. Nervous, Tovin smiled a bit.

"Is this a game to you, Tovin?"

Normally, Tovin thought the queen's massive spread of hair was quite lovely; a glorious mass of unapologetically assertive spirals challenging the room for dominance. It made her look like a cobra spreading its hood. The fact her upper fangs protruded outward amplified the image.

Weariness found Tovin again. "No," he assured her. "But it is what it is."

"Meaning?"

"I can't change what the ghost is or what she says to me. Do you want me to lie to you to make you feel better?"

Destiny wanted to hammer in the point. *Now tell her she should know better.*

Haranguing the powerful queen beyond what was necessary felt risky. Eresna's face started to soften. Tovin forced his voice to be reasonable as he explained, "The ghost is real. She shares what she wants when she wants. I don't have control over it."

"The vampire was real." Nadine crept into the conversation in a meek voice that clashed with her very colorful outfit.

Yuri agreed. Her voice was calm and steady when she added, "We should proceed as though the ghost is too."

Eresna, though she didn't directly say she was wrong, did continue on as though Tovin could be right. "I have concerns, Tovin. Quite a few."

Cheered by her change in tone, he listed off concerns of his own, starting with how to free himself from the ghost. He was in the middle of a few suggestions when she cut him off impatiently.

"Did you touch the portal?"

Tell her the truth, Destiny advised him.

"No, no. I... uh... that's against the rules."

Nooooo, Destiny said in a way that would have paired nicely with clanking chains.

Eresna wasn't much more impressed. "Then why feel so guilty whenever the word 'portal' is uttered?"

He didn't really have an answer except to feel wicked. Sensing it, her expression lost the softness and once again, her gaze locked with his, moving wherever he moved.

Tell her, Destiny advised again. *Do what I say from here on out.*

Gulping, Tovin went in with both feet. "I did. I did touch it."

"Umhm," Nadine said to fill the giant chasm of silence opening up between all of them. "And that was very bad. But—"

"Nadine," Eresna warned, her eyes golden. Nadine collapsed back against the wall, trying desperately to blend into a shadow that wanted no part of her. "We're done for now. Yuri, take Tovin someplace he'll be safe. Make him comfortable."

She's ordering her to kill you, Tovin. Tell her I'm not a lifestealer.

Tovin blurted out the information as Yuri placed a hand on his shoulder.

Eresna looked him up and down, her mouth pinched, her face extra tight. "What is she? What does she want? No more tidbits of information. I want the whole story."

Destiny's responses were clipped in her anger. Since time was an issue, Tovin didn't bother dressing the dictations up to sound polite. He spoke them verbatim.

"She says she's told you the truth. And if she were a lifestealer, this would be over by now. Your arrogance saw to it centuries ago after the first human you killed touched the portal. She wants you to know she's the only hope you have of stopping the infection the vampire brought with it before it spreads. And killing me means you're on your own. Good luck with that."

Part Three

Transformation

The Varcolac

Chapter 28: Family Dinner

AMBER AND LAVARIO

Werewolves must have tall tales the same as humans. Lakes that allowed you to speak to the dead were one of them. Wraith Loch was a lie. Ghosts didn't exist.

Part of Amber's ritual was to repeat these lines to herself at least five times. Despite the mantra, she visited Wraith Loch almost every day for a chance to see her slain family. What felt like decades ago, she'd been living a normal life—college, visits home, boyfriends. Then, things changed in the blink of an eye. Werewolves, actual monsters, had come to her home, killed her family, and taken her captive. Since that day, she'd been adrift in a violent world, still clinging to the past for comfort.

Unnatural plant life lined the lake's shore. Stagnant water humidified the air in the cavern to the point it felt almost tropical. The stench of the place stuck to her skin. She'd smell it on herself all through the night and into morning, sometimes giving her a headache. Put all together, the pieces of the experience were disgusting more than they were supernatural. She wasn't sure why Lavario found it so pleasant.

Amber sat on the shore and pulled out a peanut butter and jelly sandwich. Daddy's favorite.

She talked to her family. "Hey, it's me. I'm still not swimming in stomach acid."

In Amber's imagination, her mother gave her an indulgent smile. Her brother didn't understand but giggled anyway because he was young and carefree. Her little sister rolled her eyes and pulled her headphones back over her ears, far too cool for everyone else. Father, even in her fantasy, remained aloof. Impossible to please past his dying breath.

Amber sniffled. Behind her, Lavario—after confirming she wasn't in danger—wandered off, probably to nap.

"You'd love Lavario," Amber told her sister when she was sure Lavario was out of earshot. "He spends money on all sorts of frilly nonsense. Plus, he's hot. If you're into tall, muscular men with piercing eyes."

Master of couth and subtly, her sister would respond with something like, *Yum, I'd hop on and ride that dick all the way to happy town*. At least that's what she said two years ago about Tyson, a boy they'd crushed on but who didn't give either of them the time of day. Of course her sister couldn't say anything anymore. She was dead.

Amber stifled her tears. Her voice got snared in emotions when she tried to continue. Finally, she was able to choke out, "I miss you all so much."

Expecting silence didn't make her disappointment less crushing. It felt like a cold shoulder. Dead air. She could keep going with those. A crackling noise off to her left stopped her. Close after it, there was a wave of hot energy.

Living with werewolves reconnected Amber with the fragile animal inside her that didn't want to end up on a dinner plate. Something was there with her, an unknown with the calm, muggy feel of a Southern graveyard. She'd gone there for the chance to speak to ghosts. Now that she felt a presence, her mettle wavered.

With forced resolve, she whispered, "Daddy? Mom?"

The strange energy intensified. Goosebumps puckered out of Amber's skin. Shaking, she increased the volume of her voice and spoke the words of every doomed horror-movie idiot ever.

"Hello? Is someone there?"

An image of a door answered. It popped into her mind, accompanied by an impulse stronger than any she'd ever felt—*touch*. Unaware of her own actions, she reached for the strange doorway in her vision. She kept walking forward as it got farther away. Vines tangled up in her foot and she pitched forward, falling in the lake.

Water closed in around her. Muscle memory compelled her arms and legs through the movements of swimming, but nothing she did propelled her forward or upward; the water held her in place. Soon after, it turned opaque. Amber didn't know up from down, left from right.

Inside the suspended world, eyes assessed her in a detached, clinical yet also somehow intimate manner. It wanted to know every part of her being and would dissect her layer by layer until her frame lay bare and broken in its hands.

The presence pulled away. The water cleared.

Amber clawed her way to the shore. The moment her knees sunk into the slimy soil of the bank, she collapsed. Instinctively, her body wanted to yuck up water. There wasn't any in her lungs—sandwich came up instead.

She lost track of how much time she spent clutching her sides and panting. The strange, hot energy remained there too. Its heat vibrated, its frustration, its hunger. In some ways, its desperation mirrored her own. She was connected to it. And that's what terrified her most of all.

LAVARIO NURTURED HIS finicky plants. Dissatisfied with their previous room, he went and got himself one with a few small windows to let the sunshine in. The previous occupant was somewhere below in the vast underground complex. Lavario acknowledged Amber's presence with a quick side-glance but remained bent over his garden.

"Everything okay?"

Relief washed over Amber upon hearing his voice. Guilt followed. She reminded herself her family's blood was on his hands, but she didn't believe it was true anymore. Anger wouldn't come. She chewed on her bottom lip and debated whether or not to tell him about her hallucination.

When she could finally answer, her words came out through a strainer. The heavy stuff got left up top. What trickled down was thin and only had the flavor of truth. "Yes, I'm fine."

Lavario stood up. "Did someone hurt you? Did Mazgan?"

"No."

The protectiveness in his eyes made her face flush. Ever since Mazgan threatened to eat her alive, Lavario stepped protectively between the two of them whenever the Mazgan came near. Terrifying as the Alpha Guardian of the Varcolac was, Amber feared whatever she'd felt at the lake more. It was stupid, she thought, to dread a figment of her imagination.

He continued to stare, raising a brow as he looked up and down at her wet clothes. *Explain*, he commanded without saying it.

She didn't know what happened. She couldn't articulate it. "No, no one hurt me! I fell... I fell into the lake! Happy now?"

He came forward and grabbed hold of her hand. His thumb glided gently over her broken fingernails. One was far worse than she'd thought. It had bent almost fully backward. Swollen and purple tissue repaired under his touch. Healing her was one thing he never asked her permission for. He just did it.

She snatched her hand back. "Like I said, I fell."

Lies. He knew it. He wasn't the type to press for details. Rather than busybody his way into her life, he fetched towels—the fluffy ones he kept hidden for himself because she always tossed them on the floor.

"Take a warm shower, Amber. I put your pajamas near the tub."

By the time she came back into the room, he'd returned his attention to plants. Each small movement maintained precision, but it didn't look like he was actually accomplishing much.

"Is that new?" Amber pointed at a fragile sprout.

"Yes."

"Does the thing even bloom?"

"A Rothschild Orchid is not a thing. And, yes, every fifteen years or so."

"Aha. How much money did you waste on it?"

"Six grand."

Amber whistled. "So you bought yourself an expensive lifetime chore?"

"Yes. I named it Amber." Lavario congratulated himself for his joke with a tilt of his lip.

Amber hummed her disapproval. To her ear, it sounded like a hive of bees. She hoped that's how he heard it too.

The levity lasted as long as her resolve to be strong held out.

"You are shaking, Amber."

"Right. Because I fell into the lake."

Even his sighs felt ancient, like a noise released after sliding back the lid on a sarcophagus. "As you say."

Amber nested herself in one of the deep chairs he'd bought, liking the way it closed around her. She kept Lavario in view, following him with her gaze and panicking whenever she thought he might leave.

She knew he could sense her desperation to stay near him. She worried he'd make her say it. Worse, explain it.

He stayed without questioning her. Late into the night, she kept him awake by tapping him with her foot. Grumbling, he blinked, yawned dramatically, and shifted to wolf form—or, as Amber called it, his nap form—in a seamless gesture. As soon as he hit the floor, his big eyes closed and a snort-snore hybrid escaped from his maw.

"Lavario?"

Tired-Lavario lacked social graces. "What?"

"Are there ghosts?"

He chewed on her question for a good while. "I know of at least one ghostlike creature."

"What would you do if you thought you saw it?"

"Run. Very far, very fast. Run, run, run."

Chapter 29: Frilly Crap

AMBER AND LAVARIO

There was a door on the other side of Amber's consciousness. *Touch*, it demanded. Tiny shocks ran the length of her arm, compelling it upward. Fear brought it back down to her side. There was something else with her. She couldn't see it. It couldn't see her. But it was searching. Eventually, it would find her.

She woke up panting, chest heaving. Cold sweat skipped the length of her spine, hitting each vertebra like a stone on water. Her limbs trembled as she stood, but she managed to get to the bathroom before she threw up.

"Get it together," she told herself. "There was nothing by the lake. There's nothing here now. You're losing it. Find it."

Ritual, she hoped, might ease her back into typical. She hummed gently to herself while she showered and then brushed her teeth and hair. Fearing what she'd see, she avoided looking at herself in the mirror. Tears slid down her cheeks. She wiped them away with the back of her hand.

Lavario was nowhere near as affected by the events of the night before.

His slippered feet kept *tap-tap-tapping* as he sipped from a fruity pink drink that even had a small umbrella tilting jauntily to the side. The blue-and-white robe he wore was bunched up to conceal his crotch. Amber assumed he was naked beneath, which excited her more than it annoyed her anymore. What really got her goat was how he wore it like a sultan rather than a giant wolf sitting around watching celebrity dance contests.

For the most part, the two of them had made peace. Lavario made it clear she could leave at any time and he would even do his best to keep her from getting killed in the process. Amber didn't want to leave. There was nothing left for her in her old life but questions she didn't want to answer.

"Hmm," he considered the scores the same way others might consider whether a wine paired nicely with cheese. It aggravated her to see him so blasé.

"I was having a nightmare. Could have woke me, you know."

"Last time you punched me in the face."

"You're a werewolf!"

"A werewolf who doesn't like getting punched in the face." He turned up the television volume.

Exasperated by Lavario's chill attitude, Amber angry-walked to the other side of the room, audibly huffing the entire way. She was equally noisy when she brought out her paints and began her efforts to capture the fears from her dreams on canvas.

Lavario had bought her the painting supplies after a woman, who'd assured her she was not a therapist, suggested art projects to help Amber focus and relax her mind. Grudgingly, she admitted it worked. Most of the time. She mixed together some darker colors and began an abstract piece. While she worked, she watched Lavario from the corner of her eye. He was as cheerful as she was on edge.

Unable to maintain focus, she huffed at him. "Everyone here wants to hurt us."

"I am aware." Threats were not something Lavario took seriously. He turned up the volume one more notch.

"You're not worried. At all?"

"Why would I be? No one has ever defeated me."

Amber made a face at his arrogance. "Pink drinks and frilly crap are things you might want to avoid if you are looking to stress how badass you are. You know, send a don't-mess-with-me signal."

"Do you think anyone in this pack approves of my frilly crap?"

"Nope," she responded.

The Varcolac wolves had made it pretty clear how they felt about Lavario's stuff. Each time a wolf came into their apartment, it bared its teeth to pretty much every decorative item in the room as though lamps, chairs, tables, and cushions were living things capable of feeling fear.

Rather than discourage Lavario, the snarling sped up the renovation process. Sparse transformed to luxurious within months. Laminate floors turned to bamboo. Generic white-popcorn ceilings and walls from the eighties were retextured. Chairs straight out of an 1800s schoolroom were replaced with stylish sofas and lounge chairs. And, of course, a television.

All of it was nice, but Amber's favorite thing was the wardrobe. Divided into two sections, it housed clothing he wore for anytime occasions and clothing he'd be fine ripping if he needed to turn into a wolf on short notice.

It was an odd sort of mood ring—right side, nonwolf day, left side, wolf day. There'd been a lot of wolf days recently.

Lavario gestured to all of it with a sweep of his hand. "And yet I still have my 'crap.' Know why?"

She saw where this was going. "Because you're a badass," Amber responded dryly.

"Correct."

He took another sip from his pink drink—a longer, pointed one, Amber thought—then went back to his show. She sighed at him and crunched the brush into the canvas. The bristles buckled, some broke in the gooped-on paint, sticking out like the unwanted hairs on her grandmother's lip.

"You're the worst."

"You are nervous." He finally sounded sympathetic.

"Yeah, well. They're going to kill us at some point."

His face looked reproachful. "Nonsense. Wolves do not murder each other. Still, you want a way to contact me if you think you are in danger?"

Yes! She wanted to shout it at him. Instead, she pointed her finger gun at him and pulled the trigger. Her shorthand for *nailed it.*

He grabbed the grocery list she'd pinned on the fridge. "Stay here. You must sleep. I will go to the store."

"I woke up an hour ago! I don't need to sleep again."

"Disagree." He placed his hand on her forehead, muttered a few words, and pushed her backward onto the couch.

"You son of a bitch!" She didn't know if she said it or thought it.

Once she was asleep, the door reappeared. *Touch.* Beside it, a landscape painting. Somehow, it seemed larger than before. Behind it, the lurking unknown fixed its eyes on her.

Chapter 30: Not the Same

AMBER AND LAVARIO

Moonlit lines emerged: dark masses between sharp silver edges that Amber told herself she would paint later. Hazily, she looked at them through the fog of sleep, trying to capture the bends, the angles, and the colors of her dream.

They kept moving, twisting away from her before she could commit them to memory. Amber wasn't afraid anymore. At least that's what she told herself. She had canvases of conquered demons.

"Hold still!" she told the image. The dream whirled on her and moved forward very slowly. Those lines vanished the closer the form came; the dark mass became fur, the silver lines the edges of a body.

"Lavario?" she said hopefully, now very much aware she wasn't dreaming.

The figure growled.

No, not Lavario. His growls were more like half-hearted reminders that, yes, he was a giant wolf, and no, she should not move his furniture around, eat in his bed, or touch his precious television. This was deep, guttural. Unfriendly. Amber got up and ran toward the kitchen. She grabbed the nearest item available to defend herself.

Iron skillets were not silver bullets. After she swung at the encroaching werewolf with one, the monster blinked its golden eyes as though it couldn't believe what happened. It continued to advance while Amber scrambled backward to put more distance between herself and it.

Futile as she knew it was, she swung again. And again. She kept at it— her eyes closed, heart racing—until she finally made contact. The metal shivered in her hands. The monster snarled, pressing its muzzle right into her ear. Terror was part of the game the werewolf played. If it wanted her dead, she'd be dead.

"Where is Lavario?" it asked her.

"I don't know," she told it. "Not here."

"Good," it snapped back in a gravelly female voice, jaws clanking. Spittle hit her cheek. A large paw shoved her backward against the cabinets. "I want him to feel your terror before he comes in here."

"Claws off my floor, Vanu." A lazy, dry voice interjected itself into the conversation.

Amber opened her eyes. Behind the interloping wolf, Lavario stood in the doorway, several bags in his hand and his eyebrow arched upward in the prissy, superior way she knew and didn't totally hate anymore. She even felt a smile tug at her lips when he sat down the bags with a florid, dignified scoop of his knees as though he didn't have a care in the world.

Vanu grabbed Amber by her throat and pulled her forward. "Back."

"Or?" He gave Vanu a slight flip of his hand.

Amber rolled her eyes the best she could. "You've seen this on a billion shows."

Lavario nodded as though he were uninterested in the entire ordeal for that exact reason.

Suddenly, his nostrils flared. Amber took this as a good sign he was about to do something to help her, but then he spoke. "I said claws off my floor. The wood is quite delicate."

"Such an ass!" Amber yelled at him.

The werewolf holding her agreed. It squeezed Amber's throat until she squeaked her distress.

Lavario's eyes narrowed, teeth flashed, and Amber swore she could even see his ears flatten although he was in human form. "You test me."

"I came here to claim this room. Its contents, Lavario."

Instead of getting upset, he gave her a gesture that pretty much said he had zero interest in why she was there. It was beneath him to worry about such things. "By attacking my bloodservant, Vanu? Food is off-limits. Rules, no?"

"You always said rules are fluid."

This amused him. "Quite true. Quite true. Drop her and challenge me for it the Varcolac way. I am prepared to fight."

Finally, Vanu pushed Amber back against the cabinets. With shaking hands, she grabbed another item from the kitchen counter. She didn't even bother to check what it was—it was enough for her to hold it.

Vanu's calm terrified Amber. Most wolves who met Lavario slunk away, avoiding eye contact. Those who gave him orders—sweep the floor, drive me here, pick up the dry cleaning—did so in a voice shimmering with hesitation. For good reason. Lavario obeyed patiently, but the look he gave them said, I'll remember. I'll collect. Vanu didn't seem to care.

"Take my property if that is what you came here to do, Vanu."

She charged. Lavario idled. Midleap, he suspended her in the air, levitating her in stasis all the way out the door. Once he released her, she continued her charge right into a wall, which broke into several plaster chunks around her.

"The wall is yours, my dear," Lavario told her. "Patch up the hole or live in it."

The door slammed, then his footsteps sounded as he came back to the kitchen. He didn't ask her if she was all right as he unloaded the groceries. A slight smile peekabooed the corner of his lips.

"A skillet?" he finally asked her. "And you're wielding a spatula."

"You left me!" Tears stung her eyes. Angry at herself, she wiped them away, crushing the delicate flesh of her cheek against bone in the process.

"You are fine despite it."

The condescension in his tone made her tears dry up fast. Bristling, Amber grabbed at a few of the items she knew were for her. Paintbrushes, canvases, ice cream, Midol... and Fruity O's?

Air puffed up her cheeks. "What the hell is this?"

He gave the box a dismissive glance before answering. "The cereal you asked for."

"I asked for Fruit Loops. *Fruit Loops.*"

"Same thing. Bright candy circles."

"They're not the same!"

A quick flick of his wrist waved her away.

"You probably spent two grand on that shirt you're wearing. Don't act like you're some bargain-conscious shopper all of a sudden."

"You know me far too well for such a ruse."

She agreed.

Amber looked through the bags again. Before he left, he'd made a promise to give her something to contact him if danger ever gnawed at the door. Possibilities whirled in her head: magical rings, necklaces, or maybe even a watch. She imagined herself summoning Lavario in an instant; her very own fashion-forward genie to smite enemies while wearing a special suit he'd set aside for ass kicking.

Too proud to beg or remind him of his promise, she harrumphed until he gave her a slight smile. His green eyes flickered with devilish good humor. Right. Her thoughts. He could hear them. Amber felt heat rush to her face.

"Open it," he told her.

Eagerly, she did. "This is…" she couldn't believe what she was seeing.

It was a bright orange and only had two blockish buttons; one of them said Mommy, the other one said Daddy. Up top, FirstPhone was written in motherfucking comic sans. Bears hugged around the frame, cheery looking little things with symbols on their heads. Some of them were doing handstands, others were hula-hooping. The one on the back had a giant bouquet of daisies.

"What the hell?" She held the device up to his face. A package of stickers fell to the floor. She looked down at them. They were bright, glittery.

"It's a phone. Mommy and Daddy are both me. You can press either and I'll pick up."

"You got me a kid's phone with fucking Carebears all over it?"

"Feelings bears," Lavario corrected her.

"Same thing!"

"They are not the same thing," he assured her with a grave authority.

The longer she looked at him, the more self-satisfied his smile became.

Fury bubbled up inside of her until she finally realized it wasn't anger at all. She thought it was funny. She'd be damned before she told him that.

"The Fruit Loops. You have to go back. I *need* those."

"It is late." He waved her off again while he put some fancy butter that probably cost a fortune into the fridge. Amber eyed it with growing wrath.

"I know how *Lost* ends."

He straightened. "You wouldn't."

She pointed at the door.

"And if Vanu comes back?" He gave her a sly, toothy smile.

She smiled back. "Give her these." She pressed the box of generic cereal to his chest. "Then levitate her off to the store with you."

Lavario growled as he picked up his keys. Amber swore something heavy was being dragged off in the distance. Noise faded. Amber collapsed in the corner. Her lips trembled.

"I'm going to stay here. I can do this. I can be alone." Sooner than she liked, she got up and bolted down the hall, frantically trying to catch him before he left. As she ran, she glanced at each door with a suspicious eye.

Chapter 31: Karate Chopping Through It

AMBER AND LAVARIO

Makeshift punching bags hung along the wall—little more than trash bags filled with flour. Once one broke, its contents slumping to the ground in a silky-white torrent, Amber moved to the next. Slick with sweat, her fists slid when she made contact; burning, chaffing her flesh as though it were snakebitten. Her knuckles were red, raw meat.

Occasionally, she looked over at Lavario to reassure herself he was there. Paranoia plagued her after he'd left, leaving her vulnerable to Vanu's attack. Sleep became near impossible. There was always the door, always what lurked behind the door. And when she woke, werewolves took the place of the unknown.

At least one of them was sort of on her side. For all the good he did.

There was a time when Lavario only showed her a very polished version of himself—as a man he was refined, as a beast he was majestic. Not anymore. He'd shrunk to the size of a normal wolf. He slept on his back atop a mound of pillows. A giant back paw shot up in the air. One toe was white, like a mountain summit.

Sometimes his tail wagged. The first time the damn thing hit the wooden floor, she'd thought they were being shot at, so she'd flung herself to the ground with a screech. Now this was her new normal. If he wasn't napping, he was watching television, eating, shopping, fucking, or getting ordered around by smug assholes, some of whom he'd just fucked. When he got too noisy, she threw a fruit loop at his head and thought about how much he looked like a giant—

Languid green eyes opened into a small slit. "I am not a collie."

She harrumphed at him. "Good dream? Find something on sale?"

"Yes, it was wonderful. Your hideous chair was soot and ash."

She patted her La-z-boy recliner, which was swathed in a large, bright art-deco print she'd picked out. Lavario side-eyed it whenever he walked past, along with the rest of her junk scattered haphazardly on her side of the room. Whatever. Her space was comfortable—lived in.

She continued to glare at him.

"Do you want something?"

"Oh no! You go right on with naptime while I train myself."

"Train yourself?" He fully opened his eyes and sat upright, taking stock of the disaster around him. "What... what is this mess?"

"Me doing something."

"Appears to be all you do, a long list of *something*. Is that my garment bag?"

"I ran out of trash bags," she explained. Knowing what he'd say next, she continued, "Your garments are on the floor somewhere."

He growled at her. There were teeth this time.

"Show me yours, I'll show you mine." She growled back, teeth flashing. She threw handfuls of flour at him. Fuck physics. It dispersed into a spattering of powder by the time it reached him. The look he gave her sneered at the ineffectiveness of the gesture. "Yeah well. Now you look like you have dandruff. Don't act like that doesn't bother you."

His ears flicked like a horse's tail swatting at flies. A tiny fraction of the substance fluttered down to the floor. Dissatisfied, he lifted one massive paw off the ground, suspending it temporarily behind his ear.

"Don't you dare think it," he warned her and kicked himself in the head like a damn.... "I am NOT a dog."

"Uh-huh. If you're bored, you could teach me how to fight. You promised."

"Oh, yes. That. I thought we agreed it was not working out."

They hadn't really agreed on anything. She wanted him to teach her how to kickbox, sword fight, use nunchucks. Violent things. Stuff that would make her fists collide with bone, split open flesh. Since he was alive and everyone seemed to hate him, she assumed he'd be good at it. Possibly the best.

Instead, he'd fortune-cookied her with lectures about finding what worked for her. When that failed, he bought some beginner DVDs. One of them was actually a jazzercise tape. She grumbled at the memory.

She thought she saw Lavario's canine lips twist upward and jabbed, "Maybe dogs do smile."

He sniffed at the slight but didn't deign to respond. "You cannot karate chop your way out of trouble."

"Better than doing nothing. At least I'm going to fight them, maybe kill one or two before they get me."

"I will advise them to hide the silver and wolfsbane," he responded. Yawning, he stretched, curling his claws away from the floor like a cat might do, before bombing to the floor. A mushroom cloud of flour whooshed out from under him.

"How are you even alive! Everyone wants to kill you, yet all you do is sleep!"

He hooked a claw under his gums, pulling upward to show off his fine, sharp white teeth: thirty-two pointy reasons for his self-assurance. "Instinct. Throat, belly, thigh. And magic. Mostly magic."

"I don't have giant fangs! I can't do magic!"

"Glad you finally understand the gist of what I am telling you."

She was about to snark back at him but came up short. Amber could ill afford to be cavalier about her situation. She was as hated as Lavario but nowhere near as powerful. It pissed her off.

He flattened his ears and hunkered down, anticipating a tirade. Although she wanted to follow through with his expectations, she couldn't bring herself to it. Mind reading wasn't an ability she had. She couldn't sense his emotions, and his motivations were largely a mystery to her. But she somehow knew he spent nearly every waking minute with her because she was afraid. He was guarding her.

She couldn't rely on him forever, though. "I need to learn how to fight." She stressed the importance again by smacking her fist into her palm.

He gave her a doubtful look. "Physical strength is a tenuous power, Amber. Your father boxed in college. He knew how to hit people. How well did that serve him?"

Thinking about her dad brought on a shot of guilt followed by a chaser of pain. It burned. It muddled her senses. Worse than any of that, it made her cry. Last time she'd seen him, he'd only mumbled a condemnation for her whorish ways. The tepid, lifeless accusation had more effect than any of the times he'd shouted it at her.

"The fight wasn't fair."

"Nor will it be for you. You are not a brawler, at least not yet," he informed her in a dry voice after she didn't respond. "But you are strong."

Amber averted her face to hide her discomfort.

Sometime while she was lost in reflection, he'd turned into a human to boil water for his tea. He covered himself in a loose robe only because she constantly objected to his nudity. Slowly, like an old man, he moved around the kitchen as though he couldn't remember where he put anything.

"Your mugs are to the left," Amber told him to work her way back to a conversation without having to acknowledge what he said before. "What do you suggest I do, then? Toss my hands up in the air? Laze around the—"

"Learn what you can. Control your fear."

He dipped the bag into the boiling water.

"That's it?"

"Until you become wolf, yes."

What seemed like ages ago, Kijo had told Amber about her days before becoming a werewolf. There was an inconsistency there. Amber grabbed at it. "Kijo said you taught her to be a Varcolac wolf, which—if you'll remember—included lots of physical violence. What are you teaching me to be exactly?"

"Alone."

"Like you?"

His eyebrow arched at the association, but he nodded. "Yes."

"Alright then, take me shopping."

He considered her request. "You cannot tell anyone what I am. If you wish to return to your human life, I can—"

"I don't want to return to my human life." Guilt clawed through her again. She wanted to become a werewolf. She wanted to become the same creature that had destroyed her family. It was just as well her loved ones never visited her at Wraith Loch. What a sham she'd become.

Sensing her anguish, Lavario approached and placed his hand against her cheek. Although it was a comforting gesture on his part, Amber still felt her body tingle in sexual awareness. She leaned into his embrace, enjoying how his large hand eclipsed half her face.

Lavario gave her a fond, awkward pat and said, "I will make arrangements."

Chapter 32: The Natural Process

AMBER AND LAVARIO

From what Amber could see, parallel parking must have been unconscionably difficult. *Pull up to the mirror of the other car. Back up. Stop. Turn the wheel. A slight bit of gas. And...too far. Again.* Seventeen attempts later, Lavario still couldn't get it right. She gave him her best you-sure-tried-buddy fist bump to his shoulder.

People honked their car horns behind them. A few shot off to the side, haphazardly avoiding pedestrians and oncoming traffic. One of the drivers, a young man in a try-hard sports car, really nothing more than a Honda with a fin, leaned out his window to squeal curse words at them.

Lavario hit the wheel in frustration.

"Do not frenzy," Amber scolded him.

"Yes, thank you, Amber."

Stoic on the surface, the werewolves in the back seat kept peace as their disgraced guardian struggled to complete yet another simple task. One of them checked his watch. His lips curled into what might qualify as an expression, but when he caught Amber spying, his features realigned themselves back to deadpan. Amber never knew if they were amused by Lavario's ineptitude or saw it as an affront to practicality. She supposed both could be true.

With a bite to his voice, Lavario turned her direction. "You could offer your assistance."

"I'm only here to observe. Doing anything else subverted the natural process," she responded in a voice saturated with detached pseudoscientific grandeur. Those keen eyes of his continued to dig for another response until she swiveled her head toward him, eyebrows raised to her temple. "Do you even have your license?"

"For what?"

Amber gave him a long, hard glower. For extra insult, she turned around to look at his two packmates in the back seat as if to say, *Can you believe this guy?* They could not. One of the warmer of the Varcolac wolves shook her head a bit to acknowledge the outrage of it. Lavario caught her reflection in the rearview mirror and showed her his teeth.

"Stop being such a grump," Amber chided him when she saw it. "It's not her fault that you're the—"

"Yes, I know. The *worst*. As you say."

Amber made her finger into a gun and pulled the trigger. "Blammy, right on the mark. Honestly, even Dip can do this."

Snobbery was something she could always count on from him. The mere mention of the other werewolf's name—a creature Lavario described as a mongrel unfit to even be called a False Moon—made his green eyes turn a little bit golden. Each time Amber saw the slight change in color, she felt a small thrill. She could nettle him unlike any other.

"Stop smirking, Amber."

"Bet you wish you could hocus pocus your way out of this one, huh?"

"I do. I really do." Witnesses put a kibosh on any magic. Otherwise, Amber knew he could have lifted this car and placed it in its spot a billion times over. "I have a different type of power to use on humans."

Lavario rolled down his window to address a young male with a hat on his head, an attendant of some sort.

"You," he shouted at the man.

The guy pointed at his chest to say, *Me?*

Lavario confirmed it. "Yes, you. Come." When the young man was close enough to the car, Lavario took a hundred dollars out of his wallet. "I will give you this to park our car."

Ten embarrassing seconds later, the car was parked. Lavario opened the door for his packmates the way Dip had done for him so many times before. They got out and went on their way without so much as a glance at either of them.

Lavario placed his hand on Amber's chest before she went any farther. "Remember—"

"Yes, I know. If I say anything, you'll have to kill them all."

TWIRLER WASN'T A word Amber would have used to describe herself. She couldn't restrain the impulse anymore. She'd never looked so good. Her hair curled in short, tight spirals along her temple, accenting the strong angles of her face and the wide, brown eyes, which lit up attractively each time the assistant brought another fancy garment for her inspection. Young, fun, vibrant: the dress she wore was a fifties throwback with its high, scooped neckline and large floral pattern. Perfect fit for her. So, yeah, she twirled.

"I can't believe this is me!" she gushed at the saleswoman. She turned around to inspect her bum. "Oh! I want to wear this one out."

"You look stunning," the woman assured her smoothly.

Lavario scrutinized her selections. "Lavish, a dash of functional—very little in between. Appropriate for you. You will want shoes as well?"

"Fuck yes, I want shoes," she confirmed. "No heels please," she told the saleswoman.

Excitedly, the paid-a lot-to-be-so-bubbly woman took off to fill her request. Her head bobbled as she looked for items of interest, and when she dove down between sales racks, her rump stuck upward like a duck in a pond.

By the time Amber's shopping spree was done, her arms were so overloaded her eyes barely peeped over the edge of the various boxes. She walked out of the store using her elbows to notify her where the walls were.

"Ouch!" It wasn't a perfect system.

"Mind the walls," Lavario warned her.

"You could help, you know."

"Here to observe. Natural process, you understand."

Amber gave him an unladylike grunt. By the time she got to the car, her arms ached from the strain of carrying so much. Unexpectedly, the expressionless werewolf from the back seat assisted her in getting the purchases into the trunk.

"What a gentleman!" Amber praised him, surprised.

"Yes, well done, Fredrick," Lavario said dryly.

Younger than Lavario, at least that's what Amber guessed, he looked at her with new eyes, which Amber suddenly noticed were a lovely warm brown. Not knowing quite why, she grinned at him from ear to ear.

Lavario chuckled. "You'll be a dog walker yet."

Fredrick made no comment. As they drove home, Amber met gaze with his from time to time in the rearview mirror. Flirting, she realized.

For now, she didn't feel afraid. But she knew that time would pass. Soon, she'd be back in their small apartment, hostile werewolves all around them waiting for their chance to get her alone. Well-dressed food was food with an expensive wrapper on it.

Lavario knew her mood changed. At some point, he turned to her, taking his eyes off the road. She was ready to be curt when he confronted her about it, but he only took her hand in his. There was nothing possessive about it. It was like a little note in a bottle washing up on her shore. When she read it, it said, *Be still, be strong, do not frenzy.*

Chapter 33: A Tenuous Power

AMBER AND LAVARIO

Prettifying herself made Amber feel better on a superficial level. Fragmented as her mind might be, she appeared polished, put together. Sane. "Ha-ha. As if. Quaking in your boots at a ghost that didn't even boo at you."

Her self-chastisement didn't sting or stick. Undercutting her fears, pushing them off as superstition, wasn't working. Each day, she woke to the same sense of the hunt, the same sense she, the ghost, and the strange door were three points about to converge.

"The incident at the lake has troubled you for a while."

Lavario's voice startled her out of introspection. Hearing her own fears out loud made her feel ridiculous, like a child running to flip on the light. "Stop mind-spying!"

"Perhaps we should talk about the ghost?"

The image of the door hopped into her head.

Lavario straightened. He looked alarmed. "A door?"

"Yes, I'm about to walk through it." She pushed past him and did just that.

He followed. "Apologies for prying, Amber. I am concerned."

"Me too."

"About?"

She didn't want to answer that question. Not yet. "Going to take a walk."

He reached for his coat, which Amber assumed he wore because it was fashionable. Weather didn't exist in the Varcolac compound, which was mostly underground, and Amber damn well wasn't going outside.

"Alone."

"They will accost you, Amber."

"I know. I'll take my phone."

"Wait."

She stopped. Assuming he'd disagree and possibly try to stop her, she prepared herself for an argument. Hands firmly planted on hips, she indicated he could continue with whatever it is he was going to say.

"Remember, you are a fighter. Be still. Be strong. Do not frenzy."

The unexpected reassurance undid her animosity. More than that, it reminded her there was a lot left unsaid between them. Amber hugged him. The embrace felt awkward until Lavario wrapped his arms around her and patted her back.

She mumbled a question into his chest. "You didn't have anything to do with my family, did you?"

"Not directly."

She wasn't satisfied with the answer. "How?"

"My inaction drove Kijo to an extreme response."

"I want to kill her. You cool with that?"

"I see it as understandable. I wouldn't go so far as to say I was cool with it."

Amber pushed away from him. Worried, proud, slightly fatherly, his expression made her a tad uncomfortable, considering how he affected her. "I'm not your replacement kid either. Alright? Look, I'm also sorry about all the—"

"Should I get you a priest?"

"Trying to make nice here!"

"No need."

There was a need. Talking about how she felt wasn't Amber's thing, so she pushed up on her toes and pressed her lips against his.

Bold had described her since the day she could remember words. Demanding a new seating arrangement in kindergarten was bold. Wearing her hair short and natural instead of straightening it the way her mom and sister did was bold. Moving so far away from home against the wishes of her father was the boldest of all. Bold was never a compliment. She was an excess of stubborn, opinionated, and aggressive.

Lavario didn't return her kiss. Amber broke away and prepared herself to hear some variation of she was too much of something or other.

"Right now, you are too *vulnerable*." He rested his thumb on her lower lip. "I would be taking advantage. Give it two days serious thought. If you still have these feelings, kiss me again."

Amber sigh-groaned at the imposition. "Nothing will change in two days. I'll want this."

"You nicknamed yourself 'daddy issues.' Forgive me for wanting to be certain."

Heat rushed to her cheeks. "Stop mind-spying!"

Lavario ignored her outrage. Serious faced, he gave her shoulders a squeeze. "Go on your walk. Be bolder than you ever thought possible."

COURAGE LEFT HER when the first werewolf she encountered showed its teeth—long, white, and very sharp. Snarling, it cornered her against a wall. Another joined, slamming its clawed fist right next to her head. Plaster got in her eye. Next to them, she was reminded of how small she was, how soft her flesh, how delicate her pulse.

One of the creatures cupped her cheek, twisting her head to whisper in her ear. "Where's your keeper?"

Thoughts piled one on top of the other, gridlocked. Unjamming them seemed an impossible task. She wanted to say clever things, but her uncooperative mind shouted *fuck* repeatedly instead.

I am a fighter, she told herself even though her eyes were squeezed tight enough for tears. *I am strong. I'm not going to frenzy.*

"Probably shopping," she told the monsters. She forced herself to wiggle through the small gap between furry bodies. She moved forward one step at a time, her gate inconsistent and staggering like the beat of her heart.

Somehow she managed to keep herself from running until she was around the corner. How far did she jet afterward? She couldn't guess. Dizzy from the exertion, she put her hand to her chest and panted.

Touch. The thought came from nowhere, an electric whiffle through the otherwise idle air.

Amber teetered. The familiarity of the sensation made her nauseous. Long ago, to keep herself sane, Amber had determined her dreams were symptoms of stress, little more than terrifying reminders she'd been through hell. She wasn't dreaming, at least she didn't think so.

She knew this place, right down to the landscape painting, completely out of sync amongst all the look-alike, xeroxed walls. As she did when she was sleeping, she wondered which werewolf put it there. It was way too cheap to be Lavario. Still, he was the only werewolf she knew who valued aesthetics.

Touch.

The directive came again. Telling herself it was no big deal, Amber gave her shoulders a shrug. Uneasiness didn't leave her. Her hand inched upward to touch the door.

"What are you doing here?" Kijo's voice startled her.

Amber had no real idea. "Use your eyes. I'm looking at a damn door."

Kijo turned her head to study it too. Her eyebrows drew together tightly like they were holding up the middle finger. Amber couldn't fathom why there would be so much hostility between the perpetually nettled Kijo and a piece of wood. Maybe it was bad at staying shut.

"It is not a door. You know it isn't."

Amber began a denial. "I—"

"You know it isn't," Kijo asserted again. "It called to you? Invited you to touch it?"

Amber nodded. There was no sense in denying it. Nothing escaped Kijo's black eyes—not light, not laughter, certainly not white lies. Anything drawn into them got dissected with the precision of a scientist but with the careless zeal of a child.

"Come with me. Now," she growled when Amber failed to move. "Get away from it."

"Goddamn. You have no chill."

Kijo didn't respond. She grabbed the sleeve of Amber's shirt and pulled her along down the hall. Amber walked as fast as she could, occasionally trotting to catch up.

Whether Kijo noticed Amber lagging behind was open for debate. Her head never swiveled back. Straight ahead the entire way until they stopped.

"Never go back there alone."

"I wasn't going to go back there at all."

"Good. Tell Lavario what you saw. Your room is all the way up the hall, to the left, then another direct left. You should know where you are after that."

Then their conversation was over.

Or was it? "Amber," Kijo called when she was halfway down the hall. "Remember to tell Lavario. Use the word 'lifestealer.' He will know it."

Amber almost asked her why she didn't do it herself. Snide comments slid back down her throat. Kijo's face, normally so resolute, had a hint of vulnerability to it—a small crack in the otherwise tight, marble-like structure. For once, it didn't feel like Kijo was ordering; she was practically begging.

"I'll tell him," Amber promised.

Chapter 34: Little One

AMBER AND LAVARIO

Same, same, same. The Varcolac compound wasn't the friendliest place for a person who navigated using landmarks.

"Fuck it all." Amber tossed her hands in the air and lashed out at the nearest object, which was another damn wall. What else would it be? She allowed herself one hysterical laugh.

A hand touched her shoulder. Amber twirled around, ready to fight.

"Hello, little one."

Gorgeous didn't begin to describe the she-wolf who came into view. Shoulder-length blonde hair framed her delicate face. Features so precise, so symmetrical that they could have made anyone believe in a higher intelligence graced Amber with a view of paradise.

Like all the other Varcolac wolves, she wore simple clothes—a cotton blouse, beige dress pants, zero embellishments or ornaments. Inexplicably, she transformed the drab garments into complementing outlines that accentuated the curve of her hips, the steep slope of her long legs. Instead of hiding her bust, the shirt she wore pushed up her breasts, which peeked over the top as if to catch you looking.

Clever things abandoned Amber, gliding right out of her head, no doubt to breeze back in when they'd only be useful for replay fantasies. "H-hi," Amber babbled.

"Get lost?"

"Sure did. Nothing here changes."

"I'll take you back to Lavario."

"He changes least of all." Amber belted out an awkward guffaw.

"Indeed so." The werewolf' beautiful mouth laughed. Her eyes did not. She reached out her hand and touched the side of Amber's cheek. There were a few soft words that sounded like a lullaby to Amber's ear. She forgot them as soon as they were spoken.

"Now come with me, little one."

Amber's legs moved forward without asking her brain's permission.

Unlike Kijo, the gentle-seeming she-wolf regularly checked over her shoulder to make sure Amber stayed close behind. Her gait was relaxed. Occasionally, she'd play the part of tour guide, letting Amber know where they were in the massive compound. None of it stuck. She could have said, *And here's our slaughterhouse*, and Amber would have uh-huhed and shuffled along after her.

What was wrong with her? Amber shook her head, but the cloud didn't pass.

"Shush, shush. Almost there."

"Okay," Amber mumbled, stunned by her compliance.

She told herself it was okay. The werewolf guiding her wasn't all fangs and grump like the rest. Statistically, it seemed unlikely Lavario would be the only reasonable one of the bunch. At least that's what Amber told herself. The farther they went down the hall, the more apprehensive she became.

Amber stopped. "I don't recognize any of this."

"I know. We're in my room. Do you want to come inside?"

"N-no, I should get back to Lavario. He's probably worried."

"He isn't the worrying type. He has no reason to be. Bloodservants are off-limits." The beauty entwined one of Amber's small curls around a long, elegant finger, tugging playfully. "I only want to know what you and Kijo talked about. That's all, little one."

What happened next flabbergasted Amber on every level. A tender hand stroked her face, her brow. Brushed up against hers, the she-wolf's lips— even with teeth—seemed sweet, not scary. And Amber liked it. She really, really liked it. Without thinking, she grabbed the back of the woman's head, pulling downward to deepen the kiss.

Surprised, the she-wolf stepped backward to break the hold. "Goodness. Quite a bit more receptive than I thought. Can't say I mind. You are a lovely young girl."

Amber gave her a dazed grin.

The she-wolf opened the door to her room, held out her hand. "Would you like to come inside now?" The woman cocked her head to the side as though she were about ready to indulge a childish whim.

Inside was the hip place to be. Amber decided this was true once both their shirts were off. Teeth nibbled fleetingly as the she-wolf stroked upward along Amber's inner thigh, teasing at where it was heading but never quite getting there. Disappointed moans did nothing to speed the process along.

"Patience. Patience. Tell me what you and Kijo talked about."

Amber licked the smooth line of the she-wolf's neck. "A door. And something she called a lifestealer."

She puckered her lips and furrowed her brow. "Goodness. Very troubling. The door...did it call to you? Did it ask you to touch it?"

The continual interruptions irritated Amber. She tried to guide a hand back to her breast. "Yup, just like I'm asking you to touch me."

The she-wolf broke the hold in an instant. "Put your clothes back on. Come with me."

Once again, Amber did as ordered without complaint, without challenging the werewolf or even asking for her name. It felt so unlike her. Questions certainly came up in her head—lots of them—but somehow they all got marked off as satisfactorily answered.

The two of them walked out of the compound. Air hit Amber with the force of a blow. The sensation was unfamiliar, a throwback from a past life.

She shook and folded her arms across herself. "Cold out here."

All the sweetness was gone from the she-wolf's voice. "Walk out to the woods. Stay there. You're sad. You want to end your pain."

After the werewolf's footsteps faded, there was no sound in the forest except for the Amber's chattering teeth and the occasional rustling of leaves on nearby deciduous trees. It was Amber's first time in a real forest, not the manufactured ones of city parks. She already hated it.

Her inner thoughts were nowhere near as quiet. *I want to live, I want to live, I want to live.* She continued to stand in the same spot. Those thoughts slowed down. Everything else slowed down too.

Chapter 35: Upstream

AMBER AND LAVARIO

Memory didn't give a shit about inconveniencing her. It came to Amber at her worst—when she was shivering, nearly beaten and dead. It freewheeled on one of the rare breezes to deliver an unwelcome reminder that her will once belonged to her.

Amber's father's advice was simple. "Don't drown."

He'd left her on the bank while he and her uncle walked upstream dragging a small raft filled with their fishing gear and one case of beer. They'd float down later to collect her, they had said. Meanwhile, she was to practice math, catch minnows, and not die.

Amber wasn't satisfied with the shallows. When she sat on her small innertube, which was decorated with cartoon starfish, it sank to the bottom. The rocks stuck to her water-slick bottom.

"I want to float!" she told the universe.

As was often the case, the universe didn't care, so Amber usurped its burden. She took the drawstring from her swimming trunks and tied a knot around her innertube and dragged it upstream. She'd go to deeper water. She'd float.

She fought the current. Slippery rocks and fast water ensured a lot of falling. Bruises started to show; evidence, her father would later say, of her hubris. Later in life, the word for that same dogged persistence, her stubbornness and guile, became bitch. Or bold, if the teller were feeling generous.

Back in the present, the forest closed in around her.

Survival notions darted away like a memory she couldn't quite grab hold of. She stood there knowing she needed to do something if she wanted to live, but each time she tried to formulate a plan, her brain told her to stay, end her pain.

"I'm not in pain." Her lips were too cold to manage anything above a murmur. She was too cold to do much at all.

The memory of the river came back to her, her short legs slicing through the water. She had felt the way she thought Moses had, parting the Red Sea. At some point, she'd even gone to the shore to get herself a junior-sized staff similar to the one she'd seen in Sunday school, complete with weeds wrapped around the top to symbolize the snake.

Her own memory played like a movie.

This time, the rest of her body took the hint. Her foot inched forward. Amber gasped at the pain. Her other foot followed. Once again, there was an immediate stab. This was working—kind of—but the going was slow and torturous. Each step made her whimper or suck in air.

She regained total mobility when entering the compound. Whatever spell she'd been under broke its hold. There was still a dull throb, similar to exercise fatigue, when she moved.

"Ouch, ouch, ouch" wasn't the most heroic mantra for her victory march down the hall. She was too annoyed to care. The sharp teeth and shitty dispositions of the werewolves she encountered didn't faze her.

"Shut up," she told the first one who growled at her, "find a new noise to make. Oh, and which way back home?"

The angry one didn't answer, but another did. "Come with me. I will show you."

Amber massaged a charley horse out of her right calf and limped forward, following the beast in front of her.

Once they were in a familiar hallway, he pointed the direction she needed to go. "Down the hall. Yours is the next to last on the right."

There was something about his voice. "Are you the gentleman from the shopping trip? Fredrick?"

"Yes."

"Cool. Thanks, Fred." She half waved, half saluted him.

It annoyed her a bit when she didn't find Lavario wringing his hands in concern. As usual, he was taking himself a nice nap. He shot up quick enough with the click of the door as it shut.

When he saw it was only her, he yawned and scratched his belly. "You are back. Good."

"Thanks for worrying."

"You are too capable for me to worry."

Amber was about to argue more.

Sensing it, Lavario waved her objections away. "Wait here. I have something for you to mark the occasion."

He came back with a smartly wrapped gift. It looked like a garment box from a high-end retailer, but the phone incident jaundiced Amber to outward appearances.

"What's this? A backpack with a leash attached? The ones that help parents keep track of naughty children?"

"Nothing quite so useful. Open it."

Cynical of what she'd find beneath, Amber undid the bow, lifted the lid, and pushed back the tissue wrap. She gasped in disbelief. She'd seen this robe during their shopping trip and fell in love with it immediately. Pure silk looked flimsy to her eye. This garment was a blend of fabrics, all of them soft to the touch but firm. Delicate pearls made looping floral patterns alongside embroidery. It was exquisite girly, something a queen might wear. She'd been so afraid he'd laugh if she asked for it.

She kneeled on the floor and clutched it to her chest. She felt its smooth lines, enjoying its elegance. No one else but Lavario had ever indulged her frilly side. "Thank you. It's beautiful."

"Not half as much as the one who will wear it."

"Oh, you flattering old horn dog, you."

Lavario chuckled. "Did anything happen on your walk? Your thoughts are tangled."

One of the first lessons she'd learned was to keep weaknesses—fears, woes, and emotions—to herself. Otherwise, they became weapons used against her. *There,* they'd say, *you're not as strong, smart, or brave as you thought you were, are you? You needed to be taken down a peg.* There was a deep pit inside where bad shit got buried. Lavario sniffed around it, pawing at the loose dirt.

"I won't hurt you. I won't laugh."

"I feel safe with you," Amber told him. "Yeah, something happened. Lots of things. Lavario, I don't know if I'm losing my mind. I think I'm being chased by a ghost. Or a...I dunno. A demon. I wake up each night worried that it finally found me. Are you going to ship me off to the loony bin?"

He sat on the floor and pulled her against his chest. "You are too hard on yourself. Your family was slaughtered in front of you. You were kidnapped and abused. Each day, you wake up surrounded by deadly threats. Those who come to us under similar circumstances are off in a corner gibbering nonsense by now. Understandably so."

Amber let herself lean totally into Lavario's body. He supported her full weight.

"I'm tired."

He rested his chin on her head. "I know. Rest."

Amber closed her eyes. "Something else happened too. I met another werewolf."

"Fredrick?"

"No, a beautiful woman. She, uh…" Amber paused, embarrassed. "She kissed me."

Lavario tightened his arms around her. "Did she hurt you?"

"No. Well, it was strange. We kissed…a lot. Some other stuff happened. And then I was in the woods, and whenever I told myself to leave, all I could think about was ending my pain."

Lavario went quiet. So quiet Amber thought at first he might have drifted off on an impromptu nap.

When he spoke again, his voice startled her with its force. "The werewolf. Describe her to me."

Chapter 36: Control Spell

AMBER AND LAVARIO

Morning wasn't Amber's best time. Understatement. She groaned and rolled back over, resistant to Lavario's prodding finger. Seeing no result using the gentle approach, he grabbed her shoulder and shook.

"Amber, I must know why Vanu cast her spell."

Fatigue made a chore of mockery, but she gave it her best shot and adopted his snooty accent. "Must you now?"

"Yes."

"I think not, sir. Good day."

"Get up."

She tugged a pillow over her head and pulled her knees up to her chin. Last night's ordeal exhausted her. She felt like she'd run a marathon. "Go. Away. Collie."

He growled the way he always did, a low thing lacking bite that reminded her of an old man fed up with the youth of the world. Before she could retort, he carried her to the bathroom. Heated tiles spared her bare feet the realities of early morning, but the cold air bit into her skin. She dropped to the floor and curled up there.

"You are impossible, Amber."

"The giant blood-drinking werewolf thinks a sleepy woman is impossible? It's dark. It's cold. This chick is a night owl. Straightforward stuff in an otherwise complex world." Amber yawned. "Where is the sun anyway?"

He drummed his fingers on the frame of the doorway. "East. Now arise, fair sun."

"Flattery isn't going to cut it. What else you got?"

"Claws. Teeth. Rapidly thinning patience."

"Pretty weak skill set. Why don't you go make me some pancakes? How about the fluffy ones with the strawberry sauce? Those sound good."

He growled again.

"You do that so much you may as well not bother with it. Seriously, you're some sort of growling sprinkler. Grrr, this direction, Grrr, that direction, Grrr, grrr, grrr, and then you're back at the start."

He started to do it again but stopped himself and muttered. The glint in his eyes told Amber to stop pushing. The previous night's misfortune was forefront on his mind.

There was no wry humor in his voice when he said, "Five minutes. If I do not hear water, I will bathe you myself."

Threats shouldn't make her wet. She showered imagining his hands running the sponge over her midriff, her thighs, her breasts. Amber turned the nozzle toward cold, which only made her horny and freezing.

"You." She pointed at herself in the mirror. "Get a grip, girl." Something impish within her responded, *More like get yourself some, girl. Grip everything you can, whatever he'll let you.* Amber rolled her eyes at her sex-craved self. She winked back.

Lavario told her to wait two days before kissing him again, but one felt sufficient. At least that's what Amber thought until she saw his face. The sensual line of his mouth tangled in a frown and remained snagged there.

She tried to lighten the mood. "Careful, you'll brood yourself into wrinkles."

He ignored the dig at his appearance. She could tell he forced lightness to his voice when he said, "We will talk when you are done, Amber. Take your time." He gave her cheek a gentle pat. Amber assumed the sweet gesture was to make up for his earlier grump.

She gave his hand a squeeze and sat at the table. Pancakes were a favorite food of hers. Lavario's tasted spectacular. Light, fluffy, buttery—everything delicious pancakes should be. Lumps of glue might taste better today. Amber pushed her fork around on the plate.

Reading minds fell outside her abilities. She depended on patterns of behavior to guess Lavario's moods. When angry, he hunkered in his chair and tried to wait it out, which was what he did. Claws flexed in and out with each scrape of her fork. His aggravation wasn't directed at her, so Amber didn't take it personally, but she didn't like seeing him so worked up. Calm and steady, he was the eye in a continual storm. His choler brought the harsh winds inside.

She gave up and apologized. "Sorry. Yeah. Can't eat. Thought I could."

He jumped up and scurried right over. Amber had never seen him move so fast. He got right up in her face and began some type of assessment.

Amber coughed, uncomfortable with the direct attention. "Please tell me this creepy prolonged eye contact is—"

"Functional. Yes. Your permission to intrude?"

"Do you know what you're looking for?"

"Somewhat." Frustrated by the prolonged stretch of silence afterward, Amber prodded him to elaborate. He finished his thought after a sigh. "You overcame a control spell."

Amber shrugged, uncomfortable with the warmth flowing through her body in response to the praise in his voice. "I guess that's what I did. You'd know."

"How did you do it?"

"I stopped thinking about what I needed to do and let my body tell me what it wanted."

The answer didn't sit well with him. Intuition was for fucking or fighting. Decision-making was more of a cerebral affair. "What do you mean you stopped thinking?"

"That's it. I just stopped thinking directly about it."

He was aghast. He even lifted one hand to his chest as if he were in dire need of a fainting couch. "But you're so smart."

Amber gave him a shrug. "Call it a different type of thinking, then."

Lavario dropped the puzzle. There was a tilt to his eyebrow, suggesting he put a pin in it for later. "I know you overcame a control spell, but I do not know why Vanu cast it. So, your permission?"

"Okay. Sure. Go nuts."

He sandwiched her head between his big hands. Eye to eye, the intensity he went to such great lengths to hide was obvious. His pupil palpitated to the rhythm of her heart. Amber's mind started to drift. She relaxed in his hold, like sliding into a warm bath.

"Concentrate," Lavario said. "Focus on the night you saw Vanu."

Amber tried to do as he asked. She focused on Vanu's face, her lips. Heat rushed up inside her, coiling in her belly. Amber was sure Lavario felt it too. If he did, he brushed it aside.

"Your mind is clouded. She wanted to know what you and Kijo talked about? Did you two talk?"

"I don't know," Amber answered automatically.

"Try to remember."

"I can't."

"Try harder. Put yourself back in the room with Vanu. Tell me her words."

Tingling sensations along the tips of her fingers transferred to her lips. She was back out in the forest freezing to death. Nearby, there was something with her. The ghost from the lake. It got closer and closer and closer. She felt its hand reaching for her.

Amber jerked herself away. "Lavario, Stop!"

He withdrew immediately.

Trembling, Amber used one shaking hand to clasp the other. "Did you get what you wanted?"

"No, you cut me off. Your mind went back to the ghost." He sounded disappointed in her.

"Sorry," she apologized, a bit hurt.

"It is not your fault. We have to go to the source. Get ready and come with me, Amber."

"Why do I need to go?"

"To keep me from killing her."

Chapter 37: The Smudge

AMBER AND LAVARIO

Hard, glassy amber flecks in Lavario's eyes reflected light. Whenever Amber caught a glimpse of his expression, she knew he wasn't kidding about the whole keep-me-from-killing request, though she didn't know how she'd quell a ginormous werewolf. She was surprised when he remained civil enough to knock.

Vanu did a slight double take at Amber's appearance but regained her composure. Coolly, she greeted them as if the mere opening of the door were a colossal favor.

"May we come in?"

She stepped back and extended her arm.

Lavario dropped pleasantries once they cross the threshold. "You brought Amber here last night?"

"We got to know each other a bit. You cozied up to a great number of my bloodservants over the years."

"My motivations were always pure—"

Vanu cut him off with a guffaw. It thinned out toward the end, making her sound more nervous than amused.

"Purely sexual," he finished.

"As were mine, Lavario."

He slowly shook his head. "She remembers the woods. You were sloppy."

All semblance of calm vanished. She transformed. She lifted her lip to show the tips of her fangs. "You don't understand, Lavario. Amber is very dangerous."

"Is she now?"

Vanu must have seen a hidden sign of aggression Amber wasn't privy to. She coiled up and backed away. Teeth out, shoulders hunched, she paced in an arch from one side of the room to the next. Lavario followed her movements with his gaze.

Anticipating that the two werewolves would fight each other, Amber wasn't prepared when Vanu leaped in her direction. Also seemingly taken aback, Lavario delayed his reaction long enough for Vanu's claws to graze Amber's collarbone.

In a blur of movement, he jerked Vanu away and lunged. His jaws bit deep into her stomach. Yelping reverberated off the walls, surprisingly high-pitched.

Wincing, Amber inspected the damage to her shoulder—a few scratches, not really much deeper than a cat's.

She inserted herself into the fray before Lavario went in for another bite. "Hey, remember when you told me not to let you kill her?"

He chomped Vanu again anyway.

"Okay, that's bad. Get off." Amber kicked Lavario's haunch. He flattened his ears. "And don't you dare growl at me again. You told me to do this."

Nice and slow, he stood up and backed away from Vanu. Amber stayed behind him. Only when Vanu returned to her human form did they both relax. Lavario stayed wolf.

"Explain," he demanded.

"It would be treason."

"You just tried to kill my bloodservant. Exile is the punishment."

"I doubt I'd get more than a reprimand."

"Rules are rules, Vanu."

"I'd lie about the incident, then."

"How un-Varcolac of you."

Amber took offense to how impressed, even happy, Lavario sounded. Actual smoke might have billowed from her ears when he asked Vanu if she was okay. Spittle definitely flew out of her mouth when Lavario went to fetch her a bathrobe. He wrapped her up and lifted her to unsteady feet like a parent sending a child off to try again.

"Keep away from Amber." Lavario saying it felt like an afterthought.

The look in Vanu's eye said she couldn't promise anything. "She's dangerous, Lavario."

"How so?"

"Go talk to your daughter."

Lavario chuckled at that and gave Vanu a friendly wave goodbye.

Amber verbally pounced on him once they were out in the hallway. "Whatever happened to 'Don't let me kill Vanu?' I'm surprised you didn't tell her, 'Don't worry, you'll get her next time!'"

Lavario huffed at the accusation. "Back when I was the second in this pack, Vanu—"

"Ah, memories."

"—was one of my few allies. She wanted to warn me. She knows not to come after you again."

"So we going to talk to Kijo?"

Lavario waved the suggestion away. "Vanu would like that very much."

"Oh?"

"It puts Kijo in a very poor place politically," he explained. "She can't be seen as allied with me."

"Right. Don't want that. So what are we going to do?"

"Use technology."

AMBER DIDN'T KNOW what he meant until they were knee-deep in security tapes. Lavario fumbled with the controls. "Use technology" apparently didn't mean use it proficiently or use up-to-date technology. There were a bunch of tapes, a VCR, and the struggle was real.

"Do you want me to do that?" Amber asked him for the fifth time.

"No, no. I have it." He pushed the wrong button, rewinding the tape instead of fast forwarding. He gave the device a narrow-eyed glare and an eyebrow raise as though everything was its fault. "Why is this thing so stubborn?"

"Because you're doing it wrong. Really embarrassing considering how much time you spend watching TV. Glad for you I'm the only one here."

He started a growl but stopped himself. Self-conscious ever since Amber called him out on always using the noise, he kept busy trying to find himself a new way to express displeasure. He messed around with growling's close cousin, grunting.

Amber gave him feedback on his process. "Now you sound like a goat."

And he went back to growling. "Very well, you do it."

"I will. First, what are you trying to find?"

"Your walk."

"Ah." Amber hit the fast-forward button until she saw herself leave their home. "And there it is. Now what?"

"We follow your path. I want to see where you went."

The two of them sat side by side on the uncomfortable wooden bench. Being so near Lavario made her acutely aware of the stubble along his jawline and how his lips curled whenever he caught her fantasizing. That's what she was doing now. Part of her hoped he'd say something, but his attention remained fixated on the television screen.

He bent forward to wipe away a smudge. It didn't go away.

"What is that? Some type of glitch with the tape?"

He practically planted his face directly on the screen. "No. It moves with you. Find the next tape. It will be hallway 767."

Amber switched tapes several more times until Lavario asked her to stop. She saw herself chatting with Kijo and then she dragged Amber away. The strange smudge followed along. Something finally clicked in her head. The thing she'd thought was a product of trauma could be real.

"Please tell me that's not a ghost."

He didn't answer that. "Come with me. I need to look at that door."

Chapter 38: Dangerous Ones

AMBER AND LAVARIO

What she saw didn't match either of their moods. Beige walls as far as the eye could see. A friendly landscape painting hung on the wall. And a door. A plain, wooden door. Innocuous as shit came.

Shock, disgust, fury, exasperation, panic. Amber struggled to define the emotion in Lavario's face. His angular features, normally elegant, appeared downright 2-D cubeish under the force of his tension. His mouth worked open as though he were going to ask a question or make a comment. Amber turned to him, expecting some dry remark, but he clanked his jaws back together.

"It's only a door," she ventured, knowing full well it wasn't true.

Lavario remained silent. He didn't need to say anything. *Touch* came off it, wave after wave, and pulled at her control. Her hand twitched at her side. She almost surrendered to the impulse. Lavario pulled her back, gently taking her hands in his until she was once again herself.

Amber had enough of being quiet. "Tell me what's going on."

For the first time since they came there, he faced her. His words were strained. "I should have felt its presence. Kijo was right. I am becoming domesticated."

Amber thought his tense choice was interesting there. As far as she could tell, he had corks on his fangs the day she met him. "Yeah," she told him, "you are the worst."

For once, the comment appeared to sting. His jaw popped. There was atypical desperation in his voice. "This door. It calls to you?"

Vanu's words came back to Amber, *She's dangerous, Lavario.* She changed the subject. "What do you think the painting is for?"

"To demarcate this location. Someone wanted to be able to easily find this place." His answer was brisk and he was back to questioning her. "The door, Amber, it calls to you?"

"You already know the answer. Tell me what this damn thing is."

It turned out to be a portal made from dragon bone, wrapped up inside a wooden door to appear, as Lavario said, harmless. Amber listened to him describe what it was and what it did with a calm she didn't really feel.

When Lavario was done explaining, she snapped her attention back to the start, back to what really annoyed her. "Why the hell do you want them to appear 'harmless'; I'd slap some warning label on my magical, highly dangerous world-traveling death portal. Besides, it hardly passes as 'normal' when it tells you to touch it."

"Because," Lavario snapped, "if we left a bunch of portals made from dragon bone lying about, humans would have tampered with them long ago. Better they look like normal doors. And it speaks only to certain humans."

"*Dangerous* ones?"

"Yes, dangerous ones."

He went back to being quiet. Although he kept his gaze firmly locked on the door in front of them, Amber could tell his thoughts lingered on the exchange. The sorrow in his eyes had her stomach in a whirl. She reached for the comfort of his hand. It took him a bit to return the hold, but when he did, his grip was strong and warm.

"Whoever brought it here wasn't human, Lavario."

"You are right. It was a werewolf."

Judging from his expression, he knew which one. The muscles in his face twitched. Tiny rivulets of gold sluiced the green from his eyes, leaving behind a cold, dead anger.

There was nothing to say to such stark fury. Nothing except for, "Probably shouldn't frenzy."

LAVARIO TOYED WITH an ornamental knife, digging the point into his thumb as if testing its mettle and his. Like everything else he owned, it was beautiful without being ostentatious. Apparently, the knife was also functional. Red beads of blood welled up around the fine silver point.

Seeing the blood made her queasy. She thought about her throat, her stomach. *She's dangerous, Lavario,* Vanu had said.

She pulled the robe he'd gifted her tightly against her body. "Enough, it's a knife. It cuts. I get it."

His quizzical eyebrow arch gave her some hope.

"You've been playing around with it for the last hour or so."

He glanced down as if seeing the knife for the first time. "Yes."

As it always was with Lavario, the word could mean everything or nothing at all. There was a vast chasm between where they dumped everything unsaid.

Amber admitted to herself she didn't want the gap to widen. "I need you to be honest with me. Are you going to kill me?"

His skin, normally a warm olive tone, turned ashen. The knife clattered on the floor. He stooped to pick it up reflexively, as if he didn't quite know what he was doing.

Amber knew what the answer was before she asked but seeing the truth in his eyes hurt more than she imagined. "Why? Why would you kill me? Why am I dangerous?"

"There is a good chance your ghost is a lifestealer."

Amber gave him a blank, angry glare. She felt the lines on her face slope into a full-fledged glower the longer he stood there without giving her an explanation. "Oh yeah, I know what that is. We talked about lifestealers in my werewolf occult class."

He gave her sarcasm a tired sigh. "The soul of a vampire, a creature that feeds off energy." He took a pause, holding up his hand to indicate he was gathering his thoughts to continue. "Few humans and even fewer werewolves possess a genetic anomaly that makes them suitable hosts. One of your ancestors must have survived an early vampire attack. Once the lifestealer manifests, stopping it is very difficult. It can jump to any host and will once it consumes the life of the previous."

Suddenly feeling so much colder, Amber shivered. Her voice trembled when she asked, "So what's the thing waiting for?"

"For its host to touch the door."

"And what does that change exactly?"

Lavario gave her a series of gestures that equaled out to one giant shrug.

"That's what you've got for me? You're ten billion years old or whatever, and you're telling me, 'Gee whiz, I dunno, Amber'?"

He wasn't even apologetic when he said, "Unfortunately."

"Okay, then. How do you destroy it?"

"You cannot. It is magical energy. We have only ever been able to contain it."

"In the portals?" Amber guessed.

"Yes."

"How?"

"The dragon bone. Think of it as a wire that absorbs, conducts, and traps magical energy. A closed system. You are an open system. You can absorb but also conduct."

Hope welled up inside of her. "Okay, so, couldn't we theoretically trap it in something else made of dragon bone?"

"Yes. Or a dragon can consume it."

Excited, Amber clapped her hands. "Right then, in all the stuff you hoarded, there has to be something we can use."

Lavario appeared uncomfortable. Anger, not directed at her, made his voice a sharp edge. "My belongings were confiscated. I had something, but I do not know where or how to find it. I don't even know where to begin."

"We'll look for it. What is it?"

He didn't answer her question. "The lifestealer will manifest soon, Amber. It is in here now searching for you. I can feel it. Once it finds you, it will drive you to insanity. It will bring you to the door one way or another."

She made her eyes lock into his. She forced her voice to be steady despite the rapid pounding of her heart. "If things look bad...you can kill me then. But let me try to fight it. Let me try to live."

The look he gave her was like no other she'd ever endured. Detached emotionally, he considered her merits as if assessing ripe from rotten fruit. It was a cold and slow calculation. Amber felt herself whither under the intense scrutiny and she knew the conclusions he'd come to were against her.

She backed away at his approach. Fearing he'd strip her of her robe before he killed her, she pulled it tighter around her body. "Lavario." She hated how the way she said his name sounded like pleading.

He hated it too. He flinched but kept moving.

Handle out, he gave her the knife. As she drew the blade away from his hand, she could see a red slash trail along on the palm of his hand. "Know I will try to kill you when it becomes necessary. This knife can kill me. Use it if you believe yourself in danger. Fight for your own life as I will fight for mine." His large hand cupped her chin and tilted her face upward. "Neither of us is strong enough to face this alone, Amber. Perhaps we can find a solution together."

Carefully, she put the knife on the nearest shelf. Not so carefully, she entwined her fingers at the nape of Lavario's neck, loving how soft and uncooperative to straightening the curls were there.

"It's been two days."

Chapter 39: Beautiful

AMBER AND LAVARIO

Boys kissed her with mouths saturated with beer. They'd been sweaty, fumbling. Perhaps she hadn't been much better back in her college days when the thought of touching a man felt taboo. Maybe she wasn't any better. Her mouth worked against Lavario's; her tongue licked his bottom lip, her teeth playfully nibbled the soft flesh. His response remained tentative—not quite accepting, not quite rejecting.

Disappointed by a second lukewarm reception to her advances, Amber dragged herself away and thought about the attractive blond man who was meant to be there instead of her. Those green eyes of his were probably better looking than her whole body. She imagined he wouldn't have to work so hard to get Lavario to fuck him.

"Nonsense," Lavario told those thoughts. He grabbed her hand and placed it on his erection. "I have no desire to fuck you, Amber, or anything so crass."

"You just put my hand on your—" She cut herself off after looking in his eyes. *Slow and methodical*, they said, *like the way I tend to the needs of my garden.*

Lavario closed the gap between them, tugging her back against the length of his body. "Are you sure this is what you want?"

She felt the heat of him, the length of his arousal against her stomach. "Yes."

He nuzzled the slope of her neck, breathing her scent at the same time. "Kiss me."

He bent to accommodate her height. This time, his lips gave a warm welcome, surging back against hers with an enticing and frustrating tenderness. She wanted to talk to the animal inside him. She wanted it panting.

"You do not want the wolf. You want the man."

"You said you were both. It's both I want."

He gave her an airy chuckle. Amber loved how breathless it sounded.

Hurry wasn't a word in his vocabulary. Lavario's mouth took its time opening. When she finally got access, his tongue pressed back against hers, giving no further ground. They stayed that way for a bit, letting their bodies sort it out for themselves who was in charge. Eventually, her tongue slid past his, and her self-satisfied murmur vibrated in his mouth.

He broke the kiss to give more instruction. "Touch me."

Her fingers found the top button of his trousers. More eager than skilled, she twisted and pulled haphazardly until the pant legs were cuffs around his ankles. Lavario assisted her toward the end, pulling his long legs free from the fabric.

His exposed skin felt unnaturally warm under her fingers, warmer when she got to his inner thigh. The sound he made when she rubbed her hand up the outline of his cock through his underwear was half purr, half growl. His lips kissed the line of her throat while she massaged him. Each time he bent toward her, his mouth outlined a path for the tip of his tongue to follow.

She tugged harder on his shaft, enjoying the friction between the cloth and his flesh. His body arched toward hers. "Amber. Amber."

"Um?"

"My shirt."

"You want it off because you think you look funny standing there without any pants."

Lavario lightly bunted his head against Amber's and brushed her temple with his lips. "Stop mind-spying."

Another kiss caught the laughter between their two mouths. Amber did as he asked, unbuttoning his shirt with as much care as her trembling fingers could manage. It was a nonwolf day; he wouldn't want it ripped.

"There," she said and ran her hands up the length of his torso. Under her fingers, the muscles of his stomach pinched together.

Wordlessly, somehow knowing she wanted it, Lavario lifted her off the ground and carried her to the bed. She enjoyed the sensation of her own frailty. Up in his arms, she felt like a breeze.

Confidence abandoned her when he placed her on his bed and she could view the chiseled length of his body. Next to him, she felt doughy, gauche.

"Nonsense." The admonishment sounded a bit growly.

"Come here." She held out her arms. He came into them with his typical grace.

Beneath the expensive, subtle smell of whatever product he used, there was the natural wild scent of him. Try as he might to cover it up, Amber knew she could find it along his inner thigh, all the way up to his groin. She licked a path to it, enjoying the way he tasted.

Insecurities plagued her undressing. Where she had been rushed—getting her hands over a hurdle more than savoring the moment—he was deliberate, relaxed. Playing with bra straps, tracing the outline of the bones of her shoulder. He sampled newly discovered territory with his lips, planting small kisses and nibbles as he went. He nuzzled her skin with care using his long, aristocratic nose.

She moved to flip off the light. Lavario grabbed her hand, kissing it gently.

"Stop," Lavario told her. "You are beautiful."

"My butt is—"

"Beautiful," he told her, kissing her above each cheek.

"Big," she corrected him. "My skin is—"

"Beautiful."

"Dark," she corrected him again, hearing the voices of all the men in her life who came before Lavario. "I am—"

"Beautiful," he told her with gravel in his voice. "Any man or woman who told you otherwise was a fool." When she started to list off more things wrong with herself, tears welling up in her eyes, he groaned deep in his throat. "Amber, Amber, Amber. Look at me."

Eyes, normally a light green, ran veins of gold throughout. Canines cut outward from his gumline. He was as much a wolf as she'd ever seen him without being wolf. "I feel like I am arguing with the mysterious smile of the Mona Lisa. Or an orchid. One of the most glorious, temperamental flowers is asking me to find fault with the color of its petals because fumbling, stupid boys could not appreciate them. You are exquisite. Everything here bows to you."

He closed his mouth over hers. Amber surrendered to the very persuasive case he made. She decided it was best to concede the point entirely when he stroked his fingers between her legs at the same time he nibbled on the tender peak of her breast.

He took his mouth on a relaxed tour of her body, stopping at her clit. Surprised at how good it felt, Amber gasped at her own pleasure, at the warm, coiling heat building between her thighs and in her stomach. She expected him to stop long before she finished. She was wrong. Near her climax, his tongue went up inside of her, simulating the thrust she wanted from his cock.

She tangled her fingers in his hair. "Lavario."

It was his turn to give her a self-satisfied murmur.

Her body shook. And he began all over again.

When they were done, she rested her head against the curve of his pelvic bone, facing upward so she could watch his expression while her fingers ran through his belly fur. Voices inside of her head made apologies for not being the handsome blond man he'd wanted.

Lavario's response to those thoughts remained the same. "Nonsense."

"Stop mind-spying!" She gave him a friendly bite on his inner thigh that made him groan in a way she liked.

Something occurred to her. "Wait. How old are you?"

Lavario snorted. "Very old."

She pulled on one of his stomach hairs. "That's not a number."

"Very well. On a scale from one to ten, where one is old and ten is very old, I am ten."

She gave him a dirty look. "Do you even know?"

He gave her a sly, secretive arch of his eyebrow rather than an answer.

"You're the worst," she told him with a huff.

"I assumed as much." He stroked his fingers along her cheek, played gently with one of her springy curls. "Were you pleased despite it?"

Very. Her entire lower body throbbed with how pleased she was. Pressing herself up against the length of his leg was almost enough to send her over the edge again. "You did okay."

He responded with his typical dry, tired tone. "Such flattery."

"Can't let you get any more arrogant than you already are. You'll be insufferable."

Too late, his eyes said. Somewhere midbrag, his expression changed. He stroked her upper arm with gentle fingers and said, "Get some rest. We have a long day tomorrow. Many after."

She opened her mouth to ask him why but realized she didn't want to know. Soon enough, their changing world might put a knifepoint at the other's throat. They were warm and safe for the time being. The lifestealer could be a problem for another day. And many days after.

Chapter 40: A Long Day

AMBER AND LAVARIO

Lavario didn't bother knocking on Kijo's door. He jerked it open and walked inside as though the room were still his. Kijo, seated on a plain wooden chair, glowered at him—her teeth were fully exposed, her bright eyes boiled gold. In response, Lavario pulled his lips back in a snarl. The gesture had real anger to it, not at all like the same old song and dance.

Amber didn't think the two of them were all that similar until she saw them side by side. Small gestures, like the way they tapped one extended claw on the arm of the chair, stood out.

Kijo cocked her eyebrow in the same dismissive way Lavario did and said, "Leave."

"Tell me you did not know about the portal, Kijo."

"I knew of it."

His voice dipped lower. "And you knew about the lifestealer?"

"Inkling, yes. I was never sure."

Lavario lashed out at the nearest wall, striking it hard enough to carve out veins.

Unimpressed, Kijo dismissed them with a wave of her hand and another terse, "Leave."

"You put pack before the survival of all."

For a second, it looked like a fight brewed between them. Kijo rose from her chair, instantly wolf. Lavario's teeth, normally holstered in his gums, were out and loaded. The two of them circled, posturing in a way the sane versions of themselves would think of as stupid.

Amber stepped between, holding out her arms. "Chill. Both of you."

"Put your pet on a leash," Kijo spat out.

To Amber's credit, she thought about what she did next for a good minute. She came to the conclusion that, left unchecked, Kijo and Lavario might end up killing each other and perhaps her in the process.

Gulping down her fear, Amber strode up to Kijo and forced herself to push her away, gently as she could while still getting the point across. "You two don't have the time to sit here and bicker."

As always, it was difficult to assess what Kijo felt outside her ever-present anger. The slight tilt to her lip suggested some amusement, if not the grudging admiration for her gall. She regarded Amber thoughtfully—making the same kill-or-don't-kill calculation Lavario made earlier, except without any trace of sentiment. Amber slipped out of her sight.

Twisting her lips, Kijo brushed her aside and addressed Lavario, "You brought us to this place. Had you defeated Mazgan as I said, the lifestealer wouldn't be here."

"I cannot lead—"

"Not now, no. You *could have* led the Varcolac. You elected not to. Now you are here, tainting what remains of my authority with your presence."

Amber agreed. "She's got a point."

Redirecting Kijo's attention back to her wasn't wise. Kijo's golden eyes flared. "And you slept with this human instead of disposing of her. You put her above pack, above all others. I should kill her for you."

Amber peeped out from behind Lavario. "But you won't?"

Kijo showed her teeth as if seriously considering it, but then—in an odd turnaround—shook her head and snorted.

Once again, she refused to directly respond to Amber and faced Lavario. "I trust you to carry through if necessary."

"Yes." Lavario's calm admission made Amber's stomach muscles clench. She'd grown accustomed to him sounding slightly perturbed but gentle, as affectionate as he could get without being a condescending sort of indulgent. Amber studied his face, searching for some sign he didn't really mean it, but his demeanor was every bit as cold and determined as his daughter's.

They went quiet. Between the two there lurked a mutual sadness and the weight of a lot of unsaid bullshit. Amber knew the look from experience. She'd shared one with her own father not long before he died. Eventually, Kijo broke her gaze away from Lavario's and once again commanded him to leave.

This time, he spun on his heel, following her directive.

Unlike Lavario, who kept his back turned on his daughter and strode out with confidence, Amber didn't fully trust Kijo. She kept glancing over her shoulder as they left, somehow very sure Kijo wouldn't allow them to barge into her house and leave unscathed.

Thudding footsteps confirmed her worst fears. She yelled, "Look out!" at the same time Kijo slammed into Lavario's back.

Stunned, he didn't spring back up the way Amber expected. He made a few attempts to rise, getting as far as his knees, but Kijo's assault was relentless. She bit into the side of his stomach; teeth cut deeper at each new puncture. Her claws grappled into his sides, tearing up rivets of flesh whenever he tried to shake her off.

Lavario mustered enough strength to fling her off his back using magic. It didn't have much force to it. Kijo landed nearby and completely recovered moments later. Cautious, she squatted low in a defensive position—eyes fixed, ears up and alert—and assessed Lavario's condition with wary, calm detachment. Satisfied, she crouched, building up energy for another charge.

Lavario looked up at Amber. Apologetically, blood running from his mouth, he told her, "Run."

Chapter 41: And Many After

AMBER AND LAVARIO

Doing what she was told didn't suit Amber, never had. Running was out of the question. She'd already determined they'd chase her down wherever she went and kill her. Whatever else she could say about the Varcolac, they kept the asshole promises they made.

Amber took out the knife Lavario gave her, figuring it could kill one werewolf as well as another. Kijo paid her no mind. She kept right on snapping her jaws toward Lavario's throat.

"Run," Lavario told Amber again, sounding furious and desperate at the same time. He held Kijo back with one paw. It shook, rapidly losing strength.

Amber followed the order, only she booked it straight toward Kijo, throwing in a battle cry for no reason other than it felt good to yell. Hell, doing anything other than waiting for her life to end felt wonderful. Her first blow ended with a thud, and Kijo absorbed the impact of her body without comment. Amber might have been a screaming child in the grocery store. Clearly, it bothered her, even pissed her off, but Amber wasn't hers to scold. Not yet.

Amber slapped her upside the head and demanded, "Let him go."

She didn't say no exactly, but her next bite went through bone. Amber heard it crack.

Okay, fine, Amber thought to herself. *Be that way.*

The knife went in easy between Kijo's shoulder blades, sliding to the hilt. The second time was just as effortless. Fur and blood gunked up the works on the fourth and fifth stabs, causing the knife to veer outside her grip and clatter on the floor. Unpracticed in the art of murder, Amber chased after it, accidentally kicking it away. Her heart pounded in her chest.

Behind her, Lavario groaned. In pain or at her efforts, she wasn't sure. She assumed the latter. "I'm trying."

To up the threat level, Amber stuck the blade in Kijo's side, close to where her heart might theoretically reside. She gave Amber's attempt a growl and finally pulled away from Lavario, who lifted himself off the ground only to fall. His ragged breathing huffed from his lungs. He blinked his eyes open and shut. Amber saw the white bone of one of his ribs.

"Can you heal?" she asked him.

"Yes." It was Kijo who answered. The knife, which she'd extracted from her side, fell to the floor. Blood flowed freely from the wound. Kijo paid it scant attention, nothing more than a quick assessment. "But you cant."

She lifted her paw upward, readying it to sweep down in an arc.

Mazgan, a voice Amber never thought she'd be glad to hear, cut in, "Here she is with the Boo Hag and the Boo Hag's pet. They work together now as they did before."

Flanked by four other werewolves, two of which Amber knew—Oscar and Vanu—Mazgan entered the situation with a sneer and a grand sweep of his hands. Perhaps it was her imagination, but his clothes appeared far more bombastic than they had before. Kingly gold, bright whites, and royal blues popped amongst the browns and tans of his dour companions, who scowled at Amber's presence by Lavario's side. Vanu's glower was darker than the others, tinged with disappointment. Her eyes met Lavario's, reasserting, *She's dangerous.*

He was in too much pain to care, assuming he even noticed.

Vanu took stock of the rest of the situation. She managed to sound respectful while she disagreed. "This does not have the look of conspiracy, Alpha Guardian."

He hated to be contradicted. Amber could tell by the irate glower, but he had to concede her point. Either Kijo and Lavario weren't colluding as accused or both of them had a woeful dearth of knowledge on how to collaborate.

"Explain yourself," Mazgan addressed Kijo. "What happened here?"

She lied. "Lavario came to retake his dwelling. He failed, Alpha Guardian."

The Alpha Guardian turned to Lavario, "Well?"

"As she said," he wheezed, sounding more like an old man than ever before.

Mazgan tilted his head upward to look down on them all. His neckline reminded Amber of a rock-'em-sock-'em robot on the wrong end of an uppercut more than a proud lord. "I do not believe you. And you will address me by my proper title, Lavario."

Mutiny boiled up in his eyes. He glanced in Amber's direction and doused it. "Yes, Alpha Guardian."

Kijo continued. "Alpha Guardian Mazgan is correct. Lavario did come here for another reason, but it is too foolish to mention. He has gone mad, no doubt from his own hubris."

Mazgan chided her. "Let me be the one to determine its merits."

"Very well. Lavario told me there is a vampire walking in this world. He claims you brought a portal here, Alpha Guardian, and that your tampering released a lifestealer—"

Lavario's eyes widened at the mention of a vampire. Amber could tell its presence, if there was one, was news to him.

Mazgan shouted, "Enough!"

Perhaps he thought it sounded authoritative. To Amber's ear, it was well above the hysterical threshold. The werewolves by Mazgan's side exchanged glances. There were more than a few raised eyebrows.

On the floor, Lavario chuckled appreciatively. Under the circumstances—with a rib exposed and a broken leg—he could apparently still appreciate a good maneuver.

"There is much more, Alpha Guardian. Lavario has committed treason against us."

Lavario's laughter stopped.

Mazgan swallowed. Amber could tell he didn't want to hear what came next, but he told her, "Continue."

"He claims he bid a Moondog to take the vampire to the Isangelous stronghold and release it there to force war between our packs. He wants us to fall with him."

Oscar rolled his eyes. "None of this can possibly be true. Still, it speaks volumes about his lack of loyalty to the Varcolac."

Kijo agreed. "Indeed. I propose we bring his crimes before the pack and let them decide what to do with him."

Tellingly furious, Mazgan bit out, "Did he say whether or not the vampire was destroyed?"

"He did not, Alpha Guardian."

Mazgan paled and licked his lips.

Weakened from the fight, Lavario could only glare at his daughter from the floor. Fury unlike Amber had ever seen contorted his features. His chest heaved. Blood came out in flecks from his nose. His eyes were still green, which gave Amber hope he hadn't totally lost control. Kijo regarded his fury with amusement.

The other four werewolves waited for Mazgan to make a decision. "Very well," the Alpha said and tried to straighten his shoulders.

"And the girl?" Oscar asked.

Kijo said, "Bring her. She might be privy to Lavario's schemes."

Oscar grabbed Amber roughly by the elbow, lifting upward so she had to stand on the tips of her toes or let his nails dig into the tender flesh of her underarm. No doubt he longed to repay her and Lavario for the humiliation of losing his rooms. Retribution was a fixation in the Varcolac mindset.

Excitement made a small, keen light stab through Kijo's eyes. "Tomorrow, we will convene." Kijo's eyes bore into Mazgan's. "And then everything will be out in the open, as it should be, Alpha Guardian."

Chapter 42: Legs of its Own

KIJO

Lavario would survive his injuries. The Varcolac medics would make sure of it.

Beaten wasn't an adjective that sat well on Lavario's shoulders. The other pack jeered, lining up for the chance to be one of the few who got to drag him away. Weak from blood loss, Lavario allowed himself to be arrested without protest. Struggling in his condition might lead to humiliation beyond what already happened. Above all else, he was practical. He taught her to be the same.

The other werewolves in the Varcolac couldn't find it in them to be similarly matter-of-fact in their dealings with Lavario. Protocol didn't require them to treat an accused traitor with stoic, steely resolve, so they didn't. The repressed hatred they felt toward him materialized. *Frenzy. Frenzy. Frenzy.*

Oscar, whose chambers Lavario had taken so easily, gave the claw wounds in Lavario's side a savage kick. "Where is your magic now, exile?" he spat in his face.

"It will be back. Rest assured, Oscar."

Alyssa spat on him next, adding, "You will burn for your treachery."

Gene rushed to join in on the camaraderie. He got so few opportunities to take part in pack events. "It'll be hard to cast spells without hands, exile. We'll take them before you're executed."

"Redundant."

Kijo smirked at Lavario's calm, steady-eyed dismissal of their taunts. She knew him well enough to observe the set of his jaw, the dismissive quirk of his lips. He didn't bother wiping off their spittle. He lifted his head, meeting each of their eyes until they looked away.

And then his eyes met hers. *Goodbye, Father,* Kijo tried to convey the message using the strength of her will. His murderous expression said, *I'll remember this*. Kijo didn't mind. She needed the animal inside Lavario out in the open, wanting blood. Either that or dead and out of the way.

"Take him back to his chambers," Kijo instructed her underlings. She thrilled to see them snap to attention, once again responsive to the command in her voice. "I suspect he'll be thirsty after all this. Put his girl in there with him."

They grinned. Bloodlust following blood loss was common. Lavario might lose control and eat Amber. Kijo doubted it, but the thought appealed to the Varcolac enough to go along with her suggestion. Smarter wolves would have seen the foolishness of it. None of them were especially smart wolves. None except Vanu.

Mazgan coughed. They were alone in the hallway. He felt free to place one of his big, meaty hands on her shoulder. A thumb stroked her collarbone. "Guardian Kijo." His voice oozed, once again laden with the false promise to love her. His foolish yearnings sank to the bottom of her feet and she walked on them.

"Alpha Guardian."

"The Varcolac are grateful for your diligence, Guardian Kijo. You chose pack once again."

"There is nothing but pack."

"Spoken like a trueborn guardian."

"I like hearing the edge in your voice, Alpha Guardian. Reminds me you can cut."

There was surely a great deal more Mazgan wanted to say. No doubt he had endless questions about the vampire, the undead cog in his masterful plan to take control over the bloodservant trade. Where was the rotting creature now? Was it really inside the Isangelous compound? He could only stand there and scowl, those questions eating him up inside.

"You'll put this all at your father's feet?"

"Yes."

"I will not exile him, Kijo. The sentence will be death."

"I'm sure he'll submit to the pack's wisdom, as he always has."

Violence flashed in the Alpha Guardian's eyes. Jagged, ready to rend flesh, his teeth protruded from his gums. Kijo took his face in her hands. His features softened under her touch. One witnessing the exchange could even describe him as tender.

Kijo whispered in his ear, "Be still. Be strong. Do not frenzy."

Of course he wouldn't heed the advice. He was a fool.

FOR KIJO, IT was a rare and welcome thing to be happy. Unsettled by it, Gene stood a wise distance away and observed with care. Learning boundaries by trial and error had been a difficult process for the charming pup, who relied on seduction rather than deference to get his way.

Eventually, he gathered the courage to ask, "You got the big wolf to the table. This going to be his last meal with us?"

"Likely, one way or another. And what does Vanu say about this?"

"She's not happy."

"Why?"

"She sees your move for power."

Kijo extended her long fingers and slowly curled them back into a fist. Yes, her move for power. Counting on Lavario to storm to her door, all teeth and accusations, paid off nicely, but not as well as Mazgan's pomp and arrogance. Accusations were out in the open but not from her lips. Of course the pack guardians would still be duty-bound to investigate. Kijo suspected they'd find something.

Gene wasn't finished. "Vanu wants me to find out..."

"Yes," Kijo prompted when he trailed off.

"She wants me to find out what your plans are for the lifestealer."

"Something she could ask me herself. We are still on those terms last I checked."

He straightened, trying his best to appear taller, more imposing. "She knows about, uh..." He licked his lips. "She knows I've been talking to you."

"How useful you are to me. As promised."

Gene flinched at the snub. "She offers an alliance against Mazgan. You two can sort it out after his fall."

Kijo drummed her fingers on the arm of her plain wooden chair, considering. She had offered a partnership not too long ago. Vanu all but sneered at it, preferring to see how things played out. Now the situation had changed and Kijo had the upper hand and Vanu came along with it. It wasn't cowardice but caution. Kijo admired caution.

"Tell her we'll sort it out on a condition."

"Which is?"

She'd left the stab wound from Amber's dagger strike unhealed. It itched. "Bring me the girl. Bring me Amber."

"You put her in with Lavario, Guardian Kijo."

"Yes, and now I want her back. Make this happen."

Chapter 43: Bloodlust

AMBER AND LAVARIO

Amber didn't know what to do. The werewolves who brought them back to their apartment mended the most severe of Lavario's wounds but left him close to death, weak and barely conscious. His blood soaked through the silk fabric of the chaise, a surer sign than his ragged breathing of exhaustion.

Amber wet a cool rag and held it to his temple.

"Stay back." Lavario held out his arm and pushed her away gently.

"Let me help you." She dabbed his face, taking care to get all the spittle from his swollen skin.

Lavario allowed her to clean him with minimal interference. As soon as she was done, he gave her another gentle push away from him. "Thank you, Amber. Now move back."

She perched on her La-z-boy and hovered, ready to run and fetch whatever he asked for. He lay there and said nothing, did nothing, looked at nothing; his eyes open wide and unblinking. After a while, she leaned back in the chair and fidgeted. He needed her. She could tell.

"Tell me how to help you, Lavario."

Refusing to answer, he bore his teeth in pain and closed his eyes. Was he embarrassed by his failure? Possibly. Such a thing must be new to him, strong as he was. "You shouldn't be ashamed, you big proud baby. Kijo blindsided you. It wasn't a fair fight."

"I am not ashamed. Stay back."

"Why?"

He didn't turn to face her. "I might hurt you."

"You wouldn't."

"Not on purpose, Amber. Never on purpose."

She expected a follow-up to enigmatic remark. Common as carbon, lectures and explanations came from his mouth on the second. Maybe he'd gone green. He remained silent.

She stood and shouted at him, "Blood, you need blood, right?"

He had asked her if she preferred to be awake or asleep before he fed the first time. Afraid of exactly what feeding entailed, she'd told him to let her sleep through it. She didn't feel the same anymore. She'd gone too far, seen too much, to dread a few teeth pricks.

"Take it if that's what you need. Do it."

He kept his voice calm and low. "If I drink from you, I will kill you. Stay back."

"They'll kill me anyway. Mazgan will torture me. You remember?"

Lavario closed his eyes. "You are strong. Stronger than any of them, stronger than me in time. You shook a control spell by force of will alone. Endure what Mazgan throws at you. Come back as wolf after they end your human life. Come back and live as you should."

She couldn't believe what she had just heard. "You're going to let Mazgan feed me to Dip?"

"'Let' is not the word I would use, Amber. I cannot fight in this condition. Whatever death waits for you waits ten times over for me, rest assured."

"You're a fool if you think that makes me feel better. Take my blood. You turn me."

"I am an accused traitor, Amber. You would be reborn as a False Moon. I cannot do that to you."

"You're a giant fucking snob, you know that?"

Humor crept back into his voice when he admitted, "Yes."

"Garvey. You loved him as a Moondog."

His voice turned into a growl. "I love him still, the fool. Try as I might not to."

Tears fractured Amber's vision. It wasn't the time to be jealous, so she swallowed it down. "Then you can love me as a Moondog."

"This is not about love, Amber. I made a selfish decision when I turned him. I will not make the same mistake with you."

She touched his face, stroking her hand up the length of his elegant jawbone. "I will never forgive you if you don't take my blood and fight. Take it please, please." She kissed him. "We don't have to be alone."

"I do not have fight left in me."

She kissed him again, working her warm lips against his cold ones until he surged back. Time nipped at his heels a bit more. His tongue moved inside her mouth, incessant and needful. A big hand wrapped around the nape of her neck, pulling her forward.

Amber lifted her lips from his and grabbed hold of his cock. "Seems you have blood left enough. Enough to fight if you can—"

"Do not use that word between us."

"Okay, I won't." She bit her wrist, holding it to his mouth. His nostrils flared at the smell. "Drink," she commanded him.

He fell back against the chaise. "Your future is brighter than this. You are a guardian. I feel it."

"Fine. I'll be a guardian of the Moondogs."

"There is no such thing, Amber."

"I'll make it work. Drink."

Temptation prowled behind the armor of his protectiveness; it was a dangerous animal with bent shoulders and sharp teeth. He wanted to live. There was a keen, calculating edge in his eye that told Amber as much.

He blinked it away. "You are the future."

"I'm not asking you. You're going to drink one way or another."

"Rob me of my choice, you mean?"

Amber laughed at how indignant he sounded. His lips puckered at the noise. He wasn't too far gone down the path of woe-is-me to arch his eyebrow either.

She put her hands on her hips and told him, "You told me I could only be neutral in my head. Choosing means acting. Well, in my head, I respect your right to be a stubborn, elitist asshole who hates Moondogs and doesn't want me to be one. But I'm not neutral on living. I want to live. I don't see myself living without you. You're going to drink on your own, make it as dignified as you want, or I'm going to grab a funnel and a club."

"You are the worst, my dear."

Amber shrugged. "Club then?"

"No. Bring me clean clothes."

"Left side?"

"Yes."

"That's the spirit."

He struggled to pull off his shirt. Limbs didn't quite cooperate the way they did before Kijo tore tendons in his back. "Help me," he finally asked her.

"Can you stand?"

He nodded and pushed himself to unsteady feet, bracing most of his weight against a wall. Careful to avoid any wounds that might open, Amber undressed him as fast as she could while still being mindful of his condition.

Getting him dressed again proved to be a harder task. Simply pulling his arms through sleeves had him panting.

"Sorry, almost done. There."

"Thank you."

He leaned against her and something sharp stabbed into her jugular. Teeth? No, too thin.

She slapped her hand where it pricked her and glared Lavario, who was holding a syringe. "You son of a bitch. You have magic."

"This lasts longer and you are determined." He guided her to the chaise to keep her from falling on the floor.

The drugs made her tongue heavy, her limbs nonexistent. Worry and grief took away most of the sharp things she wanted to say.

Feeling helpless, dreading the future, she asked him, "What will I do without you?"

Lavario gave her a long, appraising glance. He wiped away a tear with his thumb and twined one of her curls around a finger. "One day," he told her, "you will forget about this. Come back to me in your thoughts that day. There is a place in my heart for you. Keep one for me."

She wanted to tell him to fuck off. Drugs slurred it to "Fo of."

Lavario smiled a bit. He got the message.

Chapter 44: Weapon

AMBER AND LAVARIO

Hazy lines and muffled voices penetrated the thick cloud in Amber's mind. She groaned. The room went still. Footsteps pounded toward her. It wasn't Lavario's light, careful stride. It was the walk of someone who gave zero shits who heard her coming. Amber guessed Kijo before she saw her.

Amber forced the tremble out of her voice and said, "Hi."

Kijo hovered. There was a light in the black of her eyes, a hole in the thick tarp. Amber's future shone through it, and it didn't look as bright as Lavario had described earlier. "You are a lot of trouble."

They'd dressed her in colorless rags. Amber sniffed at them but refused to say anything about it. "Mad about the stabbing?"

Ludicrous, the expression on her face said. The mouth followed up with *no*.

"Well, that's good. Where is Lavario?"

"Moved to a cell before the trial."

The lack of emotion in Kijo's voice brought a hot wave of anger through Amber. "Do you even care what happens to him?"

Kijo dragged a nearby wooden chair toward the futon where she stored Amber. She sat with an easy grace and confidence Amber envied. "There are more important things than my father right now. What did he tell you about the lifestealer?"

"He told me it's the soul of a vampire that feeds off energy. It can't be destroyed, only contained, and once it finds me, it will—"

"It already found you." Eager, Kijo leaned in, her face as hot and intent as an interrogation-room lamp. "Can you follow it?"

Amber didn't even try, partly because she was scared and partly because she didn't want to play at Kijo's game, whatever it was. "Nope. Why hasn't it shown itself if it found me?"

"I sense it latching onto your energy only to pull away as if stung. I believe it fears you."

Astounded, Amber could only blurt, "Why?"

"I don't know." Kijo tapped her fingers, then considered each one individually. "Curious that one of the few things that can bring it into the world is also a weapon against it."

Amber digested Kijo's theories in silence. Everything Lavario had told her about the lifestealer didn't suggest it was vulnerable to a twenty-one-year-old kidnap victim. From how he described it, the entity seemed invulnerable to everything but dragon bone. But why would Kijo lie? What game could she possibly be playing? Amber didn't know, but she distrusted Kijo's motives.

"Sounds strange for something like that to be afraid of me," Amber said.

"We only fear things that can harm us, and it fears you. Its hesitation is the only reason I don't kill you now."

Well, that settled things. "I'm convinced. It's terrified of me."

Kijo snorted. "Reach out to it. Use your mind."

Questions dried up on Amber's lips. The whys of what she was being ordered to do no longer seemed important when she took Kijo's unpleasant mug into consideration.

Amber inhaled as much air as she could. Rolling her shoulders calmed her a bit. It was how she'd gotten in the zone for tests during college. The strategy failed here. Nothing came to her—no feelings, no inklings, no mystical vibes. Well, nothing other than Kijo's presence, which dominated the entire room.

Daunting as it was to snap at Kijo, Amber did it anyway. "It would help a lot if you'd back up out of my space."

She scooted the chair closer. "There's no time to coddle you. Learn. Search the room."

"I'm trying to relax here."

Kijo grabbed her hand hard enough to hurt. Scornful, she pointed out the errors in Amber's thinking. "You're being hunted and you try deep breathing and mediation? No. Don't relax. You can feel my eyes on you, sense where I am in the room. Find the energy of the lifestealer. Seek its eyes. You did it at the door. Do it now."

Amber tried again. This time, she didn't force herself to a calm state. Instead, she tensed her body until every muscle ached and concentrated on the nooks and crannies of the room. And then she felt it. And it felt her.

Kijo's somehow knew it. Instinct, Amber supposed. Kijo squeezed her shoulder and said, "Good. Walk to it."

Amber forced herself forward despite her body's many objections. Her heart proved to be the biggest traitor out of all her organs. It pounded, skipped, then somehow hopped up in her throat, where it conspired against her with her lungs. Suddenly, she couldn't breathe either.

Unable to move, she stopped and apologized. "I can't."

"Be still, be strong, don't frenzy."

"You don't get to say that." Amber whirled and went the other way, right back to Kijo. Finger extended, Amber got up close and snarled, "You're not his daughter anymore. You're a power-hungry, backbiting—" Amber searched for a word. "Coyote."

Kijo didn't blink. "Your anger over my betrayal better serves you when used against the lifestealer. Learn its mark. It's learning yours. I admire your courage, Amber, but it won't save you."

"And getting into a pissing match with magical energy will?"

Tired, Kijo continued the lecture. "Would it help if I said your life depends on it? If you're not a weapon, you're a liability and its means to enter the world. I kill liabilities. Right now, I'm trying to teach you. Throw it in my face for loyalty's sake if you must, but consider how Lavario will feel hearing you died by my hand, in his old rooms, wearing rags."

Yeah, he'd hate everything about that, especially the rags part. Amber kicked her anger to the curb. Working with Kijo was the logical move. Lavario wanted her to be grounded, not impulsive.

"No sensible animal would go over there. Isn't self-preservation about as base as it gets?"

"Sensible animals destroy their enemies. Be as strong as its fear of you promises you'll be. Confront it while respecting its power."

Amber straightened her shoulders and walked so fast she practically trotted. Her heart beat just as fast, but it felt natural this time. Fear made sense in the context, so she allowed herself to feel it. At the same time, she pushed her body forward through the barrier.

She stood face-to-face with the lifestealer. She couldn't see it, but she felt its eyes. They'd found each other. She forced herself to be calm through its investigation, to stand still as it wrapped around her limbs. And then she pushed back against it, shoving all her fear down its throat. It slunk away. Amber followed its path to the other side of the room.

"Good," Kijo congratulated her, sounding impressed. "Remember its mark. It will try to hide, to deceive. You must always be able to lock onto it. Never forget it's there. Never let it slip behind other predators or other pleasures."

"Yes." Amber swallowed and grudgingly added, "Thank you."

Kijo gave her a stiff nod. "Do you want to save Lavario?"

Sensing a trick of some type, Amber studied Kijo's face, searching for some sign of deception. Whatever else Amber might say about Kijo, she was usually very straightforward. Usually.

"Of course I do." An idea occurred to her. "You, you can turn me into a werewolf and I can—"

Kijo barked out a laugh. "No. That will happen in time, but not today. I ask you again, do you want to save Lavario?"

"Yes."

"Then you'll have to get very good at finding the lifestealer. Practice."

Chapter 45: Trial and Error

AMBER AND LAVARIO

Dirt-covered clothes hung off Lavario in threads. New injuries marred his refined features. A deep, ugly gouge on his forehead hid his stunning green eyes. Amber knew that would bother him most of all. Lavario wanted to meet his end with dignity; he'd told her as much when he asked for a change of clothes. Judging by Mazgan's puffed-out chest and extra haughty demeanor, even that small courtesy wasn't to be granted.

But why didn't Lavario transform? Why didn't he put all the young upstarts who taunted him in their place?

Mazgan saw Amber. "Ah, there you are, pet. I have something for you." He handed her a chain.

Horrified, Amber realized it connected to Lavario's neck. That connected to hand shackles, which linked to bindings at Lavario's feet. Beneath the restraints, his bruised skin swelled and puckered.

Mazgan clucked. "Take him to the stand, pet. Let us all see him for what he is."

"No." Amber dropped the chain. It clattered on the floor.

Towering above her, he walked up to her until their toes touched. "Take it."

Amber forced herself not to move an inch. She tilted her chin to meet Mazgan's stare directly. "No," she repeated.

Lavario grabbed her hand. With a slight smile and a gentle hand pat, he reassured her it was okay. *Do what I say*, his eyes begged. Grudgingly, Amber bent and took the chain. Best he could with his hands restrained, Lavario gestured for her to continue forward.

She kept her pace slow, allowing Lavario to shuffle along after her without stumbling. The wolves on the left side of the courtroom didn't make it easy. They jeered and spat. Those on the right contented themselves with witnessing the spectacle. By the time they'd made it to the stand, both of them were breathless and filthy.

Amber tried to help Lavario sit on the plain wooden chair. A rough hand shoved her toward two guards. Heavy and ill-fitting, the shackles they clamped down on her wrists rubbed Amber's skin raw.

Mazgan kicked Lavario's chair to the floor. "Go fetch it, dog."

"Yes, Alpha Guardian."

Amber shook her head. This was all wrong. *Fight.* She thought it hard enough for every wolf in the place to hear. Lavario didn't turn her way, though she swore she saw his ear lift slightly. He bent over the chair and did his best to sit it upright, but failure was a foregone conclusion. Top-heavy, he pitched face-first to the floor where he landed with an undignified thump. He hit the chair, sending it farther away from him.

"Crawl to it, Lavario. Try again."

"Yes, Alpha Guardian."

Amber couldn't watch. She turned her head toward Kijo. Kijo watched Lavario humiliate himself with stoic indifference. Amber wanted to imagine there was outrage there, hidden deep beneath the calculated apathy, but that was probably wishful thinking.

Help came from an unexpected source. Vanu stood and spoke out against the treatment. "Lavario's crimes are not proven, Alpha Guardian. Protocol demands we treat him in accordance with our laws." The wolves on the right side nodded their agreement. Those on the left frowned.

Mazgan conceded, a disappointed frown tugging his meaty lips downward. "Very well, for protocol's sake."

Lavario sat on the chair after one of the other Varcolac wolves sat it upright for him.

Mazgan took his place on the bench above. "Let's begin."

Tense already, the mood in the courtroom worsened the more Mazgan and Lavario spoke. The differences between were stark. Shouting, sneering, the Alpha Guardian of the Varcolac rambled—his words came quickly, one tripping over the next. Unimpressed, Lavario spoke in a calm, measured tone laced with scorn.

Amber cringed. Nearby, two Varcolac wolves twisted in their seats. Displeased with Lavario's answers, they got growlier and snarlier. It didn't help that his defense so far boiled down to, *I don't care enough about this pack to conspire with Garvey to destroy it.*

Mazgan wasn't interested in any of the conspiracy charges. There was one question he kept coming back to. He asked it again, "Where is the vampire?"

Lavario gave him the same answer. "Ask Kijo, Alpha Guardian."

"She is not on trial."

"I am aware, Alpha Guardian. But ask her just the same."

Mazgan's face reddened as he yelled, "Your insolence will no longer be tolerated! Your contempt for me and this pack ends tonight."

Lavario's tone veered away from the submissive direction it had taken the rest of the trial. *At last.*

"Alpha Guardian, a greater enemy than me is at your door. It cares less about your titles and rules than I do."

"Very well," Mazgan said after a pause, "is there anyone who wishes to present evidence to back Lavario's claim that this powerful enemy walks amongst us?"

Vanu stood, as did Oscar. Mazgan stared at them with red-faced fury. The sides of his cheeks huffed in and out, like the sides of a dying animal.

Protocol forced the Alpha to say, "Present your evidence for consideration."

Oscar addressed the court. "I have no love for Lavario, as many of you know. But I am a guardian of this pack. As such, I put aside petty differences for the greater good of the Varcolac. There is evidence Alpha Guardian Mazgan met with Garvey, Lavario's progeny, and that Garvey returned with the vampire. Lavario's claim that Mazgan tampered with the portals is most certainly true."

"Do you have anything to prove this, Guardian Oscar?"

"Yes. Tapes."

A few of the gathered wolves gasped.

Mazgan visibly paled. He probably thought he'd destroyed all the evidence before the trial. "That can't be true," he stammered. He straightened, clearing his throat. "There are no tapes."

"How do you know this, Alpha Guardian?"

"Do not take that tone with me, Oscar. Remember your rank."

"I always remember my rank. And duty. How do you know there are no tapes, Alpha Guardian?"

Mazgan indicated his displeasure by lifting his head and pinching his lips.

Undeterred by the hostility on display, Oscar asked him the same question a third time. This time, he added, "The pack demands a response."

Lavario gave Oscar's persistence a slight smile. Amber couldn't tell if he was amused by the other guardian's bravado or if he was actually impressed by the gumption on display. Sorting the nuances of emotion from Lavario's battered face proved difficult.

Mazgan finally answered. "There are no tapes because I am not guilty."

Oscar shook his head, disappointed. "Bring the footage, Vanu, and tell the pack your story."

There was a neat bow wrapped around the entire ordeal. Amber had an idea of who had tied it. Kijo picked invisible debris from under her fingernails. Judging from her expression—a mixture of haughty scorn and triumph—she imagined they were bits and pieces of Mazgan.

Chapter 46: The Lifestealer

AMBER AND LAVARIO

Once the screen went blank and the tape stopped, the only noise was the clicking of Lavario's chain on the marble flooring. A bride ousted at his own wedding, Lavario sat off to the side, forgotten.

All eyes were on Mazgan. Unsure what to do now that his denials proved to be lies, the Alpha Guardian licked his lips and stuttered, "That was not official security footage."

"No, it was not." Although it was a direct response to Mazgan's comment, Vanu addressed the entire group, snubbing the Alpha with her posture and body language. "I placed new cameras when you told me of your plan to kill off humans using vampires, Alpha Guardian. Though I was moved by your declaration of love, my loyalty is to the pack."

Amber expected her to continue but then remembered the Varcolac, with the exception of Mazgan, were not big grandstanders. Vanu, done with her story, sat.

Mazgan's attention snapped on Kijo, who didn't react at all. She stared straight ahead as if deep in thought, considering the veracity of the testimony.

After a long pause, her authoritative voice—void of frenzy or any other emotion—cut through. "We must decide what to do about the Alpha's transgressions."

A werewolf Amber didn't recognize stood to shout, "We are trueborn wolves! The portal is ours by right!"

From talking to Lavario, Amber knew the pack was divided between old and new guard. She'd never seen the split herself and had doubted its existence until now.

The stiff and stoic demeanor, a point of pride in the Varcolac, vanished. The room erupted as they played bumper cars with their voices. The wolves on the right side of the aisle jeered at those on the left, most of who bellowed about procedure, tradition, and caution when it came to meddling with forces none of them fully understood.

Kijo waited for the clamor to die down before she continued. "None of the pack's guardians were notified of the portal's presence. We are its custodians by virtue of rank."

The same unknown rabble-rouser fired back. "The guardian title is no more than a contrivance to keep us underfoot. Those who split from the Isangelous cling to its traditions and ridiculous superstitions. We should continue to free ourselves."

Lavario, forgotten, snorted.

The rabble-rouser seized the opportunity Lavario's scorn provided. "Our disgraced Guardian is a prime example. What did he protect this pack from all those years? We hear how dire it is to tamper with the portals, yet nothing happened. Now that he is about to be exiled or killed, he warns us of an unseen threat. No doubt only he can protect us from it."

"Nonsense, Charles. I will do no better against a lifestealer than you."

"Then what is your purpose?"

"To keep brash young wolves from doing stupid things. The portal is not a right or a trophy to possess. It is not a pawn in a game for political power. It was a prison. Now the gateway is open."

"We don't believe you."

He lifted his chains and cocked an eyebrow. "Yes, I grasped as much through context clues."

Charles shook his head, disgusted by the wry humor. "Guardian Kijo, you agree with your father?"

Terse, Kijo responded, "In this matter, yes."

The crowd muttered. Charles smirked, believing the point he wanted to make was proven. "We all know you wanted him to challenge Mazgan and lead the Varcolac."

Kijo didn't lie. "Had he done so, we wouldn't be in our current situation."

"And what is our current situation?"

"Dire." Kijo did not elaborate.

Mazgan broke his silence to bellow, "You all see this is a plot. Kijo and Lavario want to rule this pack according to Boo Hag rules."

Now that Amber knew what to listen for, she could hear the uncertainty behind the priggishness. She noticed several wolves exchanged dark looks after his outburst. A few shook their heads. Maybe they, too, finally heard his bluster for what it was. Amber could hope.

"Yes, Alpha Guardian." The heckler, who Lavario identified as Charles, acknowledged Mazgan and continued, "Let's not be distracted by this ghost Guardian Kijo and Lavario brought out of the closet to frighten us. We are Varcolac, not weak humans who hide from shadows. We do need to evolve as a pack."

The last remark got an emotional reaction from Kijo. Her lip raised upward, exposing sharp canines. "I am happy to settle our dispute the Varcolac way whenever you'd like, Charles." Her level stare bore down on him until he turned away. "No? I didn't think so. But you're right. The wolves in this pack don't run from shadows. The lifestealer is here."

A sea of heads turned left, then right. It was Charles, the elected mouthpiece of the unbelievers, who asked, "Where is it?"

Kijo marched to Amber. Piercingly hostile, her tone demanded results, "Do as I taught you. Find it."

She didn't want to perform her new trick in front of everyone. She couldn't even pee in public restrooms. Uncomfortable being the center of attention, Amber popped back, "Why don't you do it?"

Kijo refused to explain. Typical of her, she leaned forward and barked the same order. "Find it." The accompanying squeeze wasn't gentle.

This wasn't the time or place to argue. She'd grown up enough to realize some battles could wait. Amber surrendered to what she had to do. Her first impulse was to relax. She shook it off and tensed her body. *You're being hunted,* she told herself. *Hunt back.*

The energy of the lifestealer ballooned out over the crowd. Sensing she was also on the prowl, it wove in and out, mixing amongst the Varcolac. It wanted to lose her in the energy of the surrounding werewolves, who were every bit as hostile.

Seek its eyes, Kijo had told her earlier. Like a tiger in a zoo cage, it paced back and forth, changing its location, never its focus. Feeling a tad bit predatory herself, Amber ignored its slight alterations and locked onto its steady glare. She knew she had hit the right spot when she felt like she might pee herself in terror.

"Here," she told them.

"Stand next to her, Charles," Kijo ordered. "Tell me you don't feel a presence."

Slightly less sure of himself, Charles stood where Kijo pointed. Amber studied his features, feeling a smug sense of vindication as the mocking tilt to his lips evened out. He rocked backward on his heels as if dodging a blow. If he felt a fraction of what Amber did, he'd be terrified.

Triumphant, Kijo squeezed his shoulder. "You feel it."

Even if he tried to deny it with words, his dry mouth and nervous facial ticks ratted him out. Swallowing, he admitted, "Yes."

"And what does it feel like?"

Charles said the exact word that flashed through Amber's mind. "Death."

Kijo nodded. "That's what it is for all of us, Varcolac and Isangelous, if we don't stop it."

Charles backed away, practically tripping over his own legs. He whirled around to face Lavario. "Use your magic. Get rid of it."

"Use magic. Throw water in the river to stop a flood." The respondent wasn't Lavario. High and tinny, its voice carried throughout the courtroom and drilled its way right through Amber's bones. It was the lifestealer, she realized.

Frantically, the wolves of the Varcolac searched for the source of the noise. Some sniffed, others flitted corner to corner, snarling as though to cow it into submission. The energy swirled around them. And it changed from menacing to...amused?

Charles's voice was almost as high as the lifestealer's. "Throw water in the river to stop a flood? What does it mean?"

"Magic is useless against it. It *is* magic," Lavario explained.

Chapter 47: The Challenge

AMBER AND LAVARIO

Sensing a change in the temperature of the room, Mazgan stood and puffed his chest out. Creatures of habit, the wolves of the Varcolac stopped searching for the lifestealer and turned to face their leader.

"Lavario, I demand to know why you didn't tell me of the presence of the lifestealer before today. Such vital information should be relayed immediately," Mazgan hollered.

"I was unconscious after Guardian Kijo beat me nearly to death, Alpha Guardian." Lavario delivered his response in the same submissive tone he'd used all night, but Mazgan heard a slight in it.

His face turned red as he shouted, "Dip, take Lavario's pet. Place her in the dungeons."

Dip, who'd been sleeping through the proceedings, jumped to his feet. Slobber dripping from his maw, he gave her a wet, full-toothed grin. From where she was, she could smell the rot on his breath. Long ago, Mazgan had promised the filthy mutt he'd get to eat Amber alive. Looked like today was the lucky day.

Lavario stood, dragging his chains with him. "We had a bargain. Amber was not to be harmed."

Amber's heart flipped. That's why he'd been so docile.

Mazgan continued. "As always, you broke the rules, Lavario. Your contempt for me ends tonight."

"I would have less contempt if you were marginally smarter."

And just like that, he was back to normal. Amber was happy for him, except his defiance fortified Mazgan's resolve. He snapped his fingers and pointed at Amber. Two wolves shot up and hustled her direction.

"Enough." Kijo's voice broke their argument. She motioned for the werewolves chasing after Amber to sit. Surprisingly, and without quarrel, they obeyed. "Your personal disagreements take back seat to this threat, Alpha Guardian."

Mazgan slapped his hands against the podium. The force of it vibrated through the walls. "You have no authority to chastise me or block my orders."

"I challenge you for this right. Formally. Now."

Amber inwardly scoffed at Mazgan's surprise. The fact he didn't expect events to backfire so horribly was a testament to his intelligence. Or lack of it. She snuck a glance at Lavario, who wasn't smiling.

Kijo continued. "Charles, you speak for the younger wolves. Do you back my challenge?"

The expression on Charles's face suggested nothing was going the way he desired. The wolves on the right side of the room, previously so ruckus and disagreeable, watched their representative in silence.

Charles eventually said, "Yes. Yeah. I support you." A few exchanged angry glances. Most nodded their agreement. Bolstered by the generally positive response, Charles's voice gained confidence, "I support your claim, Guardian Kijo."

Kijo turned to the left side of the room. "Do the older wolves of the Varcolac support me?"

Vanu stood. "Yes, we support your claim."

Kijo thanked her and redirected her attention to Mazgan. "Name the day and time, Alpha Guardian. That is your right."

The Alpha Guardian of the Varcolac jittered to his feet and fled.

"Ha!" Amber couldn't help herself. It was funny. Lavario joined her and the two of them filled up the silent room all by themselves.

"QUIET." KIJO SETTLED the room with a word.

Befuddled, Charles asked, "What do we do? Chase after him?"

Amber expected the fearsome rule-driven Kijo to run Mazgan down and drag him back to settle the date and time of the challenge. Instead, she waved it off and told them, "The lifestealer is priority number one."

Despite what Charles said about guardians being useless, he was the first to ask, "How do we defeat this thing, Lavario?"

Draped in chains and covered in spit, some of which was sure to be Charles's, Lavario pursed his lips and refused to answer. As the number of wolves seeking his counsel increased, the more agitated he became.

Finally, he bit out, "Maybe the lifestealer is adverse to khaki and posturing. Don an itchy shirt and challenge it the Varcolac way."

Kijo's lip twisted. "That was not a guardian's response."

"Guardian is no longer my rank—stripped from me, if you remember—by combat. Given my status as pack outcast, I do not believe I have any obligation."

Kijo's eyes turned golden. Her nails turned into claws, which curved inward to her palm. Drops of blood fell to the ground. There would be an ugly, deep wound the moment her fist unfurled.

"Perhaps you could see this as an opportunity to earn back your rank."

"I earned my rank a long time ago, just as you earned yours."

Amber had never seen such animosity between Lavario and his daughter. Had he been unbound, she'd halfway expect it to come to blows.

Kijo put her face in his and asked, "And so you turn your back on all of us?"

"And so we stand back-to-back."

"Very well. Forsake your kind. We must attend to the final matter of your sentencing."

Lavario arched an eyebrow as if to ask, *Seriously?*

Yes, seriously, Kijo's glower confirmed. Something similar came out of her mouth. "As the acting Alpha Guardian of the Varcolac, it is my recommendation Lavario be exiled. Perhaps, in time, he can find his way back to us when he can be a proper guardian. How votes the council?"

The panel of judges stood one by one—voting, Amber realized—until all of them were counted.

"It is unanimous. Lavario, you are stripped of your titles as well as your place here. We give the bloodservant to assist you in your search for the dragon bone amulet."

Bruised, beaten, Amber limped to Lavario's side. She didn't need to be an empath to feel his fury. Gold didn't touch his eyes, none of his teeth pushed past the barrier of his tightly drawn lips. He didn't even growl. And he always growled. The energy around him changed, hostile to the point it rivaled the lifestealer in its intensity.

"I regret not killing you," he told his daughter loud enough for everyone to hear.

A ripple of emotion quivered the normally tight lines of Kijo's mouth. Lavario had often talked about Kijo as Jun, an abandoned child left to freeze and starve in the wilderness. This was the first time Amber thought she could see such a girl. The moment passed quickly enough. Kijo—hard-eyed and unforgiving—took over.

"You'll have a long time to mull over your poor decisions as a False Moon, Lavario. I give you a month to sort out your affairs."

None of the other wolves of the Varcolac rushed to undo his chains, so he dragged them along with him. Occasionally, he stopped to catch his breath, placing his hand against the wall to support his weight. Any offer to help him got a steely glare.

"Sorry," Amber said to the last one. "It looks like you're struggling."

"I am."

They hobbled along in similar fashion all the way back to their apartment. Once inside, he did everything relatively like normal. He checked his messages, watered his plants, took a quick glance at his mail.

While he drank his tea, Amber asked him, "You going to take those chains off?"

"Too weak. Recovering."

And then he stood and walked to the bedroom. Not caring where he landed, Lavario fell on the bed and slept.

Chapter 48: The Worst

LAVARIO AND AMBER

The manic energy of the lifestealer palpated in the room. Dreading the thing might speak at any moment, Amber clamped her hands over her ears, squeezing to the point it hurt. She didn't sleep—eyes wide open, dried out, and probably the color of rust—until Lavario woke midafternoon. He broke his chains and sauntered to the kitchen without uttering a word or sparing her a glance.

Amber didn't feel much like talking either. She curled up in her chair, close enough she could see and hear Lavario, plummeted into an uneasy slumber, and woke to the sound of bacon sizzling. It felt like she'd only slept for moments, but it must have been hours. Shadows blanketed the hallways.

"Sleep well?" Lavario asked her, thumbing through the paper like some television dad from the 1950s. Only he was shirtless and fine as fuck. Daddy issues indeed. He gestured to the stack of pancakes waiting for her on the counter.

Not quite trusting how normal his voice sounded, Amber hesitated. "No..."

"I imagine not."

"Has *it* done anything?"

"Eat before we talk."

Amber kept one hand from trembling by tightly gripping it with the other. Lavario assessed her over the fringe of the paper, calculating—from the looks of it—how soon she might fall apart on him. Two bloodshot eyes plus two trembling hands equaled a meltdown. While she ate, she kept her head down and her eyes averted. She didn't want her merits judged. Not in this moment.

"Pancakes are good—as always."

Lavario held up a stainless-steel serving dish. "Would you like some cream for your coffee?"

Amber placed her hand over the cup. "No, thanks. Black pairs nicely with my mood."

"I put whiskey in mine."

"That sounds fantastic. Send it over."

He reached inside his tweed jacket and pulled a flask from a silky inner pocket and slid it over the table toward Amber, scratching the delicate wood in the process. She put the tips of her fingers on the shallow grooves and traced the path as far as her arm could reach.

Lavario watched her hand. "We leave soon."

"Assumed as much. A month grace period is probably more like twenty seconds in Kijo time."

"Generous."

Amber pushed the bacon around on her plate, dragging it through maple syrup until the sweet goo cooled and solidified around the pork fat. She held the abomination up to her nose and sniffed. With a sigh, she let her newest mistake plop between her fingers.

Lavario's newspaper ruffled. "Pack for our departure. Limit your effects to the size of a small carry-on."

Nothing there held sentiment other than the robe Lavario gifted her. "Easy enough."

He kept staring her direction like he expected her to say more. When she remained silent, he continued, meeting his eyes with hers, "I spoke with Kijo while you slept."

"And..."

"She presented an alternative to fleeing. You can stay here amongst the Varcolac. Enough of the pack are impressed by your courage to allow it."

The clang of Lavario's coffee mug as he all but dropped it made her jump in her seat. Liquid sloshed over the rim, seeping unchecked into the porous surface of the table.

Anger threatened to steal the breath from her body. "You're being... careless."

Lavario continued, "She will turn you immediately after my departure. I recommend you accept the offer."

"Did you hear me?"

His bland expression didn't change. "I heard."

Amber uncorked the flask and guzzled what she assumed was expensive booze. The burn down her throat brought tears to her eyes. Trying to act cool through the pain, she put her hand over her mouth to stifle a coughing fit. Snot bubbled up in her nose. She was a real mess.

Lavario studied her bloated face. "Go ahead and let it out, Doc Holiday."

"Shut up," Amber wheezed between hacking fits.

He waved his hand in dismissal and went back to taking dainty sips from his porcelain cup. When her lungs cleared and she quit spasming, he tried again. "Accept Kijo's offer, Amber. Stay here. Become a true wolf."

She crinkled her nose at his nagging. Well, he'd probably call it reasoning, but that was his word for whenever his mouth opened and words came out. At least in that regard, he was like any other man she'd ever met.

"I don't care about that."

"You assume now but—"

"I won't care later, either. I'm used to people like you sneering down their noses."

"Such hogwash." He shook his paper with enough force to make it sound like a bird taking wing.

"Not really."

Lavario tapped his fingers on the table and huffed at the indignity of being lumped in with the dregs of humanity—racists, sexists, bigots, halfwits. "You rebuke me for insisting you reach your potential. Accept Kijo's offer, Amber."

Amber picked up her fork just so she could let it clatter back to the plate. She let the ruckus signal a change in topic. "Did the lifestealer do anything while I slept?"

"Hunted."

Amber assumed the creature had moved past that already. It had her and Lavario in its sights. "Why?"

He amped up the volume of his finger tapping to max irritation. "Because that is all it does. Secure your interests, Amber. Stay here."

"What about you?"

"My time is done."

He took another sip of his coffee while Amber stewed and contemplated the exact meaning of what he said. Finally, she barked out, "Done *done* or... see you later."

"The future is open."

"Do you get paid to be enigmatic?"

That earned a slight lip quirk. "If only."

Lavario stood and walked over to the sink. *Plop!* That was the sound his dishes made as he dropped them in the water. He didn't rinse off any possible stains the way he normally did, nor did he cradle the delicate china on a spongy drying mat. Why did it bother her so much? She didn't know.

"You're being careless again."

He braced himself against the counter. The muscles in his back were tense, gorgeously taught. A massive sigh rippled his smooth skin. *Clink-clink*. His claws clicked on the tile. He was about to huff and puff and annoy her again.

"Amber—"

"Stay here. Got it."

"So you will?"

She hated how hopeful he sounded. "*Maybe*. Let me go talk to Kijo."

He faced her. "Remember, be sub… calm."

Submissive. That's what he nearly said. Amber harrumphed at the temerity of such a suggestion. After all, it was him who'd told her to be bolder than she ever thought possible. She was supposed to go to his temperamental progeny with her tail between her legs?

He gave her an unapologetic snort. "Avoid confrontation."

"Right. I'll be back."

Amber left the apartment, thinking about her relationship with Lavario. What long-term potential did they have? What were they going to talk about as things progressed? Certainly not the times when peasants came to their castle with pitchforks and torches. And she could picture Lavario leaning against the stone arch of a castle window, waiting for his dinner to come to him.

He's the worst, she said to herself. He probably heard.

Chapter 49: The Hair of the Dog That Bit Her

AMBER AND LAVARIO

Go to Kijo? What on earth put that stupid notion in her head? Amber couldn't quite piece her own logic together. Certainty—the overwhelming sense of rightness that brought her this far—failed the closer she got to Kijo's door.

Seriously, what was she thinking?

An image of Lavario popped into her mind: the smooth lines of his muscles, the way the dip in his back vanished inside his waistband. It was a perfect line begging to be traced with tongue, finger, toe.

"Right. You were thinking about sex. Idiot."

Amber didn't know if Kijo would let her have the best of both worlds or not. If turning her meant she had to stay with the Varcolac, she'd just as soon be a Moondog. Maybe, though, she'd allow her to leave with Lavario. Long shot. Amber kept her fingers crossed.

At least she had the dagger Lavario gave her. That was something.

The lifestealer trailed behind. Fear tangled inside Amber's nerve endings, making her fingers tingle and her skin twitch. It felt like a crisp fall day when there were a billion webs floating in the air. To calm herself down, Amber imagined her sister beside her; she'd say, *Don't get worked up over spider ejaculate, fool.*

Amber laugh-snorted at the memory and opened her eyes. And stopped midstep. "Shit!"

Getting lost in the Varcolac compound was easy enough to do without daydreaming. She forgot to count the doors on her way to Kijo's room, and she couldn't get her bearings any other way. Nothing changed from one wall to the next.

"How do the werewolves even navigate this mess?"

Behind her, a voice answered, "By smell."

Amber greeted the newcomer, "Vanu. Fancy meeting you again. Almost like you followed me."

"A lot like that, little one."

Amber blamed her initial attraction to Vanu on magic, assuming she'd spelled Amber into fixating on the soft mounds of her ample cleavage. That wasn't the case. Her attention snapped onto Vanu's breasts like it was the opposite end of a magnet. Apparently wanting both men and women was another thing she and Lavario had in common.

"Careful," Amber warned her. "I'm dangerous."

"I haven't forgotten. Difficult to do with the lifestealer here with you."

They stared at each other for so long Amber almost wanted Ben Stein to appear with eye drops. Finally, Vanu dipped her head as if in defeat. She vanished behind the frame of the hallway, only to reappear moments later holding a red umbrella covered in black polka dots. Somehow, the contraption took top marks for the strangest thing she'd seen, not to mention the most garish, while living amongst the Varcolac.

"Walk me outside."

Amber's memory wasn't that short. "Yeah. No."

"You're safe."

Amber turned around to leave.

"Amber, talk with me. I promise I won't hurt you."

"Oh, well. If you *promise* this time."

Vanu gave her attitude an undignified sigh. She tapped the metal-capped tip of the umbrella on the tile floor. A crack splintered from the center, coiling back in on itself. Vanu studied the damage with a grimace and shot Amber a dark glare.

"Don't look at me. That's on you."

"If I still wanted to kill you, I'd do it. Kijo says we need you."

"And you trust her?"

"Yes. She serves this pack. Walk with me."

Amber hated reminders her life was at the discretion of any werewolf she came in contact with. Frailty sucked ass. But she had to concede the point. She touched the handle of the dagger in her pocket to reassure herself it was there.

"Fine."

Vanu's umbrella left Amber anticipating rain, but she wasn't prepared for the torrential downpour that assailed them the moment they stepped outside. It blew sideways, pricking like needles into her skin. Anything more than five feet from her face was a washed-out blur. The whole world was drowning.

Vanu turned the umbrella, shielding Amber the best she could. She pointed. "I have something to show you. This way, to the shed."

That's the last thing Old Yeller probably heard. Amber staggered her steps, idling behind while she decided whether or not she wanted to outright flee. She didn't care for the way Vanu peeked over her shoulder to check on her. It was the mark of a guilty conscience.

"You'll be fine, Amber. I only want to show you some old records."

She gripped the knife tighter. "If you say so."

Dilapidated almost to the point of collapse, the wooden shack made a ruckus in the wind. Its door thump-thump-thump-thumped like the tail of a giant dog. The rest of the structure creaked and groaned. Whenever the thunder boomed, the glass from the broken windows vibrated. Water dripped on her head.

"Shitty place to store anything," Amber commented.

"Yes, well, no one else knows they're here."

Vanu got down on her knees and lifted a loose floorboard, which she set off to the side with far more delicacy and care than the warped, splintery plank deserved. Amber struggled not to notice the white lace of Vanu's bra as she felt around for the records. Occasionally, there were wet, slopping sounds. Vanu pulled up a fistful of gunk and shook her hand, splattering it into Rorschach patterns against the wall. Amber looked at it and saw wasted time. Whatever she hid down there had to be rotted.

"You sure what you're looking for is down there?"

"Yes. Be patient, little one."

Amber made herself comfortable while Vanu determinedly pawed through the muck. There was a tinny noise.

Right after, Vanu gave a triumphant, "Aha!" and stood. In her hands, she had a small metal box, which she opened by sticking her claw into the keyhole. Inside, a flash drive rested on a bed of velvet like some sort of electronic vampire.

"Very old-school."

Vanu didn't address the remark. She held the flash drive up in front of Amber's face and said, "This has information for all Lavario's items we sold instead of burned. One of them is listed as an item made of dragon bone."

"What is it?"

"I don't know. That part was deleted before I found this. I need you to get Lavario to tell you, and you two retrieve the item. Work your magic on him, Amber. Win him back to our side. Right now, it's the only thing I know of that can contain the lifestealer."

Amber reached out to take the flash drive, but Vanu pulled it back. "Keep it here until you two are ready to leave. We can't risk losing it."

Wordlessly, she placed it back in its hiding spot for safekeeping.

The two of them walked out to a chaotic world. The metal from the roof screeched the way Amber imagined a banshee might. The rain still poured down sideways. Water dripped from the leaves above them, pattering on the ground. A fat drop splattered on Vanu's skin and ran the couture of her breast. Its path held her rapt attention. She really was a hornball. She had to admit.

Vanu, her eyes suddenly blacker, grabbed Amber's hand and pulled their bodies together. Her voice was heavy when she said, "Little one."

Amber pushed her away. "Stop the fake shit like before. And I'm not little. We're pretty much the same height." Maybe Vanu was a little taller. Maybe.

Vanu placed her hand against Amber's face, letting her thumb trace a tender outline of her entire mouth. "It was only fake at the start. It didn't end that way. Your beauty is unreal, little one. And your taste." Vanu licked her lips. "Let me show you how real it can be between us."

Confusion made Amber stammer a reply she didn't hear. Was it yes? It must have been. Vanu's mouth closed over hers, and her tongue immediately followed. Well, Lavario told her to be submissive, so Amber leaned against the somewhat taller Vanu and allowed her to tilt her head backward and lick raindrops from her throat.

So far, Lavario was the only other one to ever call her beautiful. She wasn't accustomed to the salacious attention the werewolves gave her. It dizzied. That was why it barely registered in her mind when Vanu suddenly jerked out of her arms and seemingly flew off in the distance. Behind her, a shadowy figure lurked.

Chapter 50: Rejection

AMBER AND LAVARIO

Amber closed her eyes and visualized a rain-swept Lavario with his dark, wavy hair blowing in the wind and his green eyes alight with devilish good humor. Ideally, he'd be jealous but not so much so he wasn't open to a three-way. Amber crossed her fingers and hoped for that exact scenario. When she mustered the courage to actually look, an unknown werewolf came forward.

Well. Fuck.

"Vanu?" Amber called out. Was she dead? She couldn't see through the sheet of rain or hear anything over the downpour—no footsteps, no shouts, no life. Around her, the world continued to boil and swirl.

Holding up his hands to assure her he was no threat, the newcomer moved forward and said, "I thought she might have been trying to kill you, like before. Did I misread the situation?"

The imprint of Vanu's lips on Amber's ached. "Not entirely."

"Kijo sent me. She assumed you got lost."

Back in the old days, the musical way he spoke his words might have charmed the heat to her loins. Now it just made her suspicious. She hadn't aged much, but she'd grown up beyond her years.

"Who are you?"

"My name is Gene. As I said, Kijo sent me to make sure you got to her quarters safe and sound."

He stated his name and purpose in the same singsong voice, but Amber detected a hint of annoyance behind the melody. Maybe it was the way his chin tilted or the hard, focused way he assessed her. Amber put her hands in her pockets. One squeezed the phone Lavario had given her; the other grabbed hold of the knife.

"Don't you want to be one of us?"

Amber told the truth. "Not really."

Gene gave her candor a wide, toothy smile. Although the words he spoke were ones of encouragement, Amber only heard, *The feeling is mutual.* "This way." He gestured with his hands.

"Thanks, I'll find her on my own."

Gene tried a different tactic from music. He grabbed her by the elbow and pulled, making it clear she could go along willingly or he could drag her the entire way. His tone hadn't changed; it was still a cordial melody. Even as he jerked her inside the compound, causing her to stumble at the threshold, he kept his speech light and airy as though everything he said was inconsequential. Rivers of water ran from their clothes onto the stone floor beneath them, but Gene didn't even give the mess a second glance as he led her forward.

Smirking, Gene glanced over his shoulder and said, "Lavario wants this for you. He's certain you'll be the next great guardian of the Varcolac."

The pressure on her arm cut off circulation to her fingers. Amber hated reminders her life was at the discretion of any werewolf she came in contact with. Frailty sucked hardcore.

Amber capitulated. "Fine, lead the way."

He smiled again and gave her a charming bow, directing her to walk ahead of him. Even the way he moved set her on edge. The *clack-clack* from his dress shoes reminded her of a tap dancer's step. The empty hallways magnified every noise. Amber ground her teeth and searched for an escape route. Inside her hand, the handle of the dagger burned.

"GET DISTRACTED?"

Normally, the way Kijo simultaneously assessed and dismissed her would have goaded Amber to flippancy. Wiser than she was, Amber held back and simply nodded.

"Thanks for helping me find my way back!" she said to Gene.

Kijo gave her comment a wry twist of her mouth. "You understand becoming Varcolac is a great honor?"

"Of course."

"Hm." Kijo tapped her nails on the arm of her chair. Deep grooves in the plain wood suggested Kijo often used it as a scratching post. Her eyelids hung low over her black eyes. "What did Vanu want?"

"Nothing."

"She brought you out in the rain against my express orders for no purpose?"

"Yup. Weird, huh?"

"They were kissing, Guardian Kijo," Gene supplied.

Kijo turned his direction. "And where is Vanu, our ally, now?"

Gene gulped. His Adam's apple bobbed. "Unconscious."

"Hm," Kijo said again. "Curious."

Gene straightened and tried his best to seem imposing. "She'll be fine. I wanted to rebuke her for leading our new daughter away."

"I don't need you to discipline my subordinates. When I send you to fetch, fetch."

"Of course."

Lips tightened, Amber reflected on whether or not being immortal was worth the cost of being Kijo's progeny. Exactly how close would they become after the transformation? Amber had no real way of knowing. She could only hope not very was the answer.

As though sensing Amber's thoughts, Kijo turned her direction. "Is this what you want or what Lavario wants?"

"Lavario mostly."

Her long fingers tapped on the wood. "He explained the alternative to you?"

"Moondog."

"You have the ability to become true wolf. I am as sure of it, as is Lavario. There is no need for you to fear the test."

"I'm not afraid. I don't want to be Varcolac without Lavario. I'd go for true wolf, though, as long as I can leave with him."

Kijo tilted her head to the side as if she couldn't quite believe what she heard. She hung her fingers suspended above the arm of her chair. To her, the Varcolac represented everything worthwhile in her life; the beginning and end of who she was. Despite their differences, Amber admired Kijo's dedication to her family. It was one of her few good qualities.

"I'm sorry," Amber said. "I don't mean it as an insult, but I don't belong here."

Kijo's blinked. When her eyes reappeared, they were golden. "Where do you belong?"

"I don't know."

"With Lavario, you believe?"

"Yes. That at least."

"He left."

Startled, Amber shook her head a few times. "What?"

Surprisingly graceful for someone prone to violence, Kijo kicked out of her chair in one fluid movement. She pulled two glasses down from her cupboard and poured booze. Gene held his hand out to take the offering, but Kijo walked right past him to Amber.

"He left," she said again and shoved the glass to her breast. The liquid sloshed against her. "Drink."

"Wh—when?"

"Right after your exit. He wants you to move forward, Amber. Can you?" Kijo sat back down.

She pinched her eyes shut. Beneath her lids, a vision of her future lurked, ready to tug her heart back in Lavario's direction. She'd been thumbing the dagger he gave her all day. She reached for the phone. With certainty, she knew he'd answer if she pushed one of the glittery buttons.

What should she do?

Other men in her life sought to smooth her into a presentable lady. The jagged, untamed parts of her that others called bitch. Lavario loved those best. With him, she could be as bold and brash as she'd ever wanted.

"Amber?" Kijo's pragmatic voice brushed aside the romantic notions filling Amber's head. A little frown creased the soft hairs of her brow. "Can you move forward?"

"I want to go my own direction."

The crease became a canal. Anger was what Amber expected. Instead, Kijo responded by sighing and slapping her hands against her knees like a fed-up grandmother. "May your stubbornness be rewarded in time."

Amber thought she knew what surprise meant, at least the dictionary definition. She came to understand it firsthand as Kijo's paw came down across her neck and the whole world went red, then black, then white.

Chapter 51: Trap

AMBER AND LAVARIO

As Amber fell, she grasped for anything solid to hold onto, but the world around her revolved around chicanery. Objects slipped through her fingers the way airplanes went through solid walls of cloud. A presence in the white haze caught her attention. It had no form, but she knew the eye of her hunter. The lifestealer.

Its voice called to her, *Amber, touch.*

A massive archway appeared. Unlike the doorway hidden in the Varcolac compound, this monstrosity convinced her of its otherworldliness. The gleaming white bone, supposedly dragon, crackled with energy. Sparks flew upward only to roll back in on themselves like a sun loop.

Amber recoiled from the heat.

Touch. The impulse overrode her survival instincts to the point she reached out to obey the command. Expecting to grab hold of nothingness, Amber was surprised when the door pushed back, jarringly solid. Electricity shot through her body. Fire coiled in her stomach, boiling her bones and innards into a sludgy soup.

Caught in a surge of centrifugal force, Amber struggled to remain whole with something ineffable pushing half of her off to the side.

She jerked upward, panting. After a while, she realized the ground beneath her existed. She touched herself and enjoyed the feel of her own body—real, corporeal, breathing. Amber huffed in and out to make sure. Yup, all three were true.

"Amber, you're awake."

"Vanu....? Is that you?"

"Yes."

Amber tried to blink away the fuzziness in her vision. "What's wrong?"

"Tell me you wanted this for yourself, little one."

"Want what?"

Vanu didn't respond. Amber heard her breathing change from slow-and-steady to quick-and-angry, but she didn't have the energy to investigate it. Amber's head throbbed. She used her hand, oddly cool when the rest of her body felt like it was on fire, to squeeze her temple. Pressure didn't work.

She couldn't remember anything either. "This feels like how classmates described drugs. Did I do drugs?"

"No." She went quiet. Amber started to nod off to sleep, but Vanu inserted herself between Amber and peaceful oblivion. "Come on, I'm to transport you once you wake."

"Transport me where?"

"Just come on." Vanu held out her hand. "You'll be fine."

VANU DROPPED AMBER off in the middle of the forest and left her to wander like some disgruntled, groggy red riding hood. Minus the basket of snacks. The throbbing in her head continued, and it only got worse each time she tried to remember what happened.

"Fucking thanks!" she screamed to no one in a bout of angst.

A large thing moved after she spoke. The noise, louder than normal, echoed in her ears. Smells followed; it was a barrage of scents Amber couldn't identify. She sneezed over and over again, each one stronger than the next. By the time the spell ended, her sides were sore and the tender ridge under her nose ached. Why was everything so intense all the sudden?

"Kijo?" Amber whispered and clutched the phone and the knife.

The thudding, which already sounded like pounding war drums in her ears, increased in volume.

"Erm. Vanu? Kijo?"

Amber backed up when no one responded. She tossed her head left, then right, and ran. Doglike, she stuck her nose up in the air. By taking deep breaths, she got a sense for where she was. A river ran nearby. The thudding faded the closer she got to the rapids.

Amber stopped to get her bearings.

Things cleared up considerably after she heard, "You're only half the deal."

Mazgan's bloated white face floated in front of her. It wasn't until he fully stepped out of the shadows that Amber saw the outlines of his pure-black James-Bond-villain suit. She snorted a bit at the drama, which was absolutely the wrong thing to do.

He pulled his lips from his teeth, exposing a mouthful of pointed incisors. "Where is Lavario, you fucking little..."

Amber tuned out the last word. Why bother hearing it? "I get it. You're trash. Why are you here?"

His face turned red. "Don't you dare question me! I am Alpha Guardian of the Varcolac, I—"

Amber didn't want to make time for his bluster. She cut him off. "Yeah, you're the best. That's why you're out here chasing the likes of me instead of fighting Kijo."

"She made a deal."

"Oh, I bet. Kijo is all about compromise."

The muscles in his face twitched. His eyes turned golden, glowing like brake lights in the darkness. Amber should have stopped. Instead, she gripped the hilt of the dagger and said, "Shouldn't you be founding a predatory loan company? Or a used car lot? You know, something low stress but douchey?"

She didn't have time to rethink her actions. All she could do was hope her goading had its intended effect and pricked the ex-alpha's ego to the point of recklessness. Yup. In a blur of fur, tooth, and claw, he transformed and charged headlong without thinking. Paws slogged through the mud, flinging earth behind him and sideways.

Be still, be strong, do not frenzy. Amber repeated the advice until her pounding heart slowed to a persistent whimper.

She waited until the smell of wet dog clogged her nostrils before jumping away. Mazgan, who expected to collide against Amber's body, slid on the wet earth, rolling over a few times until he noisily slopped into the water, which went over his head.

"Damn," Amber congratulated herself. "That worked out."

But she needed the next part of her plan. And fast.

She thought back on the altercation with Kijo. No matter how many times Amber had brought the knife against the thick fur along Kijo's back, the blade never penetrated skin—at least not deep enough to do any real damage. Her attempts to cut Kijo's throat got the same result.

She needed a vulnerable area, like the eyes.

Amber crouched low, knife in hand, and waited for those yellow orbs to show themselves. She'd have seconds to land the blow before Mazgan regrouped and was ready to charge out of the water.

"Ahhh!" Amber's battle cry sounded more like a cat throwing up than a barbaric yawp—she really needed to work on that—but it pumped her up. The moment he got to shallow water, she hopped and swung. The point of the dagger hit its mark. Mazgan reared back his head and bellowed.

Amber yipped at the noise and skedaddled, pulling the dagger with her.

She didn't exactly know where she'd go. Faster than her, Mazgan could easily run her down. Another trick was unlikely to work.

Damsel in distress wasn't her normal MO, but she was up against an irrational, homicidal blowhard who could also turn into a giant wolf. She felt around in her other pocket for the phone Lavario gave her and pulled it from her pocket. Suddenly, she was once again Mrs. Butterfingers. The damn thing slid right out of her hands.

Calm and not at all panicking—*ha-ha*—she screamed, "Son of an actual bitch!" and got down on her hands and knees to find the accursed device. Luckily, she found the bright and glittery phone without too much of a hassle. Unluckily, she'd dropped it in a nest of wet deer poo.

She pushed one of the garish buttons and prayed he gave it to her as an actual security provision rather than joke. The line clicked. "Lavario?" Amber whispered as forcefully as she dared.

He answered. She knew he would. "Hmm?"

It sounded like he'd just got up from a nap. "Wake up and help me, you overglorified throw rug. Mazgan—"

"Mazgan what?"

"He's after me."

A long silence followed. "Where is he now?"

"I don't know. I stabbed him in the eye and booked it."

Lavario chuckled. Actually chuckled.

"This isn't funny. He's going to kill me."

"Are you near the compound?"

"Yes." Or at least she thought so.

"Stay on the move. Scream after a minute or so. Keep at it until I find you."

The line went dead.

Amber glared at the phone as though it were Lavario and cussed at it the same way. Once she worked all the rage out of her system, she got up and kept running. Some people were graceful under pressure. Other people stabbed themselves in the eye with their own fingernail and stumbled. Amber was the latter.

She hit her knee on a downed tree while trying to climb over it. "Youch!"

Had a minute passed yet? Amber didn't know for sure. She had a terrible sense of time. She took in a deep gulp of air and shouted, "Lavario!"

There was a very nearby growl and another thudding noise.

Amber screamed again. "I'm over here, collie!"

Maybe she'd end up dead, but he—either Mazgan or Lavario—would hear that and seethe.

Chapter 52: Transformation

AMBER AND LAVARIO

Amber'd like to say she waited a respectable amount of time before she shrieked for help, but that would be a bald-faced lie. Truthfully, she shouted until her voice croaked and it felt like she might cough up blood.

"Lavario! Collie, collie, collie! Over here!" Toward the end, she whistled.

There was no way to know whether he heard. Kijo said he'd left right after Amber did. How far away had he traveled? She fretted while she ran.

Behind her, twigs snapped, bushes shook, and wet leaves rustled the best they could with the rain pelting down on top of them. Mazgan crashed through the bramble. When he saw her, he showed his teeth. Amber forgave the redundancy. Dumb animals had a limited range of gestures.

"Found you."

"Noticed." Amber took an involuntary step backward.

Mazgan sniffed the air. An odd expression crossed his face, but he shook it off along with the raindrops on his mangy fur.

Although it grossed her out, she took satisfaction in noting his injury. One of his yellow eyes dripped red. Beneath the laceration, his brown fur matted in a sticky tangle. He approached at a slow, steady pace; his head down and ears flat on his head as though he considered her a threat. Generous of him, Amber thought.

"Lavario...?"

"He isn't wolf enough to track you. He probably stopped to get a manicure."

Shit. That might actually be true. It didn't take too much effort for her to imagine Lavario picking out a dapper murder outfit before sauntering lazily in her direction. He overestimated her independence and ability, which was only flattering when she wasn't facing certain death.

"Lavario!" Her voice squeaked this time.

"I was upset at first. But now I'm glad he's not here yet as promised. Oh how his heart will ache when he finds you..."

Amber scooted sideways from one end of the clearing to the next. Mazgan followed her, pacing alongside. Then, without any of his typical posturing and warning signs, he sprung straight at her. Amber barely ducked to the ground in time to miss the full impact of his body. Claws scrapped her upper back. Adrenaline held most of the pain at bay, but the blood trickling down her back catapulted her over mildly concerned straight toward freaking out.

"Lavario! Where are you, you damn collie?"

Almost instantly, Mazgan pounced again. This time, he pinned her to the ground. His jaw came for her throat. He snapped, laughing each time she whimpered. Closing her eyes, Amber waited for the killing blow to land.

"Get off her."

Lavario. It was about damn time. Mazgan's body tensed and shuddered as her own relaxed.

Mazgan seemed to try to keep his voice level when he said, "Here at last, Lavario… just in time to watch." But there was a tremble in his words.

Lavario tapped under his right eye. "What happened there?"

Mazgan responded to Lavario's jab by whipping his jaws back toward Amber's throat. A tooth scrapped her chin before the weight of Mazgan's body was lifted. Not by magic. No, Lavario went wolf and tackled the former alpha to the ground. It was dirty, sticky, sweaty brawling. That's how much Lavario hated the guy.

Either that, or he was too tired for magic.

His sides heaved in and out at a faster pace than normal. His steps were staggered rather than fluid. Signs pointed to exhaustion.

Once Mazgan was a safe distance away from Amber, Lavario backed away and said, "Kijo is back at the compound. I believe you two have pack business to conclude."

Mazgan flinched. "She betrayed us both… We're allies in this fight. Can't you see?"

Lavario shook his head very slowly.

"Kijo promised me she'd let me kill you. You and the girl."

"Not the best argument for our being allies."

"I wouldn't have led with that," Amber agreed.

"Kijo is—"

"On her way," Lavario finished for Mazgan. "She lured you from hiding." He thought for a moment and added, "Idiot."

Openmouthed, Mazgan stopped himself midretort to sniff the air. Amber did the same without quite knowing why—it just felt natural, like she'd always been doing it—and caught a whiff of something familiar but unknown. The odd contradiction baffled her, but she understood it was someone she knew, even though she couldn't pin a name on the scent.

Mazgan flinched. Amber assessed his posture and surmised that the odor belonged to Kijo.

"Amber..." Lavario's expression changed as he watched her continue to smell.

"Shush, I want to live in this moment."

"Amber..." Lavario's eyes were huge. He kept gawking at her like he'd never seen her before.

"Shush! Oh, look, here she comes!" Sure enough, Kijo, with the rest of the pack fanned out behind her, marched forward. Amber clapped her hands and did a few hops. "Damn," she said to Mazgan, "she got you good."

A deep growl emitted from the depths of the ex-alpha guardian. He leaped toward Amber, only to be intercepted by Lavario, who slammed him on the ground. Lips curled above his gums in a feral snarl, Lavario struck with a viciousness she'd never seen from him before. The black fur along the ridge of his spine mohawked all the way to his tail.

"Did you do this to her?"

"Do what to who?" Amber didn't know what Lavario was talking about.

Mazgan didn't appear to either. Grunting, he snapped up toward Lavario's throat, trying in vain to make contact with the flesh beneath. Lavario held him back with one massive paw and kept asking him the same question over and over: *Did you do this to her?*

Amber tried to interject. "Uh, I don't think he knows what you're talking about, Lavario. I don't either."

But Lavario kept on asking.

Amber enjoyed the Mazgan Suffers show until the manic, out-of-control, glint to Lavario's normally bored, matter-of-fact eyes became apparent. They were glossy, like two very green apples, and wet around the edges. Under the strain of anger, Lavario labored to breathe. The worst of the wounds from his battle with Kijo, which were now mere scratches, trickled a small but steady stream of blood.

Kijo herself now stood nearby. She assessed her handiwork with cold detachment. "Lavario." Her calm and certain pronouncement of his name served as a greeting and an order: *Get off, he's mine.*

"Kijo's here. Let her have him. You need to rest." Amber shook Lavario's shoulder gently. In response, he gave her one of his old-grump growls. Amber took some comfort in the normal noise. "Seriously, you're in no condition to keep fighting like this. You're wheezing."

Lavario's features were pinched, but he pried himself off of Mazgan, then turned to his daughter. "Kijo, what happened? When did he do this to Amber?"

If Kijo cared about him dropping her title, she didn't show it. She gave Lavario a blank, emotionless stare. "He did nothing. I turned her."

"What?"

"I turned her."

"Turned me?" Amber yelped.

Kijo gave her a tired, exasperated yes.

She almost asked, *Into what?* But she shoved that dumb question right back down her throat before it could see the light of day. Pain cut off her next words and brought her to her knees. Grinding her teeth, she tried to keep from screaming out by shoving her knees into her chest, restricting the flow of air. She huffed instead. Not exactly more dignified.

"What's happening, Lavario?"

He knelt beside her, human again. "Your body is responding to your stress. Let it take its course."

The next pained scream came out of her mouth as a howl. Low, then high, it was a grotesque noise that was soon followed by gangly, furry limbs.

Amber understood now what Lavario had tried to protect her from. Her new form felt the way mixing oil and water looked. Nauseated from the pain, she rolled over to her side and panted like a dog. Oh god, he'd been right all along.

"Lavario," she whimpered.

"Amber." He stroked her head.

"Is it always this bad?"

"No, no. Only the first."

Kijo towered over them, casting a shadow. "Take her and leave. Your time with the pack is done. You two can be False Moons together, as Amber wanted."

Lavario's body tensed. The paw rubbing her back balled up, pulling a bit on her fur. A low, animalistic growl reverberated against Amber's chest. Although she'd made fun of him for continually falling back on the noise, this time it sounded different. Amber forced herself to leave his protective grasp and look into his eyes, which were golden. No. Molten.

Fearing what he was about to do, Amber whispered his name. "Lavario."

He gently pushed her aside and stood. Wolf again in seconds, he crouched low in a battle stance. Very nonchalant, Kijo echoed the gesture.

Lavario darted right past her and took Mazgan by the throat, pulling him up as though he weighed no more than air. A loud snapping noise split through the air. Thousands of wolf ears perked up at the noise and flattened. Mazgan fell to the ground. Dead.

Chapter 53: Energy Transfer

AMBER AND LAVARIO

Kijo's golden eyes widened in something resembling an expression, turning from stunned to homicidal in mere seconds like some sort of ultra-souped-up rage machine. Even the energy of the lifestealer dwarfed in comparison. Amber sensed its presence. It lingered in the background; its eyes—as always—fixed on her.

Father and daughter stared at each other through narrowed eyes. Breathing heavily—out of anger or pain, Amber couldn't tell—Lavario flung saliva from his jowls in a way he would have normally considered beneath his dignity.

Vanu stepped between them, her arms extended as if to hold them apart. "Lavario, this is crass behavior, indicative of a False Moon."

He growled out something resembling, an *uh-huh*. His golden eyes flashed.

Seeing a dead end there, Vanu grabbed Kijo's arm. "Walk away. Lavario is in no position to challenge you. He's not Varcolac."

Kijo shrugged out of her grasp and said, "Move."

Exasperation evident in her voice, Vanu appealed to duty. "Settle your individual grievances later. We'll need the both of you to defeat the lifestealer."

Kijo repeated her command. "Move."

Outside threats forgotten, the Varcolac pressed in on the outskirts of the makeshift arena. Eager for things to be settled between their new Alpha and her outcast father, or just to see bloodshed, they licked the pointed white incisors hanging from their open maws. Amber would have given anything for one of them to cut its tongue.

Vanu turned to Amber with an unspoken plea, *Talk sense into him.*

Amber, trying her wolf vocals for the first time, whimpered. Rather than calm Lavario, the noise incensed him to the point he practically foamed at the mouth. Vanu glowered as though Amber purposefully stoked his anger when the last thing she wanted him to do was fight. That's not what she wanted. Not when Lavario was recovering. And never for her sake.

"Lavario, let's leave." Embarrassingly high, her wolf voice startled Amber. She tried to turn back to human but didn't quite know how, so she gave up and used her squeaky-wheel voice to get some grease. "Please. I asked Kijo to make me a Moondog."

"Leaving is not an option anymore," Kijo said. "Pray he wins or you'll die right after. Run if you want. I have your scent."

Actually having hackles was novel. It tingled when they rose, and the sensation wasn't entirely displeasing. Amber found herself throwing in a snarl at the end, letting Kijo know she had no intention of running and she had all the fight in the world left in her.

Kijo gave the brave display a short nod and a "Pity you wanted to go your own direction. You could have been magnificent."

Amber didn't have anything to say to that. Well, she did, but not in her squeaky-wheel voice, so she shuffled her feet and put on her best menacing glower.

Ears flat on their heads, jaws snapping, Kijo and Lavario circled like it was high noon at the O.K. Corral. Their hands hung at their sides, fingers twitching as if reaching for an invisible gun. Posturing churned Amber's stomach. Sooner or later, actual fur would fly. Amber had grown quite fond of Lavario's magnificent coat—so soft and fluffy—and she wanted him to keep it.

Lavario didn't seem as keen on remaining intact. He taunted Kijo, "Come on then, pup."

Shit, Amber thought as a blur shot past her. Wailing a battle cry far superior to Amber's—she had this whole howl, growl, and whoop thing going—Kijo beelined straight toward Lavario. He crouched, waiting. When she hit him, he lifted up, tossing her over his shoulder. It wasn't quite hocus pocus, but it felt kind of magical when Kijo hit the ground and slid in the muck.

Lavario whirled around fast enough to pounce, pin, and rend. Amber felt the instinct well up inside. She performed the action in her mind, visualizing herself in Lavario's position, going straight for the exposed throat. Her whole body felt alive—blood pumping oxygen, and pure, brilliant light.

Lavario walked a lazy loop around his daughter, giving her time to stand. The hubris of his dismissal struck a raw chord in Amber. *Come on*, she thought, hoping he might hear. *End it quick.* If he got the message, he gave no indication.

Instead of going in for the kill, he went in for a cutting remark. "How similar we are. Almost family."

Mud clung to Kijo's fur, indeed making it appear as dark as Lavario's. Except for the height difference, they were virtually identical.

Kijo shook off the dark silt. Lips curled backward, she gave Lavario's goading a snarl. Pure fury, no sense, she charged again. On collision, they wrapped themselves in a death spiral—Kijo's claws dug into Lavario's sides, his into hers—and they rolled on the ground until they were coated in muck, twigs, and leaves. It wasn't too long before they looked more like swamp monsters than werewolves.

Behind Amber, energy amassed. She'd forgotten about the lifestealer, which was a dangerous thing to do. Curiously, it wasn't hunting her anymore. Amber did as Kijo taught her and pinned down its location. It was right beside Mazgan's body.

That had to be bad. Amber tried to get their attention. "Guys."

Amber turned in time to dive out of Lavario's path as he toppled backward. Kijo came crashing down on top. She lifted her paw and gave Lavario a clawless slap across the face. And then she used claws.

The lifestealer syphoned energy from the brawl. Excited, it pulsed nearby and pooled the resources. Amber felt it getting stronger, stronger, stronger.

"Uh, guys."

Lavario snapped his jaws upward, catching Kijo right below her chin. Wailing, she reared backward. Lavario gave her knee a savage kick. There was a *pop!* and Kijo fell backward.

"Guys...stop! The lifestealer. It's..." Amber searched for the appropriate word. "...excited by this."

Lavario shoved her out of the way. It didn't hurt, but he wasn't as gentle as before.

Amber came right back. "Listen! The. Lifestealer. Wants. This."

The truncated version of the same information didn't have any effect either. Kijo, limping and grimacing, dug her claws into Amber's shoulder and chucked her like a bale of hay. She landed with a *thump!* and rolled a foot or two, eventually hitting a tree. Pine needles rained down on her head, along with water from the evening rain.

"Stay," Lavario barked at her.

"Damnfuckshitsticks." Amber clumped all her swears into one pile. Holding the gash on her shoulder closed with her hand, she marched back to the arena with determination.

She got up in Kijo's face and shouted, "Listen!" She turned to Lavario and did the same.

There was more to her speech, but Mazgan, dead no more than a few moments ago, moaned and rose from the ground. Pure white, his eyes scanned the crowd as if searching for someone he knew.

Vanu whispered a question. "What is this?"

Reanimated-lifestealer Mazgan jumped in before Amber could say, *What the fuck do you think it is?* He smeared a mocked smile across his face and said, "Hungry."

Chapter 54: From Beyond the Grave

AMBER AND LAVARIO

And just like that Mazgan was back to be douchy from beyond the grave.

Lavario, bloodied almost beyond recognition, gaped at the reanimated Alpha with increasing dread. Amber remembered what he said a lifetime ago when she asked what he'd do if he ever saw the ghostlike creature he described to her. *Run*, he'd said. *Very far, very fast. Run, run, run.*

His feet twitched as if flight was an option on the table. Being afraid must have been as novel for him as Amber's wolf form was to her. Judging by flattened ears and black, wild eyes, he seemed to enjoy it about as much.

The rest of the Varcolac varied between awe and terror. A few of them—the dumb, Amber decided—whipped their heads between Kijo and Lavario, sneering at the temporary truce.

One of them went as far to say, "End this, Guardian Kijo. You're not the alpha until you do."

Kijo's eye and lip twitched simultaneously, but she didn't resume hostilities with Lavario.

He tried again. "Guardian Kijo—"

"Shut your mouth, or it will be your body on the ground."

Apparently, Kijo was alpha enough after all. He slunk behind the rest of the crowd.

The lifestealer, unaccustomed to its new body, stumbled forward. In its current form, the creature didn't seem much of a threat, more like an old man too stubborn to ask for directions. It even shook its head as if saying *no, no, no* the way Amber's father did whenever anyone asked if he was lost.

Seeing a fumbling, doddering corpse rather than an enemy, the wolves of the Varcolac laid their ears flat and pushed forward, snarling the way they always did to cow their enemies.

Kijo pulled them away with a barked command. "Move back." To Lavario, she said, "What do we do?"

Lavario answered, "Its host is dead. It needs energy to sustain its form. Keep away, let it die out."

Amber could tell by the way his lips pursed and how he his gaze darted from the creature to the surrounding area that he didn't really know if his strategy would work. Whenever the lifestealer moved, he moved, if only slightly. His version of freaking out, Amber supposed.

Lavario turned to her. "The dagger. You had it before. Do you have it now?"

She nodded.

"Where?"

Fuck. What had she done with it? "It's here. Somewhere. Last I remember, I pulled it from Mazgan's eye. After that, events got blurry."

Lavario stuck his nose up in the air. Elegance apparently wasn't a luxury afforded by the situation. He snorted the air like doing a line. Afterward, he even shook his head like the tweakers on television programs. He must have caught the scent.

He sauntered off, calling over his shoulder, "The rest of you grab long sticks."

No one grabbed long sticks.

The creature raised its head. Its milky white eyes fixated on Amber. Something like recognition—an *aha!*—crossed its features and it staggered toward her. Slow at first, then with increasing speed. Not knowing what else to do, Amber kept a good distance between herself and it.

The lifestealer's flesh dried up; dehydrating at an accelerated rate. When his mouth moved, flakes of skin peeled off. What was underneath was more of the same. Layer after layer of gray scale skin.

The creature spoke. Its murmurings hissed like static. "Amber. Touch."

Her squeaky-wheel voice ticked up in pitch. "Lavario...any suggestions here?"

"Keep it at a distance."

"Okay. Thanks."

Of course Amber couldn't see herself, but she could imagine how ridiculous she looked—a giant wolf stumbling away from a reanimated corpse. It trailed after her, asking her to touch in its creepy disconnected tone like no one's favorite uncle.

Gene, the werewolf who always hung around Kijo, observed the scene with an academic curiosity. "Okay, I think I know what to do here," he said. Magic pooled around him. Amber felt it coil inside her. It had a heat. The air hummed.

"No!" Lavario shouted. "No magic. No magic."

Too late.

Fire shot from Gene's fingertips. Air wooshed away from Amber's face as the lifestealer ignited. Kindling burned slower in comparison. In the blink of an eye, the creature vanished into the smoke. *Poof!* Gone.

Admiring his work, Gene said, "There. It wasn't quite the big deal Lavario made it to be."

The other wolves of the Varcolac nodded. A few muttered, "Right." They crowded around Gene and congratulated him for dealing with the situation like a true wolf, unlike their useless guardians. Amber got the sense Gene wasn't accustomed to the positive attention. Under the praise, his chest puffed and his satisfied smile morphed into a satisfied grin.

Shock wore away from Lavario. "Get away from him! It jumped. It used Gene's magical energy as a passage."

Gene's scoff cut itself short. His eyes turned yellow. It wasn't the gold of the wolf's form, more like urine or jaundice. His lips twitched. Acidic-smelling bile bubbled from his mouth. He spewed it out, projectile style. Dribbles of the green sludge splashed near Amber's foot. Nose crinkled at the smell, she scooted away.

"Get away from him," Lavario repeated. "Now, now, now."

Those who had ignored Lavario's earlier warnings—the dumb ones, Amber once again noted—scrambled away from Gene their tails tucked between their legs.

"Keep him at a distance, but kill him!"

Keeping him at a distance proved difficult. The lifestealer, now in Gene's body, charged at the crowd, which split like a flock of sheep in its wake. Each time one split from the group, the lifestealer pursued the straggler. Hands outstretched, it kept trying to close the gap between it and its prey.

Amber remained stationary, following the lifestealer's movements carefully. She looked to Lavario, who was also watching events unfold with a critical eye. She shouted at him, "What happened? It moves a lot faster."

"Its host was living, but it is not at full strength yet. It needs to feed."

The moment he said it, he sprinted off after the thing, holding the dagger in a striking position.

Amber balled up her fists and shouted, "Shit!" But what did she do? Did she stay put where she'd be safe? Nope. She ran after him.

Chapter 55: Alpha Enough

AMBER AND LAVARIO

Amber'd never seen Lavario run before, she assumed it was on a list of things he never did—underlined. His speed surprised her. Struggling to keep pace, Amber trailed after him the best she could while keeping track of the lifestealer at the same time. There was no need toward the end. They were both on its tail.

"Lavario! Do you have a plan?"

"No."

Reassuring. Amber suppressed the urge to dive for his feet to tackle him to the ground. Acting without a plan was outside of his normal methodical approach. For all her wild impulses, Amber didn't like to see him going off half-cocked, not when sloppiness meant death.

There wasn't time for suggestions. Lavario dove at the lifestealer as it grabbed for the werewolf ahead of it. He swung the dagger, lodging the blade inside the skull of the creature. It stopped in its tracks. Thin streams of blood drained from the wound. The unnatural color, coupled with the strange, pungent acidic smell, made Amber gag. Thanks for nothing, heightened senses.

When the creature pulled the dagger from its head, more of the thin, barely red blood poured out. It held the weapon in its hand, turning it over as if cataloging the item for future study.

"Amber," it said. "Touch." And lunged.

Lavario put himself between her and the creature. It hit him with enough force to knock him to the ground and the two of them fell with a thud. Feeling helpless, Amber stood by while the thing used its nails to scratch at Lavario's already battered face.

She had no idea what to do but felt pretty sure gaping at him and shuffling her weight from one foot to the other wasn't helping. The dagger he'd used to stab the lifestealer had gotten thrown off to the side. Amber lunged for it. Experience told her the handle was a slippery devil. She tightened her grip.

"Get away, Amber. Kill me right as Gene vanishes. Take out its host."

Amber, dagger in hand, shook her head. *No, no, no.*

"Yes. Get away."

No, Amber said to herself and waited until she had a clear shot. This time she left out the battle cry when she charged. She did yell, "Stay down!" when she slammed into the lifestealer.

Lavario didn't seem to hear her. He'd gone very quiet, deathly still. His fingers, covered in blood, twitched.

She rammed into lifestealer again, using her shoulder to push it to the ground. With a half growl, half-frustrated yowl, they toppled together, rolling on the slick earth in a tangle of terrified cries and guttural yips.

At least she had gotten the lifestealer away from Lavario. That was the good news. The bad news was that the creature fixated all its energy on her, and her chest tightened under the pressure.

"Amber. Amber." The way the creature said it suggested it only wanted to talk to an old friend. It was like they knew each other. In a strange, horrifying way, Amber guessed they did.

Quick as a blink, it climbed on top of her. Its urine-yellow animal eyes inspected her face with a lover's touch. The intimacy of its gaze disgusted and terrified her, but it also felt exciting in the way all forbidden things did. She was wanted. Desirable.

The creature locked its focus on her and whispered her name. "Amber."

Trying to recover her senses, which got blunted and more sluggish by the second, Amber shook her head and shouted, "Off."

Nearby, Lavario groaned. Amber strained for some sign, any sign, of the creature's voice from him. There was none. She held onto the hope he wasn't infected.

"Amber," the lifestealer said.

The handle of the knife felt warm in her grip. She raised it up and swooped her hand down in a short arc. The blade embedded in the creature's head all the way to the hilt. No more blood came out. The lifestealer stayed suspended above her, mouth hanging open as if in dismay or shock. A drip of spit fell on her cheek.

"Amber."

"Shut up! Stop saying my name!"

"Amber." It pressed its cold lips against her mouth. Her mouth. Her human mouth. Life left her in sips. The creature's eyes changed color slightly, turning mustard yellow. Gulps next. Dazed, Amber tried to quantify how much vitality she had to spare, but there wasn't exactly a meter she could read. She got weaker and weaker. She groaned.

"Amber," it said again.

"Stop saying my name!"

"Amber."

Okay, now she was pissed. Growling in a way that would have put Lavario to shame, Amber pressed her lips right back against the creature's and, well, sucked. The thing jerked backward. The putrid yellow eyes widened. Hissing, it bared its black, slime-coated teeth. Skin along the gumline sloughed away in thin, white ropes. The long claws on the tips of its fingers extended farther, right into the soft flesh of her wrists.

"Amber," the lifestealer snarled.

"Fuck you," she snarled back.

Its mouth descended on hers and bit. Blood filled her mouth. Amber tried to scream and kick, but it was no use. She was losing no matter how hard she fought or how much she wanted to live.

Suddenly, the weight of its body lifted from hers. "Amber," Kijo called to her. "Get up."

Amber tried to roll over and hide instead.

"Get up," Kijo snapped. "I can't hold it forever."

Amber looked up. Kijo held the lifestealer in a firm embrace. The thing struggled and kicked against her. "Whatever you were doing was working. Keep going."

Amber flinched away from the filthy, blood-coated mouth. Visualizing their lips touching again was enough to nauseate her. She shook her head.

"Amber," Kijo snapped. "Get up and get to it."

Kijo really was alpha enough. Normally prone to argument no matter what, Amber hopped to obey. She squeezed her eyes shut, pushed their mouths together, and tried her best to replicate what she'd done before. It wasn't working. She could feel it wasn't.

"Use your instinct. Seek it out in Gene's body. Do not let it hide. Hurry."

Amber shelved her disgust and her thoughts about how the wormy lips beneath hers felt like they might set off a chain reaction of atrophy. It hid from her, bolting away whenever she got close.

"Hurry," Kijo stressed, gritting her teeth.

Then it dawned on Amber where it was; it wanted to jump hosts. She followed it straight to Kijo and vacuumed—a word she decided she liked better than sucking—the thing up, using her mouth. When she felt it slip inside of her, she swallowed. Gene's limbs stopped wiggling. The body slumped in Kijo's grasp. Kijo tossed the used-up shell off to the side.

"What do you feel?"

"Its claws inside me, trying to get out. But I don't think it can."

Kijo's face pinched. It was as close to saying yuck as she'd probably ever get. She put her hand against Amber's breast and said, "What are you?"

"A Moondog. I guess."

"No."

That conversation ended there. She turned her head toward where Lavario lay, still unconscious. Feeling protective, Amber moved to stand between daughter and father. There was an ocean of history between the two, but neither would take up sailing anytime soon.

"He'll be fine," Amber assured her in a very low voice. "I'm going to take care of him."

"Tell him I gave you what you wanted when I made you a Moondog."

Amber couldn't remember. "Is that actually true?"

"Yes."

"Okay, I'll tell him that, then. Anything else?"

"Tell him he can never come back to the Varcolac." She lifted her eyes to Amber's. "But you can."

"But I'm a Moondog," Amber reminded her.

"No," Kijo said again. "You'll go your own path, as you wanted. I wish you a safe journey."

Part Four

Blue Moon

The Isangelous

Chapter 56: Tovin, Vampire Hunter

TOVIN

Fuck pep talks. What good had they done him up until this point?

Tovin washed himself for the hundredth time. Scrubbing the hard-to-reach places with a loofah he'd tied onto a stick. Had he been on speaking terms with Eresna, he would have asked for something a little bit more dignified to clean himself with.

Destiny peeped in on him, her eyes appearing in the billowing steam. *At least stop washing your hands. They're bleeding.*

"How do you know I'm not infected?"

You'd be a vampire by now.

"You're sure?"

Yes. Eresna let you live, didn't she?

"Grudgingly."

You're not a vampire, Tovin. It didn't bite you. None of its saliva got into your system.

Well, she was the expert. Tovin tossed his makeshift-grooming contraption on the shower floor. He half slid, half walked his way to the walk-in closet. Hand extended, fingers twitching midair, he planned his outfit for maximum safety. Destiny indicated bites transmitted the sickness, so he selected every long-sleeved, thick-fabric garment he owned.

You look ridiculous.

Tovin ignored her critique. He felt safer. "Okay, I have to make this work until Garvey comes back for me, and then I'm getting out of here. You said you could find vampires. Can you actually do that?"

Yes. You think Garvey is actually coming back for you?

The way she said it suggested he was a naive fool if he did. Tovin agreed in spirit. Garvey was a lot of things. Above all else, he was an asshole.

Tovin explained this to Destiny, adding, "I think he'd enjoy telling me he wasn't coming back for me. He didn't do that before he left."

What a dreamboat to sail away on.

Unexpectedly, his heart flipped and his mind rushed to make excuses for Garvey's churlish manners. The werewolf's tender lovemaking, gentle and considerate of Tovin's needs, contradicted the seeming lack of civility. Who was Garvey really? Tovin wasn't sure.

Arguing the point would have been foolish, so he shooed the ghost away with his hand and said, "Yeah, I know he's terrible."

She sighed at the lack of certainty. *Company coming.*

For once, Tovin actually appreciated the ghost's early-warning system. Completely flustered, he took a moment to calm down, inwardly chanting that Garvey was indeed coming and getting out of this nightmare was possible.

"Okay," he told himself, "get ready."

Good luck. Destiny didn't sound especially optimistic.

Tovin matched the ghost's lack of enthusiasm. "Thanks."

The loud slap of Nadine's combat boots tipped off the identity of his visitor. Soon after the footsteps stopped, she busted through the door, banging it against the wall.

Tovin plastered a smile on his face. "Hi, Nadine."

Eyebrows drawn down and body taunt, she gave him a stiff nod. Her voice, void of its usual good cheer, drilled right to the point. "Hope you and your ghost pal can kill vampires. Otherwise, this visit will get real awkward real fast."

"Understood."

Nadine's nostril flared as she assessed his clothes. Tovin glanced down at himself as well, feeling pleased with his selection. He thought the black-trench-coat black-sweater combo was practical, considering the bite risk involved. Could he help it if he looked edgy, dangerous, and maybe a tad fantastic?

"It's practical," Tovin assured her.

"You're some black eyeliner away from being on your own."

Tovin gestured to the intricate network of buckles and spikes on her boots. "Tell me those are must-haves for vampire killing."

Some of her humor came back. Her tongue edged out and licked her tooth. "Being fucking awesome is always mandatory. Now let's get going. Kurt and Yuri are waiting. Not patiently, knowing the two of them."

They walked down the hallway to meet up with the rest of the elite vampire-killing squad. Yuri snorted when she saw them. She'd gone with galoshes. A garbage bag with holes cut into it for her arms and head covered the rest of her body.

"This isn't a fashion show, you two. We have a job."

Kurt, who was dressed as he always dressed, wanted a game plan. "Exactly how is this going to work?"

Destiny gave a vague explanation. *I'll know the infected when I see them.*

Tovin, doing his best to sound confident, relayed the information. "Go door-to-door. Let her get a look."

Nadine, satisfied with general directions, plowed forward.

"Whoa, Whoa. Hold up." Kurt grabbed her sleeve. "We can't go to every apartment looking like a death crew. It'll cause a panic. Nerves are already frayed after the lockdown."

Yuri agreed. "Best to make this appear as a friendly visit from Eresna's companion." She lifted the garbage bag over her head. "Tovin, go put on something bright. Nadine, just wait in the hallway. We'll call if we need you."

Nadine stuck her thumb in the air, indicating she understood. "Roger, boss wolf."

Tovin ran back to his room and quickly put together a chipper costume and hoofed it back. Panting, he asked Yuri and Kurt, "This better?"

Kurt straightened Tovin's bowtie.

Yuri smoothed out the wrinkles of his shirt. "There. You'll do. Make sure to smile."

As much as he wanted to appear confident in the whole process for the sake of job security, he couldn't repress the feeling things were ripe for going awry. Tovin managed a shaky grin.

Nadine sighed. "Doubt he'll get more convincing the more we stand here."

Yuri agreed, but she had a bit more advice. "Remember, we're going door-to-door as a courtesy. We want people to feel better, not worse."

"Got it," Tovin responded.

Their first visit of the day was a nervous young woman whose voice had the force of a breeze. "Who is it?" One large, blue eye blinked at them from behind a cracked door.

"It's Tovin," he told her. "Eresna's companion. I wanted to check in and see how you're doing."

Yuri and Kurt both gave him an approving gesture. *Doing great,* Yuri mouthed.

Jesus. He felt like a kid who had to be coached along. When the woman didn't open the door, he continued to soothe her, "I have some good news I'd like to share. Can you open the door?"

Slowly, she obeyed and invited them inside.

Lydia, sweet and good-natured as her name suggested, offered them a seat. While they drank some lemon tea—terrible, watery—she mumbled about how happy she was to finally have some time with Tovin. Never once did she raise her head to look him in the eye. Shy like him, she kept her responses to a minimum.

She's infected, Destiny stated.

"Oh, uh. Thank you for being so kind, Lydia. Your good cheer is *infectious*."

Very subtle, Destiny snarked.

Yuri stood. Her movements were casual as she circled around to the back of the couch. She snapped Lydia's neck in one jerky motion. The woman fell over dead. Her cup clattered to the floor.

Tovin jumped up in his seat. He couldn't believe Yuri could be so cavalier about taking life. The look he gave her must have conveyed his surprise. Though she looked back at him with the same kind expression he'd grown accustomed to, there was a tinge of sadness to it now.

"This is what you signed up to do, Tovin," she told him. "Better she die now than kill others."

True as it was, he still wanted to see some trace of sympathy from his companions—tears, apologies, prayers. They'd taken a life. In the end, Tovin was left alone with the body and the unsettling knowledge of what his role was in this mess.

Kurt said, "I'll take a blood sample back to Eresna to verify the infection. Keep Tovin here until we get results."

Nadine entered the room as Kurt left. She leaned against the door, blocking him from running.

Yuri gave his shoulder an awkward pat that morphed into a gentle shove. Tovin fell back into the dead woman's plush chair and stared at her body. It wasn't going anywhere, nor was he.

Chapter 57: Poor Planning

GARVEY

"I need a plan," Garvey told himself, hoping that might kick-start his brain into the activity. Didn't work. He remained stumped.

Thus far, he had piggybacked on the schemes of others, ruining them when the moment felt right—or amusing. He'd resigned himself to dying a long time ago. His cowardly self welcomed it, courted it even. Failure meant he'd witness the slaughter of his pack. His own demise spared him that, among other things, such as planning.

His outlook had changed.

After the promise he'd made to Tovin, living through the ordeal mattered again. Without Garvey's help, Sweet Treat was most assuredly doomed. At least Garvey couldn't foresee a future where Tovin developed common sense. Hell, he couldn't even imagine an alternate universe where Tovin wouldn't be the first person to abandon in the zombie apocalypse.

"First," he said to himself, "I got to figure an escape route."

Garvey swiveled his head left, then right, No open doors or windows. Goddamn, planning was hard.

Isangelous werewolves scampered here to there, trying their best to bring order from the confusion. Single wolves stopped passersby to ask for reports from the guardians. Soon enough they'd group together and form full-fledged patrol units. Afterward, they'd be sure to ask him what he was doing there, and Garvey didn't have a good answer.

"Hold up," one of them shouted.

Garvey cringed and contemplated running away, but the voice, while stern, didn't sound hostile. At least not yet. "Yes?"

"What word from Eresna?"

"Keep sweeping to identify threats was the last I heard."

"The threat was identified as vampire hours ago."

"That long?" Garvey swallowed the impulse to ask the Boo Hag why they were all still so discombobulated. He supposed finding an enemy you thought long dead might cause a bit of a clusterfuck. Realizing his last response might have been lackluster, considering, Garvey added, "Wow, do those even exist?"

The Boo Hag narrowed his eyes and nodded.

"Welp, my bad. Sweep for vampires, then."

"We don't have the tool yet. We're confirming its use."

"The tool?"

"Guardian Eresna's bloodservant. Hold up here. I'm going to check your clearance."

So Tovin was a vampire hunter now? How quickly things changed in the span of a few hours. Garvey chewed the inside of his cheek, contemplating his situation. Whatever Tovin had gotten himself into, Garvey hoped he could get himself out. Not only was Garvey a reluctant savior, apparently, he was also a bad one.

The Boo Hag came toward him like a sheepdog looking to herd cattle, as Mercy might say. "Eresna wants to see you, False Moon."

"Hard pass," Garvey shouted over his shoulder as he booked it.

He didn't expect to get too far. Honestly, he wasn't quite sure why he ran away other than the aforementioned survival-bent animal inside him put it in the suggestion box and took the wheel.

"Stop him!" the Boo Hag behind shouted.

Elated to be lasting so long against one of the so-called true wolves, Garvey perked up and took the corner wide. His claws left skid-lines in the marble flooring. One of the lower-ranking wolves would have to polish for hours to smooth it out. Hopefully Anton. Garvey hated that dick.

He kept getting away.

Fresh air filled his lungs. Bright light made his pupils dilate. Around him, the wind whipped through his hair, amplifying the smell of his lovemaking. Tovin. Garvey, remembering his promise midflee, slowed his pace.

It's daytime, so technically the moon isn't full... The animal inside him was a lawyer too. Apparently.

"No," he told himself before he listened to it. "Not again."

He spun around to face the oncoming horde. He was sure they'd be right at his heels. Instead, they were off-in-the-distance silhouettes, trying their best to close the gap. Garvey could have gone out in that moment—feeling free and smugly certain he'd surprised them all.

THE BOO HAG who brought him before Eresna pushed him forward. "Hello, hi!" Garvey said to the scowling queen.

"Karma finally caught up to you."

"I thought his name was Bob."

Eresna didn't smile.

Garvey repressed a sigh. Self-described "good" people, or in this case werewolves, invented the concept of karma to explain why bad things happened to those they hated. Garvey didn't believe in a justice system balanced by a sentient universe with an innate sense of right and wrong. He believed in probability. *It's like this*, he remembered explaining to Phil, *you stand in the road, you increase the odds of getting hit. Don't tell me to lead a more vitreous life. Tell me how to get to a sidewalk.*

Dumb luck, random chance, and—of course—opportunity were friends as well as enemies in this system. Problem was, Garvey was fast running out of friends and the sidewalk was nowhere to be seen.

Eresna's fangs were already out. Her golden eyes told the tale of an irate she-wolf. Although she reclined in an overplush chair with stiff wooden arms, her body was taut, ready to spring up and strike at a moment's notice.

"Why are you here, Garvey?"

"Love..." he ventured.

Her eyebrows sloped down. "Try again."

Garvey licked his lips. "That's mostly my reason, Guardian. Yuri said Tovin needed help. I came."

Eresna's nails clicked on the arm of her chair. "Because you love him?"

"Yup."

"And does he feel the same?"

"Nope." Garvey felt a pang in his heart. Both answers were true. Goddammit.

Eresna leaned forward. "Did he ask you to kill Jerald?"

No doubt his scent at the murder scene betrayed him. There was no use lying. "I gave him that for free. Love bonus. He'd probably be horrified if he knew. Lots of moral high-ground things to say about it."

"You killed him. Not a vampire?"

Yikes. He didn't think that one through. Eresna locked her gaze with his, studying each movement he made. "Must have come in after. I didn't know about the vampire."

She leaned back again. "You said Yuri contacted you?"

"Yes."

"What type of trouble did Yuri say Tovin had?"

"Ghost."

"Be more specific. And by 'more specific,' I mean all of it—no quips, no half truths, no double meanings. Go."

Garvey walked Eresna through his entire phone call with Yuri, making sure he included every last detail he could remember. At the start of the story, Eresna's nostrils flared. By the end of it, she was full-on hyperventilating in anger.

Terrified of pushing her over the edge but knowing he had to anyway, Garvey shrank back and concluded, "And so she asked me to swap boxes."

"Where are the death records?"

"No idea."

"You weren't, out of your great love for Tovin, going to swap them?"

"No, I was going to take him with me."

Eresna laughed. Earlier, he'd been surprised when she let the vampire thing drop so easily. Now he understood. The absurdity someone like him—a bastard, a nothing, a False Moon—could pull off something so brash was laughable.

Screw lying, he wanted her to know, "I brought the vampire here. Me, a Moondog. Guess karma caught you too."

After his confession, Garvey expected a tongue-lashing followed by a literal lashing. He doubted he'd make it to trial. He straightened himself, ready to face his end in a dignified fashion.

Her eyes took a sad, unexpected turn. "Oh Garvey. Why?"

"Mazgan asked me to do it. He wants the bloodservant trade. He wants guardians dead."

The fury he expected still didn't come. She didn't even look particularly surprised, only tired. "But why would you do his bidding?"

Time to lie again. "Revenge. Against Lavario."

Eresna sighed and pinched the bridge of her nose. "I know that's not true, Garvey. I already moved your family out of the queue. I did it the moment I saw them come up in the register. You've served my pack well, and I did you that courtesy."

"You...you didn't tell me."

"I was going to the moment it became official. I had to get the approval of the other guardians."

She rose from her seat, dragging yards of purple silk fabric with her as she moved. Even back in his human days, he'd held Eresna in awe. She'd been kind to him, even gentle, after his transformation.

She took his hands in hers. "Your grudge against Lavario can be the stated reason for your transgressions, but I can't promise the Isangelous won't retaliate against your pack."

Garvey backed away from the hand stroking his cheek. He was befuddled. "Why?"

"My reasons are my own."

Garvey accepted it without comment. Really, he didn't care about her motivations, not really. "What about Tovin?"

"I can't help him."

"Can I talk to him?"

She shook her head. "I'll let him know you tried."

"No," Garvey said. "Don't say that. Tell him the moon is full."

Chapter 58: Sixth Sense

TOVIN

The ghost vanished, leaving Tovin behind to wonder if she'd duped them or if she really could detect vampires. Nadine focused on her phone. Yuri evaluated her manicure. Neither met his eye. This gave Tovin a good idea about what they thought of his odds.

"Not good." Nadine's comment, which addressed Tovin's thoughts exactly, made him spasm in his seat. "Sorry," Nadine apologized, holding her hands straight up in the air as if anticipating arrest. "I didn't mean to startle you. Just lost a bet to Garvey. Don't go track-star mode on me."

Did Garvey take odds on whether or not Tovin would fall into bed with him at the promise of safety? Was he the bet?

Panic wasn't quite scrubbed from his voice when he asked, "Oh. Oh. Is he...is he talking to you now?"

"Nah. But he'll rub it in later."

Probably. Garvey did seem to be the type who couldn't pass up a boast. "What...what was the bet?"

"Hookup on a television show. I said never, but Betty doesn't love herself. Also, we all know Garvey nailed you last night." She tapped her nose. "But, no, he didn't take odds on it. He does have limits. Sort of."

"Oh. Right. Good. Good about the limits."

Nadine chuckled and licked her tooth.

Yuri's mouth puckered. The chilly, critical glare he got from her said he needed to play things closer to his chest. His apologetic shrug didn't quench her ire, so Tovin decided his lap was super interesting and put his mind to studying it in detail.

Things between them stayed awkward until the door behind Nadine rattled, popping open a crack. She gave it a hard kick shut. "Who is it?"

"Kurt."

Nadine opened the door for him and waved him inside. "So...how did our boy do?"

"She had the infection." Kurt delivered the news in an unimpressed monotone. He shot Yuri a quick side-eye.

The ghost reappeared. Feeling vindicated by the positive news, Tovin abandoned subtly and spoke to Destiny in a normal voice, "Where did you go?"

To eavesdrop. They have Garvey. Yuri is in trouble, Tovin. Eresna knows she withheld information.

"What?"

Tell Yuri to run. Tell her now.

Tovin obeyed the urgency in her voice. "Yuri! Get out of here!"

He didn't have to say why. Normally eerily calm, Yuri's demeanor did a one-eighty. She popped up and hightailed it so fast Tovin's expression did a graduated three-sixty. That is, he went from looking shocked and stupefied to looking slightly more of both those things.

Kurt and Nadine stood perfectly still, probably wondering what the hell to do. Eventually, Kurt came to his senses and gave the dazed Nadine orders. "Take Tovin to find the rest of the infected. Eresna said to call in a search if Yuri ran." Kurt's tone became somewhat apologetic when he said, "You're to keep away."

Nadine's pale face turned red. Tovin couldn't tell if she was embarrassed or furious.

"I'm just the messenger, Nadine."

Her nostrils flared. "Come on, Tovin. Let's get this over with."

NADINE DRAGGED TOVIN along, pulling his arm whenever he lagged behind, which was pretty much constantly. "Come on," she tugged him forward. "Hurry it up."

"Where are we going now?"

The fury in her eyes and the way her reddened cheeks swelled with each new breath was response enough to stop any further questions.

"Okay, okay. I'll walk faster."

Tovin didn't take her mood personally. Nadine and Yuri were good friends, and Nadine—more sensitive than she let on—must have been heartsick and worried. Signs of her grief, a quivering lip and watery eyes, became more visible the longer the silence continued.

Voice thick with unshed tears, Nadine told Tovin, "We're in a mess here, kiddo."

She's right. You need to get away. Eresna's going to kill you as soon as you weed out the infected.

He must have given some indication the ghost spoke. Nadine smiled and asked, "What's Casper got to say?"

"Uh. Oh. She says I'm fucked. Pretty much."

"Observant ghost."

One of us has to be.

"What did she say there?"

Tovin repeated Destiny's slight.

Nadine barked a slight laugh, but her same raw, expansive humor wasn't there. Sadness clipped it short. "I like this ghost. She and I should hang out."

Tovin quirked his lip. "You two would get along very well."

"No doubt," Nadine agreed.

Once they were downstairs in the living quarters of the scrogglings, bloodservants of low-ranking wolves, the conversation turned to the business at hand. They were still on lockdown, so they went door-to-door. Nadine, who was blunt on her best days, was apparently on level fuck-it in whatever game they were playing.

"This one infected?" she'd ask Tovin. If yes, she'd gesture for them to go back inside their room. If no, she'd say, "Good, less work for me."

"Do you think you should use a word other than 'infected'?" Tovin asked her between rooms.

"Like?"

"Oh. Um. I dunno. Compromised maybe?"

"Sure, why not."

For the most part, she stuck by the agreed terminology. It's just the way she said it made using euphemisms nonsensical. Expressions on the faces of those they visited went from curious to petrified. So much distress nauseated Tovin. Nadine's indifference infuriated him.

"Do you have to take such delight in this?"

"Delight? Roundin' up the lambs for the slaughter has to fall on someone's shoulders. Did it ever occur to you that I'm tired of doing the job? That it sucks being the go-to when it comes to killing?"

"Ask for a different job," Tovin suggested, his voice tilting up toward the end like he was asking a question.

"Yeah, I'll do that. Let's keep going. Need this done tonight."

The upper floors went roughly the same way—Tovin identifying the infected, Nadine keeping an internal list of the names. Hours later, they were on the final leg of the excursion.

You need to make a run for it, Destiny reminded him. *Once they don't need you, they'll bleed you.*

"Did your ghost friend tell you to flee? I wouldn't listen."

Tovin stumbled a bit, getting his legs twisted on themselves like the clumsy idiot he was. "Do I have a tell?"

Nadine licked her tooth. "Several. Plus, I'm an animal. Sixth sense, you know."

"Nadine…" Tovin drifted off, realizing what he was about to ask her.

Nadine's wolf senses, or whatever the hell she wanted to call it, were on point. Or maybe she was just a good guesser. Either way, she addressed his thoughts exactly. "I can't let you escape, Tovin. What am I going to tell Eresna? That you overpowered me? That you outran me? That you outsmarted me?"

Tovin's ego smarted a bit. "The last could be true."

"If it were a school quiz, sure. But knowing the circumference of the earth isn't going to take you 'round the world, kiddo."

Tovin frowned at her candor.

"Look, I'm not saying the information isn't useful at all. But it's not for this situation."

"Right…" Tovin went back to his current dilemma. "So…send me on an errand. Tell Eresna you didn't know her plans."

"So…play dumb?"

"Pretty much."

"That's really dumb, Tovin. *Unbelievably* dumb."

"Last I checked, she didn't think too much of your intelligence. Isn't that why you're running around doing grunt work?"

"Ouch, kiddo."

Nadine tapped her foot while Tovin waited around for her decision. Destiny occasionally reminded him of his predicament. Tovin wasn't sure why. Not like he had anything else on his mind. He'd try to give Nadine the slip only after she told him there were no other options. He wasn't at all optimistic such a strategy would work out for him.

After thinking it over awhile, Nadine surprised him by saying, "Okay, I'm going to do this. One condition."

"Name it."

"Do you like cats?"

Chapter 59: The Unintentionally Helpful Mr. Fluffbutt

TOVIN

Guilt slowed his pace to a crawl. Last thing Nadine said to him was that she knew this ended badly for her. She didn't care anymore. Yuri was her friend, and Nadine wouldn't forget it. *She knew what she was doing,* Tovin told himself, trying to shake the feeling he'd somehow betrayed Nadine.

Okay, the last thing Nadine actually said was, "Ghost is in charge. Do what she says." Trouble was, Destiny didn't want him to keep his promise.

Stop worrying. Turn around. Get out of here.

Tovin argued with the ghost. "I told Nadine I'd get Yuri and her cat. I gave her my word."

Break it.

"No."

Look at it this way; she put an entity she wasn't even sure existed in charge of you. Her expectations aren't high.

Ouch. But true. "I promised. I have to at least try."

You really don't. It's a cat.

The way the ghost said cat, an utterance full of disbelief, doubt, and underlying horror, was the same way people said ghost. Ancient mythology said the animal traveled the realms of life and death. Some legends said they even saw spirits. Knowing cats, they didn't *help* the dead. None of the lore pegged them as good Samaritans.

"You know," he told Destiny, "the Chinese believed cats scared away evil spirits. Worried the kitty will banish you?"

They also believed you could tell the time of day by looking into their eyes. When you look into Fluffbutt's, you'll know it's time to die.

The sting was somewhat lessened by the cat's name, but Tovin took her point. He wasn't the type to have instantaneous witty replies on hand. He'd think of a zinger later, assuming he wasn't dead as Destiny predicted, which he probably would be. Why was he doing this again? Oh right... guilt. Tovin owed Yuri. Big-time.

Destiny stopped. *This is her apartment. Open it up.*

Fastidious almost to a fault, Yuri had labeled and color-coded each key, so it was easy enough to tell which one fit the lock. Tovin appreciated her thorough nature more than ever before. Otherwise, he would have fumbled around forever. Even now, his hand shook as he put the key into the lock. It jumped up and down, scratching the door. He had to stop and take a few deep breaths before he was finally able to stick it in and twist.

It's some type of heavy-handed metaphor for your sex life.

"I hate you so much."

Ditto.

"Updating your vernacular. Good for you."

Tovin pushed the door open and walked inside. Lavender and a pleasant citrus scent wafted to his nostrils. He swatted his hand against the wall and dragged his fingers along the smooth surface, searching for the switch. Once he'd found it, he flipped it up and breathed a sigh of relief when the lights turned on and there was no creepy shit, only an immaculately cleaned, homey apartment.

Well, nothing creepy except for Mr. Fluffbutt, who sat on the kitchen counter grooming one paw. His long, black coat gleamed as if it had been polished. When he saw Tovin, he blinked his green eyes and said, "Yow."

"Hey there, handsome fella. My name is Tovin. Your mommy sent me."

"Yow."

"Yes. Yow to you too. She said you're due for your snackum. You want a snackum?"

"Yow."

Careful not to startle the cat, which Yuri had described as persnickety, Tovin tiptoed over to the sink and opened the cabinet very, very slowly. The turkey n' tuna treats were up front. Tovin grabbed hold of the bag and pulled out a few foul-smelling kibbles in the shapes of fish.

"Whew!" he said, waving his hand in front of his nose.

The cat jumped down from his perch. Mewing, he bumped his head against Tovin's leg and purred. Tovin ran his hand along the cat's silky back. Mr. Fluffbutt arched his spine under the petting. The mews came louder and faster the longer Tovin held onto the treats. Rubbing and clicking his strange purr, he bopped his head against Tovin's closed fist, his knee, his thigh.

"Friendly little guy. I thought this would be a lot worse. Here you go. Here's your snackum."

Tovin dropped the treat.

"Yow!" Mr. Fluffbutt picked up the tidbit and hightailed it under the chifferobe.

"Shit!" Tovin crawled after him.

Okay, we tried.

Tovin ignored Destiny and tried to appeal to the cat. "Psst! Here, kitty kitty. Nice kitty kitty. Come on."

"Yow."

"That's right. Yow. We're friends. Now come on." Tovin beckoned the cat to him by fanning his hands toward his chest. "Nice kitty kitty. Come on. Your mommy sent me. I have another snackum for you."

The damn beast blinked his big green eyes, stood up, turned around, then flopped back down on the floor. "Yow."

You're a real natural with animals, Destiny said.

"I'm doing the best I can. It's a mother-fucking cat."

"Yow!"

"I said what I said!" Tovin whisper-shouted back at Mr. Fluffbutt. The creature flicked his tail.

Hurry this along. They're searching for you.

"Grrraaa!" Tovin bellowed and then tried to reason with the cat. "If you don't come with me, you'll be skinned. You're with werewolves. There can't be many who like cats."

Mr. Fluffbutt was not open to hearing arguments. The thing lay there and acted as though Tovin were some annoying dinner guest who wouldn't take the hint and leave. Pointedly, he cleaned a paw. His fuzzy black tail swished.

Tovin tried again. "I'm here to save you!"

Voices outside startled Tovin. He jumped and knocked over a bowl on the counter, which clattered on the floor. The spoon slid somewhere under the table. The cat finally came out of its hiding place to chase after it. *Fucking cats.*

The voices stalled outside the door. "In there. I heard something."

"Yur, that you?"

"She's in custody."

"I keep forgetting. Things feel so wrong."

The other werewolf agreed, actually sounding shocked. "You think he's dumb enough to hide out at her place?"

Destiny gave him a dark look. Tovin didn't have time to snark back or reflect on his poor decision-making skills. Catlike himself, he crawled underneath the bed and pulled the skirt down for additional cover.

Good thinking, Destiny told him. *No one ever checks under the bed.*

The doorknob twisted. Footsteps echoed on the floorboards. True to Destiny's prediction, they headed straight for the bedroom and would no doubt check under the bed first thing.

Get ready to run.

Tovin got readyish.

Suddenly, the footsteps stopped. "Hear that?"

"Yeah. Kitchen."

Tovin risked lifting the bed skirt to watch their progress, hoping for some type of miracle. What he got was Mr. Fluffbutt swiping the spoon, batting it from one end of the room to the next. Bounding and pouncing, he attacked like he thought he was an apex predator tackling a water buffalo. At the end of the display, he pulled it against his stomach and kicked his back legs.

"It's her stupid cat," one of the werewolves said.

"What do we do with it?" the other asked.

Tovin could hear the shrug in the man's voice when he said, "Leave it."

They walked out. The door clicked.

Coast is clear.

Tovin squirmed out from under the bed but kept his body low and took his time sneaking up on Mr. Fluffbutt, who continued to swat the utensil and growl. Right before the cat caught onto the ruse, Tovin flopped down on top of him. Surprisingly, he didn't squeal or hiss.

"Yow, yow, yow!" Mr. Fluffbutt protested, then went protester limp.

"Thanks for helping me. Good job, Mr. Fluffbutt. You're such a good boy."

I'm pretty sure the cat didn't mean to be helpful.

"Of course not. It's a cat."

Chapter 60: Deathmates

GARVEY

Side by side, their cells offered a good view of the other's suffering. Feeling regretful, Garvey noted how Yuri wasn't even trying to clean her tarnished silk dress. Filthy, she hunkered on the floor and waited to die with her legs sprawled out in an undignified fashion. Garvey sat so his back touched hers through the bars.

When she didn't pull away, he offered her an explanation. "My pack is going to be culled."

She snorted. "False Moons."

"To you. To me, they're my brothers and sisters. Family."

She heaved out a great sigh and halfheartedly kicked at a rat sniffing around her foot. After a prolonged period of quiet, Garvey prepared himself for an uncomfortable wait. But she spoke again, revealing she'd been deliberating rather than ignoring.

"You love them. I can understand why you felt you needed to do what you did."

Her admission touched him. "I always liked you the best."

"Not Nadine?"

"Love her free spirit. But no. You were the only one who ever saw me as a threat. Hell, you actually tried to thwart me occasionally. Best compliment a Moondog ever got from a Boo Hag."

He could hear the smile in her voice as she said, "Lavario wouldn't fall so hard for someone dumb."

"Bet he'll be mad when he hears about this."

"Livid."

"You could say that with less pleasure."

Her laughter sounded more hysterical than amused. It broke off toward the end to a choked cry she'd probably been holding in since the day she was born. Out of respect, he acted as though he'd only heard mirth.

Garvey tried to cheer her up. "Guess you can hope they'll kill me first and let you watch."

"That would be a treat."

"They might even allow a kick or two."

"Don't be a tease. Garvey..." She paused long afterward, probably organizing her thoughts. Finally, she pushed out what she wanted to say. "Do you love Tovin?"

Uncomfortable with the personal question, he toyed with a sarcastic response. Typically, Moondogs didn't share feelings with Boo Hags. In this moment, he wanted to believe they were deathmates if not packmates. "I think so, yes. It's hard to tell. I want to protect him, and I want to be near him."

"He's so *moral.*" *You're not* was heavily implied.

"Tell me about it. If he'd been any less adorable that night in the woods, I might have eaten him."

"You constantly put him in danger."

"Yes. I know. Family first. I owe them that much."

Although it wasn't intended as a slight, Yuri moved uncomfortably. Acutely aware, no doubt, that she'd put Tovin above her pack.

She pushed forward in the conversation, sounding irked. "When I told you about the ghost, you said it might be something different. What else would it be?"

"A lifestealer."

He waited for her to gasp. Younger than him, she was still by no means a pup and should have at least heard stories. But she said nothing, did nothing.

"They're said to be the souls of vampires."

"Fairy tales."

"Maybe. Maybe not."

He was about to launch into a long explanation, but it was cut short.

Holding a black cat, Tovin materialized as if by magic, an illusion that was immediately dispelled as he struggled to close the hidden door in the wall.

Despite the sloppy showmanship, Garvey still couldn't believe what he saw. "Tovin?"

"Oh!" Surprised, he dropped the cat, which must have felt like a trap door opened beneath its feet. "Sorry," he said to the creature. Unforgiving, it hissed and turned its back. Tovin tossed his hands up in the air, apparently done with the aggravating thing.

"Mr. Fluffbutt!" Yuri stuck her hands between the bars and wiggled her fingers until the cat strolled toward her as if there were no cares in the world.

"Seriously? That's your cat's name?"

Yuri didn't answer the question. She was too busy putting a *w* in front of non-*w* words like an insane person. Garvey couldn't believe he'd spent so much of his time fearing a werewolf who baby-talked to an animal so low on the food chain.

"This is humbling right here. Digging deep."

"Be quiet," Yuri advised him. "Or I'll strangle you through the bars. Yes, I will, won't I, mommy's wittle wuv wuffin?"

"Yow." The cat flicked its tail.

Garvey couldn't think of anything else to say except, "Jesus."

Tovin cleared his throat.

"No one forgot about you, sweet treat. What are you doing here?"

"Rescuing you guys."

Garvey pointed to his surroundings, namely the bars. *Get to the part where we're free*, was the general message he wanted to convey. Tovin made a face at the impatience. Soon to be executed or not, he was going to keep his own schedule.

"I have the keys. Hold on." Both Yuri and Garvey rushed toward the cell doors as he fumbled to disentangle them from his jean pocket.

Like a typical Boo Hag, Yuri wanted to know "How did you get those?"

Answering questions and opening doors couldn't be simultaneous actions from the looks of it. Tovin paused, leaving the key suspended midair, right next to the lock. "Nad—"

"Who cares where he got them? Important thing is we're getting out of here." Garvey pushed himself all the way against the bars and tried to swipe the keys out of Tovin's hands, anything to get him to hurry.

Tovin took a step back and said, "Nadine gave them to me."

Yuri cringed. Hesitant, obviously pained, she slunk back into her cell. "I can't go with you."

Garvey responded, "Why not exactly?"

Tovin's protest was more emphatic. "You have to."

"Nadine will suffer. Eresna will know."

"She'll know anyway, Yuri."

"I'll be here to take the blame. She's my family, Garvey."

Garvey doubted Eresna would buy into it. More likely they'd die together. No use telling Yuri that. He'd known her long enough to recognize the tilt of her chin, the stubborn roll of her shoulders. *Mind made up*, it said. Trying to reason with her would only cost time, getting them all killed.

He tried. "You're sure?"

"Yes."

"Alright. But...before I go..." Garvey pulled a handkerchief out of his pocket and spit on it. Permission wasn't something he thought he'd get, so he sprang forward and cleaned the smudges off Yuri's face. To his surprise, she didn't pull away when she figured out what he was doing. She stood there with her eyes closed.

"That's better," he said.

"Yes," she agreed and used her fingers to smooth her wrinkled dress. Next, she smoothed her hair into a dignified bob. She pulled her cell door shut. *Click* reverberated throughout Garvey's chest cavity. He felt it down to his bones.

He stuck his arm through the bars, resting his hand on Yuri's shoulder. "You might have been one tiny cog in their great big deception machine, but the whole system came crashing down without you. Remember that."

Tovin stuck with a simple, tearful "Goodbye."

Yuri smiled at them both. "Take care of Tovin, Garvey."

"I'll do my best," he promised her. And meant it.

YURI CALLED TOVIN back. Keys in hand, he rushed back to her cellblock, no doubt eager to add her name to the list of lives he saved.

But she hadn't changed her mind. "Take Mr. Fluffbutt."

Garvey closed his eyes and begged the universe, "No, no, no, no. Please."

Garvey heard tears in Tovin's voice. "Okay." Afterward, the irate yowl of the cat.

Quietly as he could, Garvey cursed his luck. Suddenly, it felt very much like he was in the middle of the road and standing there with him was the world's least competent escape partner and a fucking cat.

Chapter 61: Blocked

GARVEY AND TOVIN

Cat in hand, Tovin fumbled in the darkness, running his hands along the stone walls of the secret passage to guide his way. And by 'secret,' Garvey meant hidden from humans. Werewolves, who constructed it long ago, knew its twists and turns. He and Sweet Treat needed to hurry if they intended to remain hidden for long.

Garvey suppressed a sigh and reminded Tovin, "You know I can see in the dark? Want me to lead?"

"No, no. Hold onto Mr. Fluffbutt."

The cat wasn't popular.

While the damn thing didn't move much, it continually growled. Garvey held the creature under its armpits and as far away from his own body as he could manage. The arrangement worked fine for them both until Garvey had to suddenly stop to avoid ramming into the back of Tovin. This occurred often. Tovin got disoriented and walked back Garvey's direction, sticking his hands out in front of him like the mummy returns.

"You know where you're going right?"

"Nadine said the passage is to transport... uh..."

"Problem humans without the knowledge of the other ones. Yeah, I know."

Tovin's voice stumbled as much as his steps. Perhaps he was wondering how many problem humans Garvey had led through this passage. "Well, I, uh, I uh... Nadine said there were several ways out. Destiny, the ghost, was on the path to one, but..."

"But?"

"But she left."

Garvey wanted to address the ghost issue head-on, but he didn't have time for side quests. "You know I can lead and hold onto the damn cat, right?"

"Oh, of course." Tovin said it like a scholar.

"Um-hm. Grab the waist of my trousers. Really dig in there, get a good hold."

"Can't I grab your shoulder?"

"No, I might lose you if we need to run," Garvey said.

Tovin fell for it. Garvey suppressed the satisfied rumble in his chest when Sweet Treat's fingers grazed the arch of his spine. The hand rested near enough to the butt to remind Garvey he had hanky-panky to live for if nothing else. He couldn't help himself. He was an instinctual creature with base motivations.

"Squeeze a little tighter, sweet treat."

Tovin did as he was told.

Hello hi, Garvey said to himself. Out loud, he said, "Yeah, that's the ticket."

"Yow," Mr. Fluffbutt objected.

"Yowza," Garvey said back to the cat.

Garvey focused on the path ahead, not only the route of the tunnels but also life beyond the walls of the Isangelous compound. A fresh start with Tovin, whose scent permeated the narrow halls of the tunnels, waited for him. All he needed to do was convince Tovin of that. Well, first, he needed to get them out alive.

Sweet Treat's hand bumped against the skin right next to Garvey's butt. "Mmmm..." Garvey couldn't fight back the noise.

"What?"

"Mmm, we need to turn here."

"Oh." Unable to see in the pitch black, Tovin turned and hit a wall.

"Guess I was wrong. Keep walking."

Behind them, or was it ahead of them, voices echoed. The Boo Hags divvied up assignments.

Keeping his voice low, Garvey said, "Pick up the pace. Walk as fast as you can without running. They're on our trail."

Even Mr. Fluffbutt seemed to catch onto the mood. The cat kept quiet and did very little except swish his tail a few times. The growls tapered off to a series of clicks, a noise that fell somewhere between a purr and a ticking time bomb.

Garvey pushed the cat against Tovin's chest. "Sorry, I'll need my hands free to fight if it comes to that."

Scowling, Tovin tossed the cat over his shoulder and held onto it with one hand. Purring, it licked his neck and dug its claws into the fabric of his shirt. Tovin responded by raising one lip in a disgusted grimace. Maybe the cat wasn't so bad. Garvey could at least relate to the thing's one-sided romance with Tovin.

"Hold tight," Garvey said.

Garvey moved as fast as he dared with Tovin trailing behind him. Fleeing effectively—not tripping, not sliding, not getting turned around, not panicking—wasn't a skill Tovin possessed. Garvey compensated for the deficit by becoming hyperaware of the noises that proceeded clumsy moments. *Ahh, eesh*, and most importantly *oh*: whenever he heard one of those, he got ready to pry his bumbling lover, and the long-suffering cat, off the ground.

Garvey stopped in his tracks.

Tovin's voice shook. "What's wrong?"

"Path is blocked."

"Can we dig out?"

"Not that kind of blocked."

Garvey tried to not to drag Tovin, but it was difficult. They needed to move faster than they were. Behind them, wolves of the Isangelous barricaded one of the few exits Garvey knew about. Being able to hear and smell them meant they most likely could also detect Garvey and Tovin. Sure enough, footsteps followed.

Voices shouted, "This way! They're over here!"

Tovin's sucked in air so loud Garvey mistook it for the cat hissing. He clutched Garvey's waistband. This time, the touch didn't titillate.

"Get ready to run without me. Straight ahead. I can only buy you a bit of time."

"Garvey..."

The way Tovin said his name—wistful, with a hint of romance—buoyed the hope inside Garvey's cynical waters. Too bad it took throwing himself in front of death to ignite Sweet Treat's lusts. Quickly, he took advantage of the moment and brushed his lips up against Tovin's, loving the way they parted under his without hesitation. For once.

He rested his temple against Tovin's. His skin felt warm, smooth. Garvey rubbed against it and whispered in Tovin's ear, "Run."

Chapter 62: Ghost of a Chance

TOVIN AND GARVEY

Garvey had an image of Sweet Treat bumping into wall after wall like some sort of drunken Pac-Man.

Exactly what did he think his romantic gesture would accomplish? Nothing. Well, he'd get to die fighting heroically rather than scampering away with his tail between his legs. He wanted to believe he had given Tovin some small fraction of a chance, even if the odds were astronomically against him.

"This way!" Boo Hag voices carried in the tunnels, drawing nearer and nearer.

Garvey went the opposite direction, leading them away from Tovin. So far it seemed to be working. Both of the Boo Hags he'd smelled earlier stayed on his trail and left Tovin alone.

"He went this way."

They were very near. Hands pressed to his temple, Garvey squatted in the hallway to wait.

A woman materialized. Dust in the air, swirling in small eddies, blurred her features. In the dim light, and even with his heightened vision, Garvey could only make out a silhouette. As the image moved, it fragmented, breaking into bits like a shattered mirror. A familiar smell—older, stale— filled his nostrils. The ghost.

Come with me, she said.

Garvey cataloged the chill that ran down his spine into a folder that said, *Later concerns*. Immediate worries, such as being dismembered by irate Boo Hags, pressed far more heavily on Garvey's mind. That and one more thing.

"What about Tovin?"

Come with me, she repeated. *I'll take you to him. He refused to leave without you.*

He slowed the churning in his stomach and came as beckoned.

The nauseous feeling persisted. It wasn't too long before Garvey recognized where they were heading. Back up top. Back inside the main building of the compound. He sucked in air to speak, but the ghost cut him off.

Keep silent. Keep following.

Garvey swallowed his objections. Keeping track of the ghost was difficult. She tended to fade in and out of view, blending into the scenery for long periods only to materialize again nowhere near where he'd last seen her.

Over here. She called to him after he'd taken another wrong turn. *Keep a light step.*

It wasn't until he finally realized where they were heading that he appreciated the simplicity her plan. Jerald's room. The scene of the crime, right where Garvey's scent was the strongest. Problem was, he was actually mad enough to come back there.

When Garvey pushed open the hidden door inside Jerald's room, Tovin rushed forward. His blanched face appeared almost as translucent as the ghost's. The blood from Jerald's murder splattered across the room. There was a big pool of it in the middle. Tovin's eyes were almost as large.

He mouthed, *Did you do this?*

Garvey mouthed back, *Yes. You sent the ghost after me?*

Tovin put his hand on his hips. *Well, would you rather I came?*

Garvey conceded. *Point made.* To the ghost, he mouthed, *The plan?*

You can talk, she said. *Safe for now.*

"What's the plan?" he repeated in the lowest tone he could manage.

The ghost said, *I suggest fleeing.*

Tovin was a bit more creative. "We can tie the bedsheets together and climb down the walls or—"

Garvey interrupted Tovin's list of wild ideas. "Well, you know what they say, where there's a will, there's a dead human who tried too hard."

The ghost chuckled. It sounded like wind through metal pipes, a low, mournful thing Garvey interpreted it as a laugh only to avoid speculating on what else it might be. Instinct demanded he listen. This ghost of Tovin's was—at best—a situational friend.

"What's your plan, then?" Tovin's question snapped him back to current problems.

"You can see who's coming?"

The ghost indicated she could.

"Well, is there anyone coming?"

She indicated there wasn't. *Not at the moment, anyway.*

"I hate to be anticlimactic, but let's make a run for it. My old scent might trip them up for a bit, but they'll catch on soon enough."

Tovin tossed his hands up in the air. "That's not a plan."

"Okay, go tie those two sheets together." Garvey waited for him to do as told. "Good. Give me one end and hold onto the other."

"Right. What's next?"

"Hold onto it really tight in case I have to run fast. I'll drag you along the best I can."

Tovin grumbled and threw his end of the sheet to the ground.

"OW! OW! OW!" Tovin stubbed his toe on a boulder and hopped a few yards.

Garvey reminded himself Tovin wouldn't leave without him. Various other romantic notions circulated in Garvey's mind. That dulled the aching predator urge to pounce and rend whenever Tovin stumbled. Tough slog, but Garvey managed.

"Over here!"

Garvey's ears perked up. Boo Hags, a few for now but the numbers would grow as the alert spread, burst into the clearing behind them. There was no way Tovin, or any human for that matter, could outpace werewolves loping at full speed.

"Here! Here!"

The voices became a pack. The pack howled.

Tovin's eyes were green lights. *Go, go, go.*

"Without you?"

"What?" Tovin screamed back.

"Never mind!" Fighting one's nature was a real drag. Garvey stopped long enough to sweep Tovin up in his arms. The weight of his body in his arms felt like an anchor. Not in the sense it grounded him or chained his heart in Tovin's harbor. More in the sense he ran slower—a lot slower. *The moon is full. The moon is full. The moon is full.* Garvey chanted it to himself as he hobbled along.

Snarls, closer than ever before and sharper than teeth, nipped at their heels.

Garvey huffed in Tovin's ear. "Okay, we're probably going to die. You should know I care about you. A lot." Breath, quickly expelled, tickled the back of Garvey's neck. It wasn't accompanied by words, but Tovin's arms tightened. Garvey continued. "I'm sorry for the horrible first date. If we live, I'll take you on another."

"Another horrible date?" Tovin hissed in his ear. Or was that the cat?

"No, not on another horrible date. A better one."

"Low bar." Tovin clutched Garvey's shoulder. "Run faster. They're gaining."

Garvey closed his eyes and imagined the future where he and Tovin went on only semidisastrous dates. At the end of the night, there'd be another hunt. Tovin would run—well, jog—through the forest, Garvey close at his heels. After Garvey caught him, they'd go at it all night.

"What's that?"

Garvey whipped his head the direction Tovin pointed.

Headlights cut holes in the darkness, and all Garvey could think was, *Holy shit, a miracle.* Visitors to the remote forest road were rare but not unheard of. Most of the time, they passed without ever giving the compound a second glance. Magic negated its interest but couldn't quash its existence.

The Boo Hags didn't quite know what to do. Naked, they lingered at the edge of the forest, out of sight of the unknown motorist. Humans—Garvey smelled them. But something else. Hairspray. Lots of it. Mercy. He suppressed a grin.

"Hello!" One of the humans, a leggy blonde wearing high heels, stepped from the vehicle. She was on her phone. "We're lost. Can you tell us where we are?"

The Boo Hags withdrew farther into the tree line. Technology made life a bitch. A couple of snapshots of something unexplainable and a few deaths later, they'd be front-page news. The area would be swept. Everything might compromised.

"Yes," Garvey shouted back. He wanted to hammer in the point. "I know exactly where you are."

The leggy blonde clasped her hands together in a thank-you prayer. "Why don't you hop on in? It's freezing out here! We can share the Uber."

"Sounds great!"

Garvey hopped in the front seat. Tovin slid in back and ended up sandwiched between the two women, who immediately got the wrong idea and began combing their fingers through his hair. After Tovin's poor reaction, they pawed at the cat instead, who growled low in his chest.

Mercy introduced them. "This is Alex and this is her friend... Shoot...it'll come to me, I can feel it."

"Nancy," a bubbly girl supplied.

"Of course. Nancy." Mercy gave Garvey a level glare that meant, *Do not eat them*. She said, "Alex owed me a favor and agreed to a ladies campout. No questions asked."

Alex splayed her nails. "The favor is paid in full, doll."

Mercy grinned in agreement but changed the topic with a flip of her wrist and a fluff of her hair. "Who's this young fella?"

"Mercy, this is Tovin. Tovin, Mercy."

Tovin waved. "Hi. Should we be driving?"

"Yes." Garvey emphasized it even further by slapping the dashboard.

Mercy started up the car but eyeballed Tovin in the rearview mirror instead of watching the road. "Well, I'll be. You're as cute as a june bug."

"June bugs are horrible pests. They eat roots."

Mercy risked a quick glance Garvey's direction. He gave her an apologetic grimace and inwardly begged her not to make an issue out of Sweet Treat's stress-induced trivia spew.

She gave her head a small shake. "Well, ain't you as fast as a herd of turtles."

Tovin blushed.

Garvey gave his wife a peck on the cheek. "How did you know we were here?"

"We've been out here for a spell. When I smelled you, I flipped on the lights."

"That's why I love you."

Mercy straightened the mirror and gave Tovin's reflection a cheeky wink. "Hear that, turtle dove?"

"I'm right here," Tovin responded. "Of course I heard it."

Mercy flicked her nails together. "Well, I'm going to assume he's got him a nice, big dick, then."

Garvey didn't want to justify his relationship decisions, so he gave her a big grin, a shrug, and an approximate penis size by spreading his hands apart.

Playfully, Mercy slapped his thigh. "You dog, you."

The farther they got from the compound, the safer Garvey allowed himself to feel. Under normal circumstances, Eresna would chase him to hell and back, but—with any luck—she'd be busy dealing with a war on another front. Either way, that was tomorrow, and that was as far as Garvey planned.

Oh yeah. That reminded him. "What the hell happened to Molly?"

Mercy shrugged. "I left her at home."

Tovin twisted his head left to right, considering his company. "Should you have...left her alone?"

Mercy shrugged. "Beats the devil out of me."

Chapter 63: Blue Moon

YURI AND NADINE

Yuri's hair fell in a perfect straight line that ended at the stubborn tilt of her chin. Last meals mattered little to her. She'd asked for a comb, a clean dress, and a single minute with Nadine. Appearing her best was the only way she could stay calm through what she needed to say.

"Don't blame Tovin or Garvey. I told them to leave without me."

Nadine's mouth tightened. "Is that what you wanted to tell me?"

"No."

Nadine's chin trembled. The combat boots stomp-stomp-stomped. "Get on with the reason, then."

The attempts at disinterest and hostility didn't fool Yuri. Nadine needed to salt her heart and wrap it in a shroud to halt the decay. Later, in private, she'd weep and probably crush the fragile memories dwelling in Yuri's apartment. A cleansing. Like fire wearing thick-soled shoes.

"I want you to keep the Swarovski crystal hedgehog at least. I bought it because it reminded me of you."

Nadine lifted her hands and slapped them against her thighs. Her eyebrows rose along with the angry red in her cheeks. "That's what you came here for?"

"No."

"Tell me!"

The boom didn't startle Yuri. Her heartbeat was calm, her voice level when she said, "I came here to say what we never talked about. I know how you feel. I would have given almost anything to make that real between us. Your heart is a special one to give, and I treasured it in my lifetime. Find someone else who deserves it."

And the minute was up.

EXECUTIONS OCCURRED ONCE in a blue moon. The last one Yuri remembered took place almost two hundred years before after a jealous lover murdered a rival. After the ceremony, Yuri became a memory her kind carried forever. Younger wolves would recall her name, synonymous with treachery and execution.

Rolv, one of the guardians, introduced her. "The condemned."

The pack, as one, turned its back on her as she'd turned hers on them.

Undecorated, almost empty, the courtroom of the Isangelous contrasted from the opulence of the other pack common areas. There were no chairs except for the bench where Eresna sat. It was carved over five thousand years before by an expert hand. Despite its plainness, it possessed a symbolic grandeur. Behind her stood the council, the other guardians, and one representative from the lower-ranking wolves.

As she moved forward, Yuri's steps echoed.

Made from endless slabs of white marble, the rest of the room chilled occupants to the bone. It was a vast sterile room where justice, not vanity, reigned.

A dark, sensuous shade of red glossed Yuri's lips. The same lucky color swept through her dress's floral pattern. Confidence mattered. She wanted to get through this without breaking down, dignity intact. The entire pack came to watch her execution. She expected no less, but seeing all their stiff backs dried her throat. Swallowing a few times, Yuri forced herself to continue forward.

"Traitor."

"Coward."

"Ingrate."

The comments hurt, but not more than the silence from the wolves who said nothing. A turn of the lip or an averted gaze, and the lack of respect that signified, cut through Yuri's composure. She nearly fell, but a steady, familiar hand caught her elbow. Nadine.

Nearby wolves glowered at Nadine, sniffing in disgust.

Yuri forced herself to jerk out of the comforting hold. "Earlier, you made your contempt for me—"

"Don't spare me their anger, Yur. I'm here for you." Nadine's voice carried across the hall. There'd be no shielding her from the pack's backlash, especially not after Yuri was dead. Yuri allowed Nadine to guide her the rest of the way.

Eresna, her voice colder than Yuri had ever heard it, told Nadine to leave. To Yuri, she said, "Kneel down."

Eresna continued once Yuri knelt before the bench as told. "Today, we have a grievous task ahead of us. An Isangelous wolf placed her affection for a human above the safety of our pack. As a result, a possible lifestealer is on the loose with a viable host."

Few knew what that meant. Those who did couldn't contain their shocked, horrified gasps. Someone in the back shouted, "We must act now, even if it means humans learn of our existence."

Yuri flinched. Even under current circumstances, she couldn't keep her heart from squeezing. *Tovin is safe*, she told herself. A very large asterisk hovered next to the statement. Mutterings of his escape with Garvey had reached her ears. The order to stand down raised hackles. Quite a few believed they should have risked detection to apprehend them both. The Isangelous wolves wanted Tovin dead.

Eresna stopped their clamoring by lifting her hand. The sleeve of the simple white robe she wore folded down to reveal the elegant sweep of her arm. "We will deal with Tovin and Garvey soon enough. We must come together to hunt down and eliminate the threat. Today, we tend to our house. Yuri, step forward."

Yuri lifted her chin when Eresna read off the charge. Treason. Guardians—who made up the council—stirred in their seats. The only other time they'd considered such a charge was when Lavario created Garvey. Their resolve faltered then. But not today.

"We accept the charge," Rolv said. "And the proscribed punishment, which is death."

For Nadine's sake, Yuri kept her gaze fixed ahead of her, never wavering. Any sign of panic might spark her friend's protective nature, putting both of their heads on the chopping block.

"Stand. Come forward," Eresna beckoned her. "Howl at the moon?"

A death sentence was said to be as rare as a werewolf howling at the moon. The first one they'd executed had done just that, part as a joke, part because it was something he'd always wanted to do. Ever since, howl at the moon became a proxy for last words.

Yuri scanned the crowd. She found Nadine. Lip twisting upward in a half smile, she said, "Seriously, don't break the hedgehog. Her name is Nads."

Eresna's eyes moistened, but her voice remained cold. "Kneel."

Yuri did as told, just as she'd done for most of her life. Obeying orders came to her so naturally, she anticipated the next before Eresna spoke it, sparing her from having to ask it. She placed her head on the block and pulled her hair away from her neck.

Chopping off heads, while antiquated, was the most merciful way to kill a werewolf. Special weapons embedded with powerful magic were made long ago for the purpose. Very few still existed. Werewolves, practical minded and fastidious, didn't leave behind many tools of their own destruction.

Eresna, the alpha of the pack, wielded hers with grace. Her shadow fell over Yuri. Eresna's breathing quickened. Yuri felt certain she was the only one who heard it, but her gasps fractured into pants.

"I understand," Yuri told her. "You have to."

Eresna's breathing leveled.

She focused on Nadine's eyes. Two blue moons setting over a vast ocean. Welcoming, it swallowed her whole.

Epilogue

MOLLY STAGGERED THROUGH the woods, looking for a meal. She had no concept of time, but it was dark again. It had been dark many times before.

There was a name for herself she couldn't quite remember. The boys who held her captive called her Molly, as did Garvey, who broke her out of the prison. It was wrong. She searched herself for the name her parents, whose faces she occasionally remembered, gave her.

Only one word came to her. "Hungry," she said out loud and continued to walk. Silent, the forest's animals holed up in her wake. Driven by instinct, they lived by imperatives, none so strong as stay alive. Molly felt that need.

The deep snow broke Molly's uneven gait. When she stumbled, the powder stuck to her palms. Balls of it wadded in the frozen fabric of the long, baggy pants she wore. Although a primal part of her understood the substance should sting her skin, she could no longer imagine the sensation of cold.

She only knew one thing. And it kept her moving forward. "Hungry."

Food hid inside buildings. But not the pitiful shacks in front of her. Undead like her, the abandoned structures emitted no light or warmth. A nearby woodpile smelled promising. Molly clawed through it, grunting when splinters lodged under her swollen nails. It smelled like food, but there was nothing to eat. Mice didn't even scurry.

"Food." Molly scolded her surroundings for the lack of cooperation. "Hungry!"

A high-pitched whine caught her attention. Off to her side, the noise persisted. She followed it to its source, a furry animal cringing inside a small enclosure. Molly liked this creature. It reminded her of Garvey, the strange monster who hunted food for her.

"Hungry," she explained to it, hoping it would hunt for her too.

It whined again.

Molly understood fear. "No eat. No eat," she assured it.

This time the creature said another noise—loud, like thunder. It said it too many times for her to count. Spittle flew from its mouth. Its teeth snapped. Why was it angry? Molly covered her ears, growling and baring her teeth.

Suddenly, the whole area was awash in her food source's artificial light. A low voice cut through the animal's curious jabber. "Baker? Is it you out there?" He patted his leg and whistled. "Baker? Come here, girl."

Molly ran at the noise, plowing through the snow until she saw her food haloed in a doorway. Unlike the small animals of the forest, the man didn't immediately flee once she came into view. He backed up toward the door, uncertain but willing to give her the benefit of the doubt.

"Hello? Miss? Are you okay?"

"Hungry," Molly shouted back, part warning.

All his weight resting on his right leg made him vulnerable to attack, easy to topple. Molly crashed into him. They went down together, sliding on the hardwood floor until the friction of their skin stopped them. Molly put her teeth right to his throat and bit down.

Predators knew a fatal wound. This one would bleed out.

Somehow, the man still had the energy to kick her off his chest. Molly fell back into the snow and rolled, leaving blood, red and brilliant in the fresh white of the snow. She moaned in frustration when the door slammed.

Inside, a woman's voice shrieked, "I can't stop the bleeding. I can't stop it. I can't."

The creature was at her heels now. The noise it made increased in pitch and it wove between her legs, nipping and snarling. Molly waved it away, but it kept coming back. "No eat!" she told it. "No eat you!"

The man gurgled. The sound went straight to Molly's gut, where her hunger hurt the worst. Hissing, she got up and charged the door. It didn't budge. Molly tried to open it the way Garvey did, twisting the knob. Locked, inaccessible. Molly rammed herself against the fragile wood. Each time she hit, the woman inside screamed. Molly associated this noise with success.

The two heartbeats inside became one. Molly wailed. Fresh food tasted better. Blood flowed, hot and soothing. Molly kept trying. There was still one more. The woman. Her heart beat. Her blood flowed.

"Harold!" she wailed. "Get up! Get up! Please get up."

"Hungry," a male voice said from inside. The food was inedible now. Afterward, the woman's screams were pained instead of aggrieved.

Molly rammed herself against the door—harder and harder. "No, no, no," she cried when the last heartbeat faded. "No."

The door wouldn't break. Outside, things only got colder. Soon, everything there was dead like her.

Baker went from the door, then back to Molly. It whined and spun. Oddly, she understood the creature's sadness. Stranger, she felt it too. "Sorry," she told the other animal, using one clawed hand to smooth its fur. "Sorry, Baker. Hungry."

Molly patted her leg the way she'd seen the man do. The smaller Garvey whined but approached her—its head low, tail wagging slightly. She assured it, "No eat, no eat you."

Snow fell. Beneath it, the voices of the undead were muffled. But Molly heard their names, the same as she heard her own. They banged against the wooden door, crying out in the night.

"Hungry."

Acknowledgements

As always, I want to thank all my friends who have supported me along the way.

Cody: thank you for letting me chase after my dream. Maybe one day you'll get to start your streaming career and teach stats to nerds on the internet. First, I'll have to stop writing Christmas stories that use the word "fuck" twenty times. It might be a bit is what I'm saying.

Amy, Shaffer, and Milo: Thank you two for always inviting me to the party but understanding why I don't want to go. Most people don't even accept that contradiction, and you guys always go a step further and embrace it.

Joanne from Outback: You're a critical part of date night. I'm delighted if you actually do enjoy my books, but I'm equally happy with the cheese fries and smart banter.

My parents: Thank you both for raising me to be the type of person who works hard and pushes herself to achieve her goals. Dad, in an odd sort of way, gathering rocks for the fountain taught me that beautiful things come from mundane parts. I also learned that creative endeavors are achievements in and of themselves. Mom, I grew up admiring all your different skills. I tried learning some of them. I still can't paint worth a damn, but I can bake now. Kind of. Thank you for sharing that with me. Without you two, I'd be a much different person than I am today.

I'd also like to thank my editor Jason for all his hard work and NineStar Press for giving my books a home.

About the Author

Jackee Rohrbach is a writer from Washington State.

She has a loving husband, two dogs (Mulder and Nibbler), and two cats (Zinsser and Nova). Yes, Mulder is named after Fox Mulder. It fits because he's a really paranoid dog.

She grew up thinking she'd be a judge or a professional in some other law-related field, but ended up as an academic for a bit and taught criminal justice courses. She got her graduate degree from University of Cincinnati. While getting her degree, she worked on an assessment project where she interviewed offenders.

She found her way back to creative writing sort of by accident, but she's glad she did!

Email: Jackeeroh@gmail.com

Twitter: @JackeeRohrbach

Website: www.Jackeewrites.com

Other books by this author

The Worst Werewolf

Speak with the Dead

"Vampire Hours" within *Into the Mystic, Volume Two*

Also Available from NineStar Press

Connect with NineStar Press

Website: NineStarPress.com

Facebook: NineStarPress

Facebook Reader Group: NineStarNiche

Twitter: @ninestarpress

Tumblr: NineStarPress